Inheriting the Sleigh

THE APOSTOLIC LINK CONTINUES...

Inheriting the Sleigh

by
Morgan Vance

\

✳✳✳✳✳✳

Dedicated to anyone with the courage to read something new. To explore something new. To think and act anew. To those willing to get lost in the written page—and most importantly, to any and all endeared by the holiday season.

Prologue

For a man who stood heartbroken upon Golgotha's hill, he'd certainly seen a lot. From the Black Death to the near demise of the Jews, his observations of personal tragedy extended a mile deep. And yet, this moment was as daunting as any he could remember.

The hallway was quiet and long. Every 75 feet stood another door where a bearded but comely man took note of each number on his way past. Apartment 5116 caused his eyes to change. He stopped between potted trees, near a golden knob.

The gentleman had something gripped in both hands— gently setting the fine wood over the welcome mat. Pulling a silky sheet off the top, the baby inside was content, lifting its feet and fingers with a smile. The newborn loved the bearded gentleman holding the hand carved cradle— one with trains chiseled out each end used as carrying handles.

Kneeling on one knee over the hospitality carpet, he looked past the classy door, as if able to see right through it. He was in a meditative state, absorbing every second of the emotional task.

Pulling a glass ornament from underneath his coat, he nestled it into the blanket as a ding from an elevator caused the man to turn. A laughing couple in fancy evening wear exited through the parting doors. They should have taken note of he and the baby both but on their way for an ensuing hall—acted as if they weren't even there.

"Are you sure this is it?" the man now had his eyes tilted up, as if gazing through the ceiling and into heaven itself. If he received an answer, it didn't come verbally. "Take care of this one, then," he whispered with a submissive tone, suggesting he couldn't shake all of his doubt.

But following one final coo, the teary father forced his gloved index finger over the doorbell, vanishing ever so quickly.

Chapter 1

The control room was black, with only glimmering buttons and monitors adding light to the darkness. Faces with headphones were corresponding. They were focused, though far from overwhelmed, clearly having performed this task many times before.

"Tell the crew to clear the dock," said Isaac.

"Clearing, now," another retorted below. Hoods with mink trim were pulled overhead in the exterior night. There was a frosty glow on the outside, with colorful flare lights outlining the runway.

"Sleigh Bell number 327 now ready to launch. Is Kris ready?"

"Ready," the response was relayed via a small microphone underneath the furry hood and through the headphones of those inside

But following one final coo, the teary father forced his gloved index finger over the doorbell, vanishing ever so quickly.

A tall steel door slowly lifted to bridge the interior and exterior portions of the runway with reindeer bobbing their heads in the now-brisk air.

"Prepare to deactivate the Wall," came Isaac's order. "Oh, and Cross," added the Chief of Staff.

"Yeah," Blaine's bright red sideburns stood out between the sides of his hood as he performed one last sleigh inspection, merely as a precaution to satisfy Isaac's overbearing attention to detail.

"Did you …?"

"Did I, what?" he playfully retorted with a smile. "Double-check the power head? Of course."

"And …?"

"Test out the exhaust nozzles? Yeah. Did that too."

"Thanks," Isaac hated to ask, but knew it was his job to pester people at such an important time of the year.

"Deactivation complete. Wait … now … complete," a third voice interrupted their exchange from his control room cubicle; this one a geek with stringy bangs. Blimm reached up to a higher board to pull one final shiny, red lever.

Isaac approached with a handful of others to observe the ensuing moment of truth through a large, translucent glass window. A streaking hum was heard until it gradually faded. A flash of pink accompanied near the edge of the invisible wall as a beating windstorm—once contained— suddenly swept in with fury over the runway. Elves at snow level were covered head to toe in fresh frost as they waited, the anxious reindeer more than ready to elevate.

"The countdown begins at ten … nine, eight, seven." All eyes watched alongside Isaac with routine fascination, as if relieved the culminating day was finally here. "Three, two … Sleigh bell launch."

Bells chimed as the glistening runners slowly moved out into the open runway before morphing into an inclining dash.

"Penetrating Wall," Blain sounded from below. "Penetration complete." Despite their protective gear, those outside could hardly stand the extreme temperature, anxious to retreat indoors.

Inheriting the Sleigh

"Activate Wall."

"Activating," a few hand strokes of a keyboard sent the red streak the other direction as the suffocating climate was once again trapped by a protective, yet unseen bubble.

A jubilant clasping of hands erupted inside the control room to celebrate the annual success of the launch. And just like that, unsure what to do next—following a grueling, year-long cycle, all Isaac could think to do was breathe. His traditional, two-week-long vacation had finally begun.

High above in the twinkling night, a relaxed Claus watched dots shuffle around a digital dashboard. They morphed into images at his command. A row of hot green playing cards—Santa's biggest vice was then spit over the wide screen to set up a fresh round of Solitaire to pass the time—all as the reindeer casually provided their transport. But down below, the only elf scheduled to remain inside the control room was rarely content. "Alright, it's been long enough. Say something. Even so much as a grunt—I'll take it," a fidgety voice, whose job it was to monitor sleigh routes, eventually radioed up. Blimm naturally twitched over his polka dot overalls and mismatched socks pulled up well past his knees.

"All is good," he heard Santa in a voice both calm and content. "Off to the Marshall Islands we go."

There was a reluctant pause. "One thing we might ... you know, consider."

"And what is that, Brother Blimm?" Kris was a little annoyed by the never-ending extra whip of caution.

"I know you want to avoid military surveillances, but we're receiving reports ... and credible ones," he rustled through some notes spread about his cluttered desk. "The Southern Pole is undergoing a period of hostile visibility. It might be worth, you know, shortcutting through the Outback. We could initiate the drone wave frequencies to avoid detection."

"Don't be silly. There is no need to teach this old dog new tricks. We'll cut across the southern oceans as we've done the last 150 years on our way for Micronesia."

"As you wish," Blimm relented with headphones and a thread-like mic dangling near his mouth. "Let's hyperflight then, just to make sure we arrive at House One on schedule. The storm could slow you down by as much as 30 percent at the pace we're on now."

"Hyperflight ready," Santa's white gloves pulled up on a small lever near the dash. Additional flames shot out the back of the glistening sleigh as the reindeer were excited to pick up the pace.

With darkness having since been replaced by murky, gray light, Blimm had his eyes glued to a monitor. The blue oceans had turned into thick ice with visibility now nothing but a blockage of fog. The sleigh lowered, though the fog remained.

"Everything still cheery?" asked Blimm. He knew the rough conditions on their own were no reason to panic but even semi-bad weather naturally made him nervous. But as he leaned back in his chair, received no response. "I said, everything still ... OK?" He was forced to test his mic with a tap.

Only the wind now howled through his ears, but it wasn't the lulling rustle he was so used to. Blimm instinctively hopped to his feet to size up the very nightmare he'd often lost countless hours of sleep over. The mere thought of it had caused him great anxiety over the decades. In fact, several times he'd nearly quit his demanding job as Launch Operations Engineer, only to get drawn back in by the decent salary.

Inheriting the Sleigh

It wasn't uncommon for Kris to ignore Blimm out of habit, but not after a string of repetitive pleas that would usually force him to break from his game of cards. "Please talk to me!" the elf mumbled with a nervous tick. "Cause if this is merely another attempt at getting a rise of my neurotic disorder, I'm warning you. I simply cannot stomach it!"

The red button on Blimm's desk was big and blaring, and yet it had never been pushed before—until now. The elf didn't have to think about sounding the alarm, as Santa, already more than 9,000 miles away was unintentionally veering for a thick slab of ocean ice. Blimm couldn't make out the details from his station monitor, but the live audio feed was more than enough to paint a picture. It was the terrifying sound of a plummet, as the man on the other end could only cry and nothing else through the muffled drop.

Lit with a red glow on the opposite side of the Mayday the reindeer tried to pull up, though the sleigh wasn't cooperating as the runners abruptly cracked hard against the frozen surface. The towering sack of presents all carted and neatly harnessed, suddenly tipped, as did Kris with a jolt and a smack.

And then, the ensuing quiet haunted the mess of an elf as a wide flash of hot green, much like the wondrous aurora borealis, magically shot over the surrounding ice. Penguins dispersed from the brutal impact, while the startled reindeer were forced to abruptly touch down in a barren arctic wilderness, void of any thought as to what to do next.

Staring aimlessly into the glowing machinery, a numb Blimm now sat curled up in a helpless ball under his desk. He nibbled at his already sawed-off nails with the crash now just a sour moment of the past. The screaming alarm continued to beat across his shocked temples before a door suddenly split open, a taller figure barreling through in little but a colorful robe.

Vance

"Blimm!" Isaac was in no mood to locate him. But the twitching elf didn't answer with his arms wrapped around his scrunched kneecaps. Isaac had the wherewithal to know where he might be and urgently crouched down. "Blimm, tell me," Isaac asked softly, as not to frighten him anymore than he already was. All the while, he could only hope the warning was merely some big, innocent mistake. "Why did you sound the alarm?"

The damaged elf continued to say nothing, though slowly tilted his gaze up to stare into Isaac's commanding, dark brown eyes. Unable to take one more second of silence, he whipped his hand across Blimm's pale cheek to slap him back into the moment.

"It appears as if we've had a terrible accident … sir!" Blimm finally revealed with a surge of fresh guilt.

Isaac finally froze himself, as if needing a second to process the worst-case scenario; one he so desperately feared every step of the sprint in from his warm bed. His gaze finally left Blimm's to aimlessly pan across the quiet control room, before issuing one last instruction. "Deploy a rescue unit. And emphasize this is no drill."

Isaac took a deep breath to gather himself before exiting back through the doors.

"Chief," Blimm caught him before he could go. "Is this … you know. The end?"

Isaac's handsome face was clouded over by uncertainty, choosing to ignore the question he had no answer to.

Chapter 2

The quad of long, narrow vehicles kicked up heaps of snow as they found the sleigh tipped and damaged.

"Deploy!" one instructed as a large team raced for the open cracks in the glacier.

Some lingering penguins watched in concern as the divers, all with thick whale skin suits, dove headfirst for the holes. But there was no need to drop much further into the depths of the frigid sea as another team quickly found Kris lying on the surface, crushed by the weight of his own vehicle.

"We've got him," the message was immediately radioed through the speakers of each mask.

Kris lay motionless, with a streak of blood frozen permanently to the ice. In fact, so was his short beard, which needed to be trimmed. A hose ignited a flame to melt the ice around his swollen cheeks.

"What is it?" asked one medic to another. Both lenses shot from his protective goggles like a folding scope to get a better look in the bitter cold. But all he really needed was his pulse to know the truth.

"Deceased," the elf whispered as he held the Claus' head, while another respectfully scooted to pick up the burgundy hat off the insufferable ice. The fuzzy, white ball dangled off his glove as he felt uncomfortable even touching such a sacred relic. "And the reindeer?"

"Looks like Donner might have a sprain," another elf radioed to the rest of the group—lifting a limp leg. "But the other eight appear to be … just fine." The deer stood still together to avoid more slippage as only a flat expanse of endless nothing surrounded the many shocked faces.

Then, one by one, the rescue unit fell to their knees in an awful moment of truth.

"But … I was under the impression the ol' man couldn't die," whispered an elf with a plump build. He was the first who dared speak around the glowing conference room table. The group of admirers were dressed for bed, and sat stone-faced back at the Pole, listening to every word of a rescue that wasn't meant to be. "Or was it all just a fib? You know, so as not to bring any unwelcome questions along with it?"

"Gib, you know as well as I that Kris didn't lie," the tallest elf in the room uttered softly—offended by the thought—all while trying to stomach the horrifying confirmation. Isaac paced about, torn by precisely how to feel.

"Notice I didn't say, lie," Gib, one to eulogize in his own way, stroked the ends of his walrus mustache. "Just, you know … trying to protect us from the truth, that's all."

Isaac, unable to stay in one spot for very long, sat again with his elbows propped and his fingers clasped. "The truth is … he was as mortal as you or I. Death just couldn't come of natural causes."

Ezra defogged his glasses around the creases in his mature face. "Then you're saying he may have been … murdered?"

Every curious eye shot toward Isaac to gather his anticipated response—the word "murder" feeling nearly tornadic to their troubled hearts. The elf was put off by the pressure of needing to theorize a thought so terrible. "Why couldn't it have been something so simple as driver's error?" he thought to himself. It was a reason that was much easier to accept.

"Do you really want me to provide you with the numerical odds on that?" Ezra inquired to a host of befuddled stares.

"No," Silva immediately raised a hand, as if annoyed to hear the oldest elf in the room crunch numbers. "We don't."

"And the sleigh?" Isaac turned to Blaine, sitting quietly at the opposite end of the table.

Blaine was still as emotional as he was shocked, though managed to hold back the tear that desperately needed to cross down his cheek. "I've gone over the launch report several times. Negative 23 Fahrenheit. Wind, nothing out of the ordinary. Of course, there was freezing fog, but certainly not atypical this time of year inside the Antarctic zone. Perhaps when they haul the sleigh back, we'll find a malfunction, but to think that even the backup engine wouldn't kick in, seems highly improbable to me. Especially considering everything checked out," Blaine wracked his brain with his fingers pressed deep into his befuddled skull. The crash was personal to him.

"But even if there were problems," Corbin piped in for the first time. "The reindeer are trained to ensure safe emergency landings, are they not?"

"The truth is," said Silva. She ignored the speculative point, only adding her own. "There's a lot we can all claim we don't know—but a pilot who has logged an infinite number of hours in the skies—crashing so abruptly … it doesn't add up."

"Oh, I can imagine what the world is bound to think about this," Gib smirked, finally bringing up what everybody else purposefully avoided as long as they could. "Every spoiled little rug rat from here to Hong Kong …." Silva wanted to smack him across the neck, but her glare alone was enough to get him to stop talking.

Isaac stood, as if unable to take much more of the hypothesizing. He approached a clear, glass wall—gazing out into the sleepy, dark city. "After 2,000 years, the apostolic reign has come to a bitter end." He cupped his astounded mouth in disbelief, twitching in the process before a group of disconcerted elves.

"Who then will tell the matriarch?" inquired Silva. She had an attractively narrow face, with silver and black hair and a sophisticated scowl, but in this moment was genuinely concerned.

"I will do it," stood an anxious Blaine with designer sideburns that swirled like exotic snowflakes along the sides of his pale face.

"I know you would, Cross," Isaac turned back, using his pet name as a sign of respect. "But this is something I must do myself. The rest of you oversee the return of the body. Write up news of the obituary for the High Council to approve and read before the public. The autopsy is important, but perhaps not as important as what must be done next." Isaac sucked in his grief just long enough, knowing full well he had essential chores to perform in the moment.

"Isaac?" called Gib with the rosiest of cheeks, stopping him before he could step out the door. "I assume you will discuss Kris and Martha's … you know … direct kin?" It was the million-dollar question every elf wished to know, but as usual, only Gib had the nerve to ask it. Isaac thought hard but said nothing before slowly scooting the latter half of the door shut.

He proceeded out a little-used back exit for a narrow, brick street—through a quaint grove of trees, past a short white gate, and then lastly through the locked door of a charming, two-story residence. The jog took a while, but now fully inside the isolated cottage, Isaac's somber trek resumed only a few more steps—over a narrow hall with a creaky wood floor. He grabbed a kerosene lantern up a flight of stairs, before arriving upon another closed door. He knocked to no reply though could hear faint tears. Slowly inching it open, he peeked his head through the crack to see the shadow of a woman standing with her back facing. She was staring through a small, octagon-shaped window next to a canopy bed. The full moon reflected brightly through the glass. "Martha," he called softly.

The woman appeared 50 or so in age. She was attractive and dressed in a flowing nightgown with her hair wrapped in a ball. She turned with a depressed eye to behold Isaac, his head tipped down toward the floor and his hands respectfully gripped behind his back. "Mr. Newell," she called.

"I'm so sorry to intrude, Mother Christmas. But I have some news. Some very … terrible news."

"Oh?" Martha shrugged.

"Yes. I must inform you …." Isaac paused for longer than a second or two; long enough to convey just how hard it was to complete the sentence.

"Thank you, Isaac, but I know exactly why you're here."

The elf squinted with confusion. "You do? I mean, did someone …?

"No," she shook. "Nobody need tell me a thing. Martha tilted her head back up toward the bright full moon. "I can feel it across my chest. The hour has finally come. After all these centuries, I can feel his spirit once and for all being reclaimed. The great bearer of gifts—my dearest Kris has finally been taken up."

"Shall I give you time to grieve then? You know … to sort through your many thoughts. I can only imagine …."

But Martha was already nodding. "I'm afraid there's no time for that."

"No time?"

"Yes. For Kris' death means mine is equally near. My sister, Mary often quoted it. She heard Jesus say it himself. You know—that we would go together."

"I'm sorry," Isaac remained confused. "But you didn't go together. In fact, you were precisely 9,682.1 miles apart when he perished," Isaac rambled with a portable gadget in hand; one to help him gather the exact number. For it was his job to point out every technicality.

Martha gazed deep before turning to resume with the truth. "I guess I don't have long then, now do I?"

Isaac was more befuddled than ever but continued the best he could. "What now? The High Congressional Council will certainly meet first thing in the morning to discuss it. But just in case what you're telling me—heaven forbid—actually happens, I need to hear it from you."

"I think you know, don't you?"

"And yet, I think I need to hear it," he gulped. "Or I'm afraid I'll never build the courage."

Martha's emotion was fixed. "Go get him, dear Isaac. Get the boy and bring him back. Bring him back at once."

Chapter 3

The Communion lines were long at St. Patrick's Cathedral. The Neo-Gothic landmark faced Rockefeller Center in the downtown Manhattan glow. Festive horse-drawn carriages passed over city streets and a chestnut vendor was among those set up near the iconic spires. It was all part of the splendor of Christmas Eve—though the rumors were already beginning to whirl.

Nick Crest is subdued inside the house of worship, waiting for the adorned Priest to slip the Sacrament wafer into his mouth. The teenager reverently took in the words of "O Holy Night" next to his mother. She modeled an expensive fox fur coat, and earrings that brought immediate attention to her fortunate place in life. Nick touched his heart with a grimace, though Vienna came prepared. His mother knew exactly when to dip into her crocodile skin handbag to sift for a canister of prescription pills. "Aren't you glad I brought them?" Nick knew better than to argue, twiddling his fingers to imaginary keystrokes. "Hurry and swallow—it's your turn soon."

Nick peered around, looking for something or someone. "Where is he, anyway?" he tried to get his mother's attention.

"Who?"

"Who do you think? He told me himself he was coming."

Vienna scoffed. "You act as if your fathers never said that before."

"But this time he promised to donate a thousand dollars to a charity of my choice if he didn't make it."

Vienna smirked, as if clearly able to picture Arthur Crest making such a loose promise with his time. "Mass isn't really his thing, Nick. Don't worry," she could tell her words weren't helping. "I'm sure he'll be here. And if he isn't. Look on the bright side. The Ronald McDonald House just got a whole grand richer. Now, hands out of your pockets," Vienna scolded as the Holy Eucharist was just feet away.

Nick accepted, extending the sign of the cross, in wait for the annual holiday tradition to resume.

"Nick?" He didn't even have time to turn back before a gushy spit wad landed wet in his right ear. Nick managed to scoop it out, flicking it onto the floor before turning back with a bothered stare. "Did you hear?" Loopy, as he was called, annoyingly whispered over his shoulder.

"Hear what?" Nick was aloof. "About that grand plan of yours to prank the Gershwin Theatre. Setting off the fire sprinklers during Mamma Mia? Oh, you told me. And more than once."

Loopy could hardly contain his chortle. "Yeah, what an epic idea that was," he admitted. "And we're still doing that by the way."

"You need to be quiet," Nick could tell they were drawing attention. "Besides, I have to concentrate."

"Yeah, yeah. Big shot musician, I know. But I'm talking about the Big Guy here."

"Big Guy? What … Big Guy?"

Loopy kept his mouth hovered close to Nick's ear as the women seated next had a stern, shushing finger. "Wow, you really have left planet Earth, haven't you? It's Christmas tomorrow."

Inheriting the Sleigh

"I'm aware," Nick assured, swiveling his neck halfway around for only the second time.

"Then you'd know I'm talking about the Boss Claus, the chronic home invader. You know, the world's greatest ho. Get it?" Loopy smirked. His fist playfully skimmed Nick across the shoulders, hoping to eventually get a rise out of him—which he soon did.

Nick tried hard to appease the immaturity. "Again, what have I not heard?"

"You really don't watch much television, do you?" a disappointed Loopy's eyes rolled before resuming. "News cut-ins everywhere. Santa hasn't been making the rounds."

Nick paused to digest the unexpected declaration. "What are you saying?"

Loopy was bothered to have to spell it out for him. "I'm saying, there's been no trace of the man."

Nick thought for a moment before scoffing. "Nah, I don't believe that. What tabloid you been reading?" Nick knew Loopy had a track record for being the first rung of the rumor mill.

"He's supposed to start showing up stateside in the next ... I don't know—few hours," Loopy nervously looked down at his Hulk themed wristwatch. "Sydney, Moscow, London. I'm telling ya; the dude's disappeared."

At this point, Loopy had Nick mildly believing he was at least telling a fraction of the truth. "Can you imagine—all those disappointed kids halfway across the globe—waking up to empty trees. That could be us tomorrow." Nick said nothing with his dazed stare stuck down at a racked hymnbook. "Then again, look who I'm talking to," Loopy resumed his quiet rant, always content to hear his own voice. "With a money-flush pops sure to come through, you may not need Santa Claus, but I've got a 3D gaming system on the line here. A Crop Cube Max with my name all over it."

Nick glanced back a third and final time, relieved to finally see Loopy leaning back in his pew.

The presiding Cardinal and Archbishop of New York, Timothy Dolan, stood before the televised proceedings. The historic edifice was dolled by a showering of wreaths and poinsettias.

He walked from the checkerboard marble, onto the red carpet covering the steps of the Cathedral platform where the white altar was trimmed in swirling gold and chiseled with the faces of deceased saints. Dolan's cross-topped staff led the way—his red and gold robe equally splendid.

"John's Gospel summarizes best why we receive the blessed Communion," said the Cardinal between flickering candles. "Truly, truly, I say unto you. Unless you eat the flesh of the Son of Man and drink his blood, you have no life in you. For this day, we celebrate the historic birth revolving around the originator of that quote. A pregnant, unwed mother who bore the extremities of the day, she was forced into the outskirts of the city to a humble place called Bethlehem to give birth to her child. Though not in any proper clinic, or even an inn. But a lowly stable where the animals lived out their chilly nights."

Most were now focused on the sermon, though not Nick. His eyes were two rows ahead staring at a petite girl walking in late. She followed behind her parents, cramming into a small, reserved gap in the pew. Nick's face naturally changed and simultaneously went to work creasing a piece of paper originally used as a ceremonial program.

"Mary giving birth to a giver," Dolan resumed. "The greatest giver that ever lived. Giving that would breed even more giving." The Cardinal then took a long, sweeping pause, as if conflicted on how to proceed. He could tell his audience was distracted and soon couldn't remain silent any longer. "Which leads me to something I don't do very often. Changing topic for a moment, if I may." A surprised stage director was caught off guard by the impromptu gesture, unconducive to live television. "For I suddenly feel a need to discuss the unique circumstances pertaining to today," Dolan turned to address a camera before slowly swiveling before the congregation once more. "To the great philanthropist we have all come to know over time as Santa Claus."

Every patron swiftly lent an even more attentive ear; so much so, they failed to recognize Nick releasing his paper airplane that skillfully sailed a few feet ahead. Its momentum stalled directly over the shoulder of Marie Bayliff.

She was pretty as her hair was long and looked the part, with knee-length socks and a plaid scarf to match. She barely felt the plane slowly glide over her left shoulder, only noticing the tip of the cockpit out the corner of one eye. She knew immediately what it was, flattening out the artwork to discover a note.

"Not sure I can do this. Pray for me."

Marie slowly turned to acknowledge Nick. He was staring, only to see her more than happy to smile back.

"But may it not discourage the true meaning of Christmas," Dolan's voice continued to sermon, though Nick had since managed to tune half of it out. "For it is about so much more than receiving that which we hope to receive. It is about the joyous moments of watching our loved ones unveil gifts we have sacrificed so much to give. And Santa Claus or not, that tradition will certainly never go away."

The archbishop transitioned as Cardinal Dolan—relieved to get that off his chest—subtly walked out of view. An African American priest in a tall, triangular hat, resumed by drawing out every word with prolonged pronunciation. "And now, may we receive inspiration from the sweet sounds of our Lord."

A choir in white aprons struck up near a barnyard Nativity to the hymn, "O Come All Ye Faithful," while an usher in a traditional suit subtly signaled Vienna from the nearest isle.

"OK, here we are. You ready?" she, as mothers instinctively do, straightened out the collar sticking up out of her son's V-neck sweater—dabbing down his hair. Nick took a deep breath before scooting past several sets of knees toward the discreet outer aisle where he was guided up to an awaiting Steinway. But his fingers didn't feel right; and even worse, his mind soon began to veer.

"Nick, is this piano charade really your only extracurricular? Who you trying to be anyway? Liberace or something?"

"I don't know. For whatever reason it comes naturally."

"Naturally," Arthur shrugged inside his swanky, downtown office. "For 25 grand a year, or whatever I'm pay'n … I would hope it does."

"So, are you com'n to the Arts Center then?"

"In Brooklyn? Tonight?" Arthur squinted back in his chair. "I don't know, Nick. It is Tuesday. Best day for the markets." The unpleasant memory picked a bad time to resurface.

"But this time I actually composed a number myself. Been working on it for a year."

Vienna purposely stood outside the office door, listening to every word. She was heartbroken by the softness in Nick's plea. He wanted his father there, despite the puppy stare being lost on his distracted mind.

"You know," Vienna couldn't stand not intervening any longer. "I really do think you'll like it, Arthur. He does have a gift. And it's not just me saying it," she proudly held a copy of the Times. It had a one-word headline. **Prodigy** was stamped in bold, black ink atop the flattened-out paper—one since tossed onto his desk.

Escorted to the front of the Cathedral, Nick's confidence was rattled. In his last moments away from the spotlight, he cracked his knuckles before scooting over the bench, wondering how to handle the pressure he hadn't fully considered until now.

As the choir concluded its final verse, there were a few more lingering seconds of silence before the musical director cued Nick—just as rehearsed. "Ladies and gentlemen," spoke a deep, unseen voice. "Let me introduce the reigning Young Pianist of the Year. 14-year-old, Nick Crest."

Nick exhaled once more before laying his fingers over the polished ivory. They effortlessly began to glide across as he played his own composition. It was a caroling piece with classical charm. His skill was hard to ignore; that is until a sudden freeze of movement made the audience wonder. He didn't need sheet music, but the typical notes inside his head were no longer relaying signals to his hands, forcing Nick to stop cold. The boy was now left alone in a heavy sweat, with a confused congregation sending those in charge, scrambling.

People were now only a blur—Nick left to rely on the awkward collection of noise to gauge a reaction. "Is everything … alright, boy?" the musical director scurried over.

"Are you having a stroke or something?" added a concerned priest as Nick said nothing, only rubbing away at his eyes.

A body soon stood from the congregation. Marie didn't hesitate to merge onto the carpeted steps leading for the stage. She was stopped by security, but after a few words was eventually permitted past.

Nick waited as Marie kept walking until she was directly at his side.

She didn't say much, rather using her soft, caressing touch to pat at his twitching hand. She then pulled out something from underneath her coat. It was a flute, and with ease began to whistle several notes. They were notes that even soothed Nick, who picked the right time to start playing again. "Silent Night" soon morphed into "Angels We Have Heard on High" and then "Joy to the World." There was a chemistry to the duet.

With the blur subsiding, he suddenly fell back into his element again. They could have gone on forever, and perhaps would have, had it all not been forced to end. Nick's nightmare had morphed into a dream; a dream that was disrupted only by the bells that clanged to disperse the standing-room only Mass.

The spotlight had since left, though Nick's embarrassment remained. He hadn't even had time to thank Marie for rescuing him before both were whisked back to their seats and eventually out into the cool, night air.

Wintry flakes magically trickled from the night sky as he turned to find his mother—since disappearing in the street chaos.

"Hey, great job, kid," uttered a passing gentleman in a vintage top hat and matching cane. "Good thing for that pretty little gal though, hey," he patted Nick on the shoulder. "Believe me, son, we all need 'em."

"Carl," his wife unlocked their arms with a rebuke as the man was amused by his own jab. Nick, bugged by the timing of the backhanded compliment, said nothing as he continued to search for Vienna.

He shrugged in frustration before pushing his way through the fleeing traffic outside the Cathedral and past some ensuing skyscrapers. "Wo!" a couple he knew stopped him before he could go a step further. "Is that you, Nick?"

"Mr. Walker. Mrs. Walker," he respectfully tipped his head, though clearly in no mood for small talk.

"Are you excited for Christmas?" Mrs. Walker asked, though hesitated once she considered the delicate news. "I mean, anything special on your wish-list this year?"

Nick wanted to answer but couldn't, instead overrun by his own thoughts. "Have you seen my dad?"

"Funny you'd mention it," Mr. Walker failed to think prior to his quick retort. "Just did, and not long back."

"So, he was here," Nick computed.

"Here? No. Down at Madison Park, I believe. Having dinner."

"Dinner?" Nick's curiosity heightened. "With whom?"

The country club gentleman finally came to the realization he'd been caught in his own trap—knowing just enough of the truth to believe it wasn't what Nick needed to hear. "Um, yes ... he was with someone. Who was that, dear?" Mr. Walker snapped his fingers near his better half, as if unable to come up with a quick-witted lie.

"A business partner?" Nick paused to gather himself before completing the question. The Walkers awkwardly looked at each other, without a response.

"To be honest, I'd never seen her before, Nick," the flustered gentleman was left to wonder if he'd inadvertently said too much.

Nick took a second to digest the truth. Mrs. Walker could tell something was wrong and motheringly placed a hand over his shoulder, only to see him dash off without the courtesy of a goodbye.

His jog lasted several minutes down Fifth Avenue, past several last-minute shoppers on his way for the golden Trump Tower.

The elite hotel and residential complex had a sprawling and pristine lobby, with a golden hue. But for Nick it was just home. Up the elevator he went to the 51st floor. Barreling past actor and neighbor, Bruce Willis, he failed to say, hello. The truth was, with a handful of Hollywood types living on the same floor, it failed to impress him much. Nick used his key to enter apartment 5116 where a shouting match had already ensued. Vienna had beaten him there.

"How could you do this to me again!" she rebuked as Arthur apologized—though failed to admit much detail.

Used to seeing his parents argue, Nick listened before deciding this was not the time to step in. He tiptoed into the gaudy apartment. A perfectly clean oasis presented past some potted ferns—a fantastic view of the city displayed beyond the tall sky window drapes.

Nick sighed, plopping onto a couch cushion with a remote that just so happened to be within arm's reach. Taking Loopy's advice, an enclosure opened in the middle of a large bookshelf, presenting a 90-inch flat screen. He turned it on to randomly see the infamous frozen tongue scene from *A Christmas Story*. He welcomed the comedic relief but kept flipping until stumbling upon Fox News.

"And more on the unusual no-show of Santa Claus," read Shepherd Smith from a teleprompter. "Adam Housley has new details from Sao Paolo, Brazil ."

"Thanks, Shep. As has been tradition in years past, this is precisely where the man internationally known as Santa Claus should have been not long ago. But just as we've been reporting all over the globe, there is absolutely no sign of him making an appearance anywhere thus far." Drone video of the landmark Christ the Redeemer statue looped over the reporter's voice as he interviewed a family.

"I'm here with the Rochas, who have just woken up, along with many others here in this quaint neighborhood along the south side of the city. The Rochas do speak a little English along with their native Portuguese—and granted, it is still very early here in Brazil. First, give me your reaction when you entered the family room?"

The man was barefoot near the front lawn of his modest home, wearing little more than a white t-shirt and soccer shorts. "Well, first thing I thought, we must be robbed, you know. Because he always come. Never had he not come."

"So, your first impression was to call the police then?" Housley turned, holding the stick microphone under Mrs. Rocha's chin.

"Yes, yes. Call police. But when we walk outside, we know entire neighborhood been robbed too."

"Though it wasn't that at all, correct? Because nothing to rob had ever arrived to begin with."

Nick absorbed every word of the report; at least the best he could overtop a heated debate he could faintly make out through the apartment walls. He muted the TV, turning back toward a 15-foot-tall Christmas tree that was lit and decorated, as if intended for professional display inside a Macy's department store.

Vienna then burst through the master bedroom doors where both she and Arthur stormed out to an unpleasant surprise. Nick was waiting—patiently, in fact—more than ready for a much-needed explanation.

Chapter 4

Mourning bells chimed in the misty morning swells. It was a triple pang that didn't take long to awaken the entire island city. Chaos and speculation quickly spread about the Pole's dark cobblestone streets, with nearly everyone slumbering out of their homes and dormitories to gather for themselves. They wanted to know if the terrifying chatter could actually be true.

Isaac desperately wished he had the time to console the public but simply did not. The trusty Chief of Staff hardly had gotten a full hour of sleep. Disheveled and on a clear quest, he did his best to push through the cluttered street traffic, ignoring the many cries on his way there.

With a hood to conceal his face, he jogged past a sign and vintage lamppost that read, "Holly Street." He was heading straight for the tall building in the middle of Candy Cane Square. The exterior steps to the Congressional House were high, and Isaac sprinted up every last one, past the columns and through the tall doors with a festive wreath that split in two as it opened.

To satisfy protocol, he flashed identification past every secure checkpoint, proceeding higher and higher up more interior stairs before stopping upon the edge of a circular drop in the center of the giant building. He eyed the abyss—one that extended further down than he could possibly ever see—and up hundreds of feet more. It was topped by a glass dome where the sun, though entirely absent in the winter, was intended to provide natural light.

Inside the hole was a giant tree where the scent of pine was thicker than a forest. It looked like a mammoth spruce—the height of a sequoia and the girth of a small hill. But what made the tree even more spectacular were the countless glimmering bulbs that filled the needled branches—large swashes of decorative mesh and icicles to compliment the grandiose display.

Several vehicle ports surrounded the tree from the circular isles at an equal distance apart. They were perched on many different levels and provided an entryway to inspect the tree. Small, waist-high vehicles awaited at each passage. They had no tops and could've been stripped right off glittery carnival rides.

Isaac entered the closest one—a wide monitor at the front. He typed in a security clearance, and a few more numbers after that until a picture of Nick's face appeared over the screen. It was more like a slowly developing image that turned and flashed to all sides.

Isaac operated a foot pedal and joystick until the vehicle began to glide. It was like an advanced crane system, leaving the platform and extending out toward the tree—smoothly weaving up or down or wherever Isaac wanted it to go.

The handsome elf was in search of a particular bulb, which he'd only found due to a series of specific coordinates next to his picture. The crane suddenly stopped in front of one near the large, golden angel that hovered over the rest at the top. The bulb sparkled of lime green with decorative grooves, but if you looked close enough—just as with every bulb, you could see moving images playing through it. It was the inside of the Crest's sky-rise apartment in real time.

Isaac squinted to gather a better look, before slowly reaching for the medicine ball-sized bulb. The focused elf needed both arms to wrestle it off the branch. The image was a panorama view of the living quarters. Isaac slowly turned it a full 360 degrees. He saw Nick, which startled him; only because the boy wasn't merely drifting about his normal routine as he expected he might. Whether he knew it or not, Nick was peering directly at Isaac.

The boy's eyes were locked in on his family's own Christmas tree—more specifically an exact replica of the lime green bulb. The only difference was it was five percent the size. Extending a hand, the outstretched palm was coming straight for Isaac's view—as if three dimensional. Out of eerie discomfort, the elf immediately took a red cloth to cover up the bulb, wiping a stream of sweat off his cheeks, as if hating to be so intrusive.

Swiftly gearing back for the platform, the large ornament was now in his possession. "I'm taking this with me," he told security before the officer could beat him to it with any inquisitiveness—as it was his job to know what Isaac was secretly supporting underneath his armpit.

"There's a procedure for that, you know!"

Isaac ignored the concern, instead hurrying down another formal hall. He was nervous, knowing the ensuing confrontation might not go well.

Taking one last deep breath around a corner, he stepped inside to confront the many voices. They were taking their seats inside a dual-level meeting venue. It was circular with primarily wooden architecture that appeared American Revolution in period. Each row was higher than the one before it, with another deck up top where mature elves chattered about in wait. Many were dressed in wool trousers, vests, and coats; some with gold chains, lockets and funny clocks hanging off their pockets.

Isaac finished his trek through the hall into the well-lit chamber, one with a small, empty podium in the center. The elves—many with flamboyant hair and strange beards, hushed as Isaac was finally noticed. The mature faces belittled Isaac's handsome youth with natural contempt, skeptical to say the least. The vicinity eventually went deathly silent.

"Well," stood a congressman with a large nose and whiskers. "You can imagine how we all felt to receive such an urgent distress call as this on Christmas morning. Surely you understand how much slumber was cumulatively lost here among this gathering?"

"I can venture a guess," Isaac had to bite his tongue to sound calm, knowing how little sleep he was working on himself.

"Aren't you going to speak then?" inquired another brashly impatient congressman once Isaac took a second to gather himself. His golden teeth glimmered off his pocket watch. "As Kris' first in command, is it not up to you to confirm what in holiday horror is going on here? The elves have gone raving mad. Is he … injured?" The elf, with swirls of bright white hair, leaned over a wooden rail to intrusively demand answers. "Or is he … you know, even worse … dead?"

Isaac swiveled one time around, unsure how much the powerful Elites already suspected. He assumed the question was a bad joke, only equally true at the same time. "I'm afraid the answer is—in fact—dead," he delivered the verbal blow swiftly, as if still pained to say it out loud.

A keychain then inadvertently dropped from his pocket. It was a sound heard by every ear in the ensuing silence. The Elites were stumped, processing the psychological bomb. They knew it merely by the look in Isaac's eye, and after a brief gasp, many failed to even fake their bother.

Vance

"So … there you have it," whispered a bald congressman with just a few strands of curly, blue locks sticking straight up off his scalp. "No longer just a rumor. The old man really could die. Heaven say."

"How could this happen? I mean the jolly gent was what … 2,042 bloody years old?"

"Wait, I thought it was 52," piped a senile Elite on the other end of the arena-style chamber.

"Whatever the number. I just assumed death was beneath the Claus." A rising commotion soon needed to be quelled.

"The day had to come eventually!" Isaac was quick to retort once the gathering hushed enough to where he found a window to resume. "The man the world originally knew as John the Beloved was only granted extended life. Not immortality as will come with the Resurrection. Need I remind you—you all knew this explicitly."

"That it could not come of natural causes?" piped another, arrogantly nibbling over a toothpick. "Yes, so we were told. But that doesn't mean we believed it. But assuming for argument's sake it is true, wouldn't the cause of death need then to be, murder?"

The elf shuttered, sensing things quickly getting out of hand. "Not necessarily," said Isaac. "There are other ways to die."

"I say, sabotage!" interrupted another with coarse gray hair that slicked to a triangular point out over his thick eyebrows. "For a professional sleigh driver like the Claus to crash—is unspeakable. Not to mention, blasphemy."

"Are you saying the most polished among us aren't prone to accident?" asked a more rational Elite with an Abe Lincoln top hat that rose a good three or four feet in the air. It was so glaringly tall, those behind him had to peer around just to see the grilling for themselves.

"Well, perhaps I am. In fact, I call for a full investigation. And that includes bringing in the NPIU."

"I second that demand!" cried another with a fist banging hard against the wooden ledges. "The Pole Intelligence Unit needs to have full access to the crash site, not to mention every single member of Kris' inner circle."

"And that starts with you … Isaac Newell," an Elite with a cane and long beard—one stained in swirls of purple and green, stepped forward. He had a lazy eye that caused a concerned Isaac to lean back, just as the cunning politicians wasted little time seizing the moment.

"We can hash all that out later, but right now have more urgent matters to discuss," insisted Isaac.

"Matters such as what?" raised another congressman. This one shorter than most with a large polka dot bow tie. "Christmas is done for. We have failed. Unless of course, there are proper emergency measures in place."

The Chief of Staff did his best to remain patient through the interrogation. The skeptical looks around the room were more than a few as the Elites asked the question merely as a courtesy. They had fully expected Isaac to admit his failure.

"I assume you're not about to suggest there is one," added an Elite in a red suit, with green hair spilling out his ears. "Surely, no elf is capable, trained or equipped to take over the annual delivery? Why, such a job is herculean. It simply cannot be duplicated."

After a pause, Isaac nodded. "Well, not by an elf … no."

"Good," the reassuring sighs and fake laughter sounded an alarm inside Isaac's head.

"I guess this means only one thing then," added the Elite in the Lincoln hat. "As much as it pains my heart to say it, our wonderful days committed to the toy business appear to be numbered."

More bad acting joined in a throng of agreement as others sprinkled in their own opinion.

"Then again, it was certainly a great run. Centuries long, I might add—as grueling as it was. Though perhaps we owe ourselves a vacation, anyhow."

"No, no, no," another smiled. "We could brainstorm a different form of menial labor instead. Something even more suited for the elves' kind. I can see the campaign pitch now. Replace a toy ... with real joy."

Isaac wanted to challenge the pretentious absurdities from the top of his lungs but also knew it wasn't the time. Instead, he took a deep breath. "I hope for just once we can speak free of politics. Because the grave situation at present demands it." His audience looked pained, to say the least—unwilling to listen to another word of the monologue. "Please. Nobody understands better than I the philosophical differences of the past. Those that have created a bitter divide between your persuasion—and, well ... others. You know, those who actually bask in some form of giving," he unsubtly threw in an insulting shot. "But we have to think about the future now—and dallying or opening up old wounds is unfortunately not an option either of us have."

"It sounds to me as if we've already come to a conclusion," spat an aged Elite with an unusually large chin and ugly, drooping wrinkles across his face. "That there is no future," he said softly, while casually blowing a smoke ring from a long, orange pipe.

"But that's where you're wrong!" Isaac began to get a little agitated at the fact he had not yet been allowed to bring up what he'd originally come to discuss.

"Go on then," an Elite pushed a hand forward. It was his way of offering up the floor. But Isaac was never allowed to continue as an elf stormed into the meeting hall. All eyes turned as the doors were abruptly shoved open.

"Newsflash!" he cried. "The Matriarch has just been found dead! That's right ... dead!"

Another sweeping hush followed. As for Isaac, his lack of surprise didn't make the pronouncement any easier to absorb as Martha's own admission came to pass even quicker than expected.

Accusatory eyes soon veered two-by-two back upon Isaac, biting his distraught lip.

"Kris, and now Martha Kringle ... within hours of each other? I say we have a conspiratorial assassin among us!" yelled an irate congressman before others could yell it themselves. "A sinister plot to kill them both."

"Yes, isn't it clear? The assassin wants to be the next Santa Claus!"

Gradually, all eyeballs focused in on the man standing front and center in the middle of the room. "It makes sense, doesn't it?" a raspy voice was joined by a series of index fingers shaking down at Isaac. "You're next in line, are you not?"

"What ... no," even Isaac hadn't expected to be pinned for the heinous act of murder. But more chatter and fist-pounding had drowned out his ability to defend himself.

He stood, watching the verbal ruckus—his mind no longer able to endure the condemning cries. And so, instead of saying it outright, Isaac knew of no other way. Ripping the sheet off with one swift tug, a panoramic view of the apartment at Trump Tower suddenly projected outward off the large, glass ornament. The moving picture in real time now encircled directly above Isaac's head.

Nick Crest was suddenly in view over the sparkling grand piano. He was playing a non-holiday number while his parents continued to argue in the next room. The classical piece was effortless, though it was as if he were doing whatever he could to distract himself.

"Why are you showing us this?" a skeptical Elite, with large green eyes and a puckered mouth, scoffed in boredom.

"I'm so glad you asked," said Isaac with a brief smile as Nick struck up a new number—this one resembling Beethoven's "Fifth Symphony." "This scene may very well appear at random, but what if I said you are now looking at Kris and Martha's ... one and only child." The hush was thick—a clear result of their shock.

"Need I remind you," an aghast Elite eventually piped in. His hands gripped his belt as a way of intimidating the elf. "That 14 years ago this prestigious body was assured the boy had perished at birth."

"And so you were," Isaac's guilt was mild at best.

"I mean, for one, he has a burial plot right here at the North Pole," chimed the Elite with the lazy eye.

Isaac said nothing this time. "There is no body in that sarcophagus, is there?" asked another who had yet to speak. He was taller than most, with high, lava-red hair that stood out in a crowd. Mauv Lyman's inquiry struck Isaac like a sword to the gut, forcing him to fully admit the long-held secret before the rest of the gathering.

"You're right," he shook, realizing the truth was now his only choice. "It was placed there simply as a decoy to smuggle the boy outside the Pole. An emergency measure to save his life." The ensuing silence was haunting.

"It is a conspiracy then," said another. "I can't even begin to count how many laws have been broken—not to mention—orders defied. I feel we now have absolutely no choice but to arrest this man," the recommendations flew in swiftly.

The sound from the hologram was soft, but it was enough to continue drawing in the Elite's attention.

"You want to arrest me for preserving the life of a child?" Isaac almost mocked as he pointed upward. "Especially considering it was Kris and Martha's only one. No matter what bylaw you recite—surely, even the most miserly of souls can understand why I would proceed to disregard such a preposterous law."

"You still don't see the cursed logic in deceiving this legislative body? Not even someone of your position should be allowed to get away with such heresy."

"That's right," a scribe with a feathered quill opened a large book. "Article 237 of the Constitution is paraphrased as such, with the penalty of ... immediate incarceration," he read those final two words slowly.

"Let us vote to do just that," the noise was now just a blur to Isaac. The hologram grew louder, this time demanding their attention. For those at ground level, the visual floated above their heads, while for those crowded along the upper ledges, it was below. But no matter where they sat, it was getting harder to ignore.

The Manhattan skyline seen through the Crest apartment was clear and quiet on Christmas morning—though the mood inside was not.

"What do you want from me?!" Arthur Crest suddenly burst from the master bedroom where he and his wife bickered again. He was no longer apologetic but appeared almost violent.

"I want to meet her," Vienna's tears were overridden by her own sarcastic anger. "Perhaps the three of us should get to know one another. It would be a blissful, three-wheeled marriage, don't you think?!"

"Listen to yourself, Vienna! You're tired and need to go back to bed. And why ruin Christmas for Nicholas here?"

"Oh, please! You've never even liked Christmas," she spat.

Nick suddenly stopped playing, turning from his bench. Vienna and Arthur waited for the teenager to offer up a reaction, though there was little but an emotionless stare.

Vance

Tucked inside their intricate chamber hall, The High Elite Council observed the awkwardness precisely 35 hundred miles away. Not a one said a word as Nick slowly maneuvered past a waterfall and exotic fish tank, on his way for the bedroom. It was Isaac's cue to cover the ornament back up, this time for good, causing the hologram to suddenly disappear.

Two Mounties simultaneously entered the hall wielding funny hats and clubs. "I'm so sorry to interrupt," the short, yet pleasant officer appeared uncertain at best—standing inside the now deathly silent chamber. "But I've received an urgent memo … calling for an arrest?" He gently tapped his club against the opposite hand.

"I see," Isaac uttered softly in disbelief—just loud enough for the Elites to gather his disappointment. "You secretly send out a runner behind my back. Is this how we've dealt with our business in the past?"

"I think it's obvious the rules have changed?" Mauv's pale scalp was bare in the middle like a clown, with a full set of wavy locks extending past the ears. The House Speaker strategically took his time to take control of the conversation, slowly pointing a long, disjointed finger toward Isaac.

"Isaac Newell?" the officer was perplexed. He was a man the two policemen had always respected, and even at times directly reported to.

"Yes, that indeed was the order," assured Mauv softly.

Isaac—one last time—eyed the gathering of loud suits before departing the circular podium. He was walking straight toward the two reasonable men, as if ready to succumb to his fate and admit responsibility for the sudden deaths of Kris and Martha Kringle. With his hands gripped together, he stopped only feet away.

"Mr. Newell," inquired the second officer, this one thin and tall. "Whatever did you do?"

"I'm sure should you stick around long enough, they'll gladly give you all the twisted truth your heads can handle," Isaac sighed under breath. "As for me ... I have important things to do." There was a calming reassurance in his stare as the befuddled officers both rubbed at their chins.

"Well, don't dawdle now. Where are your handcuffs?" The Elites grew impatient as Isaac abruptly offered the officers one final smile before bursting out of sight. The officers made a lunge to stop him, but nothing else as they watched the elf storm away to the shrieking cries of every peeved congressman crammed inside the chamber.

Chapter 5

W hat do you say we try talking for once," Arthur did what he could to break the ice—all three sitting yards apart around the Christmas tree. They were aimlessly staring at the many gifts with blossoming bows still wrapped underneath, wondering how to proceed on the bizarrest of years.

A mounted TV was on in the background, just loud enough to hear. It was welcome noise to Nick—anything to break up the awkwardness. "We return now to our special report," CNN came back from a commercial break. "The unusual absence of Santa Claus. With a dependable track record extending back centuries, the mysterious man was a no-show this December 25th." Nick watched, still wondering how much he cared in all his distraction. But as hard as he tried not to, was also noticing the disappearance making him think more so than usual.

Arthur reached for the remote—to his son's dismay—turning it off. "All this Santa hogwash," Arthur had his back to the flatscreen. "Everybody kicks the bucket at some point. Or maybe the man got kidnapped or something, who knows," he mocked, hoping to get back on point. "Good thing for you, you don't need him," Arthur swiveled his head—all while opening his arms to envelop the posh apartment. It was his way of suggesting his own wallet could offer him plenty more than Santa ever could.

Vienna, meanwhile, went silent and sad—for more reasons than one.

"Why don't we begin with these two," Arthur was desperate to lighten the mood. He reached down, handing a present to both.

Vienna took a couple seconds before hesitantly extending a hand to accept the small box covered in shimmering paper. "Go ahead," she signaled Nick to go first, dabbing down an eyelid with a tissue.

Nick's gift was in a much larger box—wrapped in cartoonish paper with disc jockeys spinning turntables. He was meticulous in the way he opened it, looking for a seam to preserve the paper. It was his own way of annoying his father.

"Don't you want to find out what it is by … I don't know … New Years?" he jabbed as Nick finally uncovered a shoebox. He pulled up handfuls of stuffer paper with a pair of fresh tennis shoes underneath, immediately taking notice of the signature swoosh. The midsoles lit up with a glowing mechanism, and the base of the shoe was covered in a combination of teal and pink, as if dripping in paint. Nick analyzed the groovy soles but failed to even fake the least bit impressed.

"What … those are like 300-dollar sneakers you have in your hands." Nick finally lent a half-smile but nothing else. "They're not even on the market yet. I have a client that's one of the top guys over at Nike. You're gonna be the only kid in New York wearing those. At least for several months."

"In that case … cool. I mean, thank you," Nick coughed, anxious to veer the attention away so that he didn't have to pretend like he was into trendy things much longer.

"Moving on then," a confused Arthur turned with an over-the-top smile toward his disconcerted wife, hoping for better luck. Vienna didn't even bother to look his way. Unlike Nick, she tore her paper quickly, simply to get it over with.

Bright ocean blue sparkled from the sapphire pendant, as even she had a hard time acting unimpressed. It looked like a mini disco ball, only dotted in tiny sapphires. Vienna held the jewel up to her neck as Arthur, a man with a reputation for giving away extravagant things, was excited to gauge her reaction.

"How much did it cost, Arthur?" she whispered.

"Not important," he waved a hand with a smile across his plush robe—one exposing the hairs of his chest as he took a sip of his coffee. "Let's just say it once belonged to the royal family. Princess Diana wore that very piece to a charity gala the year she died. It's virtually priceless."

A cell phone suddenly vibrated against a glass table, putting pause on the exchange. Vienna and Nick both carefully watched as Arthur reached for it, nerves inadvertently filling the creases in his face as he perused the text.

"And now it's my turn?" Vienna was bold in her request, having already forgotten about the jewel.

"Excuse me?"

"I said, it's my turn to read it." Anger was quietly building as Nick pretended to be aloof to the confrontation.

Arthur took one more sip from his mug. "But it's nothing," he smiled. "Just a client wanting to know how his portfolio fared in the wake of last week's selloff. It'll bore you to tears."

"Really? On Christmas morning?" she skeptically watched him gently set his phone back down. Vienna kept her eyes locked on the case before making a quick swipe. It was so swift and sudden that Arthur couldn't stop her.

Inheriting the Sleigh

"Vienna, have you lost your once-exquisite mind?" He stood as she raced around a potted tree into another room to gloss over the message for herself. More tears followed.

"What nerve on Christmas?" Vienna held up the phone—hurling it toward a plant. Nick watched it crack in two against a pot, having never seen his mother this hysterical.

Instead of attempting to console either one, Arthur locked onto his son's angry stare with a cynical stare of his own. "Why don't you just go play that piano of yours. Isn't that what you really want?"

The apartment bell rang and Arthur, a little paranoid it might be his mistress cracked it open just enough. A jovial Marie was on the other end in fresh leggings, knee knee-high boots, a headband, and new argyle sweater with the tag still on it. She was holding her coat and scarf. "Merry Christmas, Mr. Crest."

Arthur gazed at Marie in a stupor before realizing he was a little underdressed. "Miss Bayliff." Arthur cringed as they could both clearly hear Vienna's grief wailing across the apartment.

"Is everything … OK?"

"With Nick's mother… all bets are off."

"Time to be going now," an embarrassed Nick rounded a corner with his coat, never more ready and anxious to leave. Marie couldn't help but notice most of the gifts underneath the tree were still unwrapped as Nick quickly hooked her by the arm—shutting the door with his foot.

"I assume I wasn't interrupting anything," she asked as they were already halfway to the elevator.

"Interrupting? Yes," Nick gazed into her striking eyes. "Which is perhaps the best gift you could have given me. So, what now?" he desperately changed the subject over tiles of crown silhouettes inside Trump Tower.

Vance

"I know it's a bit cliché, but how about ice skating at Central Park? Or if it's too busy, we could just do dessert at Serendipity. You know, like we used to."

But as they noticed the sun poking through the rotating doors, Nick got distracted. He'd remembered walking outside every Christmas morning to a frolicking scene downtown, but this year was noticeably different, as if he could immediately feel the somber mood pulsate through him. A surprise, only because he hadn't even considered until now what a tragic reality this was for so many.

More than one news van was parked along the curb with their antennas raised at tree-level. Reporters were looking for emotional, man-on-the-street reaction with confused New Yorkers anxious to vent their frustrations.

A mother holding her weeping child whipped past his view. "I promise, the toy store is just down the block," the woman was clearly locked in on her own personal emergency, racing as fast as she could, desperate to satisfy a distraught toddler. Nick's bothered stare followed at their backs as he watched them scurry away into more foot traffic.

"Are you alright," Marie turned his shoulder. "Perhaps I should have warned you. You know, before we … I figured you knew."

"No, it's OK," he clarified, forcing himself to snap from the glaze. He did his best to switch topic—this time to something he needed to finally get off his chest. "And thanks for saving me last night. I mean … so humiliating," he said before Marie cut him off with a smile.

"You just let your nerves override your concentration," she turned to stroke his hand—one that every now and again, twitched at will. "In fact, I read something similar even happened to Bach once."

"Bach?" Nick laughed. "You just made that up."

"Maybe," she playfully laughed as they continued to walk, passing a collection of faces that were getting harder and harder to ignore. They were young, bitter, and sad. Nick did what he could to bypass the obvious but got to a point where he couldn't avoid the elephant outside the room any longer. "So, what are we really supposed to make of all this?"

She only shrugged. "I guess you just kind of grow up expecting certain things to happen. And when they don't," they rubbed shoulders against a profusely apologetic father doing his best to reassure his little girl. "Only then do you consider such a thing even possible."

Nick would have nodded in agreement had he been able but instead stopped to grip his kneecaps. He could feel his heart racing again.

"Where are they?" Marie had been around Nick long enough to know exactly what he needed.

"Right … coat pocket, I think," he grimaced.

"Here, sit," Marie guided him toward an open street bench and popped the cap.

Fumbling for a bottle of water from her purse, Marie was prepared. "How fast is it beating?"

"It's beating," Nick cringed while holding his chest near Rockefeller Center. Holliday music blared and the décor was festive, despite the oddities of the morning.

"You nearly passed out in chemistry a few weeks back," she smiled as he began to calm down some. "In fact, you know what I think?"

"What's that?"

"I think your heart is simply too big."

"Too big?" Nick's eyes widened. "What are you talking about?"

"I think it's too big for your own chest. Your sensitivity for others," said Marie as Nick continued to grow aimlessly lost in the current predicaments of complete strangers. "I think you care about people too much … and perhaps sometimes … it just wants to burst."

Vance

Nick tried to avoid it but couldn't refrain from smiling. "Really? That's your best assessment?" Though he wanted to appear prickly around the edges, his eyes soon took over his concentration yet again—as if having a terrible time not sharing in the holiday horror. He was helpless not to feel the pain from the dolls and balls that never came.

Chapter 6

An old, leather bag was being put to good use. Isaac, in a stretch, one-piece, raced around dressers and armoires, hastily stuffing clothes inside—before the choo of a train suddenly interrupted the quiet solitude of his windowless bedroom. He looked up to where the train was. It was the size of a toy model, chugging forward through a hole in the top of the wall. There was a set of tracks for it to follow along an upper ledge, with trees, snow piles and even lampposts positioned alongside.

Isaac gazed over at a grandfather clock, as if surprised by its timing. "What do they want now?" he sighed as the train eased down to a stop at a station ramp. A green toy soldier that looked eerily lifelike in its movement was straddling the side of the train. The soldier dipped its hand into an open box car with no top, grabbed a normal-sized letter and handed it down. Isaac was forced to stand on his tiptoes to reach it, while the train wasted little time to start increasing back up to full speed again, through another hole in the wall along the opposite side.

Isaac ripped open the official envelope—one with a golden seal. He read it underneath a neon blue light; light responsible for the only glow inside the room. The text was short, but beautifully penned with swirling cursive.

Former Claus Chief of Staff, Isaac Newell,

With an official warrant being delivered for your forthcoming arrest, we advise you quickly to the Candy Cane Courthouse. All avenues for your escape have been blockaded and it is assumed you will turn yourself in by early morning on the morrow, without incident.

Sincerely Yours,
High Council Speaker,
Mauvtavious Lyman

Isaac digested the threat before striking a match and burning the note. He'd been bombarded with a series of official messages leading up to this latest decree—all of them delivered via rail.

Briskly reaching for the bag on his way out the door, he suddenly realized he'd forgotten something. It was a wrapped gift, no bigger than a book. Isaac set the present near the top of his luggage, zipped up and entered a dark, adjoining hall into a kitchen.

The kitchen was fifties in style, with corner-round pink appliances and old red and green signage on the walls. Isaac popped a straw from an old cola dispenser and poured hot tea from a kettle. After slurping down half, he went to a small box on the wall and punched a code that immediately opened a square in the middle of the linoleum. There was a ladder, which he took down into a secret room below. The surface leveled back flat above as he descended.

Inheriting the Sleigh

Other than patches of lamplight at various workstations, the basement was dark where a team of quiet elves were focused and hard at work.

"There you are. We've been getting nervous," said Silva. The elf was young and tall, with long, shiny black hair that had a silver streak running up the middle.

"That makes two of us," Isaac sighed as he caught up to speed on the progress of the escape plan. "The warrant's been granted sooner than I expected."

"And here I thought you actually might have some good news for once," Gib quipped in passing. "Nice suit by the way. You just get out of yoga class?"

"How's that key coming, Silva?" Isaac asked.

Her workstation sloped, with Silva's focus solely on creating the mold. "Did you really not believe me when I promised to have it done by departure? You do realize I've never disappointed you before. Well," she stopped herself. "At least since the cholera vaccination fiasco of 1812. But everybody needs a mulligan now and again."

"Well, plan on bumping up the departure." Others couldn't help but overhear, leaning in closer. They got a better look in a patch of good light—now able to tell by the way he was dressed that plans had clearly changed.

"Bumped up?" said Gib, awkwardly leaping to his feet and sauntering forward. "How bumped up are we talking about?"

"Hours," said Isaac. "I leave tonight."

"Tonight?" Blaine cried as he stepped even deeper into the light in the center of the small room. "But I barely have your documentation finalized. I can get you through Finland—but probably not Norway, and certainly not the States."

Vance

"And what about you, Corbs?" Isaac turned to an elf with thick, wavy hair. He was the only one still sitting. The smart, but laid-back elf had always been Isaac's go-to. "Tell me you're more optimistic than the rest of these nervous wrecks."

Corbin typed away at an old, dusty computer, chewing sugary gum at the same time. The bunker was less equipped to advanced technology, but he preferred it that way, always nostalgic for older machinery. The font was small and neon green, accompanied by an occasional beep. "It appears as if they've got men stationed at every corner post. Our access codes for the Wall have all been eliminated." Corbin then glanced at a series of surveillance monitors locked in on various parts of the city.

"And the Tubes?" Isaac clung to his last hope.

"Yeah, they shut those down first," Corbin always had a knack for sounding more casual than he should in dire situations, exemplified by another pop of his gum. "It looks as if those odious Elites are using any legal means necessary to wipe us out entirely."

"What should we do then?" there was a pleading behind Isaac's call. "You guys' never disappointed Kris ... and please don't save any of that disappointment for me now. I need you."

"Perhaps I've got an idea," the last elf in the bunker stepped forward for the first time. Ezra had his glasses resting low over his nose as he approached with a small, pen-size flashlight in hand. "I say we create a diversion to draw everybody away from the southern end. Give Cross here ten minutes inside the control room and he'll have the Wall deactivated."

"You know, for an elf who specializes in time," Gib quipped softly, so only Isaac next to him could hear. "You'd think he wouldn't restrict himself to ten minutes to get the job done."

The group of six mulled the crazy thought, aware that nobody else had yet to offer a better proposition. "I don't know what kind of diversion we're talking about, but it's gonna have to be fairly spectacular," Isaac informed.

"For starters," added Blaine with a checklist in hand. "You'll need a seal skin suit—probably with a layer of polar bear on top of that."

"Covered," Gib's grin tilted up underneath his walrus mustache. He pulled open a tall cabinet where the specialized wardrobe hung over a rod, pressed and new with all the travel accessories to go along with it. "Call it a hunch, but I figured you might be forced out into the bitter elements as a last resort."

"How 'bout an ice runner?" Isaac moved on before thanking Gib with a satisfactory nod.

"Parked and ready," insisted Blaine, stroking his decorative sideburns. "Though if we wait much longer, somebody snooping around is bound to stumble upon it."

Isaac took a deep breath, as if to suggest he was proud of the progress and impressed by their intuition. "You guys really are the best," he breathed.

Gib nodded. "I repeat the sentiment every day in the shower."

"Since when do you shower?" Silva whispered to an unwelcome stare.

The portly elf had a bunch of small, silver precision tools at his workstation, with only a single bulb providing minimal light. Some looked as if they could've been surgical instruments, and he gave them a final polish before placing them all into a padded briefcase.

"So," Isaac resumed. "About this diversion." Ezra already had a large grin, as if proud by what he was about to declare. "Ezra?" Isaac repeated as he failed to speak. "Tell me you have something specific in mind."

"Actually … it's already happening," said the squinting elf, checking his pocket for a better set of frames to see from a distance.

Corbin curiously rushed over to the three monitors above his workstation—slapping away at the keyboard until large plumes of smoke were suddenly spotted engulfing a series of large warehouses.

"That's the plastics division," said a concerned Silva with wide-eyed intrigue. "You're burning down the plastics division?!"

"Yeah, what's next? Metals and lumber?" Gib added with a straight face.

"If that's what it takes to get me out of here," said Isaac as the others were surprised to hear him approve. Just then, a balcony collapsed down upon the snowy street, crushing a trash bin and sounding an alarm. Vintage red fire trucks barreled out of brightly painted garages toward the flames.

"Watch the guards at Central Command and tell me when they move," Isaac instructed. "It's all under Elite control now."

"Still there," Corbin brought up another monitor with his boots casually kicked up over the desk.

"And which way is that fire burning?" asked Gib.

"Southeast," Ezra informed. "Considering wind direction and speed, it could spread that way in the next ... 15 minutes or so," he calculated after a glance at his pocket watch.

Isaac yanked Ezra by the collar, forcing him to look him in the eye. He wanted to kiss him on the forehead for his brilliance. "I'm not even gonna ask how you pulled that off." Isaac quickly tugged his new thick layer overtop his stretchy one-piece, ready to climb another ladder on the far end of the bunker. "But we might as well be close when it's time to strike."

"And then be ready to hunker down for who knows how long. We're all accomplices to some class A infractions now." Silva stared down

Inheriting the Sleigh

Ezra—who for the first time was beginning to show nerves himself.

Discreetly popping up through a snow-covered lid, concerned elves were outside in the darkness, curiously looking toward the gray streak generated from the massive flames. Many were fleeing to escape the smoky drift.

With thick hoods covering their eyes and ears, Isaac led the team, minus Corbin, down several alleyways and through the back lot of a doll factory. Some gates were hanging open, while others had to be scaled and climbed to finally arrive at Central Command.

It was exotic and grand, crafted of red brick and made up of many towers. The towers were of different heights, but all topped by domes. It was as if a unique Christmas tree bulb was perched upon each one. The colors of those domes drew in the eye but were faded a bit by the incoming flames.

"Who do you see?" Isaac asked as Silva had her eye on a scope for the back doors. "Only one guard. But I don't think he's going anywhere."

"It's time for the sticky stunner then," Isaac instructed as Silva handed him the scope to confirm the need for a specific weapon.

"Great," Gib sarcastically obliged. "Why do I see a hearty prison sentence in my future?"

That was the last thing on Isaac's mind as Blaine reached for the colorful gun.

"No, Cross" Blaine was surprised to see Isaac wave him off, requesting the gadget that looked more like a toy than an actual firearm. As the best marksman of the bunch, he was the obvious choice to take the shot. "If they ask you at trial who pulled the trigger ... you can all put your hand on the Old Testament and draw it back to me."

"Superb. Perhaps they'll only give me two to three hundred years then," Gib smirked. "Which for me could mean life."

Vance

Isaac had trouble concentrating. Between the ongoing fire alarm and the nervous bickering behind him, he wondered if he could even connect with his target—pacing back-and-forth a hundred feet away.

"Steady," Blaine was nervous by his twitching shoulder as Isaac knelt on one knee—the sticky stunner still lining up. "If you miss, he'll have a chance to cry for help."

The blaster was outlined by a series of flashing bulbs—looking ready for space battle. "And make sure the scope accuracy is initiated."

A focused Isaac pulled back on the trigger, dropping his target. A vibrating pulse was felt from the gun, and Blaine shook with approval, the guard now uncontrollably convulsing against the surface. He was creating involuntary snow angels in a patch of fresh snow.

Isaac nodded, as if impressed himself it only took him one take. He turned to find Blaine; whose artisan sideburns were frosted over by freshly fallen flakes. "Alright, Cross." Isaac used his pet name. "You've got approximately …," he turned to Ezra.

"Three and a half minutes before the guard regains any voluntary movement."

"210 seconds," Isaac repeated as Blaine eyed the now-subdued security guard.

Blaine burst for the door in a sprint as the others remained stationary in a snowstorm that continued to intensify.

"Two and a half minutes, Cross," Isaac muttered with his focus strictly on Central Command.

"So, what do you plan on doing once you get there?" Ezra inquired in a short patch of downtime—his attention still focused on the inferno.

"What do you mean?" asked Isaac as he highlighted the two-minute mark under breath.

"I mean, I know you're going after the boy and all. But I'm assuming he's already involved in a pretty intricate life, interwoven by a series of ... you know ... complex personal relationships." Isaac turned, wondering why he was using so many big words. "I'm just saying that it might not be so easy to entice him to leave. We've all seen his living quarters. Seems pretty exquisite to me."

"The frivolous and superficial components to one's life can often be deceiving, Ezra. 90 seconds!" Isaac stated with his own set of big words, as the streaking hum then reverberated across the Pole. The protective barrier wall was no longer there, and the team could almost immediately feel the rush of numbing cold once blockaded from the outside. Blaine came barreling out with everyone on edge, waiting for what was next. They knew that despite the commotion, not a soul could help but feel or hear the Wall deactivating.

"Record time," Isaac congratulated Blaine as he puffed hard into his numb hands.

"Thanks, but I'm sorry about the incomplete travel documents."

"Yeah, well ... we'll have to work with what we've got."

Chattering coats rounded a corner in the distance, speeding up the escape.

"Where's Corbin?!" Isaac yelled, with their window getting thinner. A shiny vehicle, with a clear, enclosed top suddenly spun into view. It kicked up heavy slush in its wake. The runners skidded out of control, as if driven by an amateur, and stopped only after ramming a snowbank. Everyone rushed over to pull Corbin out—the top mechanically lifting up.

"Sorry I'm late," he dusted himself off, though appeared to be OK. "Had to test out the flotation device. You never know when the ice is gonna crack."

Isaac swiftly traded places with Corbin as patrol vehicles sounded in the distance. "Good luck then," Isaac waved. "And I truly do mean that."

"Wait," Silva stopped him before he could speed off. "You will come back ... right?" Her question hinted she wasn't entirely sure.

Isaac hesitated but nodded. "If I do, let's just say I won't be alone. Now run!" he ordered, twisting the ice runner accelerator at a speed the vehicle was warning him not to go.

Chapter 7

There was a lot to talk about inside Lourdes Academy. The first day back from holiday break was typically loud, but the chatter this year was high for a different reason.

"Nick," a classmate razzed, his plaid collar rebelliously flipped straight up—his green tie loose around the neck. "With no Santa, I hope daddy came through this year."

Nick usually didn't grant Victor O'Keefe the courtesy of a response but did this time. "If you equate my father's generosity being caught red-handed with a harlot, then perhaps, yes … he did come through this year."

Nick slowly turned and walked away, while Victor was clearly caught off guard. Less by the sarcasm, and more by the fact he received a retort.

Marie, with a backpack slung over her shoulder, heard every word. "Hey … you," she playfully poked.

"Marie," Nick nodded, continuing at a swift pace. She forced herself to keep up.

"You do know that Victor is still staring. Looks a little blindsided, to put it mildly."

"Good. Mission accomplished."

"Is everything … alright?" it wasn't hard to sense his testiness. "Did your mother finally leave?"

"No, but I saw a lawyer at the house the other day."

Marie shook, as if understanding exactly what that meant. They entered their classroom at the sound of a bell. It was old, with plenty of history behind it. The chalkboards were dusty, and lines of ivy could be seen curling up and along the outsides of the windows. Nick and Marie were the first ones at their desks, followed by the rest in matching forest green uniforms.

Mr. Abbot dramatically coughed with his fist at his Adam's apple, as if purposefully signaling the kids' loose attention. He had a full head of curly hair with a noticeably large and round nose, and his voice was nasally at best.

"I hope everyone has learning and more learning on their minds today, for we have lots of catching up to do. Can everyone say, midterm, midterm, midterm?" The class was silent as Mr. Abbot waved a baton to gauge a reaction. "I was serious now; I want you all to say it."

"Midterm … midterm … midterm," the group was unenthusiastic and out of sync.

Mr. Abbot tapped his baton. "Yes, well, the break has really dampened our spirits, hasn't it? Pity you. Textbooks!" He was almost ruthless in the way he so quickly changed topic. "As the most entertaining Religious Studies instructor you may ever have, I'll allow you to thank me later with a Honeycrisp apple on my desk." The students were pained by the boredom—all too used to Mr. Abbot's quirky attempt at humor. "Chapter 17, entitled 'John the Apostle.'"

"Mr. Abbot," a boy's hand shot straight up. "Speaking of John. I have to … you know … use one. In the men's room." The class snickered as

Inheriting the Sleigh

Mr. Abbot scratched his face without even cracking a smile.

"Stanley Becker, I've been doing this for over 35 years. Assume I've heard that one before. Now, one free hall pass to the first person who can tell me how many books in the New Testament were written by the beloved hand of John." Not a hand rose, Mr. Abbot eventually forced to call upon his typical safety net. "Nicholas?"

Abbot approached his desk where Nick had his head bent low—his hands covering his clean-cut hair. The teacher intrusively crouched a bit to see between the small cracks of his fingers.

Nick released his knuckles just enough to stare back. "Five. He wrote five books, Mr. Abbot," he repeated for emphasis, as if desperately hoping not to be disturbed again—his mind needing to focus on more pressing things.

Abbot nodded, fully expecting to receive the correct answer from the smartest kid in the room. Nick immediately re-covered his head. "Correct, indeed. And can anyone besides Mr. Crest here tell me something unique about John?" he asked while moseying back to the chalkboard.

There was more silence, and this time the length of it bothered the boy. He quickly scribbled a note—one he managed to inconspicuously fold underneath his desk. With a subtle flick, the plane landed two desks ahead.

Marie quietly undid the creases in the torn notebook paper, just as she had so many times before. She read the note out loud with slow pronunciation while Mr. Abbot continued writing the class's next assignment on the board. "The only original apostle that scriptorians have never been able to agree to an exact cause of death."

Mr. Abbot swiveled around at the sound of a feminine voice. "Who said that?"

Vance

Marie, in her white button-up, plaid skirt and knee-high socks hesitantly half-raised a hand.

"Very good, Ms. Bayliff," said the teacher as Marie turned to offer Nick a silent "I owe you one." "As the others were mercilessly stoned, hung, or even crucified, we still don't know what happened to the son of Zebedee and Salome—the mysterious John the Beloved. Turn to his Gospel, 21st chapter. Jesus chatting with his chief apostle, Peter in the 21st verse. Peter refers to John and asks, 'What shall this man do?'" Mr. Abbot quoted the verse from memory as a few students were still trying to pin down the page. "And the Savior's response came in typical fashion. With another question, of course. Verse 22," he tapped another shoulder.

"If I will that he tarries till I come, what is it to thee?" read a girl with her long braid slung down to her waist.

"And finally, 23," Abbot signaled a student with a lisp.

"Then went this saying abroad among the brethren, this disciple should not die. Yet Jesus saith not unto him, he shall not die. But if I tarry till I come, what is that to thee?"

"So," Mr. Abbot enthusiastically raised his hands out wide to encompass the entire room. "I repeat Jesus' inquiry. What is that to you?" As usual, nothing but befuddled silence followed. In fact, not even Nick attempted to answer this time.

Mr. Abbot allowed the silence to permeate—until Roy Sam, a linebacker on the Lourdes Academy's football team built up the courage to change the subject entirely. Sam's brown and bulky physique was difficult to contain underneath his tight polo, and his short attention span was even more glaring. "Ugh, I hate to veer off topic, Mr. Abbot ... as John certainly is fascinating and all."

"Little late for that, wouldn't you say, Mr. Sam? But yes, I agree." Abbot waved to proceed.

Inheriting the Sleigh

"It's only, ugh … did you hear the news? I mean, it's all over the internet."

"News? What, that you now own the Bureau League sack record? I believe you've mentioned that before. Or is it the full ride to Syracuse you feel a need to remind me of now?"

"No, no," Sam laughed with a guilty look that gave away the fact he had a smart phone smuggled underneath his desk. "It's just being reported, sir, that they're close to locating the crash site."

For the first time, Nick curiously lifted his head to listen.

Abbot immediately pulled down a white screen over the chalkboard to magnify the classroom projector. He read the BBC headline, now visible before the class. "Australian Research Team Discovers Evidence of Santa Crash." For once, the kids no longer wallowed in boredom, perking up with their eyes glued to the projection. It was their generation's JFK assassination, or O.J. verdict.

"Researchers on snowshoes returning from an Antarctic expedition through the Southern Pole, stumbled upon debris findings Wednesday. The team led by University of New South Wales professor, Tom Turley, reported various toys and candy stuck in the snow deposits along their path. The team was studying the mating habits of emperor penguins when they came upon some man-made objects in the most unassuming of places, the world's deep tundra. 'We even discovered shards of a foreign metal,'" said Turley in the article. "'It was light and sleek, but extremely tough and unlike anything I had ever seen before.' Turley went on to assume the metal was part of Santa Claus' sleigh, though the crux of the sleigh was never found."

Mr. Abbot reached for a terrestrial globe on his desk. The globe was so old, the country of Iran was still called Persia. He spun the tan ball until coming upon the massive expanse of uninhabited land south of the

Indian Ocean. "Well, I'll be," he whispered with a rare smile.

A secretary with old glasses poked her head through the classroom door. "I apologize, Albert," she called Mr. Abbot by his first name. "But Nick Crest's mother is here to draw him out of school."

"Mama here for your little dentist appointment," the class heckled the boy, who absolutely detested the undue attention.

"Nick, make sure and read through the end of 17 by tomorrow," Abbot instructed. "Expect to be quizzed. Oh, and don't forget that report on Paul's epistle to the Ephesians is due by next week." Nick had hardly paid attention as he grabbed his bag to swiftly follow the secretary out the door.

"May I ask what this is about?" he inquired.

But she seemed hesitant to say more than she had to. "Well, it appears as if there's been a little incident, and this is not the time for you to be here at school."

Loopy passed by with an overblown, jumbo-sized hall pass slung around his neck. He was headed for the bathroom and couldn't refrain from making a scene on his way there. "Hey, Nick! What did I tell you about the man in the hat? Pretty wild stuff, hey? Looks like they found the crash site and may be close to track'n down his ride. I wish we were both there to loot the spoil. Seriously, you should come over though. We still need to plan out our line of attack on the Gershwin."

Nick was embarrassed by those able to overhear—quickly turning the other way—relieved to round a corner and out of sight. The secretary led the way into the school office where Vienna anxiously stood up from her waiting chair. She was dressed far more casually than usual and had a patch over one eye. On top of that, his mother's cheekbones looked bruised.

"What happened!?"

Inheriting the Sleigh

"Never mind," Vienna appeared anxious to retrieve her son before having to divulge much more. "Thank you, I appreciate it," she gestured to the secretary, though unable to hide her emotion. Grabbing hold of Nick's forearm, they whisked along the hallway and down the Academy's front steps.

"Are you seriously not going to tell me what's going on here. Why are you hurt?" Nick felt like he could now raise his voice.

"I'm OK, Nick. We just have to leave, that's all."

"Leave? Where?"

"Out of the city. Out of New York. Your grandmother's waiting for us in Connecticut."

Nick stopped before they could cross the street on their way toward the subway terminal. "Dad did that, didn't he?" he now had his hands gripped over both his mother's shoulders, only letting go after she flinched in pain from the pressure of another bruise. Vienna said nothing, simply staring as the crossing signal turned white.

Chapter 8

Isaac had both heard the tales and seen it on screen many times before. But it was different entirely to be veering up at one skyscraper after the next blocking his view of the world outside downtown Manhattan. The Chrysler Building, for one, nearly appeared to bridge the hustling street with the heavens above in the overcast sky.

The mid-January weather was brisk, and life was beginning to move again following the tragic absence of Santa Claus.

The elf felt funny dressed as an everyday American. He wore a bright orange ski coat with a wool liner, jeans and a knit hat, though all lacking the brand name tags. He was taking his time to absorb the foreign vibe, something he had always been curious about. Because after listening to Kris talk about his exotic experiences year after year, he was realizing the minimal detail he'd received just wasn't enough. He had to experience the grandeur and bustling pace of New York City for himself.

Isaac was abruptly bumped backward. With his head stuck up in the gray clouds—staring at lights illuminating various high-story windows—he failed to even see the turban. The irritated man was moving swiftly, clearly not expecting Isaac to understand his mumbling rant as he backpedaled from the collision. The truth was, Isaac's job forced him to be semi-fluent in nearly 5,000 languages, including Arabic.

"Anafasa," Isaac slurred back to signal how terribly sorry he was. The Pakistani grew startled and embarrassed before quickly scampering off into more foot traffic.

Isaac slipped into a short gap between buildings to gather himself and think away from the crowds—something rarely a problem at the Pole. "Corbin, where are you?" he mumbled in frustration while pulling out a device. It was two or three times the size of an iPhone and had a stick handle on the bottom. There was no easy way to read the layout, with a series of dots and codes replacing the apps. Isaac knew he was getting close to his destination, all as his handheld machine went berserk, warning him of something.

Popping back out onto the sidewalk, the elf veered across 56th Street to see Trump Tower in golden caps above the hotel's glass entryway. Quickly merging onto Fifth Avenue, he couldn't help but notice a digital billboard with a message from an Atheist group taunting Christians. The sign, with holly, mistletoe, and a cross dissolved into view. "Where is your Christmas now?"

Isaac tried to keep his odd instrument discreet as he approached the potted boxwoods at the front entrance. The atrium was lavish and illuminated by a cascading waterfall and surrounded by pink, marble walls and brass mirrors. But all the while, the location dots on his monitor were screaming with silent urgency—causing Isaac to immediately lift his head.

Nick was now descending the golden escalator. The boy he'd studied so intently from the hologram was focused and stripped of a smile. Isaac whipped around in every direction, back-and-forth between his mini monitor and the pockets of traffic inside the hotel. Relief was only met by distraction as the overwhelmed elf was suddenly forced to juggle two trains of thought.

"Chief … you copy," Isaac suddenly heard some soft static as he pushed through the rotating doors in Nick's wake—back into the brisk air. Shoving his earpiece further in, it was exactly what he'd been waiting for as the signal gradually became more and more clear.

"Corbin?" Isaac gleaned softly so as not to draw too much attention to himself. "Is that you?"

"Yeah," he retorted. "Finally got this old satellite receptor up and running in the bunker. It's on reserve power, but it should work … for a few days anyway. You know, as much as we mock, you have to hand it to the enemy. The Elites have severely managed to disrupt our communication processes. It's making my life exceedingly difficult."

"Are you safe?" Isaac had a thousand questions, while doing his best to keep up with Nick. The boy was marching swiftly to a series of honking traffic on Fifth Avenue. "I've been trying to gain contact since Greenland."

"If 'safe' is your way of saying, undetected at the moment … then yeah, I'm safe." Isaac could clearly picture his friend blowing a massive bubble, within a bubble, within another bubble.

"And the others?" Isaac probed as he followed a safe distance behind Nick walking briskly south.

"I momentarily found a frequency good enough to reach Gib this morning. He was whining like a baby, hiding out in some factory attic somewhere—without a pantry, I might add. Hunger pains clearly setting in. As for everybody else, I assume they were left to improvise after the Guard drew in quicker than expected. Honestly, they could have spread out in any number of places."

Isaac puffed into his hands, while now struggling to keep up with

Nick. "And what about you?" Corbin changed the subject after a lull in the exchange. "Looks like you're actually there. Let freedom ring."

"Yeah," Isaac confirmed as a woman looked back, wondering if he was talking to her. "In fact, I'm following him right now."

"Wait, what?" Corbin was taken aback, having no idea the decisive moment was actually happening as they spoke. "And?"

"And I ... don't ...." Isaac suddenly stopped altogether.

Corbin waited a few seconds for Isaac to finish, though he never did. "You don't ... what?"

"I think I just lost him," Isaac vented as he ran ahead with Nick now nowhere in sight. "Yeah," he swiveled, with more street-goers intrusively pushing at his back. "I must have taken my eyes off or something. He's gone!"

"What do you mean ... gone?!"

Isaac held up his hands in disgust as he jogged ahead to see if he could catch another glimpse on the heavily used sidewalk.

"Just take a breath," Corbin soothed.

"What about the surveillance line?" Isaac snapped his fingers with an idea. "Can you activate some of those cameras?"

"Wait," said Corbin, as there was good reason he hadn't brought the idea up himself. "You know as well as I, there are some major privacy concerns with that. That was Kris' domain, and his job alone to be accessing ..."

"Corbin, you know as well as I, I wouldn't suggest such a thing if it weren't paramount," Isaac felt the need to raise his voice this time to get his point across.

Corbin bit his tongue, as if desperately not wanting to go there. Isaac listened as Corbin reluctantly slid his rolling chair back across the bunker's hardwood floor, punching up one random monitor after another. "Where exactly is your cross street?"

"Fifth and 51st, I believe. He was wearing a blue fleece, with a hood and navy scarf."

"Blue fleece, navy scarf. Blue fleece, navy scarf," Corbin whispered to himself as he typed away, trying to pull up the correct one. "I haven't used some of this equipment in ages," he mumbled while blowing some dust off an old switchboard. Isaac, meanwhile, poked his anxious head through passing store entryways. "Then again, I still got it," Corbin smiled in response to locating Nick so promptly as he watched him suddenly emerge two blocks ahead.

"Where?!"

"Veer down the alley at 49th."

"49th?" Isaac was flustered in the new terrain. Cab horns honked as he forgot to inspect a crosswalk for oncoming traffic.

"Remember ... you're dealing with streetlights now," Corbin reminded as he personally watched a taxi nearly barrel right over Isaac's scampering feet. "OK, turn there."

"Where?" he peered into an empty alleyway with nothing but piled up trash bags and emergency foldup ladders in sight. "I don't see him."

"That's because he went inside," Corbin signaled some neon blue signage above a door—one that blended in perfectly with a concrete wall. It was old and rusty compared to those on the brightly lit street. The sign looked like something plugged into an old record store window and read, "The Blue Owl" overtop some crumbling brick.

Isaac knocked but nobody answered, prompting him to eventually crack it open himself. There was nothing but a rickety staircase on the other side. "Are you sure this is where he went?" he probed, hoping for some reassurance.

"As sure as Santa is dead," Corbin confirmed with a hush.

Inheriting the Sleigh

"Unfortunately, that's where my view stops."

"In that case," an uncertain Isaac whispered as he took off his knit hat and approached the steps. "Signing off for now."

Only a single bulb dangled by a string to expose the bottom of the stairwell where a dark hallway veered deeper underground. Isaac listened closely for noise he could now hear. Reluctantly tiptoeing his way around, he was cautious as the noise gradually grew louder in the emerging neon light. It was a hidden nightspot that morphed from a crumbling mortar hallway into a swanky oasis.

Isaac, attracted to the glow, took a step forward. He followed up a short flight of steps before being swiftly stopped in his tracks.

"Hold there," instructed the baritone voice with a mohawk and quarter-size holes in his ears. His hair was pasted upright like a rooster crest, and the sides of his scalp were completely bare. He wore a wife beater exposing an arm speckled with swirling patterns of rainbow-colored artwork, and had rings punched through nearly every extremity of his face. "Name?" The flamboyant bouncer, with combat boots and military pants, pulled out a binder from underneath the desk.

Isaac thought hard about what he might say before starting with the truth. "I'm just looking for someone. You won't find me on that list."

The bouncer pretended to check his massive watch. "You've officially wasted the last 17 seconds of my life. This is a member's-only establishment," he turned his back while scrubbing down a tall, fancy glass.

Flipping around again, the bouncer fully expected Isaac to have disappeared. But instead, the persistent elf now displayed a full stack of crisp, one hundred-dollar bills. Isaac used his thumb and index finger to draw several out. The bouncer kept his eyes glued to the appetizing currency before silently suggesting he keep going. Isaac, one by one, slowly added another bill before stopping again. The bouncer, with creases underneath the tattoos in his arms, was approaching seven feet when adding his hair. He softly motioned one last bill before extending a hand for the wad. Isaac, humored by an American's gullibility for fast and easy money, then slowly proceeded forward, anxious to escape the bouncer's glare.

"Wait!" he yelled over a techno beat. "Your name!" But Isaac failed to respond, instead vanishing up a short flight of stairs.

He was used to observing the incredibly bright stars and other fascinations of nature, such as the streaking Aurora Borealis in the high northern country, but the strobing flashes and heavy beats were beginning to annoy him.

The club wasn't crowded, but there were trendy patrons perched at most of the countertops and over vintage furniture from decades past. Contemporary rods and funky chandeliers dazzled the ceilings—to a point where it almost made Isaac dizzy as he glanced around for any sight of Nick. All the while, grappling with the truth of why he would ever visit such a place to begin with.

A waitress, with six rings through her nose, met a bartender close enough for Isaac to overhear. "Take this to customer one!" he carefully instructed over the blaring music. The loaded tray contained several bottles of high-priced liquor—bottles clearly designed to dazzle.

"Mr. Crest has arrived sooner than usual?" The waitress, with a stack of loose-fitted bracelets dangling off her wrists, smirked while picking up the tray.

The last name immediately caught Isaac's attention, and he followed her as she swiftly strolled toward the very back of the spacious club— around several booths and past a stage set up for a band. Isaac quietly crept behind her before arriving upon another quaint section.

Inheriting the Sleigh

The décor was suddenly more appealing to an older crowd and looked like the inside of a castle library. Tall, cherry bookshelves rose tall above flickering fireplaces, with red cushioned furniture and exotic artwork on the walls. It looked straight out of an old speakeasy.

Isaac nonchalantly took a seat at a small, round table, watching the waitress locate Arthur. He was sitting on a barstool in a business suit, his tie loose around the collar, as if winding down from a stressful day at the office. He barely acknowledged the waitress as she dropped off the assortment of bottles; bottles that Isaac assumed would exceed a normal man's annual wage.

But Arthur was not the person Isaac was interested in, rather the boy that had somehow managed to slip all the way inside completely undetected. Arthur didn't know it, but Nick's eyes were glued to the back of his Armani coat.

The waitress finally noticed Nick. She tried to get a look past his eyes beyond a hoodie. They seemed young, though she was immediately pulled away before a chance presented itself to pursue her curiosity.

"We need a couple Vodkas over here!" the waitress scurried back out to assist several other well-dressed patrons, smoking pipes inside the underground lounge.

"Can't you wait a minute," another waitress cried, frustrated she couldn't take care of everybody's requests at once.

"I've been waiting here since last Tuesday!" the man fired back, all as Nick stepped in closer.

He peered behind his father, while Isaac veered to avoid eye contact. A sweating Nick then suddenly made his approach where Arthur sat semi-glazed and alone. After chugging a shot glass, his father couldn't help but notice his son—the straight-faced boy now that close.

"Nick? he mumbled in half-surprise and half-irritation. "What are you doing here? I mean, how did you get in here? Or better yet even know I was here?" The questions were half-sensible. Arthur's intoxicated head swiveled, with Nick, embarrassed to say the least. Isaac quickly moved closer, nervous as to what might happen next.

"So, this is your life now?" Nick said sadly, with other patrons hard not to overhear the peculiar conversation.

"Nick," Isaac closely watched Arthur want to scold him, though was in no position. Instead, he tried to explain. "No, no. What you're seeing is not who I really are. I mean … am. You know that, don't you … Nick? I'm a good person. Ask anyone here. They'll tell you," he slurred, with his glass raised high before finishing off another shot. "Go on … ask 'em."

Nick couldn't take much more of the rambling. "Are you aware that Mom is preparing to file charges against you? Does any of that register at all?" All eyes in the room were now focused on the exchange.

Arthur's humiliation was quickly morphing into anger. "Is that so?"

"You honestly believe you can buy your way out of anything, don't you? That any problem will magically just disappear."

"You really think it's wise to talk to me like that?" Arthur whispered, doing his best not to be overheard.

"How could you beat her?!" Nick yelled, not the least bit ashamed to reveal the truth in front of a room full of complete strangers. "You expect me to sit back and watch as you self-destruct, ruining our lives at the same time?"

Arthur stood, with his intoxication since turning into a drunken rage. He flipped a tray onto the concrete surface, shattering the fancy bottles. The others stood as well as Arthur suddenly pulled off his coat, rolling up his sleeves and charging like an irate bull. Nick held his stance, but being outweighed by a good 80 pounds, was helpless. Isaac immediately stood in concern as Nick was driven backwards into some awaiting chairs.

"Don't you ever speak to me that way, you ungrateful …!" Surrounding patrons, far more sensible, quickly scampered over to stop Arthur from taking another swing. Now on his back, Nick covered up his vulnerable face. "I took you in! Without me, you'd have grown up in some rat-infested foster home!" Arthur screamed in bitter rage—held back from inflicting a knockout blow. "Let me go!" he popped back up, aimlessly shoving at those daring to still touch him.

"And what, let you kill the poor kid?" asked a concerned patron.

Nick's nose was bleeding, but his reaction to the fight was far more severe. He was now convulsing, of which nobody knew how to stop.

"Excuse me!" Isaac didn't plan on stepping forward but felt like he no longer had a choice. Bending down in the scrum of good Samaritans, he gripped Nick by the shoulders, looking him directly in the eyes for the first time. Reaching inside the boy's pocket, he pulled out a prescription cannister. The others watched helplessly as Isaac forced Nick's rigid back up straight. "Water, please!" he cried as nobody thought of the obvious for themself.

Arthur was now unrestrained, watching in wonder from a distance as Isaac went to work, forcing the pills down Nick's throat. Almost immediately the shaking began to quell.

"Are you some kind of doctor or something?" inquired an observer.

Isaac turned after gently setting Nick's limp frame back down onto the cold surface. "No," he uttered while gazing into Arthur's lost glare. Once again, his mind struggled, trying to decide just how much to divulge. "Let's just say I was present at the boy's birth," he said vaguely as Arthur's bloodshot eyes doubled with intrigue.

"Present … at the boy's birth?" he squinted with a sleeve that was now partially ripped off. "That's ridiculous."

Vance

Isaac took a deep breath, wondering if Arthur might attack him too. Instead, the elf's mind suddenly drew back 14 years to a small white room with red trim. Kris and a single doctor urged Martha to keep pushing. Sitting a few feet back from the bed, Isaac held a wood bark pen, recording every detail of the delivery.

"I don't know who you think you are, but you sure as hell better be willing to provide more proof than that!" Arthur exclaimed.

"Check his lower back," Isaac calmly motioned to another patron close by in the dim light. "There's a birthmark there. It's shaped like a candy cane." A man at his side hesitantly pulled up Nick's sweater. "And if you need more, the boy's got a total of 17 freckles on his left arm. Not to mention a surgical incision just below his heart."

"What have you done, stolen his medical records or something?" Arthur accused.

But the elf didn't speak this time as Nick was groggily regaining his senses. With others quickly pouring in, Isaac had no choice but to discreetly slip out of sight. He had inadvertently said too much.

Chapter 9

Isaac mopped the 51st floor. With rolled sleeves, the janitor blended in nicely, smiling at those passing by—which included the likes of a cookie company heiress and a Saudi prince draped in a silk bed sheet and pink headdress.

As the golden elevator doors closed, the hallway was clear again. Isaac finished dusting a painting of the old Twin Towers. He turned, lifting his head to listen for any more unwelcome footsteps before standing directly in front of door number 5116.

Reaching down into a utility cart, the elf pulled out a small briefcase. Patiently waiting for a rotating security camera to veer out of view, he tried the key first, but it didn't fit. The elf wasn't rattled, choosing a pick instead.

After another ding of the elevator, a new suit sauntered past. Isaac slipped a rag out from a jumpsuit pocket, casually scrubbing against the door panel to look busy. With a pair of polished black shoes soon fading out of view, a couple more swivels from a more suitable pick was all it took for the door to suddenly inch open.

Isaac took his time to step forward—for one, to behold a breathtaking view he had only previously seen from limited angles via the ornament. And two, to absorb who might be inside the swanky residence.

The tall, tinted bay windows were without blinds, exposing a direct view of Central Park. Tree limbs hovered below, with a wall of skyscrapers beyond that in the distance. Tall vases in the entryway foyer housed decorative dry weeds, as if perched outside an Egyptian pyramid. An authentic coat of a Yankee soldier was displayed on the wall near the entryway, alongside an original bulbed poster of the Broadway show, *Rent*. They both complimented a framed, hand-written note signed by President John Adams to his beloved wife, Abigail.

Isaac listened for voices and could hear some, though they were faint and distant. He crossed underneath the chandelier into a room full of floating bubbles on the wall. Contemporary lights hung from the ceiling to provide minimal light in a dark room. Isaac recognized the baby grand and continued to tiptoe forward up a higher platform and past the fish tank—one built directly into the wall itself. A small TV was turned on at low volume above a sink in the kitchen, with a news roundtable giving their latest theories on the disappearance of Santa Claus—over a month gone by since the crash.

But that wasn't the noise he was listening for and kept going until he found it. It came from Nick's bedroom.

"I still don't understand how you could be so foolish following him there to a place like that. Dangerous and dumb," Vienna sat along the edge of his bed, taking a fresh washcloth to address a wound in her son's forehead.

"You're blaming me? Arthur's whole life has been a sham." Nick often called his father by his first name, perhaps a clue as to how he truly felt about him. Vienna was full of guilt as she absorbed the truth, only to suggest even more guilt through her silence. "What ... you mean ... you knew?" Nick asked.

Vienna tried to avoid eye contact but couldn't keep at it very long. "Well, let's just say... it's all extremely complicated."

"Complicated. What do you mean, complicated?"

"I mean, your dad is who he is, Nick," Vienna was almost relieved to say it out loud. "Extremely well-off, handsome, charming. At least when he has to be. Unfortunately, that's how many men in this town are."

Quietly standing parallel with his back against the partially open bedroom door, Isaac listened as Nick contemplated that pessimistic view of humanity.

As for the elf, he had many thoughts—including abandoning every task he had come so far to perform; but each time, forced himself to squash that second-guess. As terrible as he felt, he knew it was something that simply had to be done—swiveling without another thought for the crack in the door.

Isaac's sudden emergence was the last thing Nick ever expected to see as a small but colorful dart suddenly struck his mother's neck. Vienna's eyes froze wide before her frame dropped like a heavy ball— Isaac swooping in from nowhere to catch her before she hit the floor.

Nick instinctively sprung upward, scooting further down against the bedframe. The startled boy attempted to yell, though nothing came out as he was met by an odd gun the size of a pistol. It was teal with a large, circular muzzle. Isaac was quick to squeeze the trigger, disabling the terrified boy's lungs with a visible gas that almost immediately put Nick to sleep.

Isaac raced to open a window, covering up his own face with a cloth.

"Now I understand this must seem rather odd. Frightening even,"

Nick's transitioning mind was able to draw in only a faint trace of the voice. "Nicholas, can you hear me?" He could, but it was hard. He had no idea how long he'd been out but soon noticed a man sitting in a chair next to his bed. He was short but clean-shaven—a nice disposition to his face and appeared to be mid to late 30's in age. The last person Nick ever expected to pose a threat.

Isaac slowly moved his finger along Nick's pale face, only to see his eyes move with it. "Yeah, you'll be back to normal in minutes, perhaps sooner," he insisted with a mild shrug, using a couple more devices to check Nick's vitals.

Nick had to muse long and hard to remember everything that'd happened prior to the moment he passed out, but the thought of his mother suddenly slapped him cold. "Whoa!" Isaac braced Nick's shoulders as he slung upward, only to realize he didn't have the strength to make such an abrupt lunge.

"Where … is she?" Nick stammered.

Isaac pointed to the floor where Vienna lied—her head comfortably over a plush pillow. "She's just fine. Only sleeping peacefully, just as you were." Nick felt the need to panic but had trouble doing so, still under the duress of the gas. "I just need you to relax," Isaac gently guided him back down. "I know you're concerned about your mother," Isaac gazed up at a clock on the wall. "But you'll be talking to her again by the top of the hour."

"What … you … want?" Nick did his best to slur the obvious.

Isaac took a breath. "A fair question, indeed," he said with a look of surprise by how quick Nick was coming to his senses.

"Because you can take anything. But I promise, I don't know the combination to my father's safe, and personally all my money is tied up in the form of a trust. I can't even touch it until …"

Inheriting the Sleigh

Using a quick hand to cut Nick off, Isaac ignored his guilt. "I'm sorry to lend you that impression, but I'm not here for your money."

Nick finally had the strength to sit up. He inspected his mother—oddly smiling in her slumber. He then turned back toward the intruder, analyzing the elf the best he could. "I know you," it finally clicked as Isaac had since stood up pacing about the room. "How did you …?" Nick gulped nervously while tucking his knees up against his chest. "I mean, know all that stuff about me?"

"Now we're getting somewhere," Isaac nodded as he took a seat again, this time over Nick's keyboard bench. He glanced around the walls to see framed portraits of all the famous composers. The sketches were black and white with uniform frames. "You're quite the pianist, aren't you?" Isaac picked up one of several honorary certificates displayed over his desk. "Impressive. Then again, if you had known your father, it all makes sense. He was quite impressive in his own right." Isaac's gaze then shot back toward Nick, sweating as he waited for his previous question to finally get answered. "Sidetracked … of course. Perhaps I should start with my name." Nick's eyes were half-dipped in fear, the other half in deep confusion. "Isaac. Isaac Newell." The elf stuck out his arm, though Nick failed to complete the handshake.

"You mentioned my father," Nick, at this point seemed to have most of his normal wits about him. He was deathly serious with his newest inquiry. "What did you mean?"

Isaac appeared conflicted by how to respond. Nick had always been curious about his birth parents and intuitively beat him to it with another question. "You weren't talking about Arthur Crest, were you?"

Isaac paused before offering a confirmation. "Arthur Theodore Crest? No, I certainly was not."

"So, you know that I'm adopted then?" Nick squinted, still

wondering a million things.

"Why, yes … I do," Isaac retorted calmly.

Nick's mind drew back to the infinite number of times he'd asked his mother where he'd come from, though eventually grew tired of hearing her change the subject.

"So …" Nick, still a bit skeptical, suggested the man he'd only known for no more than five minutes to proceed. "Tell me. Who is my real father?"

Isaac knew it all needed to come out some time and figured there was none better. "What if I told you, he was a man you've always known from afar?"

Nick absorbed the clue, only to grow stumped by the riddle. "Known from afar?" he eventually repeated the last three words. "And I'm supposed to know what that means? In fact, this is all getting extremely weird," Nick began to panic again. Isaac grew concerned as Vienna's head suddenly flinched up for the first time, though only temporarily.

"The truth is, I knew your parents," it finally spilled out. "Fairly well, in fact."

Nick, at this point, added up what he could. "So, you don't want money. And you knew my birth parents. I'm assuming there was a better way of telling me all this. I mean, without breaking in. Are you here to kidnap me or something?"

"Well, yeah," his honesty was instinctive before realizing how that might sound to an uncertain child. "I mean," Isaac hastily pushed out an open palm as if calming down a feisty horse. Isaac was now standing again to speed up the revelation—one that so far had not gone well. "I'm not trying to kidnap …! Look, you asked how I knew you. You don't come from New York, Nick. In fact, you don't come from America at all."

His squint was long and deep. "Then where do I … come from?"

"The North Pole," Isaac revealed with a penetrating gaze, all as Nick took a moment to swallow the absurd thought. The declaration dangled there for many seconds.

"Is this some sort of weird prank?" he still didn't know whether he could believe a single thing the elf said. "Loopy sent you over here, didn't he?"

"Loopy?" Isaac countered. "You mean, Russell O'Brien, the annoying kid down on Waverly Place?"

"Yeah, Loopy O'Brien," Nick was taken back, as very few people actually used his given name. Nick quickly got back on point. "Look, if you really do know my birth parents, then you can tell me how to contact them."

The elves' tone changed. "I'm sorry. But I can't do that," Isaac shrugged.

"Of course," the boy cynically grew suspect. "Because you're a mile from the truth."

"Your real parents are dead, Nick," Isaac this time released his bombshell as abruptly as he knew how, tired of beating around any more bushes.

Nick bit his tongue. Though a part of him believed none of what he was told, a small piece of his heart did begin to grow excited by the thought. It was a glimmer that faded just as quickly as it came.

"Think about it," Isaac resumed. "The delivery never happened this year, and as an official messenger of the North Pole, I've come to tell you the truth."

"The truth?"

"Yes," Isaac nodded with a smirk. "As outlandish as it might sound."

Vance

Nick glanced at Vienna one final time before succumbing, signaling Isaac to continue. "Go ahead then. Tell me—what is the truth?"

"Your last name at birth," Isaac grinned, as if finally getting to the good part. He could feel the spotlight shining down on the anticipated reveal. "It's ... Kringle."

Nick finally felt as if he had more than enough strength to physically push himself up off his bed, though it was another squint that was most noticeable. "Kringle? What are you saying?" "That my father is ... Santa Claus?"

Nick said it half-jokingly, and yet Isaac's return stare clearly confirmed that was not his intent. "That's right. I'm now looking at the one and only heir of Kris and Martha Kringle."

Nick grew quiet again before suddenly reaching for his medication; pills that didn't seem to be where he last remembered—over his bedstand.

"Give me a hint," Isaac urgently asked as Nick pointed to a shelf where several new white bottles were neatly lined up between books full of sheet music. Isaac waited patiently for the prescription to settle in.

"Tell me," Nick was abrupt this time with his question. "What do you want from me? And why are you telling me this now?"

Isaac's gaze accurately reflected the empathy inside his heart. "What if I told you that Christmas was in jeopardy of forever falling apart ... and that its resurrection rested solely upon you."

Nick hopped to his feet for the first time, with the concerned elf bracing for any hasty movement. "Resurrection ... rests ... on me?" his eyelids widened with sarcasm. "What ... I assume you want to take me to the North Pole or something, is that it? And make me the next, Santa Claus?"

Isaac only rolled his eyes—to suggest, maybe.

Inheriting the Sleigh

"Please tell me that's not what you're saying. Because if it is, it's absurd."

"The truth is," the elf's voice softened with more honesty. "I hate being here right now—even more than you hate seeing me. But the world needs you, Nick."

Nick wanted to be dreaming, but at this point was confident he couldn't possibly be. "But ... my life is here," he turned again to his mother. "Granted, it's not all roses, but it's nothing I can just run away from. Specially to pursue something I'm less than certain is even real."

"I know your problems, Nick," Isaac's tone softened. "Unfortunately, most kids have them in one way or another, which is precisely why your father lived the unusual life he did."

"And yet ... he failed to come through. Did he not?" Nick this time had some bitterness in his voice. "Isaac, is it?" The elf nodded in silence, listening to Nick release what troubled him. "So, what you're really saying ... I now have two fathers who have disappointed me?"

Isaac didn't know how to respond this time, nor had he ever thought about it that way. Instead, he turned to the clock on the wall knowing Vienna would be waking back up at any moment. "Well, food for thought," he mumbled as his first crack at Nick came to an end. Whether he liked it or not, the elf was forced to quietly fade away, exiting the bedroom—followed by apartment number 5116.

Chapter 10

Vienna was awake, but disheveled, sipping a cup of coffee near a bay window. She couldn't remember a single thing about passing out, and Nick chose not to remind her, figuring she probably wouldn't believe it anyway. In fact, he made sure his mother was too distracted to notice him reading a note that was clearly intended solely for him.

The paper was old, almost like a raveled up Dead Sea Scroll—of which he oddly noticed sticking up out of his favorite pair of shoes.

I obviously cannot force you to come with me, Isaac's penmanship was close to perfect, with a large, swirling capital letter at the top. *But your father is dead, which means that Christmas is also. Good thing hope still exists to save it. Let us bravely act on that hope together.* It was signed by the elf's own hand.

A knock jolted Nick's heart, causing him to drop the letter that curled back up as it fell.

"Crest residence?" asked one of two NYPD. Nick only nodded as he pulled back on the door.

Vienna scurried over, expecting the visit. "Please, come in."

"Then I assume you know why we're here, ma'am."

Inheriting the Sleigh

"Has he posted bail yet?" she couldn't wait a second longer to ask.

"Yes," said the second officer with a hand at her hip. "This morning—but his next court appearance isn't until next month."

"But what if he comes back here? I mean he's already laid hands on myself, not to mention our son."

"Don't worry, the judge issued a restraining order. Mr. Crest can't legally come within 500 feet of either one of you."

"But he has more money than the Vatican. Not to mention, keys to the apartment," Vienna continued to plead in paranoia.

"Well then, I suggest you get those locks changed, ma'am."

Nick managed to slip past the officers attending to his mother, poking his cluttered head out the door to see into the vast Trump Tower hallway. The truth was, he was anxious, looking for any evidence of a lurking elf nearby—curious, but more frightened as to what other surprises might lay in store.

His first glance offered nothing—though as he double-checked, a second scroll, sure enough, leaned alone against a bare wall.

He looked to see if the vicinity was clear, unraveling it quickly.

As for me, I have no choice but to return. My agenda was clear. I needed you to follow, though am prepared to disappoint millions if necessary. I understand what you'd be giving up should you elect to change your mind. Don't let guilt consume your heart. May God grant you the strength to work it out. And always know, you have a trusted friend.
Sincerely,
Isaac Newell

Nick's heart sped. He paced about, eventually bending over a wine cabinet in the kitchen for support—his fingers barely clinging to the rough parchment. "I can't do this. I can't do this. I can't do this," he repeated in nervous motion as if desperately trying to talk himself out of it. "In fact, I can't even think about doing this. You're not actually considering … no, of course not," he uncharacteristically chattered to himself. "That would be crazy."

Nick's eyeline then caught something peculiar. It was the top of another scroll. Most would have walked right past it resting inconspicuously inside a vase over the granite countertop.

Vienna continued to plead her case at the door while Nick hurried toward the vase to slip off a red ribbon tying the scroll together. He hesitated but ultimately unraveled the third note.

I trust you now have had considerable time to think.

"You've got to be kidding me," Nick cursed under his breath "Who is this guy?"

And it sounds as if you are rightly easing into your decision. The Pole is a complex, but charming place. Sort of like your own life. I think you'll come to really love it there.

"Complex, but charming place?" he grimaced.

Good question, the letter read as if Isaac was verbally responding to his latest concern. *Let's just say it certainly has its share of political squabbling. Then again, name a place that doesn't. It'll play right to your strengths, Nick. Because let's be honest, the Pole is in your blood.*

"Nick, can we talk?" A teary Vienna suddenly appeared through the dining room atrium. He quickly pulled the scroll behind his back. It wasn't discreet, but due to the weight of so many other things on her mind, his mother failed to point out the strange behavior.

"I've decided we need to resume with plan A and go to Connecticut. We'll be safe there. Of course, we'll have to come back here in a few weeks when they need me to testify ... but we can talk about all that later." Vienna was rambling as Nick continued to listen—straight-faced and silent. "I think this will be good. Of course, you'll need to make new friends, but you're good at that." However untrue that was, Nick let her carry on unchallenged. "It's the countryside, Nick. You like Grandma Shriver's ranch, don't you? "Oh," it just occurred as Vienna suddenly had a renewed vigor. "And I found this great little piano studio just a half-hour away or so in Hartford. You'll just love it, Nick. You really will."

Nick wanted to offer up a dissenting opinion, but was so consumed by his own internal battle, there was no time for it. In fact, he had to rub his eyes, wondering if his medication was beginning to give into hallucinations.

Another scroll, this one resting inside a groove in the wall—one designed for a decorative piece—was now in Nick's direct eyeline. His Twilight Zone paranoia was driving him crazy, like an itch that wouldn't go away as he rushed over to grab it before his mother, or anyone else for that matter, could first.

Check your pockets, read the fourth scroll in handwritten font. Nick slapped away at the front of his jeans, before trying the pockets in the back. Sure enough, feeling hollow, rolled-up paper, he yanked it out—however confused to how it got there in the first place. "OK, just breathe," he whispered.

"Everything alright," Vienna, with an empty suitcase in hand, overheard the sigh in passing.

Nick whipped around with a pale face. "Yep. Just fine."

Vienna did a doubletake as she reached for a stack of shirts above the dryer. "I'd start packing if I were you," her voice trailed off. "We don't have much time."

Nick swiped a hand across his cheeks. "This really can't be happening. Nope, not happening." This time he hesitated to unravel the scroll, trying desperately to talk himself out of it. In fact, he wanted to toss every letter inside the living room fire—and though close to doing just that—something inside forced him to read the newest scroll.

Isaac's voice played heavily through his mind. "It's settled then. And I truly could not be happier to hear it. On behalf of children everywhere, welcome aboard, Nick."

Nick nearly froze, as if caught in the middle of a mind trick. A piece of him could see through the spell, and yet a bigger piece was beginning to overtake his typically stout mind. He swiveled several times in search of the elf, though could see nothing.

"My advice," Isaac offered. "Pack light. And don't tell a soul. Yes, not even Marie."

Nick's focus abruptly changed. There was certainly still plenty of fear and angst, but he was also responding to everything he'd been told. "Wait," he whispered to himself, finally breaking from the trance. "Marie?" he veered up mumbling. "How does he know about …?"

The thought was coincidentally halted by the Uptown Girl ringtone coming through his phone. Marie's name flashed over the display screen. Nick allowed Billy Joel to carry on for longer than usual before answering. "Hello," he slurred.

"Nick. That you?" she asked again to no response.

"Yeah," his answer was slow, still bogged down by an overload of emotion he wasn't exactly certain how to deal with.

"Where have you been? I've probably left ten messages today alone."

His glaze wasn't weakening.

Inheriting the Sleigh

"I read about the incident at the Blue Owl. Are you OK?"

"Oh. You heard about that?"

"Um," Marie chose her words carefully. "You do know your father's mugshot was all over the Times?"

Nick just then realized he was in the middle of a real-life, New York City headline. He gripped his heart, as if hardly able to take even a second more. "I'm sorry, Marie. But I think I have to … go now."

Chapter 11

The New Jersey shoreline was foggy near the industrial zone. It was early in the morning and the weather was brisk. Valentine's Day decorations were now up in an old downtown party store and padlocks were over the doors of adjacent shops. It was too early for the bars to open as some homeless bore the elements, bundled in sleeping bags near a cafe.

It was a place Nick had never been before with his eyes stuck down in another scroll. He needed his full concentration to follow the directions etched over the soft, crinkled paper, unsure if he was, in fact, going the right way.

In a bright orange, one-piece, with suspenders strapped under a warm coat, the combination was joined by combat boots and a wool hat. It was enough to get the attention of a homeless vet—watching Nick ever so carefully. "You lost, boy?" A gap in his teeth was hard to see past.

Nick remained silent with a backpack slung over his shoulder, only because he was beginning to grow frustrated, unsure which way was south.

"What you look'n for?"

"Crescent Shipyard," he said glancing down again to make sure he remembered the name correctly.

The old man laughed, leaning up against an overturned shopping cart. "Well then, you're not as lost as you think you are." He stuck his arm out underneath an old quilt to point across the railroad tracks. The morning sun glimmered off the bay, with a large shipyard perched along the shore.

"You sure that's it?" Nick didn't want to believe it.

"Think I'd know. Used to work down there assembling submarines during the Vietnam War. That is until I blew my hand right off," he proudly held up the fingerless stump.

Nick offered only a courtesy smile before hastily hurrying on past the dusty tracks.

In a matching jumpsuit, Isaac was watching. Using a pair of advanced binoculars, it was merely to confirm what he already knew. He was confident in his psychology, having studied the art of persuasion, but with an extremely tight schedule, was also highly impatient should something go wrong.

Tall ships were docked in the distance—many of them only partially complete, and Nick descended to sea level through several open wire gates. The further he walked the more hazard signs he saw, with only an occasional welder or technician at work, forklifting metal barrels onto the shipyard asphalt.

"Right on time," said Isaac from behind a cement slab. An edgy Nick leapt around in startled fright, taking deep breaths to recover. It was the first he'd seen the elf outside his own apartment.

"Oh, it's only you. I was afraid I was …"

"Late?" Isaac hopped down between a couple of toxic waste bins. "By several minutes, in fact. Despite assumptions about your father's punctuality, it's in your blood. Even he was known to be late a time or two. That's why he had me—to keep him on schedule. Good thing for us, our transport is also tardy. I see you found the uniform I left."

Nick pulled a suspender, realizing how ridiculous he looked.

Isaac was good at showing different sides to his personality, and was quick to change on a dime, if necessary. This time he was empathetic. "What you did, Nick. That was certainly brave" he said as the boy's overwhelmed gaze took in a wide view of the Atlantic. Even though Isaac had a feeling he'd show up, the elf wanted him to know he understood the sacrifice.

"Then why do I feel like a coward?" Nick gazed. "Leaving my mother at the worst possible time."

Isaac's vast memory vault couldn't help but jet back to the defining moment—the baby being dropped off at apartment number 5116. It was the warmest his heart had ever remembered feeling, watching the joy of a child light up Vienna's face.

Even Isaac couldn't help but share in the guilt of pulling Nick away. But he was also quite good at subduing his emotions; this time to satisfy the greater good.

"I said, did you not expect me to show up?" Nick had to repeat himself, as Isaac failed to answer the first time.

"Huh?" he squinted, clearly sidetracked.

Nick gulped in a breath of salty air, wondering if he could fully trust the elf. Hungry seagulls coasted low over the shipyard, with Nick only able to guess what might happen next.

"Trust me," Isaac soon resumed with a confident hue about his pale cheeks. "For me this was no sightseeing trip. I knew you would come."

A loud tugboat interrupted a lull in the conversation, and Nick, for whatever reason, seemed to know it was exactly what Isaac had been waiting for.

"That's us," he warned. "Here, you'll need this." Isaac handed Nick a credentialed lanyard. Nick's picture was on the front, though he never recalled posing for it before.

"Where did you …?" he began to ask while making sure his backpack was closed—though Isaac was already out in front, leading the way, briskly ahead.

"Just leave the talking to me," Isaac instructed as Nick caught up. "Don't leave my side. Oh, and please … do your best to act like you belong."

"Act like I belong," Nick was huffing as he jogged, though always with a sarcastic grumble. "Right."

Let's just say, the ilk you find on an oil tanker are probably not the kind you'd chose to spend quality time with over a weekend."

"Oil tanker?" Nick looked up after rounding a bend of multi-level storage sheds. It revealed an old and rusty vessel with smokestacks and cable wires connecting various beams. "You mean, you couldn't have booked us a cruise ship or something?"

Isaac ignored the complaint, instead casually stepping into a short line leading past a manned gate. Several others converged from behind, all of them dressed for the job. Nick was nervous as he stepped forward to have his own badge checked. The burly security attendant took a few seconds longer to carefully inspect his neck-up mug shot. It was different from most. Nick was smiling with a boyish haircut, one that looked as if it could've been cropped right out of a school dance photo.

"Carry on," issued the gruff voice as Isaac waited for Nick to join him toward the ship's gangplank ramp.

"Did you see the way he was looking at me?" Nick raised in paranoia. "I think they're onto something."

But Isaac was smiling this time. "The only thing they, you, or I will soon be on … is the Maslo K. Severu," he pointed to the Russian text painted across the shell of the red and black tanker.

They were a hundred yards or so from the ramp, but each step was one yard closer to Nick wondering if he might ever make it back. He was told what he was doing, but with extraordinarily little detail and with limited time to even sneak in one of his countless questions.

Hugging a chain link fence with curling barbwire at the top, Nick heard a voice from behind. It was familiar—it was soothing. But also scared and urgent.

"Nick! Nick!"

The cry persisted long enough to where Nick knew he couldn't be imagining it. He turned to find Marie in sweatpants and a hoodie gripping the opposite side of the same fence. Her hair was pulled back and she'd clearly been running.

More torn than he'd ever been, Nick glanced each way, before eventually retreating closer. Marie was frightened and shocked, Nick doing his best to avoid a scene as groggy shipmen quickly made their way up the ramp in his wake.

"What in the world are you …? I mean, how? How did you know?"

"Does it matter?" she stopped his stammering. But for the record, I'm set up to track your phone in case your heart acts up … remember?"

Nick slowly nodded, as if still fighting the urge to start climbing the fence. He wanted desperately to give her a real hug. "Which reminds me," he bit his lip, pained to be looking a disconcerted Marie in the eye. I don't believe I'll be needing this anymore," he slipped his cell phone through the fence.

Marie was pale with concern as she very slowly laid her fingertips over the case. "Wait, no," she shoved it back.

Inheriting the Sleigh

But Nick's second push was enough to end the tug-o-war. He then subtly scribbled a brief note onto a small sliver of paper he found on the ground near his feet.

"Please, talk to me, Nick. What is really going on here? Where are they taking you?" she asked as he nonchalantly handed her the token; one which he quickly folded up into an airplane, merely as a symbol.

Isaac watched with his own level of concern as Nick slowly glanced back over his shoulder again. "Wish I could tell you. I mean, I want to. Then again, perhaps this time you may have to trust me."

The girl offered up her own glance, sizing up the shorter Isaac, who only as a courtesy stood far enough away. "Don't you see that you've been lured into something dangerous. Whatever this is, it isn't normal, Nick." Nick nodded as if he couldn't agree more. "Then why?" Marie tried to contain her voice this time. "Don't you understand that people need you? Especially your mother," she paused with swelling tears. "Especially me."

Nick's guilt had reached a peak as another tugboat horn caused him to slowly take a step backwards. A thousand different sorry's were spoken through his newly developed tears. He knew it was ridiculous on the surface of it, and yet something inside was magnetically pushing him back in the direction of the elf. "I'm afraid if I don't go now … I may not at all. I simply cannot disappoint millions." It was his only clue.

Nick finally forced himself to turn to escape Marie's heartbroken glare. It all sounded illogical at best, and impossible at worst, but for some reason he was still compelled to press forward—just like that, dissolving into a blur of foot traffic.

All the while, Marie finally thought to flatten out the brittle airplane, where only two short words were scribbled in pencil—North Pole.

Chapter 12

The ship's interior was dark, damp and loud. Hollow clanks echoed through the many pipes with unsettling noise protruding out heavy machinery. And then there was the swaying of the seas, which all combined made Nick want to vomit.

"Any better?" Isaac inquired inside the mess room. Though the truth was, he could tell the motion sickness pill hadn't kicked in yet.

The passing scent of sloppy joes certainly didn't help either as veteran oilmen were quickly filling up the open mess hall with fresh trays at lunch. Nick could do little but stare and hold his gut as others occasionally stared back.

"Just keep your eyes closed," Isaac advised along the edge of the bleak room—one with large, crisscrossing pipes and obnoxious drips. Having been on the ship for many days, Nick was just as bored as he was seasick and had trouble passing the time. He could do little but fidget with his fingers that naturally always seemed to be pretending as if they were playing a concert. "Here," Isaac subtly reached down into his leather bag. It was something he'd been meaning to do at some point along the way but could tell Nick desperately needed a pick-me-up. The object was flat and well wrapped.

Nick glared at the gift, taking a few seconds to break from his lull to gather precisely what it was. "For me?"

Isaac smiled. "It was intended to be delivered on Christmas. You know, from your father." Nick gently reached out to accept the present with his hands crunching over the gloss. "You're the only one in the world to receive a gift from the Pole this year," Isaac resumed as Nick began to tear the paper apart. "Make that ... last year," he corrected.

Nick was curious as he lifted out a black tablet. "What is this?"

"Turn it on," Isaac instructed, at the same time gazing around the noisy messroom to make sure they weren't being too closely observed. "It's the face of our new Music City toy line. They call it a Key Whiz, I believe."

Nick pushed the power button to reveal a monitor with four groups of black and white keys, just as you would find on any normal piano, only they were digital. "Go ahead," Isaac signaled as Nick gently placed a finger onto the Middle C. The touch screen immediately made a sound, though the uncouth chatter throughout the room was so intense, others could hardly hear it.

"But this is only ...," Isaac stopped him before he could finish.

"Just tug on the sides." Nick reached down to slide out an end that expanded the gadget nearly two feet to the left. The other side stretching the same length to the right, completing a full-size keyboard. "It's only a prototype, but the sound I'm told is impeccable. In fact, it just might rival that grand of yours."

"Impossible," Nick shrugged, with a touch of his adoptive father's pompous pride.

But Isaac didn't take insult. His eyes were too busy concentrating on a table in the center of the room.

"What is it?" Nick watched Isaac perk up like a concerned watchdog at the scent of an intruder.

"That foreman right there?'

"Yeah," Nick responded as Isaac's eyes failed to budge an inch. The seaman had a black beard dipping well down his neck. "What about him?"

"That's Lukas Gruber."

"You two know each other or something?" Nick could only wonder the reason for mentioning his name.

"Have we met? No," said Isaac. "But do I know him? Very well. Let's just say he never did make a Nice List." Nick quickly grew intrigued by the backstory, one that was cut short as Isaac's concern intensified. "In and out of detention since grade school. Unfortunately, the rap sheet has only gotten worse as he's grown old."

"Should I be ..."

"Worried?" Isaac's neck swiveled to meet Nick's curious eye. "Perhaps. Trouble's brewing."

The sailor in question, watched as another directly across laughed in hysteria—possibly at his expense. Isaac was trained to be intuitive for odd behavior and held Nick off from asking any more questions. He needed to keep his concentration intact, with his mind at work analyzing every crevice of the sailor's face.

Nick wanted to make his own judgement, but kept his eyes glued to Isaac's instead. "Perhaps this means we should go then?" Nick was starting to grow unsettled by his eerie focus.

"I think he wants to kill him," Isaac whispered softly, as now, Nick was more than uncomfortable—he was outright scared. "In fact, I think he' s about to ...."

"About to ... what? Kill him? And how do you know this?"

Inheriting the Sleigh

"Call it a gift," Isaac shrugged. "I can see it all over his face."

Nick's retreating glance for the long foldout table took in a scene that appeared perfectly normal to him, though the other half of his brain had no reason to doubt Isaac. "So… aren't you gonna stop it then?" he quizzed.

Oilman continued to snicker in-between bites of baked beans and potato salad as Isaac abruptly leapt to his feet. "Excuse me," the elf raised his voice. Heads began to turn, but only as something suddenly disrupted the casual sight of men at break. The laughing oilman's grin quickly morphed into a cringe. Nick was fascinated by how Isaac could have possibly ever predicted it, but there was no time for that now as a blade had suddenly pierced a gut from underneath the table.

"Did he just …?" Nick stood himself, pointing with dilated eyes.

"Yep. Time to go now," Isaac warned as pandemonium replaced what was otherwise a midday routine.

The unfortunate sailor fell back onto the floor, while others sitting shoulder to shoulder with the murder victim jumped, wondering what'd happened.

Nick pushed the ends of his Key Whiz back in, tossing it into a backpack full of clothes and what seemed like a decade's supply of essential prescription, before following Isaac for the far stairwell. But the path was soon cinched shut by a herd of fleeing feet on both sides. Nick was thrust backward to the cold surface, panicked by the stampede from all directions. A descending boot nicked his face, just as another simultaneously leapt over Nick on his way to safety.

"Here, follow me," Isaac squirmed underneath the protection of a table—a prison yard brawl since ensuing in the aftermath.

"How we getting out of here!?" Nick was forced to trust Isaac's escape plan as he wiped a bleeding nose with his forearm.

Vance

"Looks like we'll have to wait for something to open up," Isaac eyed the stairwell several tables beyond. Plastic trays and glass plates slammed against the cement surface, with some lunch-goers slipping over greasy food remnants now splattered up and down the floor. Without a flinch, Isaac leapt headfirst, as if frolicking down a Slip'n Slide in the summer. He slid under and across several tables, with small space gaps in the aisles. Nick admired the beauty of the perfectly timed bolt to safety but knew his odds of doing the same were small.

Isaac curled his finger to make it quick, but Nick hesitated. Two men suddenly crashed through his table, cracking the center that nearly teetered onto Nick's now vulnerable head. In a dash, Nick sprinted right into the heart of the scrum, leaping the next table. With a man three times his age and two times his weight directly in his path, the boy was helpless.

Driven back by a stocky frame, Nick's head slammed against the surface. Isaac quickly intervened, taking a loose fork to the back of the aggressive man's neck. There was a yelp as Isaac reached for Nick's hand, yanking him up in the chaos. Dizzy but cognizant, they hurried up the windy, narrow stairs.

"I can't really feel my face," said Nick as he tapped on both bruised cheekbones. Security passed them on the way down to break up the violence, while Isaac was looking for a discreet way to return to their bunks. Only, his number one fear found him first.

"Wait," called a curious officer from the open deck, the thick scent of salt now permeating the outside. "Where are you two going?"

"Back to our rooms, sir," insisted Isaac politely as a seabird chirped overhead.

"You," he pointed to Nick, currently sweating in a tsunami of nerves. "There's blood on your shirt. Is it your scheduled lunch hour?" he looked down at a checklist, ready to ask for a name.

Nick couldn't think quickly enough to string his story together as Isaac rolled his eyes.

"The answer is, yes," the elf clarified—clearly in damage control.

"I see," said the ship attendant as Isaac shook his head. He thought again for a moment before directing the two of them to follow.

"But we didn't do anything wrong," Nick quietly uttered into Isaac's ear near the end of the tanker. "We just explain we were wrong place-wrong time, that's all."

"Of course," Isaac whispered back. "But that's not the problem. We're now under a microscope, which is not good for someone currently surviving off forged paperwork."

Chapter 13

A swirly mustache and accompanying set of brown eyes shot glaringly deep beyond a desk in the captain's chamber. The Maslo K. Severu was now docked, with the captain in white. His uniform displayed a navy-blue epaulette, trimmed with gold anchors at the shoulders. A pipe dangled off his lower lip, and his hat was resting beside him on the desk as he failed to release his unsettling gaze.

"Perhaps you have a question to ask," An impatient Isaac was forced to instigate one himself. Hours of waiting had passed since the murder, with the ship now anchored and docked somewhere in Scandinavia.

"A question? Yes," the captain dropped his pipe into a tray. "I may have many, in fact." But the captain instead took his time, releasing another puff of his pipe and creepily staring well past their bright overalls.

"Who recruited you for this job, anyhow?" the captain finally inquired as he reviewed Isaac and Nick's documentation.

"A rig headhunter, I believe," Nick was glad to see Isaac smoothly take the lead. "Came through Minnesota last summer promising steady work. Said the West Siberian Oil Basin needed roughnecks."

Inheriting the Sleigh

The captain puffed long and slow. "That is all true. Then I'm sure you were also told the work is backbreaking," he smiled, amused by the thought that most who tried couldn't handle it.

"Good thing we're both strapping and healthy then."

The stern captain liked Isaac's exuberance but soon turned his attention toward Nick. "You look young."

"Ugh, he's Russian," Isaac cut in before Nick had a chance to utter a response. The captain remained confused. "You know ... language barrier and all."

"I thought you said you were from Minnesota?"

"Well, I am," Isaac worked quick to save his story. "But Boris here's from Novgorod."

"Going home then," the captain smiled as he buried his pipe down in the tray. "You Russians certainly know how to work hard. But you also understand the world has child labor laws these days," he veered back toward Isaac.

The elf uttered no response as he thought about one. The captain's large, bushy eyebrows were scrunched together as he waited. Isaac eventually broke out in sudden laughter; so much so that even Nick was humored by it. "That was funny ... yes," Isaac exhaled. "Those rabid Communists are never shy about selling off their young?"

"Is he a friend of yours?" The captain gazed down at Isaac's badge for the first time.

"You could say Boris and I have a history together, yes."

The captain lunged back in his chair, as if less than convinced. "We could get ratted out, you know. And if that happens, who do you think the PC police will be coming after?" The captain kicked his legs up on the desk, with his outstretched hands now supporting the back of his head.

"I assume not the chef," Isaac proved he was capable of a joke; one that even the captain enjoyed, evidenced by his return grin.

"But you also understand that a man was just killed on my ship. And not to say the boy did anything wrong, but the blood on his collar doesn't look good. How am I to assume he wasn't involved somehow?" Nick hadn't so much as flinched since he sat down—and that didn't change as he digested a conversation the captain was unaware he could even understand.

Nick was allowed a few more seconds to sweat out the thought of being falsely accused when the conversation received a welcome interruption.

"What is it?" the captain sighed as a screen door swung open.

"Sir, a Norwegian police escort has arrived to assist with the investigation."

The captain pushed himself up from his chair. He stopped and turned back around to face Isaac, before exiting. "You two stay put. There's more I need to get to the bottom of before I let you go."

Nick had never been more relieved to have the freedom to speak again. "They're locking me up, aren't they?" Nick panicked. "This is it for me, I know it."

"Just take a breath," Isaac insisted with his fingers stroking his chin. He knew it was his sole responsibility to make sure nothing of the sort happened; for more reasons than one.

"I mean, why did I ever do this? Why did I follow you? Marie was right. I never should have …"

Isaac didn't even bother to respond to the streamline of complaints. He was already up poking around, slowly peeling away at the old, brown and mustard burlap office curtains to get a glimpse of the outside.

"What are you doing?" Nick's anxiety was evidenced by the paranoia in his voice.

"Trying to get us off this wretched boat, Nick. Try and keep up."

Gently pulling back on the retro cloth, Nick noticed a ship attendant keeping an eye on the deck. "Looks like we're being watched."

Isaac glanced across a series of picture frames hung crookedly over the walls. He was in search of supplies, with the interior space divided up into little more than a small kitchenette, bedroom, and office. It was cluttered with books, loose paper and all kinds of random things.

He flipped open every cabinet and drawer, taking an interest in everything from dried yeast to a bottle of hydrogen peroxide—even a box of matches. Nick only watched as the elf mixed a few contents together in some old Tupperware.

"Wait here," Isaac instructed as he slowly inched the door open, dashing out at just the right time. Nick hopped over to the window to peak through the curtain, but before he could tell what was happening, a loud explosion forced Nick to immediately cover up his ears. It brought a thick plume of smoke that suddenly washed out any sight of the guard.

With a heightened sense of fear already permeating across the ship, Isaac had added to the chaos. He came barreling back in with a cloth covering his mouth. "Here," he tossed another one at Nick as the smoky drift followed him through the door.

Nick wanted to ask how and why but knew there was no time for that. He followed Isaac back out into the salty air. "Don't worry about him," said Isaac casually as Nick concernedly pointed to the guard now crawling underneath the smoke. He was trying to find a pocket suitable to breathe in along the edge of the deck. "Simply a diversion. Expect it to subside in minutes—meaning we don't have long."

Isaac led the way down a stairwell and through a maze of traffic as another alarm sounded across the ship's dark interior. The elf knew where he was going, having studied the floorplan well ahead of time and having escape routes cleverly mapped out inside his head.

Oilmen were now bailing toward the exit. Isaac and Nick, on an overcast afternoon, blended in as they raced for the now-unmanned dock. They were happy to step foot onto the old, moist wood. It was all that separated them from the chilly waters below.

"Quickly," instructed the elf past some curious fisherman who had also overheard the blast.

The landscape beyond the shoreline was serene. A series of two-story log homes, with colorful, triangular roofs were dotted about various levels of the coastline port. A lighthouse joined the landscape—perched on a quiet island across from the sand.

"Wait," Nick hurried alongside Isaac. "But I thought we needed a boat to get there."

"Oh no," Isaac informed. "Where we're going takes much more than just a boat."

Much of the elf's ensuing movement was almost a blur to Nick. His heart was acting up, but even when alert, it was a chore to absorb what his mind was actually seeing as cat-like beelines around every corner. Nick forced himself to keep up in the chilly air, though could barely concentrate long enough to decipher words as Isaac in a foreign tongue would occasionally stop to talk his way out of a jam.

Nick's eyes slung open again—his frame lying flat in a random snowbank. Besides the outline of Isaac's face, he could see mountains in the distance, with conifer trees aligning a railroad track.

"Where am I?" he almost hated to ask with the rusty steel rail at eye level. It hadn't completely sunk in when he heard the horn in the distance.

Inheriting the Sleigh

Meanwhile, Isaac's eyes rocked upward, as if waiting for exactly that. "Fingers?"

"Ugh … three?" Nick did the best he could to see, with both eyes still adjusting.

Isaac was holding up four but assumed three was good enough. "C'mon, our journey continues."

Isaac yanked Nick up to his feet. "What happened to me anyhow?" he asked, dusting snow off his pantlegs.

"Honestly, I think you're just exhausted. But the good news is," Isaac turned back with a satisfied smile. "We're almost half-way home."

A black train, with a bright orange cab was coming straight for them, "Ugh, this doesn't look like a train stop," said Nick, searching for any indication of one; a bench, or perhaps a little yellow sign—anything to signify they were in the right place.

"Train stop?" Isaac repeated as he slowly began to pace his step forward along the tracks. "C'mon, you're an American. Haven't you ever seen a John Wayne flick before?"

"John Wayne?" Nick had once heard Arthur brag about owning an original John Wayne cowboy hat from the set of *Rio Bravo* but had never actually seen the movie.

The train grew bigger and louder fast, and it hadn't yet occurred to Nick exactly what Isaac was implying. He was now walking swiftly, with his stride covering each step between the gaps in the wooden rail supports. "Time to start running now!"

Nick picked up his pace, but only to receive an explanation as he could no longer hear Isaac over the sound of the chugging locomotive. But even in a full sprint, failed to catch up. The old boxcars soon began to blow directly past him—many with open doors, and Isaac was bold and daring as he tossed up his bag.

"Here, hold my hand!" Isaac's hair blew back as he reached for his fingertips.

"What?!" Nick felt like he was standing next to a helicopter propeller.

"My hand!"

Isaac looked behind him on the move, waiting for the next open boxcar. But Nick, rather, was highly unprepared to suddenly get slung upward with a two-handed boost at the waist. Descending in flight, his chest and face were now the only things inside the train. He was forced to disregard the pain on contact to shove the rest of his body up. Nick exhaled like he never had before—for no other reason than to make sure he was still alive.

As for Isaac, he kicked up snow as he sprinted to outrace the locomotive. He needed a running start, and trusted Nick had the strength and moxie to return the favor.

Scooting back toward the edge, Nick sat on his knees with an outstretched hand, wondering if Isaac could, in fact, catch up before the train disappeared. A nervous Nick—unable to imagine being left alone in the middle of nowhere—could now see the caboose. Isaac jumped, and the grip was seamless as Nick fell backwards to generate enough leverage to pull him up.

"Ow!" Nick winced as he rolled, banging hard against the far edge of the rusty boxcar.

"Sorry, kid," Isaac ushered in his own sigh. "Isn't that what John Wayne would say?" Isaac smiled, with Nick now lying flat over some loose hay.

"Where to next?" Nick sounded defeated—in a desperate hope they were getting closer.

Isaac pulled a sleek compass out of his bag. It was silver, with a golden map interior and black spindles that pointed up. "That would be, due north."

Chapter 14

B reathtaking," Nick observed with his head permanently stuck out one side of the open train car. "Like a screensaver come to life."

Over an arched bridge of stone, and with a frosty river stampeding underneath, Nick could feel the cold mist of the white waterfall barreling down the mountain as they passed.

"Welcome to Norway," Isaac breathed as the train shot through a tunnel. On the other side, a quaint village rested low in a valley between two mountains along the now flat river. Amidst a series of green plots, a church steeple rose a bit taller than the countless pines. "Though not quite the *Polar Express*, is it?" A sitting Isaac resumed, chewing on a stick of straw in boredom—his butt aching from the lack of cushion.

Nick leaned up against a pile of hay, sightseeing and meditating on the unknown. "Tell me. How do you know so much about American culture? John Wayne ... *The Polar Express*."

"We know about every culture. To be honest, Tom Hanks might be one of the most popular actors at the Pole. Though we do get a rise out of watching Hollywood try imagining up a place they've never been."

"And ... how have they done?" Nick sat up for the first time in hours, eager to learn something.

"Actually … not half bad," Isaac admitted. "At least in some ways. In others, not so much."

Nick was bundled up in an old tarp. He plopped back down, realizing he and Isaac had not had a whole lot of time just to talk; let alone answer his questions. But based on the elves' track record, there was never any guarantee he would give a straight answer anyway.

"So," Nick pried again. "What do we do first? You know, once we get to the North Pole? Or should I say … if we get there?"

"Honestly?" Isaac shrugged as he passed the time hurling rocks at trees. "Not entirely sure. There's so much to do, but I'm also afraid I won't be able to predict precisely what awaits once we arrive. We'll need to be ready for anything."

The vagueness bothered him, but Nick changed topic, determined to learn something. "So, did he really crash then?" Isaac had no choice but to lift his head this time. "I mean, after hundreds of successful sleigh-runs, are you telling me this time was different?"

The elf wanted to sling one last rock but stopped mid-throw. It clearly pained him to talk about it. "At this point … nobody really knows."

Nick paused again to suggest, "fair enough." "But why me? I mean, couldn't you have taken over?"

Isaac tossed his final stone, hitting his target this time—the trunk of a lone pine rooted along a stream. He pointed at his own chest. "It doesn't really work that way, Nick. Though you wouldn't be the first to suggest it."

"But you're clearly capable," Nick said casually with the wind of the moving train blowing across his pink face. "You're from there. You've been around the toy business for who knows how long," he went down the list. "And you obviously have a vested interest in keeping Christmas …"

"Stop!" Isaac caught Nick off guard by raising his voice a notch, as if he couldn't take it anymore. "I mean, please … stop," he was more polite the second time. "I know you think it's that simple—and believe me—if there were some other way."

"But there is … no other way. Isn't that, right?" Nick nodded, half-sheepishly.

Isaac said nothing before Nick leaned into the back of the bumpy boxcar. The elf eventually mustered up the courage to speak again—though as usual, was always hesitant to say too much too early. "The truth is, your father was the greatest man I ever knew. And you can imagine how we all felt when we found out that he and your mother were having a child." If ever Nick had a listening ear, it was now as Isaac finally strung more than a sentence or two together. "An old man that had already lived beyond his years, he wasn't supposed to be a father, you know. Nobody knew what to make of it—even Kris himself. And then having to turn around so quickly and just give you away. Well, that made even less sense," Isaac made rare eye contact as he took off his gloves just long enough to blow into his cold hands. "But … perhaps now we know."

"And yet, what if you have the wrong person. I mean, what if I'm not Santa Claus' only son? What if I really am just some … misfit from Manhattan?"

Isaac wanted to smile but held back. "Because a misfit from Manhattan wouldn't have voluntarily walked on that boat," he said somewhat disoriented, staring for too long out the moving train. "A misfit from Manhattan wouldn't have stepped in to protect his mother, let alone have the emotional stamina to make it this far."

"Everyone's emotional stamina runs out … eventually."

Inheriting the Sleigh

"Maybe," Isaac shrugged. "But I haven't even unlocked what's inside you yet."

Nick suddenly reached into his backpack, tossing Isaac an apple. He didn't know why exactly. It was just an impulse, as if his hand had suddenly made the decision without consulting his head first.

Isaac stabbed the glossy red apple out of midair. He perused it over by rotating it 360 degrees. It was crisp, without a single blemish. "We're getting low on food, and it could be yet a couple more days before we get there?"

Isaac wanted to toss it right back before Nick cut in, stating what was obvious to him. "But you're hungry."

The elf thought long and hard, knowing he was never one to complain about an empty stomach. But he also knew how true that was, not having had a warm meal since escaping the ship. Isaac smiled with pride—realizing his point had just been made—despite it flying right over Nick's head. But there was no chance to explain as a screech of the rails sent Isaac panicking again.

"What's happening?" Nick asked the obvious as the train was slowing down in the middle of nowhere.

"I don't know," Isaac held one hand over a handrail as he swung his body out to get a better look. "It wasn't supposed to stop until Salteven."

Voices were clamoring in Norwegian. "Do you understand what they're saying?" Nick probed as Isaac listened closely to every word.

"Didn't catch all of it, but let's just say, I did hear the word 'stowaways' uttered somewhere in there."

"So, they're onto us then?" Nick gathered the courage to muster his own look, with a rush of men converging closer to the train.

"Whether it's us, or somebody else, I don't care to find out," Isaac said as he immediately grabbed his bag to hop out onto the adjoining rocks.

"But there's no place to go," Nick eyed the never-ending forest to either side as his boots followed onto the surface. "We can't just saunter off into the woods. There could be bears out there."

"Among other things," Isaac whispered before pulling out his handheld locator—the same one he once used inside the city.

Ducking into a snowy grove, voices rounded a bend in the tracks. A series of red dots bubbled about the small monitor, though one dot now stood out above the rest. He used his compass in the other hand to decipher exactly where they were.

"So?" Nick waited for an answer.

Isaac grinned. "We don't have much further."

Nick stretched his gloves overtop his numb fingers to brave for life out in the cold—having no idea what "much further" actually meant.

Chapter 15

Nick sat alone over a log in the middle of the frosty woods—tinkering with a toy he finally remembered he had. "Rivals a grand piano," he mocked Isaac's sentiment under his foggy breath. "And I'm sitting on a beach in the Caribbean."

Turning on the Key Whiz, he stretched out the sides to get a feel for playing on a digital monitor. It was different but gave him comfort in an unfamiliar and lonely world. The movement of his fingers soon warmed up his hands enough to start improvising melodies.

"Wow," Nick was caught by surprise. "The sound actually isn't that bad." The Wedding Canon soon morphed into the Christmas Canon. It was only late February, but Nick was suffering from a sudden dose of Christmas spirit as a light snow from the semi-dark skies began to fall over his pink face.

Nick quickly responded with his own snappy version of "Let It Snow;" which then turned into "Winter Wonderland," a souped-up version of "Snoopy's Christmas," and a song his mother would always force him to play at family gatherings; "Silent Night." Once annoyed by the request, he would have killed to hear her insisting voice now.

Vance

A deep, exhaling sniff caused Nick to immediately stand up, pulling his fingers off the Key Whiz. A large set of antlers suddenly popped out of some pine, with a reindeer dipping its mouth to nibble at some tall grass peeking out the top of the snow. Nick froze as the large reindeer moved its eyes up. It grunted and bobbed, as if a little agitated, but didn't move. Nick attempted to backpedal but tripped over the log with more snow now falling over his nose from shuffling tree branches.

The deer continued to grunt while taking a few steps forward. Quickly scampering up, Nick's fingers fumbled over the keyboard. But after inadvertently punching the B-flat, the reindeer responded with a gentler breath.

Nick's own breath was full of confusion and concern as he attempted to figure out what it wanted. It rocked its antlers again until Nick played another note. 'Go away," he slammed his fist against random keys to scare it off. The reindeer rose a paw and continued to puff its nostrils, as if soured by the bad combination of sound. "I said, get!"

But it didn't budge as more snow crunched. Nick, caught in a deep patch, forced himself up in fright—only to see Isaac finally approach with a straight finger, suggesting Nick be still.

Nick stood, but slowly, shaking the ice off with his eyes going back and forth between the beast and the elf hidden in a wall of dead branches. The elf pointed to his open palm, and Nick eventually realized he was talking about the toy.

With the reindeer growing more antsy with time, the boy very gently reached down in the snow piled up around his ankles to retrieve it. It was clearly expecting to hear music.

Isaac watched as Nick resumed with his own rendition of "Silent Night." The melody seemed to sooth the beautiful animal—one with a creamy hump and swirls of black up and around its nose, legs and side.

Inheriting the Sleigh

A curious Nick stopped, only to be convinced he needed to continue again after another grunt.

Neither set of eyes left the other until the conclusion of the carol.

"Scram!" Isaac suddenly made a scene from behind as the startled deer kicked up its legs—scampering off through the trees. "Are you alright?" asked the elf as Nick used a hand to keep his heart from leaping out his chest. Nick could only watch the reindeer trail away. "I'll take that as a yes. Here, follow me. I want to show you something."

Nick caught up through another wall of white spruce, before a treeless valley opened with hundreds of like reindeer majestically migrating across it.

"Do you know what this is?" Isaac asked, pulling back on some needled limbs. "This is the very herd of which we handpicked several of your father's personal transports." Nick peered out into the gorgeous flat where the countless beasts scampered in only one direction—all as Isaac held up his locator with more news. "But even better, I've found our next transport. C'mon."

Descending through another grove, the smell of the herd was unfamiliar to Nick, but he oddly enjoyed the scent. Isaac waited for the last stragglers to pass through before moving across the wild pasture in their wake. Nick took in the sights to either side as he chugged but suddenly felt two hands forcefully push him back from going a step further. Little did he know he was about to tumble right off the edge of a cliff, where a secluded, icy ocean rocked mercilessly below.

"What now?" Nick almost hated to ask.

With affirmation from his compass, Isaac pointed northwest into an abyss of dark, star-dotted sky over the Norwegian Sea. "That's home, Nick."

Nick had trouble thinking beyond how painful it might feel to dip his feet into the arctic waters. Beyond that, his intuition was getting better, knowing exactly what was coming. "You're about to make me scale this cliff right now, aren't you?" Nick shrugged with sarcasm to no response. "Yep, of course you are."

"Here, put this on," Isaac handed him a leather belt as he detangled some rope. A metal anchor was already in place and Isaac secured the knot. "Just remember to take it slow."

Isaac tested both belts before dropping first—his legs kicking against the vertical rocks.

"So," Isaac distracted Nick as the boy eventually took the leap of faith himself. "What do you think? You know, about the Key Whiz. Our executive staff is surely going to want your input."

Focused on staying alive as his thin frame swayed back and forth into the jagged wall, Nick took his time to respond. "Actually, it's fairly innovative," he hated to admit. "That's if … you know … you're too lazy to lug a thousand-pound piano around."

"Careful," Isaac cautioned as Nick's increasing confidence was turning into increased speed as well.

"May I ask you something?" Isaac waved his hand to carry on as he was already more than halfway down. "When? I mean … when were you born?"

Isaac paused as he calculated the best way to answer the legitimate question. "During a time of conquest and war."

"Conquest and war?" Nick repeated as he swung back into a flat section of the cliff. "We're not talking about Vietnam now, are we?"

Isaac laughed as they neared the surface. "Vietnam? That was yesterday. I'm talking about the days when Vikings ruled this country. Back when Arabs took over the Middle East and the coasts of Northern Africa. Back when the Mayans were cursed into decline. Back during the days when your father was still evolving, and when the great Christmas traditions were still in their infancy."

"So, it's true then? You're actually like a thousand-some-odd years old."

"1,317 to be exact. Late eighth century," Isaac retorted with his boots now touching the sharp, slippery rocks on the surface. He assisted Nick down, with the chilling ocean tide soon pushing in at their feet.

Isaac pulled out a key, hurrying into a small cave located inside the cliff. An occasional wave crashed up against the jagged, shoreline rocks— and before Nick could even gather himself long enough to follow, Isaac came speeding out on a machine quick to catch his eye.

"What is that? Some glorified jet ski or something?"

Isaac revved up the engine with a swivel of the accelerator. "This little guy is fully equipped to get us both through and overtop any deep ice." Isaac was proud to show off its sleek features as hot air flotation bags were suddenly swapped out for sleigh-like blade runners. With the press of another button, a clear tube slowly pulled up, rocking partially backwards.

"So ... you coming? Or have you decided to turn back?" Isaac checked, waiting for Nick who was caught staring out into the endless sea.

Nick rubbed his hand against the watercraft—one with a glittery red and black shell. It was unlike anything he had ever seen before.

Pulling his pantlegs up over the seat, they strapped in under a clear shield. It felt wonderful to finally be toasty warm again from the trapped heat, with Isaac wasting no time to start crushing through the sporadic, and oftentimes stubborn ice.

Chapter 16

Isaac and Nick stood in heavy, triple-layer mink coats with goggles and thick, rabbit-skin gloves. A streaking white mist, one fed by the wind swirled about their faces as they labored amid a barren, arctic wasteland. Nick turned to his right and then to his left but could see nothing, only able to take small steps without slipping over the endless ice.

Isaac pulled out another of what Nick perceived to be endless gadgets. He was crouching to where he could see his own reflection in the glacier, this time holding a small laser to guide the dime-size dot. Nick was partially entranced, dreaming of the nearest McDonald's and a warm plate of salty fries; but a brief quake under their feet prevented a response. "Brace yourself!" Isaac warned after the laser had found the trigger—the elf's boots just wide enough apart to keep his balance. A crack was emerging in the ice.

Nick fell to the surface as the crack, only about ten feet away, grew bigger—and bigger, before soon large enough for a post to slowly emerge up out of the newly-formed hole in the surface.

When it stopped, Isaac took a second. He stepped over smaller cracks that'd formed outside the epicenter, flipping up a case at eye level near the top of the post. A series of glowing buttons awaited inside the small opening as Isaac punched in a security clearance. "Stay right where you are," the elf instructed inside an imaginary circle.

Nick once again braced his balance as the space, the size of a child's bedroom suddenly descended below the surface. The circle methodically lowered like a crane into pitch darkness. Gritting his teeth, hollow black was now all that surrounded them. Nick wondered when it might end, but the noise didn't even give him the chance to ask before a gentle rocking sensation indicated they may have stopped.

"Stay here," said Isaac as he utilized the same laser, this time for light to find his way around. They'd reached the surface in what appeared to be some kind of bunker. Locating a silver lever, he used all his bodyweight to force it down with a series of mild, fluorescent lights suddenly enveloping a room. At first glance, the area reminded Nick of his trip to Disney World, as if he were suddenly in line for Space Mountain and preparing to hop into some sort of rollercoaster tram.

"Where are we?" Nick inquired, with the trip getting more and more bizarre. The cement walls and floor were lined with strings of movie theatre lights and neon danger signs, with random barrels and crates containing who knows what. And then there was a grooved path, six feet wide, with a railing on either side and a series of odd, bubble-like enclosures resting stationary in the groove.

"This is the Tube Terminal," Isaac informed as he took off his gloves and headgear. He breathed deeply, as if dealing with his own concerns. "The last leg of the journey." Nick watched Isaac reach into a medicine cabinet hanging on the wall. "Here, take this," Isaac handed him a large, red capsule.

"Only I don't have a headache."

"Believe me, you'll have a massive one if you don't take that pill right there," Isaac warned as he opened the door to the first large bubble parked in the pathway.

Nick popped the capsule back, gulping as he swallowed. He could feel his head doing funny things, almost immediately.

Each clear vehicle contained no seat, only a cushioned backrest with thin bars and straps. Nick no longer had the mental capacity to ask questions as Isaac assisted him in, spreading his arms and legs out wide and securing his ankles and wrists. "We'll meet on the other side," Isaac promised, not hesitating to slap a glowing red button inside the bubble.

A voice that was half-female and half-electronic provided a countdown. "Your journey to the Pole begins in ten, nine …

Isaac hurried into his own bubble as Nick suddenly shot through a stone arch—as if being launched from a cannon.

Isaac awaited his own countdown, soon catapulting into utter blackness with the bubbles rolling at rocket speeds. To Nick, it was just a blur, almost like being in a dream-like state as he closed his eyes with his body in motion. And that's because his frame was rapidly rotating in three-dimensional circles as it weaved a path through the dark sea—only an occasional flare light seen along the way.

It was minutes of nausea that felt like tens of minutes before his stretched-out limbs were suddenly no longer twirling in jet-like motion. His bubble came to an abrupt stop through another arch. This terminal looked like the departure area; empty, and only lit by a few neon lights, creating just enough ambiance to see. Nick did notice a few large Christmas bows to doll up the exit port a bit, along with another track on the opposite side where bubbles would leave instead of arrive.

The underground port was also empty of bodies or voices—that is until a loud noise startled him. It was Isaac's bubble abruptly stopping the exact same distance apart from where it began.

Inheriting the Sleigh

Nick did his best to peer back, though his restraints and weary head prevented him from seeing much, if anything at all. He heard Isaac's strap release, with the door to his bubble popping open. Isaac stumbled forward, his legs nearly buckling like an aimless drunk as he somehow kept his feet. He eventually sauntered back toward Nick—beyond anxious himself to be freed, with his arms and legs stretched out into an X.

"I never seem to get used to that." Isaac hiccupped as his eyes were still adjusting. "After all these years."

"Just get me out of here—before my arms fall off, please," Nick plead in his own disheveled fatigue. Unlike Isaac, Nick plopped to the surface of the bubble with his limbs tingling. "You failed to warn me about that for a reason, didn't you?" he felt a need to state the obvious. "Don't mind if I rest for a minute," he sat up, starting to perform his own self-examination, with the effects of the pill quickly wearing off. "There's gotta be a sofa around here. Love seat, maybe a lazy boy. Even a folding chair will work," Nick tried again after no response.

Isaac stripped off more of his warm gear and immediately began getting to work. He seemed worried.

"I don't know what this place is," Nick studied his surroundings in the minimal light. "But what can I do to help?" He figured he might as well pretend to be productive, no matter how achy.

An old audio board and series of small cube monitors were stacked together above. They were resting against a wall, and Isaac was busy punching buttons—even if few of them responded. Isaac then scurried across the room to the opposite side to fire up another machine.

"Backup power," Isaac smiled. "Good ol' generator. A couple of the dusty monitors suddenly showed some black and white static before soon displaying visual images. They were random, but all the exteriors displayed a dark sky in real time.

"It's night already?" Nick seemed confused as to the exact time of day.

"No. More like late afternoon. But you won't see sunlight here at all for at least another month. It's pitch dark for half the year."

Nick was perplexed by the thought as he recalled a school report he once wrote on why Seattle was the suicide capital of the world. But then again, overcast skies seemed far better than months of continual darkness.

Isaac continued to play around with buttons, making some mistakes along the way before new views of the Pole popped up over various monitors. Most of them were too dark to see, with occasional lampposts providing only a glimmer of light. But some of the images were interior, and those were the ones Isaac seemed most interested in.

It took a while to find what he wanted, but his eyes blew up when he noticed a certain figure napping inside a small room. There was little more than a small twin bed, toilet, sink and stove inside. It was unusually tall, but void of much width and length to stretch in.

"Corbin!" Isaac called, hurrying to find a device that looked like a CB truck radio with a wound-up cord. "Corbin, can you hear me?" The confused elf, with a severe case of bedhead failed to respond at first, resting against a pillow. But Isaac's second cry definitely did the trick.

Corbin leapt in response to the familiar voice, looking for a camera he knew was propped in a corner of the high ceiling. Unsure if he was hearing things, Corbin ripped off his colorfully patched quilt in shock. "Chief ... that you?"

"Where are you?" Isaac lit into the biggest smile Nick had ever seen as Corbin's eyes elevated.

"Some sort of abandoned nuclear storm shelter, I think," said

Corbin, clearly disoriented. "It was the safest place I could find. At least one halfway comfortable."

"Well, can you locate your way out?" Isaac wondered, with Nick only a step-length behind, listening to every word.

Corbin turned his head and shook, as if never having thought about it before. "I ... don't know."

"Well, you better figure it out," Isaac felt the need to start barking orders again.

"You do understand the Elites have just cast their vote. By a near majority decree, they declared to shut it all down. You know ... Christmas."

Isaac wished he'd had the chance to read the headline for himself, but with his communication cut off much of the way home, was blindsided by his worst fear. "And the others?" Isaac inquired, but only after some hesitation. Corbin didn't have much to say in response as a confused Nick remained in close earshot to the exchange.

"It was every elf for himself. And there were times, believe me, I assumed I was burnt toast." A few more seconds of silence passed before Corbin's attention perked up. "Is that ...?" his eyes suddenly locked on to the second person in the room. It wasn't a surprise—more like happy relief as Isaac had rudely forgotten all about initiating a cordial introduction.

"Of course," he breathed softly. "Corbin ... meet Nick. Or shall I say, Saint Nick. The great apostolic link continues."

Chapter 17

The airshafts were both narrow and short. Isaac stopped crawling, but only to consult a map with a flashlight in the other hand.

"My knees hurt," Nick held back his complaining long enough.

"According to this, we should be nearing one of the original workshops," said Isaac, laser-focused on the map's detail; though he wished the font were bigger. "Then again, this guide was created about the same time as the American Revolution. I hope it's still accurate."

"You mean, we don't even know if the map's reliable?" Nick was beginning to get claustrophobic on his hands and knees, with the maze of tunnels extending miles across the Pole's intricate underground.

"Believe me," Isaac was forced to respond this time to Nick's frustration. "I would absolutely love to introduce you the proper way. You know, before a throng of jubilant applause on Holiday Row. But unfortunately, that's not about to happen. The enemy won't allow it," he sighed.

"And who are they?" Nick had to poke his head into the stream of portable light to make eye contact with Isaac. "Who is this enemy?"

Inheriting the Sleigh

Isaac wasn't sure how to answer that question, as good and sincere as it was. But he tried nonetheless, temporarily veering from the map. "An ancient hierarchy. One, for whom centuries has used intellect, and oftentimes, deceit to push for power, ultimately creating their own class. Here at the Pole, we've nicknamed them—the Elites."

"Elites?" Nick scoffed. "How much power could they really have? I thought my father was in control?"

Isaac nodded, not fully understanding all the delicate intricacies himself. "The truth is—Kris has forever been the only one standing in their way."

"And so now that he's gone ... they're abolishing Christmas altogether?"

Isaac set the flashlight down to keep moving through the stuffy shaft. "The only thing they ever enjoyed about Christmas, was profiting from it. Then again, a part of me always suspected that in their minds, the holiday had run its course. Some even believe the sleigh was meddled with. Which if true, would confirm the point."

Nick needed a second to process everything. "You're saying my father may have been ... what? Murdered?"

I don't want to believe it. But yes," the elf conceded. "It is possible. And when the time is right, we'll conduct a proper review to find out for certain. The Elites, as cunning as they are in building up power within the Congress, they've always been outnumbered. But without Kris here, the fear is, what do the working-class elves have to fight for? Who will inspire them?" Isaac paused again in the darkness, letting Nick absorb the truth. "The elves are the hardest working race on the planet, bred for charity and love. Their lives revolve around these principles. But," Isaac also emphasized as he suddenly shined the flashlight directly into Nick's curious eyes. "They won't simply continue to do that, sacrificing so much along the way if there's not somebody there to take your father's place and lead them. Someone who can do the Savior's bidding of bearing gifts on his birthday."

Nick was now sweating profusely in the heat of the underground shaft; so much so that for a moment, he'd forgotten where he was.

"C'mon," Isaac continued to crawl, anxious to find space to maneuver again. They made many zigzaggy turns until finally the shaft led into a small room tall enough to stand in.

"Oh, my legs," the taller Nick cried as he slowly inched up working through the many cramps in his joints. "I never thought I'd be so happy to use my feet again."

The room had four walls, but only one was clear. Isaac slowly approached the glass, as if knowing exactly where they were. On the other side, it dropped off into a massive enclosure extending over a hundred feet deep, and hundreds more feet long. "Do you see this?" Isaac enticed Nick closer.

The space was dark, but there was enough light to see, with a series of short and long wooden tables stationed one after the other in many rows. Old tools on pegboards were dotted about the various walls, and there were piles of un-swept sawdust on the floor. Nick and Isaac stared down at the abandoned toy factory like a couple of corporate managers examining a worksite. It was almost like a museum frozen in time.

A hollow clank was loud enough to draw both their attention away from the ancient factory and back through the small opening leading into the maze of shafts. Isaac quickly pulled out an unusual weapon, signaling Nick against the wall. It looked like an old perfume bottle with bubbly liquid inside the clear canister, along with a purple hose and bulb.

"Really?" Nick rolled his eyes.

Inheriting the Sleigh

"Have you ever been pasted with pepper spray before?" Isaac's offense was obvious as he retorted with a low whisper. "Except here, we call it peppermint spray, and it's ten times as lethal. Now, quiet for a minute."

Isaac held onto the bulb as the clanks grew louder by the second. It was now clear somebody was crawling through the shaft—the elf concerned that whoever it was, they'd been on their heels for some time.

But then it stopped. Seconds of silence permeated before a head suddenly shot out through the hole. Isaac was more than ready to pull the trigger—only to release his grip just in time. He knew the emerging smile well. It was happy-go-lucky, yet coupled with exhaustion.

"Whoa, whoa, whoa!" Corbin didn't even like the look of the peppermint spray staring him square in the nose. "Get that terrible stuff away from me, please!" he instinctively shielded his cheeks.

Isaac could have said, I told you so but instead set the bottle down to assist Corbin the rest of the way through.

"Chief," Corbin grinned. "How was your vacation?"

Isaac knew he was joking but still found it difficult to come up with a retort. "Unrelaxing, stressful, and incredibly expensive," he threw in that last part amidst a sudden flashback of paying off a bouncer at the Blue Owl.

"And what are you wearing?" he suddenly seemed puzzled by the ski pants and gift shop T-shirt that Isaac picked up at a gas station somewhere along the way. Corbin didn't wait for an answer as he drew his eyes in on Nick for the first time. The truth was, Nick was nearly as thrown off by the new elf's wardrobe choice—let alone the sudden bear hug.

"Oh, hell-ohhh," he could barely finish the greeting—being squeezed that tight.

Vance

"I certainly never imagined I'd see you again. I mean, you were the fattest little baby. Just a butterball. The biggest cheeks there ever were. Not to mention …," Isaac cut Corbin off with a finger to the neck, suggesting it was probably time to stop now. "Oh, of course. You were quite a handsome child," he grumbled with a more proper voice.

Nick took a second to digest Corbin's blinding array of color. It was quite the loud patchwork, and part of him thought he was looking at a well-used paint pallet. A soft, red cotton ball hung off the end of his knit hat. His coat was bright purple and his pants gold. But the stare-down soon became awkward, at least to Nick as Corbin never once looked away. It was one of his many quirks.

"Alright, enough of that," Isaac intervened. "Talk to me?" he pointed with a raised thumb to signal for any sign of life above. "Where are they?"

Corbin knew exactly who he was talking about; the unsung heroes and toymakers that truly made Christmas what it was. He pulled up a seat. It was the only chair in the room; an old wooden stool as Isaac braced for whatever the update happened to be. "I do have a mole feeding me what he can. Said that for weeks they locked themselves away, just waiting things out inside their dormitories. You know, obviously scared out of their wits by all the sudden changes. But last I heard the lack of food brought many back out again. Though believe me … soon," he paused. "They'll all be out."

"What do you mean?" Isaac inquired, though Corbin seemed hesitant to speak with Nick in range. Isaac asked again.

"The Elites delayed your father's burial," he veered toward Nick, as if silently apologizing for having to be the one to break the news. "Much of the labor force still fails to even surmise, let alone believe he's actually dead. They need proof."

Inheriting the Sleigh

"And?" a curious Nick calmly stepped forward, surprising Corbin by his level of engagement. "Did they? Did they get their proof?"

Corbin nodded, but slowly. "They will."

"This is our chance then," Isaac had to think for a moment, his dead-eyed stare penetrating directly through the glass wall.

"A chance for what?" Nick could only guess.

Isaac and Corbin gauged each other's reaction with silent approval before Isaac eventually declared it out loud. His eyes locked onto Nick's. "A chance to make your triumphant return. Our one and most likely only shot to convince the elves to side with us—convincing them that it's pertinent we save Christmas."

Chapter 18

The clock tower sprung tall in the center of Chimney Sweep Square. It was a glowing cube with rotating spindles on all four sides. The time was 10:00, though by the star-dotted skies, Nick couldn't decipher morning from night. Sleeping was sporadic, and he guessed morning as a hooded Isaac lifted a drainage lid exposing a cobblestone road in a quiet corner. It was Nick's first taste of the Pole above ground.

A street sign, lit by a vintage cast iron lamp read, "Bethlehem Way." Nick noticed an occasional set of pattering feet amidst the old Victorian road, one with Dickensian cottages plotted one after the next. The elves were moving toward the artificial light.

"Just follow them," said Isaac in response to another set of shadowy frames magnetically making their way toward the bright tower.

Nick grew nervous as he knew he was about to encounter a people completely hidden from the rest of the world.

The light was soon joined by a bell. It was a call for attention, and as Isaac and Nick rounded a corner through a back alleyway, there lay the spectacle. It was a city square with a white columned, Greco-Roman style structure at the center, with statues and fountains to complement.

Inheriting the Sleigh

As they slowly approached a corner between two sets of storefronts, the noise was exactly what one might expect to hear with thousands quickly converging onto the same place. Isaac was hasty as he pushed the two of them through a wall of small bodies.

Elves were quickly filling up every crevice, creatively climbing atop shop windows in hopes of finding a suitable view. Funny shoes, some with swirly points, dangled off the edges, and others held hands in a human train down a steep rooftop—the top elf locking his grip around a chimney for support.

Nick felt out of place as he made sure his hood completely covered up his forehead and ears. Even at 14, he was a good foot taller than most and was amazed at their balance and agility. There was little to no fear; and in a flash, more seemed to appear over adjoining rooftops. Nick's eyes rose with the towering clock as elves climbed its exterior. Others jammed into the stone spires of a tall cathedral as the streets were hastily being cleared below.

"Who are they?" Nick pointed at the row of disciplined soldiers. They wore fuzzy hats and long red coats drooping below their thighs.

"The Elite Guard," Isaac whispered as he worked hard to locate a suitable spot.

Nick was suddenly poked from behind by a sharp tip that felt anything but pleasant. "Move along," insisted the much shorter guard after ruthlessly sticking the musket blade into his backside.

Isaac ignored the assault as he gripped onto Nick's wrist, pulling him deeper through the chaos of fleeting feet along the south end of the square. Past a display store window with a mannequin wearing a parka, Isaac located a thin gap between two buildings barely wide enough to fit through.

Vance

"The funeral procession of our dearest Kris Kringle will begin in approximately 60 seconds," announced a voice, creating a mild panic among the crowd.

Nick and Isaac sidestepped through the narrow alley until locating a discreet ladder running vertically up one of the tall stone buildings. The bars were bitterly cold, and it felt further to reach the top than it was.

"Welcome citizens of the great North!" resumed a voice as Isaac's impatient head peeked over the ledge to get his first birds-eye glimpse. "And thank you for gathering with us at this final sojourn. A glorious conclusion to a most wonderful dispensation of time."

Nick was blown away by the aerial view. Not only by the charm of his immediate surroundings, but by the endless dots of light filling the distance. He held onto a flagpole for support, with an old banner flapping above in the breeze. It had a large golden star in the middle, with diagonal red stripes lined across the base. It was a sturdy fabric but torn in places from age.

The drumline began the parade, though Isaac paid little attention. Nick noticed his focus busily scanning the premises left to right, as if gathering for any clue.

Nick's eyes were also wandering, but for different reasons—feeling his face to make certain this was no dream.

"Introducing the magnificent Elitist Guard!" The emcee touted with enthusiasm as several uniformed lines of tall black and gold hats rounded a bend for the parade route. Some cheered while others booed as they marched in strict order. A strap descended their chins, and the buttons aligning their long coats were shimmering.

Nick appeared impressed by the chemistry as their kneecaps rose in stride, their muskets resting firm over their left shoulders. Isaac forced himself to watch, though it was clearly painful.

Inheriting the Sleigh

"How much longer?" Nick inquired. "You know ... before I see him?"

Some of the Guard were on horseback, with a band of trumpeters sounding away in a sad eulogy. "Patience. We'll let these pompous actors engage in their pony show. And then maybe they'll usher him out."

Fire breathers shot large flames into the initial rows crowding the festive, surface-level streets. Children scampered, some in excitement, others in fear as skilled jugglers caught colorful balls atop funny little miniature cars equipped with bulb horns and large exhausts.

The doors opened to the white-columned Capitol Hall in the center of the square. It was an old, ornate courthouse with round, castle-like turrets on the corners, and guards on lookout. A series of men filed out the doors to watch the parade wind down. It was as if they had come to see only the most important part.

"And who are they?" Nick could immediately tell they were different.

Isaac smiled, though it was simply to keep himself calm in the moment. He clearly detested everything about them. "Elites, Nick. But don't worry," he turned after noticing the boy's unsettled gaze. "Corbin will come through. He always does."

It was from a distance, but Nick was captivated by a blotch of color that had much more in common with a circus than a dignified proceeding. The attire was formal, yet eccentric. The many wigs poured out the tall doors with raised fists and canes, playing to the crowd while descending the capitol steps.

Some of the elves hushed as the last of them showed himself. Mauv Lyman was taller than most, but still shorter than Nick. He wore a bright purple vest topped by a green waistcoat, with long socks at the knees. His shoes were round, bulging and black with a silver buckle—and his bald head went uncovered in the brisk air.

Mauv watched as the last component of the parade was ushered in. It was a stunning white carriage being pulled by four magnificent Clydesdales with the hairiest of feet. An elf dressed in all black sat atop the plush leather, slowly steering the steeds. The carriage's large wheels, lined with green, slowly rolled over the brick roads. An impressive Christmas wreath hung from the top above the driver's head, with dashes of holly aligning various corners of the windows.

All went silent, many with reverence as they knew who was lifeless in the back. Not even the jugglers or fire breathers could deter the spotlight any longer.

Nick watched intently alongside Isaac as the mobile morgue slowly made its way around for everyone to see, before stopping directly at the grand steps. Many seconds of silence passed as the elves watched a handful of pallbearers lift out two magnificent caskets. A female elf began to sob, lifting a hand up to her mouth with a gasp.

Nick suddenly remembered Arthur once boasting about the time he personally witnessed the assassinated John F. Kennedy being displayed across the streets of Washington D.C. It was the only comparison he could draw—but for the first time, was beginning to feel some attachment in his own heart—as if seeing his birth parents suddenly made it all seem more real.

The twin coffins offered a splash of color as they were laid upon a platform in the street for all to see. Many shades of green, ivory, red and gold swirled amid bows of pine, with reflective ornaments glimmering off the streetlamps. An Elite with a long, narrow face descended a path in the white steps. "For this day, we pay our dearest graces to a man and woman the world knew as Father and Mother Christmas," rang the proper voice. It was somewhat dark and mysterious, with an old drawl. "Yes, it is he once known as the very John the Revelator."

Nick wondered if he'd heard correctly—but with so much noise inside his head—let it pass. He instead studied the strange environment, all while waiting for a clue from Isaac on how to proceed.

"Centuries upon centuries gone by—the beloved Kris Kringle—a name he would later adopt, became the very fabric of our land, culture, and way of life. He was a steward of children, and oh, how he loved to make them grin. He was a saint among saints and loved to serve his Master's calling."

Isaac could only wait it out. He was on standby, anticipating the plan to unfold, though it came in a way he wasn't expecting. An awkward screech suddenly wailed through the speakers.

The Elites jumped, many holding their ears in response to the obnoxious squeal. Mauv Lyman's communication had suddenly been cut off. He tapped the small mic that discreetly hung near his mouth, swinging around in dissatisfaction as his engineers scrambled to locate the problem.

The sound soon cleared again and went silent for a few more seconds as the thousands of shocked onlookers were rightly confused. It sounded like an old World War II newsreel—starting with a jingle that was joined by a voice.

Isaac could only visualize his friend, somewhere underground having the time of his life, while he and Nick were left to sweat it out above. "You are now listening to 101.5—your home to Celestial Radio. I am your host, Stan the Music Man, and we interrupt this scheduled program to bring you a very important announcement from a particularly important man. And no, I am not talking about Mauv Lyman."

Isaac's eyes rolled, having no idea what Corbin was doing. "What in candy cane cries," he cursed under his breath, expecting him to simply cut off the enemy's communication and leave the rest to him.

Corbin's bare feet were nonchalantly kicked up on a switchboard. He was smiling into an old radio mic still on its stand. His eyes were closed—his headphones rainbowed over his ears.

The elves above didn't know how to process what they were hearing—though knowing Corbin better than anyone, Isaac could. He was pretending to be a disk jockey, changing his voice every time he switched character.

"Greta Sinclair here," Corbin's pitch went high as he impersonated a female reporter. "Yes, Stan, from what we are hearing here high above the noonday clouds, we are now just minutes away from being addressed by God himself. That's right, the great Creator of all will speak to you, me, and all the great citizens of the Northern Pole."

"How exciting, Greta. Can you preview what we might hear?"

"Well, Stan, it's only speculation at this point. But I'm under the assumption it might have something to do with the death of Santa Claus."

Engineers continued to scramble, pulling cords and testing audio equipment above the white steps—all as Mauv did his best to remain composed, proper, and still before his befuddled audience. Isaac was equally dismayed but could only wait and see where he was going with the theatrics.

"Wait," said Greta cutting Stan off mid-sentence. "I believe he is about to begin."

"Yes, you are right. Ladies and gentleman, I present to you … God."

The elves were confused and speechless both, as another round of silence swept over the square.

Inheriting the Sleigh

Corbin's voice then went deep. "Good morning, children of the great North." Not a soul on the surface uttered a word. "I bid you assurance that I have received Kris into my own. He is celebrating in the great heavens now. But I know of what you ask. What does this mean for you and me? A worthy question indeed, and one I will soon answer."

Mauv glanced in paranoid frustration as he awaited the return of his own voice. A nod finally came from his chief engineer.

"Test. Can you hear me?" Mauv performed a quick audio check as the attention suddenly shot back toward him. "Do not believe this imposter! It is a ruse!"

"Mauv, is that you?" God's voice rose. Lyman instinctively trembled a bit, as if not completely sure himself what was happening. "It is time now to look to the future."

"What future? What are you talking about?"

"I'm talking about the future of Christmas."

"Christmas? At a time like this? I don't know who you are, but respect that this is a funeral procession."

"I know your thoughts, Mauv Lyman. You assume the tradition is over." The Speaker was flummoxed alongside the rest of the equally confused Elites; not to mention, thousands of aghast elves. "But I am here today to tell you—I have sent another to resume my ageless tradition."

"Isaac Newell!" Mauv roared with panning eyes, as if finally getting closer to catching on to what was truly happening. "You can stop with the charade now!"

Corbin's collection of voices finally went silent all at once, while Nick glanced over at the eyes inside the hood at his side. Isaac, for the first time, unconcealed his face a good four stories up. He was now staring directly at the new sheriff in town. "Corbin," Isaac whispered with his eyes failing to so much as blink. "If you can hear me, I think the game is up. You need to get out of there … now."

"I know you're out there, somewhere!" Mauv cried. "Show yourself."

An elf dangling her frosty feet off the edge of the building suddenly noticed Isaac standing beside her. With a droopy hat and rosy cheeks, she pointed. "There he is mother. Isn't that him?" Chatter quickly spread like a newly formed wave.

With the plan having gone terribly wrong, Isaac knew he had to react quickly. "Lyman!" he eventually yelled back. Unlike Corbin, he didn't have the luxury of a microphone to make himself heard. Lyman's head slowly swiveled to his left and then panned up. He'd clearly heard enough of the echo bouncing off the wind. Soon, every head in the vicinity was pinned on the very same spot as Nick sweated profusely underneath his thermals and hood. A roaming spotlight followed onto their position as Isaac now had the floor.

"So, you've returned," said Mauv with a snickering half-smile. "Defying a direct order to stay and face trial, I might add."

Despite all his anxieties, Isaac managed to smile back. "You left me no choice. Though I will say, it was all for a just cause. Perhaps you wish to meet our guest." Curious whispers struck up again across Chimney Sweep Square as Nick stood fearful and motionless.

The Elites watched with anticipation, many mumbling among themselves. They were waiting for the Speaker to act.

Mauv used a pair of fancy binoculars to get a better look as Nick pulled down his own hood. He then turned back toward the street near the grand steps to behold the decorated coffin of Santa Claus. He did so with a prolonged stare that lasted a minute, maybe more.

Inheriting the Sleigh

With shingles at their feet, Isaac swiveled his own gaze across the crowd, dreaming a movement of support might immediately rally around him and Nick both. Though time wouldn't allow it as Lyman swiftly lifted his iron fist. He declared it just loud enough for all to hear. "Those two," he pointed at the sky. "Arrest them."

Chapter 19

Nick could think of nothing else to do but sit over a wooden crate. His small holding cell was lit by only a single bulb and the cave-like walls were damp.

A guard had a crate of his own, his stacked three-high on the opposite side of the bars. His short legs dangled off the edge and his eyes oddly never left Nicks'.

"So," Nick could only fidget with his Key Whiz for so long. "Where does a kid get a good steak around here?" After hours of waiting for further word—the truth was—he was desperate for some conversation to pass the time.

But not only did the guard fail to so much as smirk at the sarcasm, he didn't budge either with his bug eyes, dead-fixed. "Excuse me," Nick now had reason to be concerned. "But are you ... alright?"

Nick pushed himself to his feet, slowly moving to one side—but the guard's gaze remained. All he could hear was the echoing chatter coming from a distant cell as a strange, purple mist was seeping both in and around the bars. It was subtle and slow but curling up and around the guard's face. It was responsible for the trance.

Inheriting the Sleigh

Locking his fists over the bars to get a better look, Nick eventually had to use one hand to protect his nose and mouth from the thickening fumes. It was difficult to see much anymore, but two bodies soon came scampering into view through the smoke. One was female—tall by their standard—coupled by a pudgy elf behind her.

"I can't bloody breathe in here," Gib cried as he swatted away at the smoke.

Nick's only thought was, "that makes two of us." But with the colorful haze slowly dissipating, he could now see the guard completely tilted to one side.

"Set the clock," Silva instructed with haste.

"Clock … set. Six minutes, 47 seconds, precisely. Ezra would be proud," the choking elf made note. He gasped between large cheeks and thick, Scottish sideburns that complimented a walrus mustache.

"Make that six-33," said Silva in slenderizing contrast. "We just wasted 14 precious seconds. I knew we should have worn masks."

"OK," Gib rolled his eyes before resetting the clock, as if knowing there was absolutely no point arguing with her.

In desperation, Nick ripped off a sleeve to cover his mouth, all while wondering if the odd tandem ever intended to acknowledge he was even there. "Excuse me?" he couldn't hold back any longer with a cough. "But may I ask what you're doing?" Nick lifted his hands from around his nose, just long enough to notice the savvy female had yet to make eye contact. Instead, she took a pack off her shoulder—placing a series of very specific things over a towel.

"What does it look like, Nicholas?" she stated, as if having known the boy his entire life. "Getting you out of here. Correct me if I'm wrong, but freedom must certainly sound more enticing than this pile of …"

Vance

"Five minutes!" Gib interrupted, all while placing a small accent pillow underneath the head of the comatose guard. "Just rest your sweet head. There, there," he gently but swiftly guided his ear back down.

"You know my name," Nick's attention had since doubled.

The crouching she-elf finally stopped to look up; for only a second—two at the most, before stating the obvious. "Why, of course we do."

"Four and a half minutes," Gib beat her to it this time.

"Oh, and I assume you wish to know ours?" It wasn't hard to read Nick's uncertain mind as they multi-tasked—conversing, and prepping tools all at the same time. "Silva," she informed. "It's Silva …"

"Bells," Gib cut her off with a grin as Silva rolled both eyes, tired of a joke she'd heard all too many times before. "Get it? Silva … Bells."

"It's actually Nyene. And this is …," Silva swung a cheek back toward her quirky partner.

"Gib," Nick said it, only so that she didn't have to. It was his way of proving he'd been listening to every word.

"Gib here at your service," he said with the ends of his mustache swaying to the movement of his hidden lips.

"OK, now that we all know each other, I guess I'll let you … get back to it then."

"So very kind," Silva quipped.

"Four minutes!" Gib nervously noted.

Silva abruptly jumped up with little bedside manner at the ticking of the clock. "Stand back! Way back," she instructed while reaching for a large, red can. The elf, with an exotic silver streak splitting through her black hair, went to work coating white foam all over a middle bar.

"Is it steel? Gib asked, watching the sudsy bubbles quickly sizzle over.

Inheriting the Sleigh

"I wish," Silva informed as an acid began to immediately eat its way through. "My job would be a whole lot easier if it were. Looks like carbon grool."

"Carbon grool," Nick uttered under breath. As a kid who aced geology back at Lourdes Academy, he never recalled learning about that before.

"That's right. A metal only found deep inside the arctic core. Nothing on earth is stronger."

"On that note, how do you possibly plan on getting me out of here?"

"Three minutes," said Gib as he obnoxiously blew his nose into a colorful handkerchief. Silva looked back, unimpressed. "What? It's flu season," he raised his flat hands in helplessness.

But Silva was more interested in Nick's sudden lack of faith. "This … is how we plan on getting you out of here," her grin was confident as she held up a bright red waxy stick. "Now go barricade yourself behind that crate over there," she cried, while taping the ammunition to the bar. "And stay as low as possible."

"Should I be concerned?" Nick now had his back leaning up against the far side of the crate—his hands pushed up against his ears.

"Perhaps," Gib was careless with his honesty as Silva and Nick both looked straight-facedly his way. Nick in fear, and Silva with a shake, wondering why he opted to say that. "Then again, what do I know? I'm just the unimportant clock manager."

"Here," Silva slid a board between the bars. "I suggest you cover your head."

Gib, meanwhile, had both pale hands propped over his own ears. His eyes were synched shut and his head bowed low, all in anticipation for the discomfort of a blast he knew was forthcoming. Nick barely had enough time to read Gib's fear before the explosion rocked the dungeon.

143

Vance

Shards from the cave ceiling immediately poured down from the top of the cell. "Oh, dear Christmas ghost," Gib muttered euphemisms to get him through it. His head was dipped toward the floor, with both arms draped over his bushy, red locks. "Please forgive me my daily trespasses. And watch over the young ones should I not see tomorrow."

The explosion was now just a flow of kicked-up dirt as Gib continued mumbling. "Hey, Findiggy!" Silva called to break the elf's lull. "Where's the clock?"

Gib leapt up, along with Nick, reaching for the chain attached to his belt. Cupping the stopwatch, he hadn't realized where the time had gone. "90 seconds."

Shooing away the dust cloud, all eyes shifted focus to the bar. It had been cracked, but not completely, now leaning at an angle. Silva tugged, but it wouldn't budge.

"What now?" Nick was counting inside his own head. They had barely over a minute left as the comatose guard suddenly attempted to lunge back up, before dropping again in fatigue.

Silva failed to answer, instead striking up a portable saw with no cord. It had a spinning, circular blade—one so sharp, one slippage would take off a limb in a flinch. The saw made a piercing sound, but Nick could still hear the faint chatter of voices gathering above. His eyes were watered over by the cloud of dust still trapped inside the semi-dark dungeon. The bulb was still on but hanging by a single wire. Silva was pushing the saw through two different cuts in the bar. It was eating the rest of the way through, however slowly.

"Got it!" Silva cried with satisfaction. A piece of carbon grool finally clanked against the surface and rolled away. To Nick, it was the most beautiful sound in the world as his thin frame hurried to hop over the three feet of bar still in place.

Inheriting the Sleigh

"C'mon," Silva waved with trouble on their heels.

Gib then lifted the guard's head to retrieve his small pillow, before following Silva deeper through the corridor. An alarm had sounded with a series of blinking warning lights now flickering in flashes, though Silva failed to stop.

The stone tunnel cornered off into different alleyways with Nick unable to tell if she knew where she was going. Gib's beachball frame hobbled behind her in the rear, occasionally turning back to see if they were being followed. Silva eventually stopped at an enclosed door. It was equipped with a keypad.

"Wait," Nick crouched, huffing with his hands over his kneecaps. "I was with someone before they separated us."

"Yeah, don't worry," Silva said calmly. "The Chief is fine. That's if the others have done their job, anyway," she purposefully whispered that second part quietly.

But from the staggered look across his eyes, Nick had suddenly grown weary. "You, OK, boy?" Gib questioned.

"I think he's starting to get ill," Silva was mildly concerned. "Could be from the gas."

Gib's head shot back around again. Encroaching voices were clearly right around the corner when a heavy door shot up. "Perfect timing."

"Hurry!" Silva cried, tugging on Nick's wrist—helping him forward. The Elite Guards looked like angry toy soldiers, with tall, wool hats and muskets strapped over their shoulders.

As one last parting insult, Gib slowly raised his arms in surrender; only to take one step back. He was childishly sticking out his tongue.

The guards readied their weapons before the spaceship-style door instantly dropped shut again, prompting a welcome sigh. A sigh both long and deep.

Chapter 20

Where is he?! Is he safe?" a disheveled Isaac cried barreling through the doors.

"Nice to see you too, Chief," Silva was slightly offended; though the truth was, even more relieved with Ezra and Blaine in his wake.

"Wow," Gib followed with his large, blue eyes veering back and forth between a roughed-up Isaac and Nick fast asleep on a makeshift cot. "We really are good, aren't we? You know, considering that an hour ago, the two of you were looking at never seeing the light of day again."

"What's wrong with him!?" Isaac approached the cot like an overly concerned parent in the wake of a tragic accident.

"Nothing," Silva insisted.

"Then why ...?"

"He look deader than a mannequin? Because we put him out," Gib cut Isaac off as he pulled his loose trousers higher up over his large waistline. "Upon examination, I found his senses to be largely ... you know, out of whack, shall we say. He's still adjusting to the Pole and needed the rest. I mean, c'mon, let's be honest. This place would make any newbie queasy."

Inheriting the Sleigh

Isaac approached his motionless frame, feeling for a pulse simply to put himself at ease. The separation anxiety nearly killed him.

"Are you OK?" asked Blaine after observing that Isaac appeared to need a long nap of his own.

"I don't know, Cross," he insisted with a bad bruise around one eye.

"What did they do to you, anyhow?" Silva wondered.

"Torture?" Gib nodded with an out-of-place smile once Isaac said nothing.

"Most of it psychological," Ezra clarified. "We found him lying face-down in a life-size marshmallow. They made him listen to Elmo and Patsy's ridiculous rendition of 'Grandma Got Run Over by a Reindeer.' Over, and over, and over again."

"You, poor soul," Silva uttered sincerely as Isaac was now doing funny things far out of character; like dusting off empty shelves once meant to store gift boxes ready for inventory.

"Yeah, I'm not so sure he is. You know … alright," Gib thumbed over at Isaac who had now moved onto polishing a scuff in the wall—a blemish nobody else but him could even see.

"The Elites were doing whatever they could to draw out information," Ezra caught the group up to speed. "They wanted to … you know, know how much the boy knows," he pointed over at Nick, frozen and flat over the cot.

"That's a lot of knows," Gib was trained to pick up on nuance.

"While we're on topic … I'm assuming he knows who his father is?" Silva probed. The group fully expected Isaac to take that one, though his trance hadn't weakened.

Blaine instead picked up from there. "It's my understanding they never made it that far. The boy remains clueless as to who he actually is."

"Well, I would hope the Chief made a point to tell him," Silva continued. "I mean, if I were directly related to an apostle—let alone a household name, I think I'd like to know. By the way, where's Corbin?" It had just occurred to ask, though neither Ezra nor Blaine wished to offer up a response.

On a dime, Isaac snapped from his stupor, proving he'd been listening to every word. "They found him," he revealed matter-of-factly with a swivel. Neither Silva nor Gib knew what to say.

"What's a third jailbreak then when you've turned the first two into a cakewalk?" Ezra eventually spoke up as Gib groaned.

"And yet, that's the easy part," Isaac revealed, striking up a match and lighting a candle for some added light. "Cause only then comes the real challenge."

"Yeah, the hard part," repeated Gib. "Let's talk about that."

"And remind me what that is again?" Blaine's voice echoed across the warehouse as the Chief got back on topic.

Isaac was quick to answer this time. "Convincing the elves that Christmas is worth risking their own lives for."

The others either bit their knuckles or kept their arms firmly folded, as if not fully convinced that was the way to go. "And is it? You know … worth fighting for?" Silva eventually posed to a host of uncertain faces. "All things considered. I mean, how much longer can we really press our luck with these maniacs? Perhaps all this change inevitably becomes permanent."

Blaine just flinched in deferral. It was his way of admitting the same point. The truth was, it was a legitimate question that nobody seemed to have a definitive answer to.

"I believe it is," a new voice suddenly joined the conversation.

Inheriting the Sleigh

All five heads turned in unison to behold Nick now standing tall behind them, clueless as to how long he'd been listening in.

"Must not have been as strong a sedative as it warned on the bottle," Gib's eyebrows rose.

Nick stepped closer to the light, looking around quickly to try and gather precisely where he was. He had trouble with the details as the massive interior was at least the size of a large department store. "Worth fighting for, I mean."

The others stood to meet him at eye level, all to convey their reverence.

"Nick Kringle," Ezra took off his spectacles, just long enough to clean the lenses, before gathering a better look. "Why, what a strapping young man you've become."

"Yes … welcome home," Blaine was equally eager to touch his hand.

"Your name?" Nick inquired as he inspected the most unique sideburns he had ever seen.

"Blaine. Blaine Richins. Though some call me, Cross."

"And I'm Ezra Tortle." Ezra himself stepped forward into the portable lantern light. He had a much cleaner look than either Blaine or Gib, with soft, endearing dimples underneath his old 19th-century glasses.

Nick veered from one face to the next, reciting their names in wonder. "Isaac, Silva, Gib, Blaine … and Ezra. My new friends." But then his gaze morphed into a squint, as if finally realizing somebody was missing. "Corbin. Where is he?"

Everyone turned to Isaac, wondering what the plan was now. "Are you ready to make your grand entrance, Nick? Cuz Corbin's in a bit of a sour pickle."

Vance

"Aren't we all," Gib slapped at his jiggly cheeks, something he often did to quell his anxiety.

Nick thought long and hard, though the group eventually was content with what they heard. "I think I am."

Chapter 21

The rusty elevator was moving up. "What's on your mind?" Isaac broke Nick's train of thought, as it was clear something had been bothering him.

"Honestly? I should be performing a concert right now. I just remembered they booked me for an event at Carnegie Hall."

But the truth was, there was much more racing through his brain. Little subtle clues in passing, as if a connection of dots explaining who he really was, finally clicked all at once.

The warehouse elevator was still moving. It was moving fast, and yet they had been inside together for minutes. "There is still a lot you have yet to tell me," Nick's eyes veered. "By design, I assume. Perhaps you want me to find answers on my own, I'm not sure." Isaac just stood and listened, giving Nick the time to say what he needed. "But there is one thing I never had the chance to ask."

Isaac was caught in a battle of his own mistakes made along the way. He had never trained a new Santa Claus before, and for the first time, perhaps questioned his own methodology.

"It's true then?" Nick's instincts kicked in again. "John ..."

Vance

The reciting of his name struck loud through Isaac's ears, as if he'd been waiting for Nick to say it on his own. "What about him?"

'He really is my father. John the Apostle. The very one you read about in the Bible. He was actually, Santa Claus?'

The air got even thicker inside the drafty elevator. The four walls inside clanked with strange sounds, and Isaac knew the time for more truth was now.

"He was the last great disciple, Nick. A man on a mission to defend Christianity."

"But this is what I don't understand. He died on the Isle of Patmos. If not there, then most likely Ephesus."

Isaac shook. "Perhaps you haven't studied the New Testament as well as you think you have."

"Believe me when I tell you, my private school forced me to memorize the entire Book of Revelation. The workload there bordered on criminal."

But Isaac brushed the sarcasm aside. "And yet you didn't understand it. Luke 9:27. But I tell you of truth. There be some standing here which shall not taste of death till they see the Kingdom of God."

"OK," Nick was feisty and quick in his own defense. "How does that imply, John?"

"John, 21st chapter. Jesus said unto him, If I will that he tarries till I come, what is that to thee?"

"Then went this saying abroad among the brethren," Nick—without hesitation—pulled the last of the verse from memory. "Yet Jesus said unto him, He shall not die." He had heard it many times, and yet there was suddenly something different in his interpretation. He paused, as if needing a moment. "If he hadn't tasted death—then why now?"

Inheriting the Sleigh

Isaac nodded as if not entirely sure. "Every good thing must come to an end ... eventually. His blood now lives through you. Don't you understand? You are now the bearer of great gifts."

"And you chose not to tell me any of this?"

"If I had," Isaac hunched with his eyes glazed against one of the four ascending walls. "Would you have believed it?"

"Probably not."

"Milk before meat."

Nick paused again, as if desperately needing to change the subject for the sake of his own sanity. Meanwhile, the elevator continued to whisk upward. "How deep underground did you say we were?"

"Deep," Isaac assured. "Though we'll be on the surface soon."

"And perhaps you can tell me what awaits through those doors?" Nick asked, as if his mind were so sidetracked by the latest reveal, he could hardly concentrate on the moment—as important as it was.

With a rare grin, Isaac resumed. "The people of the Pole, Nick. It's time to inspire them. They've all risen and need to be reminded that the same routine undertaken here for hundreds of years must continue the way it always has. They're creatures of habit, the elves. Naturally inclined to go back to work, but also not about to break any law without very good reason or the will to do so."

"But what do I say?" Nick's concern was evidenced by the instinctive reach for his pills. Isaac swiped at the cannister quicker than Nick could process. He held the bottle away as Nick lunged like a desperate addict. But instead, the elf tossed it out of sight through an air vent. "Ugh, what was that?!" Nick panicked as he heard the bottle clank away.

Isaac gripped onto his arm in a swift attempt to calm him down. "Don't you see?" he said with a smile. "You don't need them anymore."

"What do you mean, don't …?" But Nick stopped cold, suddenly realizing for the first time he hadn't consumed a single capsule since his arrival at the North Pole. His need was simply an impulse. He felt his heart. It was painless where he often felt pain. His anxieties were still real, but his dependency on the medication was not.

"Your heart has returned home, Nick," Isaac explained. "The reason you had problems, was because for years it had been calling you back. You know … where you belong."

Nick wanted to react though was uncertain how. But he also had to deal with an elevator he could tell was finally beginning to slow. "Don't think," Isaac instructed as they suddenly rocked to a halt. "Just open your mouth and let your heart take it from there. After all, it's not the worst—but the best part of you."

The doors finally parted, only to display a busy backdrop. Nick and Isaac stood still for a moment inside the frozen elevator. For Nick, the ensuing scene was like stepping back in time. Hundreds, perhaps thousands meandered about. The mixture of attire spanned cultures and time. It was odd for Nick to see Shakespearean ruffs, cloaks and petticoats intermingling with bellbottom pants and the loose fitted beads of the 70's.

"Read all about it!" an elvish newsie, with a poor boy hat and scarf held up a paper with a large black headline. "Corbin Creel Dies by Noose at Noonday!" The newsie stabbed a coin out of midair and flung a paper right back. "Former Claus Wizard, Creel to Get Slipped the Knot!"

Nick wondered if he heard correctly over the chatter, with many sitting on stacks of large crates—others simply perusing the old streets. Victorian buildings hovered over those streets with splashes of color on storefront signage and inside vendor windows.

Inheriting the Sleigh

"This is the great marketplace," Isaac whispered next to Nick—whom had yet to take his eyes off the bustling street chaos. "Where most of the elves go to get away."

An elf slid down a pole with a red light flashing to an alarm. A garage door then wheeled open, where an old vintage fire truck honked on its way out. The truck nearly ran over a young couple bundled up in thick mink coats and riding a two-seater bicycle.

"Are you ready?" Isaac gave him a gentle tug as a signal to take a step forward. River dancers skipped, while an actor shouted from a small amphitheater in a theatrical display, entertaining a fascinated group of small children.

Nick walked with little room to maneuver. Being from New York, he was used to competing against others for small spaces but was now forced to follow the only lane of moving traffic he could find. "I can't seem to …," Nick stopped, once he realized Isaac was no longer behind him.

"Keep moving now," said a friar with a thick patch of brown hair encircling a bare scalp. Nick was suddenly being shooed to keep up with the speedy flow of foot traffic.

Using his height to look for any sign of Isaac, he was desperate to find an open pocket as elves had since enclosed on all sides. "Excuse me," Nick slid past until finding a less occupied spot. There was so much noise he could hardly hear himself think. "Isaac!" he yelled, only to hear his voice being vastly drowned out.

Swiveling around, Nick's foot hit a curb, tumbling out into a street—nearly run over by a pushcart full of carrots. More feet scampered to avoid his limp frame as a concerned circle soon formed around him. Gossiping ladies covered their mouths in shock.

Vance

A she-elf in a layered dress bent to reach for his hand. "Why, you've fallen, boy," she said with a braid that brushed against his face on his way up. "Are you alright?"

"Ugh," he stammered in confusion. "I don't know. I was just … looking for someone, I guess." More and more seemed to be quickly drawn in.

"Well, you've got a mighty big hole in your trousers. And it looks as if you may be losing blood," said another. There were now too many to account for, as an embarrassed Nick plugged his nose to stop the drip.

"Don't worry, we'll call in a medic," another declared.

"No, no, that won't be necessary." Nick, hating all the attention held a hand to his forehead before nearly collapsing again in dizziness.

"I recognize him from somewhere."

"Oh, as do I," the rest of the hen chatter was now just a blur to Nick as his head continued to spin.

"You're rather right. He does look familiar."

"And so freakishly tall. Who do you suppose he is?"

"Perhaps he's some Elitist experiment."

"An experiment? Don't be silly. He just takes his vitamins, that's all."

More fuzzy faces approached, intrusively wagging fingers in front of Nick's face as he tried to shake off the spell.

"Wait, I know you," said a man with a shiny top hat. "Yeah, that's right. You're the boy, Chief of Staff Newell smuggled in here. The very one House Speaker Lyman ordered to be incarcerated at the funeral procession."

Some jeered, while others probed. "Is it true?" said another, holding up the front page with Nick's mug on the front. "Did you really break out then? Are you some kind of wizard or something?"

Inheriting the Sleigh

"Wizard? No," Nick banged on his head. He was having trouble keeping up with the sudden string of questions, soon unable to take it any longer. The chatter continued to intensify with folks pushing in many feet back to catch a glimpse of the commotion.

Nick eventually broke. "Quiet!" Every elf within earshot froze, not expecting such an impolite outburst. "I mean … if you will."

"Should we call in the Guard, then?" the whisperings resumed. "I mean, as much as I detest those pompous brutes, we simply cannot harbor a fugitive, now, can we?" a convincing woman turned to the crowd, all as a helpless Nick could only breath heavily to maintain his composure.

But another had since worked hard to emerge in the scrum. He was impolitely shoving forward, doing whatever he could to get there. "So, it is you?" asked the old man, stepping closer to quell the gossip. His face and hands were black as night, with a Billy goat patch of white hair hanging off his chin. He looked at Nick with a much different gaze than the others—with fascinating wonder.

Nick was unsure what to say as the man invaded a little too close to his personal space. "No!" he respectfully took off his Gatsby-era cap as he turned to gain control over the gathering. "We do not call the Elites!"

Nick couldn't tell whether the man had overheard or was somehow able to read minds, but did know that whoever he was, was certainly astute enough to sense the internal dilemma inside the hearts of the elves.

"But what if he's dangerous!" shot a voice from the back.

"Dangerous?" the man laughed as he rose his cane high into the air. "The very son of Kris Kringle himself … dangerous? I think not."

The gathering gasped. The music and marketplace hustle of before had long since stopped, with every eye in the vicinity trying to catch a better glimpse of the boy standing cold and confused in the middle of the marketplace. Some climbed up tall lampposts and large stacks of wooden storage crates to do just that.

"It can't be," said a woman in a Victorian gown as she offered Nick a thicker coat.

The black man, rather, kept his fixation in place. There was a certain reverence behind his brown eyes. "Do you wish to speak, my child," he asked with an exotic voice, as if having lived a long time ago.

Nick shook though was unsure. He knew what he needed to do, but was still waiting for, as Isaac suggested, something to start seamlessly pouring out. "You're conflicted … aren't you?" a few simple words were a good place to start as his eyes panned across the circumference of the crowd. The man couldn't help but smile as he heard Nick's voice for the first time, waving as a suggestion to carry on.

The permeating silence made Nick uncomfortable, but by the collection of stares, could feel every elf sincerely wanting to know what he had to say. "I was there on Christmas morning," the monologue began simply. "You know, out in the world where the children are. The truth is, it is much more than a holiday." Nick's thoughts suddenly turned to Cardinal Dolan wearing a thick golden cross as he offered up his sermon at Saint Peters. "It's a day I think we all need. You know, one to reverence his birth."

He suddenly sounded beyond his teenage years, almost as if being caught up in some epiphany of thought. "The 25th of December is interwoven directly into the fabric of the world, so you can imagine the reaction when it all abruptly came to a halt." Nick bounced his eyes off as many watchful elves as he could. "I mean, it's not really about the toys. Then again, they are symbolic of what Jesus gives back to us."

He was now desperate for somebody else to start talking. Anybody really, so he no longer had to. "You … newsie!" Nick eventually pointed at the boy with a bundled stack of fresh ink tucked under one arm. He sat atop some crates—alongside others with a decent view down. "Throw me one of those papes!"

The masses watched as the boy was quick to fling an already rolled-up paper Nick's way. It was a perfect toss as Nick snagged it mid-air. He unraveled it to reveal Corbin's picture above his own over the *Daily Icecap's* front page. He read the first couple paragraphs of old font before holding the paper out for all to see. "In the meantime, there's something even more pressing. This man," Nick pointed. "I need to know where he is." More silence permeated before the old man nodded, as if to suggest he should try again. "Corbin's in trouble, you know!" Nick resumed the second time with a raised voice.

An elf with curly hair and a mustache was the only one moving a muscle through the human scrum. A path gradually parted, before a new face soon emerged inside the small circle. He wasn't in street clothes—rather donning a bright blue uniform with a small teal cap that whimsically curled up at the top. He had bells on his moccasin-style shoes and looked ready to report directly for work. After a brief stare, the elf spoke. "I've seen, Mr. Creel."

Nick said nothing, though his wide grin spoke for him. For nothing else, it was a start.

Chapter 22

W hat now?" asked a male with rebellious hair drooping off his neck and down over his shoulders. He wore thick, but nimble white camouflage to blend in as he and Nick, alongside a hundred more makeshift soldiers to either side straddled a flat plateau overlooking a valley. It was dark, with only the lights of a fortress perched below as a contrast to the black. Had you taken away the snow, it reminded Nick of Las Vegas from the barren expanse that surrounded the neon gleam.

"To be honest, I was kinda hoping for a sign or something," Nick breathed softly, agitated by the obvious lack of communication. Within hours, he'd successfully recruited a ragtag militia brave enough to put their lives on the line but was also beginning to deal with natural bouts of restlessness as well.

"From Chief Newell?"

Nick slowly turned with cheeks that had never grown so pink. He wasn't used to standing in such frigid temperatures for so long. "I'm sorry, but I never asked you your name."

Inheriting the Sleigh

The cordial elf raised a hatchet. "The names, Germal," said the toymaker extending a gloved hand. "And it couldn't be a bigger honor to meet you, sir ... Saint Nick."

Nick eased his own hand to lock fingers of respect. Germal's expression was sincere, but equally terrified, as if ready to do something he had never done before.

As for the boy, a quiet fire lit under both eyes. Suddenly standing alone at the back of gym class, he felt silly in tiny blue shorts and a golden T-shirt, as Roy Sam wore his game-day jersey with a big 55 on the back. As a dodgeball team captain inside the Lourdes Academy auditorium, it came down to picking Nick—or a girl in pigtails. Sam, with sleeves tightly wrapped around his defined biceps, milked the moment for all it was worth. He silently pointed back and forth in a game of eeny meeny miny moe before landing on Carla Tumwater. The class laughed as Nick was once again taken dead last.

As usual, Nick showed no emotion, just as he did now. The difference this time, he was ready to battle back. "Have you ever been in a fight before, Germal?" Nick's curious whisper created a fog. "A confrontation ... petty skirmish ... maybe a tiff? Anything at all?"

"Not really," the elf sighed. "Unless you consider the one time I almost hit Arty Whipple for stealing some of my truffle quota. You know, back when I worked at the Chocolate House. This, of course, was long before my transfer to the Wood Division, and back when my temper was known to get out of hand."

Nick wanted to laugh and would have, had he not been so cold. He was ready to move—for anything else—to generate a little body heat. "Are you sure that's where he is?" Nick inquired one final time.

Germal gazed at the four corner towers inside Gumdrop Gate. They were colorful spires that drew in the eye, with the walled fortress lit up on all sides by a dazzling splash of festive glow. "Positive," the elf pointed to a trail that slithered down into the valley. I'm on that road nearly every day making deliveries. Couldn't help but notice an odd caravan moving in past the gate. It was heavily armored. Let's just say, I snuck in to get a better look. "It was Creel, alright."

Nick's nerves got the best of him every time he tried to imagine what awaited, and so, did his best not to.

"You know, there hasn't been an execution here at the Pole since the Teddy Bear Ripper of 1883," Germal resumed. "But that is where the gallows are."

"On that note. We should probably start moving."

"Of course. But you do understand …," Germal flipped his ax before catching the handle on its way down. "That if your friends don't show up as you expect them to … ?"

"Right," Nick exhaled up another draft of cold smoke. "We'll be outnumbered. And possibly dead."

Nick moved on, pacing up and down the line of elves, all of whom he barely knew. The team only had hours to assemble a plan and were going on minimal sleep. Nick took the time to make eye-contact with each one. Their weapons were simple, and sometimes odd: a shovel, an ice pick; even a pole with a lone ice skate blade dangling off the end.

"Are we ready then?" he raised his voice just enough for all to hear. "Though you must know, I cannot guarantee your safety. I mean, let's be honest, I'm no General Patton."

"You don't need to remind us, Saint Nick," a brave elf bowed with the strings of his hat drooping low into his white coat. He held two small trashcan lids—one in each hand, willing to fight in any unsophisticated way possible.

Inheriting the Sleigh

"Very well," Nick sighed with a wave of his hand. The militia immediately began to drop down a small bank, trudging in one long, horizontal line through the un-trafficked snow.

In a splotchy suit, Mauv Lyman showed his pale face. He walked out over the ornate balcony, the very one Kris Kringle often did to address a crowd. In this case, Mauv's golden eyes were focused and trained to spot suspicious behavior.

"You truly do believe this will work, don't you?" confirmed an obese Elite with his hair pulled back in a ponytail and a red belt synched tight over his round waistline. He used a bright purple cane to hobble forward, overlooking the glistening square with tall lollypops acting as lampposts, and artificial licorice strands bordering the pathways.

Mauv's flaming orange hair curled outward, and he made no visual contact with his retort. "Better than that, Jimp Ivy. I know it will."

The brash Elite shrugged. "Should I bring him out then?"

Mauv was quick to nod this time.

"You truly are a sinister son of a gun," Jimp chuckled as he observed Mauv continue to slowly pan the crowd. "After all these centuries … what you've really been waiting for was the Claus to give up the ghost. Who knew?"

The rest of the Elites took their seats upon cushioned rows, with scores of elves crowding around the planked platform. They knew what they were about to see but gasped once a cloth was finally ripped off Corbin's face, exposing his bruised cheeks. His hands were tied, with guards stationed every few feet to prevent a potential riot.

"Good afternoon," Mauv's introduction was joined by a smile from the castle-like balcony— every figurine behind him representing some form of candy. Eyes shot toward the House Speaker as a spotlight had suddenly illuminated his loud, rainbow-patterned suit. He held a matching top hat, one representing nearly every color to salute the crowd. "It is time."

Corbin forced his weak head into an awkward position to try and catch a glimpse of Lyman from behind. He had a colorful assortment of large explosives strapped around his waist.

"I hope you plan on stating your case against this man!" a brave elf was the first to speak many feet back in the crowd.

"Certainly," said Mauv. "Article 105 of the Pole Penal Code-assisting an escape. Article 229, defying a court order to surrender. And of course, my personal favorite. Article 537, impersonating Deity himself. Shall I go on?"

"And who suddenly made you king?" shouted another skeptical elf somewhere in the throng. "Doesn't the Constitution call for a majority vote in establishing order following the death of a leader?"

Mauv laughed. He was prepared for every argument. "You site Creed XIII, which clearly only references leadership from the Elvish Congressional House. It has been interpreted that Kris' power was not included therewith, but a separate branch of government in and of itself. So, in such a crisis as this, it is imperative that measures be cast to keep the peace. For your own safety, of course."

"And what does Corbin Creel have to do with keeping the peace?"

"He is a criminal," the Speaker's voice raised, as if a sensitive nerve had just been struck. "Hence, shall be the first to publicly pay for his crimes."

"What do you mean, the first?" the concerned voices trickled one after the next, though Mauv was deathly silent this time.

Inheriting the Sleigh

Nick's cheeks were frosted over in the buried snow. He was lying stomach-down outside Gumdrop Gate—close enough to a lime green fortress wall. Every elf to either side quickly buried their faces back in the snow as the roaming spotlight swung over their still positions.

"Does your perpetrator have any last words before the execution bells ring?" Nick's gut churned heavy as he faintly made out Mauv's declaration. He was deathly still, hoping for something to break up what appeared to be inevitable—all while wondering exactly how he had ever gone from a New York City high-rise to the world's bleakest tundra. His new friends were just patiently waiting out the cue.

A defeated voice interrupted the thought. "As martyrs go, I am just one," said Corbin via speaker. "Though if I may say ... Kris' death hardly represents the end. It can't. There is too much good in the hearts of those who loved him." Corbin was speaking directly to the elves, watching him being used as a fear tactic. "And my only warning to you is this. That eradicating Christmas goes far deeper than Kris' old Veteran Engineering Director of Operational Affairs. A title I always hated, by the way," Corbin managed to find humor in his predicament. "It always took me longer to say, than it did to actually fix anything."

"That's enough!" Mauv declared while noticing the elves stir.

Guards stepped in to push back the crowd with the tips of their muskets. Corbin was then thrust back over a hook in the center of the platform. Many Elites watched with quiet satisfaction; their hands clasped together from their risen rows—rows that overlooked the execution as Corbin now dangled by only his coat. "Let the execution proceeding begin!" A guard then lit a fuse that began to coil along a string.

Nick could hear the panic. The teenager was now acting on little but impulse as he slung to his feet in one swift pull. He was suddenly running like Braveheart, with more and more elves emerging behind him from the unplowed snowdrifts.

It took a team, but tall ladders were lifting out of the snow—now propped up high against the walls. A roaming spotlight eventually met the unexpected rush, sounding an alarm, but the elves weren't stopping. Many had already begun pouring up and over the barrier. Spectators were caught off guard as a host of bodies suddenly swooped in via ropes to the chaotic and frightful sound of gunfire.

Mauv looked anything but surprised from his elevated perch—even gleeful, as if anticipating such an attack.

"Speaker!" the portly Elite attempted to tug him to a safer spot inside the ensuing enclosure.

"No!" Mauv waved Jimp off. His stare was fixed as new elves continued to drop in, many getting struck by colorful musket balls. He was looking for Isaac; and more importantly, Nick.

Mortified Elites were suddenly amid the uprising—all without the chance to gather exactly what was happening. Mauv, rather, held a scope to get a better look, with elves getting crushed in their attempts to flee.

Meanwhile, Corbin nervously watched the fuse inch closer and closer as it snaked along its designed path. The Speaker adjusted his scope, focusing in on a tall elf that appeared peculiar—only he wasn't an elf at all. Nick was doing whatever he could to weave a pathway for the platform. He needed to get to Corbin.

"Child number 227491083," Mauv whispered before scurrying over to clang a mallet against a balcony bell. It was his warning cry.

Large, armored trucks soon barreled through the fortress gate, with more guards spilling out the back to join the battle.

The elves finally appeared outnumbered by the mink hats and red coats, though none of that deterred Nick from pushing forward. He could now see the fuse. Elves were getting picked off in gunfire, many by accident. The bullets were intended for Nick as the fuse was only feet from the explosive contraption—one that looked like a strand of old Chinese fireworks strapped tightly around Corbin's weak frame.

With a snowball in hand, Nick had no time to keep running. He climbed the platform as high as he could before extending his arm. The snowball was packed hard, and he knew he had to deliver his shot. Mauv tried to point through the chaos as guards finally noticed Nick emerge. They tried to enclose, but not before the icy ball managed to crush the small, slithering spark—killing it on impact.

Corbin had his eyes synched tight, only to exhale once he patted a hand at his face, realizing he was still alive.

Nick only had time to sigh himself, before being pummeled to the deck. The chaos temporarily ceased as Nick was apprehended, while most of the concerned elves had since stopped to watch their leader emerge with shackled hands.

Mauv, with a heavy escort, swiftly joined the throng. A circle opened as he approached to inspect the scene. "Child number 22749103," he muttered to himself, and then louder the next time for all to hear. "Are you not, Nicholaus Crest?" Nick said nothing as Mauv's pale face inched closer. He softly squeezed at the boy's cheeks and forehead. "I've read your file," he said with a spooky grin. "A spoiled child from the city. You know, one that has had every last bite fed to him on a silver spoon."

"It appears you yourself might know a thing or two about that," Nick finally mustered up the courage to open his own mouth as he extended a hand up the speaker's gaudy suit; one that managed to bring in every bright color. The elves oohed and awed at the bold tenacity behind the diss.

Mauv laughed. "If you only knew where I hail from and the things I've seen, you might take that back. But I am curious," he turned toward Corbin, who continued to dangle from the hook awaiting his own fate. "Why would you risk your own life for this man?"

With dead bodies strewn about the enchanting plaza, Nick quickly panned across the observing masses. He spoke the first thing that came to his heart. "Because my father loved him."

"Your father?" an Elite, with an ocean blue beard, scoffed. "You have some nerve. Number 22749103, is it?"

"Yes, you were clearly smuggled in by former Chief of Staff Newell," added a second Elite; this one with jagged white hair and an arraignment of red and green teeth. "All to propagate a message contradictory to our own Constitution."

"Speaking of Mr. Newell," Mauv glanced side-to-side. "I can't help but notice his absence. "Surely he hasn't left you to your own devices in such a dangerous predicament as is this."

"The boy's smarter than you think," Corbin piped in, simply to remind everybody he was still very much alive. "You don't have to patronize him."

"Smarter? Is he now?" Mauv raised an eyebrow and a finger both. He was struck with a sudden idea. "Then if he doesn't act like a child … perhaps we shouldn't treat him like one," he laughed. "Yes, we could punish you both, just as we would any heinous offender."

Elites, many protected from the elevation of their cushioned rows, were delighted by the request.

"What are you afraid of?" Nick's question was barely heard over the mockery.

"Excuse me," Mauv used a hand to re-silence the gathering.

Inheriting the Sleigh

"I mean, were you always such a menace when it comes to Christmas?"

The elves were shocked by Nick's brave approach; a shock clearly heard through their hush. Lyman wasn't quick-witted enough to know exactly how to respond, though he tried. "I'll have you know that Kris and I worked tirelessly, decade upon decade to build and enhance the Christmas experience. One that spoiled recipients like yourself only reaped the benefits of."

"Oh, you worked tirelessly," Corbin scoffed. "Tirelessly to build your own wealth. Congratulations on finding a way to broker the profits, manipulating the service of others for your own hustle to power."

"Corbin Creel," the Speaker slowly spread his thumb and index finger only an inch or so apart. "Need I remind you; you were this close to being roasted over a stick. Though you know me, always finding the silver lining," he grinned mercilessly. "Yes, I happen to know the perfect method of execution. For the two of you, of course."

"Are you sure you want to revert back to the Roman brand?" even Jimp was uncertain with a whisper, knowing exactly what he had in mind— all without him having to say it.

But it was already happening. A guard immediately shoved Nick forward over the platform as another pushed Corbin off the hook.

"Nick," Corbin finally got the chance to address the confused boy directly.

"Are you OK?" Nick tried to ask in the chaos of more abrupt movement.

"It was awfully kind of you to extend my life. You know, by a few minutes anyhow," the elf breathed. "But really, what are you doing here?"

"I wish I had an answer," Nick winced as he was mercilessly forced along. "One event leading to another, I guess."

"And Isaac?"

Nick almost grew angry thinking about it but bit his lip to avoid saying something he might regret. "To be honest, I thought I might find him here."

Corbin's sigh wasn't pleasant as the execution procession finally stopped. There was a level of shock in his otherwise easygoing voice.

Nick lifted his own eyes to see two wooden posts propped up inside the center of the plaza—one otherwise full of scattered statues, fountains, and lifeless trees. "What is this?" Nick grew nervous fast.

"Honestly, I think we're up against something far more sinister than even I could have imagined a few short months ago. I'm sorry for having taken a role in dragging you into it," Corbin felt like he desperately needed to apologize.

"Are those …?"

"Yeah," Corbin nodded. "If anybody would know this form of execution, it's Mauvtavious Lyman."

The color and festive glow of Gumdrop Gate typically would not have looked anything like Calvary, but with blood since dripping across the paved streets from battle, a smoky mist added to it.

Another uprising from Nick's militia was met with swift resistance as guards began to hoist Nick and Corbin up toward the T of the crosses. Their limbs were being fastened to the old planks.

All Nick could focus on was the torment. His inward prayer intensified, with his mind trying to block out all the surrounding commotion, though a loud vroom was so glaring, it made it nearly impossible to concentrate.

Dried blood stains trailed off Corbin's nose and he was noticeably bedraggled, though managed to perk up at the sound of a revving engine.

Inheriting the Sleigh

It was squealing furiously through the open gate—not stopping for anything, or anyone.

"What is it!?" Nick was trying to latch onto any hope, his back now facing the spectacle.

"The Wind Racer," Corbin managed a smile. "I'd know that engine anywhere. It's Silva's baby."

Musket balls rained down onto the souped-up hot rod, only to clank off its bulletproof shell. Silva's Wind Racer appeared like a rescue chariot, and Nick had to awkwardly arch his neck to see it zoom past.

Gib held up a large shield to protect Silva at the wheel as they barreled forward, inadvertently knocking over a statue of a reindeer on their way into the plaza grounds. Elves and Elite Guards alike were forced to dive for cover.

With one orange wheel in the front, and two massive tires in the rear, the noticeably thick tread turned over anything in its path. It was designed for not only show, but power.

"Just give 'em a second," Corbin soothed Nick's nerves as the two continued to dangle out in the open.

Nick's militia of elves were given new life as the hot rod, with a sloping frame and winter patterns of cool wind etched across its sides, continued to plow through anything with a red coat. Silva was off-roading, weaving in and out of approaching barricades, often kicking up heaps of scattered snow into the faces of encroaching guards.

With an open hood exposing its metal organs, the engine grew louder and louder, as if it might run right over Nick and Corbin both. The brakes slammed near the crosses—suddenly peeling to a stop. Gib hopped out and immediately struck up a chainsaw, slicing away at the bottom of the buried post. Nick felt his momentum falling forward as some astute elves rushed over to catch the ends as they timbered.

"Gib?" Nick couldn't hold back a smile as the elf pulled off his goggles—gripping the chainsaw with both hands.

"Laddie," Gib saluted with an Irish drawl as he cut their ropes, his mustache proudly waving in the breeze. "Mr. Corbs."

"I've never been happier to see that rotund gut," Corbin jabbed with respect, as Gib took little insult.

"And I've never been happier to see that boyish hue. But to be honest," Gib squinted after getting a better glance. "You look like you've been swimming through a meat grinder."

"Are we really exchanging good-humored pleasantries right now!?" Silva yelled, beside herself from the driver's seat. "Get in!"

Nick hurried over to the awaiting hot rod, only to get sidetracked. Germal had a huge smile as he watched Nick sprint to safety. He pulled his hatchet out of a gut, ready to use it again if need be. Nick wanted to rush over and embrace the elf with fresh battlefield scars, but Gib pulled him back as a musket ball nearly tore off his arm. Germal continued to fight, only to get rocked backwards by another ball.

"No!" Nick's wailing cry echoed as blood splattered through a snow mound.

Gib struggled this time to stop him with the suddenly dead elf now curled over a brick pathway. Corbin scurried over to keep Nick from rushing to his helpless side.

Gripping onto a bar over the back, Nick and Corbin relied on Silva to kick up the wheels again—all while Nick caught his last glimpse of Germal's motionless frame.

Meanwhile, more and more guards were now focused on the escaping hot rod, only to be met by more surprises. With a hose attached to a water tank strapped to his back, Gib released a thick spray that almost immediately turned to ice. Guards couldn't keep their balance as they slipped over the newly created hockey rink.

Silva sped away like a NASCAR driver, but even her expertise was beginning to feel the approaching armored trucks.

"Where in blasted time is Richins!" Silva griped, as she was beginning to run out of escape routes.

The rotating blades of a chopper were then heard overhead as it emerged around one of Gumdrop Gate's glowing towers. The colorful helicopter immediately drew in the enemy's attention, as Blaine dropped buckets full of a mustardy powder down into the crowded plaza. It kicked up an icy smoke as it splashed into the snow piles. The fog was suddenly so suffocating, Silva could barely see herself.

"Hey, you asked for it!" Gib reminded before she could fire off another complaint.

A loud explosion suddenly pierced their ears as the hot rod popped upward. It had inadvertently run over a heap of bodies in its path.

"The front gate's been blown up," Gib observed, as if expecting exactly that. The helicopter's bright lights emerged, and Gib had to cover his eyes to see past the blinding ray. "Just follow him! Blaine's gonna get you on out of here."

In blind faith, Silva revved on the accelerator as she sped, using the elevated light as a guide.

All the while, Nick continued to hold on tight between the rear tires. He couldn't stop thinking about Germal, nor the fate of the others who had valiantly offered up their lives to fight at his request. But all he could do now was shield his face from the flapping wind, as the hot rod furiously churned away anything in its path.

Chapter 23

"Oh, I love this song," Marie's excitement escalated inside The Poodle Skirt—just as it did anytime "Jingle Bell Rock" played from the diner juke box.

"We should decorate the tree today," Nick suggested.

Marie Bayliff smittenly sat across from Nick, her fist propping up her chin inside the glittery booth. She wore a Scottish plaid skirt with black nylons, leaving only a small gap of skin at the thigh. Her black cashmere sweater was tucked tight over a white collar and sleeves, and her hair was tied into two ponytails with stylish frayed ends.

Her eyes twinkled as she slurped a shake, captivating Nick over the checkerboard tile.

"Jingle Bell Rock" continued to play, only he wasn't dreaming that part. Nick's eyes suddenly snapped open, with the tune seeping softly through a small, classic-style radio over a hand-carved stand near his bed.

Nick took some time to digest the cruel fact that Marie wasn't there. He pulled off his bright quilt and nicely threaded silk sheets from the twin mattress, staring up at his surroundings. It was small but oozing with holiday cheer. The four walls were aligned with fun wallpaper and bright paint, with ornately carved shelves and bed frames aligned with Bavarian sketching. Nick's mind was so relaxed by a much-needed night's sleep that he'd only then remembered his near-death experience from the night before.

"Good. You're finally up?"

Nick's head jolted for a familiar voice as he only then realized he wasn't alone. Isaac was perched on an elevated mantle above a fireplace, his arms kicked back and his shoes dangling free.

"Isaac," a surprised Nick held his heart.

"Sleep well?" he asked, as if everything was normal. Nick didn't respond, but he didn't have to. Isaac already knew the answer. "Gib drugged you again with something rather potent. And this time I agreed. You needed the rest. Your eyes were spinning circles. Trust me, you'll thank me later."

"Thank you later? Wait, where are the others? And where have you been all this time?" Nick didn't even have the patience to wait for a response; he had so many questions.

Isaac lifted an eyebrow. "Which one should I answer first?"

"All of them," said Nick as he rubbed his morning eyes. "And where are we, by the way? Wait," Nick interrupted himself as another thought then struck his cluttered mind. "Mauv Lyman."

Isaac gripped onto Nick's flailing wrist to calm him down as he sprung up even higher against the bed frame. "Don't worry. At least for now. Word has spread amongst the elves."

"Word has spread. What does that mean?"

"For starters, the Elite's power grab has been stopped; at least for now. Safety in numbers," he grinned.

Nick just stared, needing to get something else off his chest. "But you left me. At the marketplace."

Vance

Isaac wasn't comfortable letting the hurt protruding from Nick's stare linger for much longer. "Remember our conversation about the sleigh? Well, long story short—let's just say—I had to go put it back in safe hands. Or how else could we perform an autopsy? Besides," the elf was quick to move onto more pressing matters. "What happened at Gumball Gate simply had to be done. Hopefully, a turning point to accomplishing every benchmark from here on out. Now," he skipped over to a rack inside the bedroom closet.

"But I nearly …"

"Like I said … onto happier things," the elf, whether Nick liked it or not, put an end to the topic. "The most important decision of the day. What to wear," Isaac held up some bright green corduroy knickers.

"Those? You can't be serious," Nick relented with a scoff, unsure he could pull off looking like a golfer from the 30's.

"How 'bout …," Nick was already shaking his head as the elf pulled out a festive one-piece that perhaps would have been better suited for Fred Flintstone.

"You're right," Isaac admitted with his head already dipped back inside the closet. "I'm not good at this. I can imagine an American boy being somewhat repulsed by Pole fashion. But believe me, it used to be worse," he rambled while continuing to throw options out onto the unmade bed. "You should have seen some of the wardrobe atrocities back during the Great Fire of London. Late 17th century, give or take a decade. Never mind," Isaac concluded he was digressing.

"How 'bout this one?" The cloak was a fine patchwork of color that dropped down to his ankles. It had fuzzy white trim around the neckline and sleeves. Again, Nick had no desire to consent but oddly held back this time as Isaac assisted him into the armholes. He eyed himself in the mirror, as if suddenly starring in Joseph and the Technicolor Dreamcoat.

Inheriting the Sleigh

The fact that Nick failed to say "no" was all Isaac needed to resume. "Alright then," the elf shrugged. "I mean, it certainly says, 'in charge,' don't you think? C'mon."

"Wait," Nick called from behind as Isaac was already out the bedroom door. "You still haven't told me what I'm … doing yet," Nick sulked as he knew better than to think he'd ever get a straight answer anyway.

"So how big was the Avalanche of 712?" Blaine inquired as Gib was in the middle of one of his largely exaggerated tales. The entire group had been passing the time around a burning fire inside a lovely living space.

"Let's just say it was bigger than my Great Aunt Marceal," Gib theatrically raised his arms out wide for effect. "Not to mention, meaner. It was racing like thunder straight headway for the village, and we only had maybe a flicker of time, before …"

Isaac coughed into his fist to signify they now had company. No one seemed bothered by the interruption. They all immediately stood in respect as Nick slowly scooted forward in his coat of many colors. Even Gib ceased speaking, puzzled by the choice.

"Hello," Nick felt a little awkward, but was quickly getting used to it. "How is everyone?"

"Just like you, laddie," Gib said softly next to Silva. "Trying to sort all this zany stuff out. Never before have times been so uncertain."

"Five minutes," Ezra updated Isaac after a glance of the pocket watch dangling off his thigh.

"Hot tea," Silva stepped in as the mother he no longer had. She was holding a carnation-colored mug over a dish. "Just the way your father liked it. With a titch of ginger."

"Here, sit," Blaine pointed to a sofa near the fire. "How did you sleep?"

"Surprisingly … well," he reflected again on his pleasant dream.

"I told you the poxxy gas wouldn't kill him," Gib smirked Silva's way—all to settle an old debate.

Nick chose to ignore it with his attention turning to Corbin. He had an arm wrapped in a sling, and a large swell around one eye. "Look what they did to you." There was anger building in Nick's voice. "I mean, they nearly …"

"There's no need to say it," Corbin stuck out his good arm. "At least we now know what those parasites are capable of."

"So, what next?"

"Great question, Nick," said Isaac, more than ready to move on as a faint trickle of noise was suddenly pushed into the room by an adjoining wind.

"What … was that?" Nick tried to find its source. It sounded like a distant crowd, with Nick naturally growing frightful again."

"It's OK. You're not in any danger now," assured Isaac as Nick fiddled with the teabag inside his mug.

"It's just the elves, Nick," Silva assured. "The tribe of Asher, they've gathered,"

"Tribe of Asher?"

"Two minutes," Ezra said as Nick was getting nervous by all the time pronouncements—not knowing exactly what they were for.

"Yeah, you know—one of the lost ten tribes of Israel," said Gib.

"This …," Nick anxiously stood up and pointed at the wood-tiled floor inside the room—one oddly without a single window. "I mean, you … the lost tribe of Asher?" Nick gathered a better look to figure out exactly where he was. He noticed a long, dark hallway adjoining the living space where another burst of crowd noise rustled through.

Isaac swung his head that direction. "We need to hurry. They're waiting for us."

"Jacob had 12 sons, all of whom formed tribes," Nick distractedly mused to himself as he suddenly recalled a report he wrote back in junior high on the Book of Kings. "The Assyrians conquered and scattered ten of those. Some of whom flee north." Blaine curiously watched as Nick passed by with his focused head tipped down toward the floor. He was connecting more dots. "800 years later, John the Apostle escapes death and is granted extended life. He also flees north and meets up with …,," he slowly pointed to every elf inside the room. "One of those ten." Gib nearly wanted to clap, impressed by the bells that seemed to go off all at once. "And it was here that you joined together to influence, mold and create the tradition of Christmas?" Nick then stopped mumbling to think some more, his reflective head buried deep in the floorboards at his feet. "A lost tribe … of course."

"To the rest of the world, we are lost," Isaac clarified. "But the truth is, we have no intention of being found. Only conducting business the same way we have for hundreds of years."

"30 seconds," said Ezra as he wiped a smudge off his glasses.

"Are you ready then?" Isaac waved.

Nick wondered why the answer was yes. It shouldn't have been, but his heart was willing him forward down the dark hallway. He began moving before being stopped by Silva.

"Wait," she called as the bottom of his fancy patchwork cloak nearly dragged along the floor behind him. She walked over to retrieve a staff near the flames. It was inside a bucket—along with other long items: an umbrella, and a bellows used to stoke the fire. The staff was chiseled and painted in candy cane stripes, with a shiny, golden ball at the top. It looked like it may have been centuries old. "Here," she hurried over to deliver the staff. "Now, you are ready."

Nick's royal stare was focused as he paced forward though the oddly positioned hallway. He soon noticed he was walking toward a mild ray of sunlight. He had never seen the sun at the North Pole before following months of continual darkness, but it was beginning to show its face again.

A semi-circular overhang at the end of the hall exposed a massive coliseum. There wasn't an empty seat inside the Roman-style amphitheater that wrapped 360 degrees around. They were patiently awaiting the figure that slowly scooted forward into view. It was the last thing Nick ever expected to see. All attention quickly perked up as the sunlight exposed Nick standing like a king, front and center. They were waiting for confirmation as Isaac eventually followed in. He stood next to Nick, panning his gaze across the breathtaking view of the full stadium—the cityscape now in the backdrop.

Isaac's preceding shout swept across the coliseum. "He's ready!"

Ezra, Blaine, Corbin, Silva and Gib now stood back in support as a roaring cheer suddenly sent Nick's heart into an adrenaline rush. It did more than take his breath away. For the first time, he felt alive, with a spark of Santa Claus pulsating through him.

Chapter 24

This is what I propose," said Ezra around a glowing table. "With today being the 18th of March, my calculations agree that we are currently off schedule by ...," Ezra had a pencil and notepad to put the finishing touches on his math. "46 days."

"And how do you gather that?" Silva naturally grew bored anytime Ezra crunched numbers. She filed a chipped nail—doing her best to keep up.

"84 days have passed since Christmas."

"85. Don't forget leap year," Blaine reminded next to Corbin fiddling with a Rubik's Cube.

"85, of course. Subtracting the typical two-week vacation to begin the new cycle, plus 12 weekends. And of course, counting February 29th," Ezra added in one more detail before updating his tally. "We are currently 47 days off schedule."

The group paused for a moment, gathering just how they were ever about to make up for the lost time. "What if we increase the workload," Isaac proposed. "You know, maybe pushing up to ten hours instead of eight."

Vance

"They're not gonna like that," Gib shook, the ends of his walrus mustache whipping as he did.

"Nor are they gonna like their Saturdays suddenly whisking away with the wind, but is there really any other choice?" Silva was always there to counter Gib's logic.

"So, at 47 days, that's 376 hours," Ezra rapidly punched numbers into a calculator. "We add approximately 20 hours to the work week. "1,930 hours, give or take till Christmas." Numbers were racing through Ezra's head at light speed, none of which made sense to the others. "So, it appears to me, and somebody please step in if I'm missing something here. At the proposed pace, if we take the square root of A and divide that by total volume of B, then we should make up for the lost time in approximately ... 19 weeks. Or in other words ... by the middle of August." Ezra paused to take a much-needed breather, all to the befuddlement of the rest. "Sound about right?"

"Sure," Gib's sarcasm was simply to move on. "The middle of August. When did we say lunch was? Or are we cutting that out too?"

One negotiator had yet to speak but cautiously listened to every word. "Nick, are you alright?" It was a question Isaac had been used to asking ever since their first meeting months prior.

"But what if the elves don't accept those terms? And what if, you know ... they hold the extra-long workweek against me?"

"Relax," said Silva. "The elves are like trained puppets. Not to say you won't have to endure a gripe or two, but now that they've pledged their allegiance, they'll do whatever you want. Trust me."

Isaac cut in quickly to suggest he might have phrased it differently. "Don't worry about that. Cross here will go hash out all the new terms with the union bosses. He's my negotiation wizard." Blaine was already out the door before Isaac could even finish his sentence. "Good," Isaac gently slapped both hands against the table. "With that settled ... for the time being anyway. We have another box to check."

"And what is that?" Nick probed.

"The christening."

"What do you mean? Some sort of baptism or something?"

Isaac pulled the key from his pocket. It was as long as it was gold. Silva got up from her chair to pull the cloth off a heavy glass case where a holiday staple was displayed inside.

"Well, go ahead," Isaac expected a reaction. "Surely you must know what this is."

"Yeah, a Santa hat," Nick eyed the soft, red cone that drooped a bit. There was the fuzzy white pompom at the top and a strip of bunny-soft wool aligning the rim.

"Perhaps you should show a little respect," Gib chimed as Nick was surprised to find his answer, insufficient.

"A Santa hat is something you might see grandpa wear playing charades at the mall," Isaac clarified. "This here is what will ultimately allow you proceed as your father's replacement. "Or, so I hope," he was crossing fingers underneath the table, as if still naturally unsure.

"I don't get it," said Nick. "Looks to me like any other hat. There's gotta be a billion of those floating around. In fact, they give 'em away every year at the Sleighride Festival down in Central Park."

"Done," Corbin emphatically declared, with the sides of the Rubik's Cube all perfectly returned in place. He'd previously been multi-tasking—only to finally join the conversation a bit late.

"Honus Wagner"

"Huh?' Gib hunched in the chair next to him as Corbin handed him the small block.

"Yeah, Honus Wagner. Don't tell me you've never heard of him."

"Should I have?" asked Nick.

"C'mon. Flying Dutchman? Shortstop? Pittsburgh Pirates? Eight batting titles?" Nick shook his head at every clue. "Baseball," Corbin grew tired, finally just giving it away.

"Sorry. I never really played sports much."

"And you call yourself an American," Gib shook his wide cheekbones.

"Didn't you ever pick up that glove we gave you?" Ezra inquired. "According to my recollection, your father dropped one off seven Christmases ago."

"And you remember that?" Nick couldn't hide his surprise.

"Photographic memory," Isaac shrugged.

"Yeah, it's a curse," Silva quipped.

"Anyway. Perhaps you've seen this before." Nick watched Corbin hold up a small baseball card. Honus Wagner's face and gray jersey, with "Pittsburgh" across the front was joined by a burnt orange backdrop and a few black spots suggesting its age. He didn't wait long for a confirmation, doubting one would ever come. "This is the rarest and most expensive baseball card on the planet. In fact, one was just sold at Sotheby's for 2.8 million dollars."

"That card right there is worth 2.8 million dollars?" he pointed.

"What? This?" Corbin laughed. "Heaven's no. This is a fake. I use it as a prop."

"And for the record, what is your bloody point?" Gib wondered as he bit into a juicy plum.

"My point is, there are thousands of these," he carelessly flipped the card to the ground.

Isaac liked the comparison but was anxious to move on. He held the key in front of Nick's face. "Though please, be gentle."

Inheriting the Sleigh

Nick wasn't sure how to process the warning but accepted the key—only hesitantly opening the glass case. With the hat resting over some green cloth, he was fully expecting something odd to happen. The others watched with intrigue, and Nick turned back to find his audience pretending to act uninterested.

He thought about it once more before extending a hand. The material was noticeably plush. Nick stroked the woolly rim, as if beginning to realize that perhaps there was something different.

"Everything alright over there?" Isaac checked in several feet back as they gave him the time and space to work things out.

Isaac bit his lip as Nick flipped his brown bangs back, using two hands to gently place it over his ears—only to encounter a strange sensation. The hat almost felt as if it was being magnetically sucked onto his scalp. His eyes immediately morphed into a squint and the bones in his face were scrunched together.

Nobody around the table knew exactly what Nick was feeling. In fact, Isaac wanted to rush over but held himself back. Nick's hair suddenly felt like it was blowing back in a mean gust of wind, only it wasn't. And his ability to think was quickly being overrun by what felt like an extreme force of nature.

He wanted to rip it right off as he struggled to keep his balance but willed himself through the storm. "Welllllllcome to the maaaaaagiccccc of Chriiiiiiistmasss," said a slow, slurring voice. "The maaaagicccc of wiiiiiinnnnnterrrr and joyyyyyyy." The verbal breezes kept pushing right through Nick's ears. "The rightful heir to the sleigh. And what a sweet inheritance it shall be." Nick rubbed his temples. He desperately wanted an Ibuprofen but did his best to make out every drawn-out word. "I need to know, are you up for this challenge?"

"What challenge?" the waves inside his head made it hard to interpret the strange voice.

"Are you ready to not only inherit the sleigh, but confront the enemy? It's lurking."

"Enemy. What enemy? You mean, Mauv Lyman?"

The response came quick. "They're coming."

Nick suddenly ripped the hat off, unable to take a second more. His breath was heavy, and his eyes red. It had taken every ounce of stamina to endure the bizarre and physically daunting spell.

He turned to find five sets of awaiting eyes—eyes that were more than ready for a full report. Gib's corneas were especially large. "Is he alive?" he asked as Nick suddenly couldn't hold his feet any longer.

Isaac and Silva lunged over to catch his timbering frame before Nick hit the floor. They gently set him down, with Isaac checking for a pulse.

Nick then thrust upward, as if suddenly awakening from a bad dream. "Still think you can find one of those in some novelty giftshop?" Corbin smiled as Nick felt his sanity slowly beginning to restore.

"Where did that come from?" Nick's heart was pounding as he wiped a perspiring drip off his forehead.

Isaac, again, plead the Fifth—only this time it was because he truly didn't know. "Perhaps in time, you can give me the answer to that question," the elf said as he helped Nick back to his feet.

Corbin, Silva, and Ezra were all huddled, though Gib had used the distraction to slip a few feet back where the hat remained on the wood plank floor. Silva noticed him reach for the dangling ball, hoping his true intention was to quickly return it right back into its protective case. Then again, she knew better as the stout elf, overcome by curiosity, froze to analyze it.

"Gib," Silva wanted him to know she was watching. "What are you doing?"

Gib lifted his bushy red eyebrows to meet Silva's stare, as if still thinking about a course of action. But his childlike intrigue suddenly became too much. He threw the hat over his own head, only to immediately slam his eyes shut—anticipating having to.

Nick was especially interested to see what might take place, while an irritated Isaac just rolled his eyes at Gib's never-ending stupidity. But with seconds gone by, Gib soon voluntarily released his squint, waiting for somebody to say something.

"So?" Ezra probed as Gib finally did what he should've done all along, however late.

"Nothing," Gib shrugged in mild disappointment—not to mention, relief as well.

"Of course," Isaac rebuked, anxious to lock the hat back up. "You're obviously not Santa Claus."

Chapter 25

I t's green," said Blaine as they pried open the electrical box.

Ezra shined a flashlight, while Corbin brushed some spider webs aside, looking for the correct lever. "Here it is."

"Good. Pull it," said Isaac as a series of massive bulbs, one by one flashed a hundred feet above inside the massive interior.

For Nick, it was the first time he'd seen it. While for others, it was simply nostalgic. "Shall we post the sign back up? Open for business," Ezra dusted his hands.

"What do you think, Nick?" Isaac probed with enveloped arms.

With a ceiling stretching to the moon, Nick's eyes gazed across the oval. The woodwork alone was breathtaking—as if standing directly inside the Seven Dwarves' cottage, only on a massive scale.

"Toy factories just like this reside all over the Pole," said Blaine.

There was a draft in the air, but the colorful walls alone didn't allow the dust to distract from the moment. Pink pathways in the hardwood floor directed traffic, while massive pillars gazed from above. They were wooden giants with chiseled faces in all four corners. A wide carpeted stairwell led up to a second level that circled about the factory, and a series of assembly lines, tubes, and what seemed like endless machinery dotted the premises.

"It's 8:00," informed Ezra, peering down at a fancy wristwatch—one with a small, colorful cuckoo that popped out the top to signify the hour.

"Yeah, 8:00," repeated Corbin, less than confident.

"Don't worry," Isaac piped. "They'll be here."

Nick continued to inspect his surroundings. He stroked the metal fence of a cage. It was the cab of an old pickup used to contain and ship out inventory. His gaze then turned to the centerpiece in the floor. A massive snowflake was etched into the wood. Nick's eyes then veered up to spot another; this one sparkling inside a grand chandelier.

"They're not coming, are they?" he turned to find Isaac, though an odd echo interrupted them both. "Somebody please tell me what that is!" said a concerned Nick, with the return of a bitter Mauv Lyman still haunting his every thought. It was hollow and coming from the walls.

"Actually, that's precisely what we want to hear, Nick Kringle," Isaac smiled as a figure suddenly dropped near the colorful ceiling above. It was so high he'd failed to even notice the oddly placed holes. An elf with flailing arms and legs was screaming from the top of his boyish lungs.

"He's gonna ... crash!" Nick pointed in grave fear as the elf was plummeting. But the others not only failed to show concern, they were smiling. The squealing body was falling behind some pipes—blocking Nick's view. But there was no thump of death as Nick expected to hear. Rather, the elf's green tights and loose-fitted blue shirt were, for only a brief second suddenly spotted again above the barricade. He was bouncing to a stop.

Isaac and Ezra led the way, with Blaine and Nick hurrying over to assist the elf up off the inflatable landing pad. "And who are you?" an ecstatic Isaac grinned ear to ear as he looked more closely at the elf's badge.

"Jindle. Jindle Page, sir," he said, standing straight and tall.

"Jindle Page. Welcome back to work. It's gonna be a short year, but I promise, a good one. Meet, Nick Kringle."

"Of course," said the jovial face with a brightly pressed suit and pointy slippers. He tipped his curly head with his hands held behind his back. "May I call you, Saint Nick?"

It felt weird, but Nick succumbed, forcing a smile, before a genuine one formed on its own.

"Where are the others?" Ezra inquired, with not much time gone before the hollow noises of before reemerged—only ten times louder. It was eerie, like a hundred ghosts all clamoring inside the walls.

"Ugh, I would back up if I were you," advised Blaine as they were beginning to pour out the many adjoining holes by the tens and hundreds from all sides. Nick scurried back for the center of the room to watch them drop like human rain. Springs sent them all partially back into the air again as within seconds, there was a bustling, city-like atmosphere inside the factory. The elves had not only reported for work, fun and fancy machinery, with carnival-like bulbs and funny sounds sprung to life all at once. The factory had gone from deathly silent to efficient chaos faster than Nick could process.

"Hello, Mr. Kringle."

"Good day, Mr. Kringle."

"We are back at it again, aren't we, Mr. Kringle?" Nick could hardly address each elf re-manning their stations.

Isaac yelled over the chatter, forcing Nick to follow. "Just watch your step there," he pulled Nick back as an elf wheeling a stack of pallets failed to see him in passing. "And here," a beeping forklift wheeled in reverse.

"OK, clear." Nick's eyes flashed back-and-forth in search of any more ongoing danger. But for those who knew what they were doing, the limited space wasn't an issue. Everything appeared to be moving seamlessly.

"Making toys!" Nick grinned as they now skipped up the green staircase, observing the intricate wood moldings. "The Pole is finally starting to make sense. What I always imagined it to be. Then again … nothing like I imagined," he turned to Isaac with the head of a robot atop a circular assembly line now in view.

"I'm sorry you had to experience so much political buffoonery to get to this point," Isaac said. "But this here is the real North Pole."

"How are toys already coming down?" Nick noticed. "Didn't things just get fired up minutes ago?"

"It's all leftover stuff from last year. We'll get that stocked and inventoried, before beginning with the new lines."

"And the gifts that never got delivered?" Isaac was impressed by his observations.

"They're all here in warehouses ready to be delivered again, though wish lists certainly change. And then you have the whole public relations grind so people know we're attempting a comeback. But enough of the technical stuff for now. C'mon, there's still a lot to do."

"Like what?"

"Let's see. A physical, fittings, a bunch of pointless paperwork … addressing the ELU."

"ELU?"

"Elvish Labor Union. Things are running smoothly now, but they'll want to hear from you personally. Simple protocol."

Nick wanted to remind Isaac he was only 14. He wasn't a huge fan of either paperwork or acronyms, and though he'd already been forced to do it before in limited fashion, the last thing he ever wanted was to give a public address. Nick, however, held back, allowing Isaac to keep rambling.

"And of course, I haven't even shown you the house yet," the elf stated casually with both hands firmly pressed over the rails.

"House? What house?"

"Your house," Isaac lifted his head.

Nick had been so consumed by so many other things—which rightly included preserving his own life—that such a thought of finding a permanent residence had never even occurred. "I ... have a house?"

Chapter 26

The street sign read, "Nazareth Way."

"Let's cut through here," said Isaac, still concerned they might encounter lurking trouble.

Through one last alleyway, it joined into a beautiful and quaint brick road; a road that eventually morphed into a splendid cottage tucked back all by itself in a snowy meadow.

Nick stood ankle-deep in powder near a bridge. A pristine blend of log and cobblestone, the residence had several elongated rooftops, each with its own chimney. Tall, forest green spruce hugged the cottage walls, with smaller trees in the front. Bulging bay windows offered plenty of light, and the steep, sloping shingles were clouded over by snow.

"Go ahead," Isaac signaled as an elated Nick made fresh footprints on his way there. The mailbox was a hollow log, and over the creek bed Nick opened a short gate. "The Kringles," was etched into a bark sign that dangled at an angle off a post.

Down a curvy stone path and up a short flight of steps, he stopped in front of the heavy iron knocker. Naturally concerned he might get ditched again, Nick turned back to find Isaac patiently waiting this time to watch him open the front door. A small avalanche of snow pummeled the boy over the head as he cracked it just an inch. Isaac smirked as Nick brushed the flakes off his face before he could step inside.

A strong whiff of charcoal and pine oozed out the interior, and Nick immediately noticed a mix of old woods. A stairwell led to a second floor, with colorful, hand-stitched rugs covering up some of the rickety floorboards. A framed picture of the nativity was the first thing he saw upon taking his initial step inside. Nick naturally stopped after encountering a heavy creak.

"Go ahead," Isaac encouraged. "You'll get used to it."

Nick picked up a trinket off a small table near the entryway. It was an old toy tractor that looked like it'd been carved straight out of a block a century ago. Dust blew back into his face as he set it down again. "So," Isaac was expecting a more positive review. "What do you think?"

Nick offered a thumbs-up this time as he peered around a corner into the ensuing hallway.

"Good. I'll leave you be then."

"Wait," it didn't take Nick long for the nerves to return. "You're leaving? But we just got here. Don't you wanna … you know, stay a bit?"

"It's day one of Operation Return," Isaac reminded. "Trust me, more kinks to wring out than Gib has spare pounds. Besides, you need some time to settle. I made sure the pantry got stocked, and if I can be candid— I really do think you need a bath." Nick wanted to take offense but couldn't after whiffing underneath each armpit. "Oh, and make sure you're up bright and early. You know, with school in the morning and all."

"Sure. School in the … Wait …?" the reminder sunk in a second or two late.

"What? You really think you can just flip a switch and suddenly turn into Santa Claus? If Ezra were here, he could give you the tally down to the nanosecond; but let's just say that over the next many months, your own personal bootcamp begins."

Nick felt uneasy as he watched the elf disappear back over the small arched bridge, and into the overcast haze. It was his moment to refocus.

Striking a match into a rusty, red lantern that hung near the door, he carried it forward to explore the old house for the first time. A fire was already popping—and a large picture of Jesus inside a splintery barnyard frame was perched over the woodburning stove. Nick's eyes gazed deep. He was drawn into Jesus' teary eyes before straightening out the off-kilter molding.

"Where is the electricity in this place?" he kept instinctively looking for a light switch. Instead, there were occasional kerosene lanterns dangling over hooks in the wall.

Soon, the inside of the cottage began to glow, revealing a beauty of the past. Down another hallway of framed portraits, and into the main living space, Nick noticed relics on nearly every shelf. Everything from old 19th century oyster cans to vintage cooking utensils. But it wasn't without its Christmas cheer. There was a decorated tree in the corner of the large room filled with porcelain angels and spiraling sash.

Nick spun a large globe next to a bright red, velvet sofa. The couch was worn, but attractive and comfortable. Enough old books to fill a small library aligned every row of a floor-to-ceiling shelf, with rocking chairs set up in various nooks for reading.

Hello," Nick's initial thought was that somebody might already be inside. He received no reply.

Embers lit up a leather history book over a coffee table. It looked as if it might have come straight off Gutenberg's press, and Nick could have perused it forever had another howl of the wind not spooked him.

"Who's there?!" Nick's head this time shot for the stairwell. His attention shifted toward the top floor where a partially open door lightly swung in and out. Nick couldn't help but make a racket with each proceeding step up—hesitantly poking his head inside. He only carefully explored his parents' old bedroom.

The top floor was all one room. It was open and free with a bed to one end, and a workshop at the other. A canopy was the centerpiece with the partial moon shining bright through the octagon window. A soft, sprawling polar bear rug was at his feet, and the largest workbench Nick had ever seen bent along a wall. It had different layers of well-used wood sloping upward and shortening in width the higher they went. Vintage tools hung from nails and pegboards, with others just strewn about the bench next to partially completed toys. Handmade clocks occasionally ticked and tocked along the top shelf as he tinkered.

Nick picked up a windup duck. It was unfinished with fresh shavings to either side. A full-size rocking horse rested by the canopy bed, along with bedstands on either side of the headboard. Each stand had a framed photograph.

Nick eyed Kris' black and white portrait. He was handsome, though not as he remembered Santa Claus from watching TV. Kris was old, but not elderly. He was fit, with no drooping white beard; rather, one gray and neatly trimmed.

"So," he stared in wonder, as if for the first time feeling a real connection. "You're my father."

But Nick's intrigue soon moved onto the next photograph. There was an envelope leaning against a headshot of his mother. He couldn't help but admire how attractive she was, with flowing brown hair only stopping near her waist. She leaned against an old fence with a warm smile.

Inheriting the Sleigh

Nick held the letter with his name on the front. A sticker of the baby Jesus sealed the envelope, while a shocked Nick fell back into the soft mattress to read—the lantern held up high for light.

Dearest son of mine,

If you are reading this letter, that is swell. You have made it home. I do not wish to fill you with unwelcome emotion as your journey has certainly been daunting and your line of questions must extend miles deep. I presume the faithful Isaac Newell has treated you well. He can get feisty under pressure but has been your father's most trusted steward for the last 350 years.

But I do wish to at least partially explain. You came as a shock, Nicholas, to not only us, but the entire Pole. Let me say that your father and I weren't supposed to have a child. Then again, neither was the aged Elizabeth before she bore John the Baptist. As a witness to many miracles over the marathon of my rich life, your delivery reaches the very top.

Though if we could only keep you. One thing I've learned over centuries of time is that often the turbulence of our mortality does not allow for what we want most. And so, it was. Though you ended up not just anywhere, but somewhere special. The 51st floor of Trump Tower. You can imagine, all this time, what it has done to me. A mother only longing to hold her son.

Nick stopped to take a much-needed sip of water, gulping through his intrigue.

But onto the here and now. You have returned with a specific and especially important job at hand. Your father was crowned in apostolic glory. His heart was full of giving, just as the Savior's was. And that same merciful and resurrected Jesus granted John the opportunity to live a life to do just that. It was Kris' request to form a celebratory tribute to honor the Master's birth, and so we joined hands with a lost people. The season was later created over decades and centuries of hard time. But after years of conceiving and fulfilling the Christmas tradition, his calling was suddenly cut short. Which means only one thing—the cherished full-time gift of giving, through a birthright, now belongs to you.

Though we have never talked, believe me when I say, I know exactly who you are. A boy with great purpose and potential, and one with that same great gift of charity in his blood. May your transformative journey always be festive and bright. For that is the spirit of Christmas.

Your loving birth mother,

Nick was suddenly more emotionally overwhelmed than he was physically drained, forced to sink peacefully away into the satin sheets. Martha's name was signed in swirling red cursive, but it was the second name that stood out like bold ink. Reading the word, Magdalene was just another shock to his already cluttered mind.

Chapter 27

A train sounded as Nick dozed. Sprawled out amidst his king size mattress, white logs above held the see-through, satin canopy sheet in place. Nick slept very well by a toasty fire as the train's horn continued to grow louder—and louder—and even louder before, just like the most intrusive alarm clock ever, he could no longer ignore it.

"Huh," he jolted up rubbing his sleepy eyes as the chugging rails suddenly screeched to a halt. Nick looked up at something he hadn't even noticed the night before. But he could clearly see it now in the morning daylight. Miniature train tracks shot through a round hole in the wall atop his workbench—the track extending well above his head. The black model steam engine, with several cars and a caboose full of real coal followed the track before stopping at a model station. It was festive and dolled with garlands and holly wreaths. Lampposts and trees were covered with faux snow, and the station port was dotted with twinkling lights.

"Morning memo! Memo for Nick Kringle," shouted an eerily lifelike toy soldier from the front of the train. It was the height of an adult hand.

A disheveled Nick scooted forward to get a better look. "I said, memo for Nicholas Kringle."

"What the …" Nick initially assumed he had to be dreaming.

"Considering we're more than ten minutes off schedule, I'd appreciate a response. Mr. Kringle. Is that you?"

"Huh," he gathered himself, standing to get a closer look. "I mean, yeah … that's me."

"Am I ever glad to hear it," an impatient forest green soldier with a World War II-era helmet wiped its brow. "For a moment there, I thought we might have to eat into more precious time tracking you down. You're a tough cookie to find."

"Are you sure you're talking … to me?" Nick pointed at his chest. His gaze was steeply tilted up toward the model displayed in the corner of the room—a moment simply too bizarre to believe.

"Of course. Who else would I be talking to?" said the gruff soldier from a beautifully painted red and black boxcar.

"And you just came from …?" Nick's eyes curiously followed the track back to the tunnel protruding through the wall.

"The soldier slowly glanced back at the hole, simply to humor him—never having been asked such an obvious question before. "Just making the daily rounds, Mr. Kringle. The same thing I've done longer than I care to count."

Nick turned for a quick second, long enough to slap both cheeks. "A toy is talking to me. A toy is talking to me. A toy is talking to me."

The soldier purposely coughed into its hand as a hint it was time to resume their business. Nick took another deep, composing breath before he did.

"Sorry. What was that?"

Inheriting the Sleigh

"Mail delivery," the soldier informed—looking down at a note it thought was already in its plastic hands. "Let's see here, I just had it. Oh, yes. Here it is." The soldier's eyes widened as he picked up a card nearly the size of its entire frame, reading the headline. "Looks like you have an urgent request."

"Urgent request?" Nick curiously reached to retrieve the postcard, as if he'd suddenly forgotten who or what he was conversing with.

Underneath was only one line scribbled in large, handwritten ink. "You're officially late for school." It was followed by a slew of exclamation points and signed by a "Passionately Peeved, Smudge Terpley."

"School?" Nick mumbled, having forgotten entirely about the night before. He turned back toward the soldier for some reassurance, only to see it shaking its tiny head.

"Yeah, and I'd hurry if I were you. Let's just say the note's author doesn't take kindly to pupils failing to show up on time. In fact, I saw him lock out an entire class once, simply for tardiness. I believe he gave himself a pedicure instead. All as many desperate hands were banging on the door to get back in." The soldier couldn't help but chuckle as he recalled the memory.

"Really?"

"Yeah. You should've seen the man, painting his toenails eggplant purple."

Nick immediately dropped the postcard. He quickly scoured a dresser, then another for something suitable to wear.

"Captain, should we fire 'er back up then!" yelled a second soldier from the caboose, as if growing increasingly nervous about the time.

"One second!" the first soldier cried back. He seemed to be enjoying watching Nick scramble about the large bedroom.

"Was that all?" Nick was surprised to notice the soldier still there as he threw on one of his father's old, musty button-ups.

"Let's see," the soldier finally snapped from his trance. "I guess it is. Yeah, turn er' up!" he yelled across the train where another soldier was quick to release the brake.

'Wait," Nick was able to get in one more question over the noise. "Where exactly am I going, again?"

"Sleigh Bell Street," informed the conductor.

Fresh steam poured out the boiler as the crew drove the bright red locomotive back out. The track hovered and weaved, over and through his bed, around a tall bookshelf and eventually out of sight through another hole in the opposite wall from whence it came.

Nick wanted very much to contemplate the oddity but didn't have the luxury. Instead, he was racing, breakfast-less down the rickety staircase, out the door and down the cobblestone road leading back into the heart of the North Pole. He ran in the chilling air until the familiar suddenly became unfamiliar again.

"Sleigh Bell Street. Where is, Sleigh Bell Street?" he searched a map near a quiet, four-way intersection. Nick followed the road until it crossed Blitzen Boulevard. And it was there he started to realize precisely how disoriented he was.

"I've seen many different expressions in my day," said a calm voice from somewhere. "And yet I could pick out yours from a mile back."

Nick attempted to find who was talking. "Is someone … there?" Nick's confusion soon morphed into frustration after he failed to find the source.

"Eyes up," he called.

Inheriting the Sleigh

Nick's head slowly veered higher—then even higher where a boy who appeared about his age had his boots casually dangling off a back-alley stairwell. "Oh, hello. I didn't see you."

"And yet I've been watching for longer than might make you comfortable," said the boy covered in many layers of leather. His black coat had a series of decorative silver rings up and down the sleeves. His hair was equally black as a contrast to his pale face. Nick disregarded the sentiment, continuing to frantically search for Sleigh Bell Street.

"Aren't you going to lose your pride and ask for help?" the boy appeared not the least bit restrained to resume his game of words.

Nick did his best to read the stranger, not to mention the map; though in desperation, finally succumbed. "OK. According to this, it appears that I should be going ... west, I think."

His hand, with a different ring over each finger was already pointing that direction. "West? Why? You off to Canada or something?"

Nick forced a smile. "To be honest, I'd probably feel more comfortable there." The dangling boots suddenly dropped to the snow with little regard for his own well-being. "Are you ... alright?" Nick's first reaction was to make sure the boy hadn't broken any bones—only to watch him land on two feet just fine.

"Sounds like not everyone's a fan of the North Pole," he laughed, now at Nick's level. "But I thought that was every American boy's fantasy, to be whisked off to some magical place." Nick knew he desperately had somewhere to be and yet chose to engage. "Starsky," he held out a hand. "Starsky Skiles."

Nick was drawn in by his mysteriously dark eyes and pointy nose, only to eventually break from his lull. "My name's ..."

"Please," he scoffed. "Don't ever think that Santa Claus needs a formal introduction."

"Yeah … Santa Claus," Nick whispered, still highly unused to being received by such a respected title. I guess I just prefer, Nick."

"Nick," Starsky shook. "It's short. Certainly rolls off the tongue. And even resembles a little nostalgic charm. I like it."

"And if you don't mind me asking … who are you?"

Starsky swung the ends of his scarf before resuming. "Me? Honestly, if you were smart, somebody you wouldn't be talking to."

Nick took a moment, wondering how much was in jest. He eventually elected to disregard the warning. "May I ask … how old you are, at least?"

Starsky wondered if Nick fired off the same question to others he met for the first time. "Honestly, I don't really keep tabs on that anymore. But to give you a ballpark, last I checked … 257."

"257?" Nick gazed. "And yet, you don't look much older than me. Shouldn't you have …"

"What? Hair growing out my ears. As you've probably noticed, there's something strange in the water here. Anyway," Starsky changed the subject. "Weren't you looking for something?"

"Yeah, Sleigh Bell Street," said Nick, though a part of him wanted to stay right where he was under the drizzling snow.

"Sleigh Bell," it took him a minute to process. "Wait, you're not off to the PTC, now, are you?"

"PTC?"

"Pole Training Center. Let me guess … Smudge Terpley?"

"How'd you know?"

"Talk about a kooky ol' geezer. Though even I'll admit, one of the most enlightened minds in the world. That's if you can stomach all the idiosyncrasies."

"Speaking of—I should probably get going. I'm beyond late as it is." But Nick failed to start walking. He had another question. "And what about you?"

"What about me?"

"I mean, shouldn't you be off making toys or something? You know, with the rest?"

Starsky glanced around the secluded alleyway, with nothing but the bland backside of square buildings in sight. He checked to see if anyone was eavesdropping before giving Nick a nasty scowl. Though Nick meant nothing of it, Starsky clearly took insult. "With the rest? The rest of whom?"

"You know … isn't that what everyone around here does? Unless you're an Elite or something." Nick began to realize he may have put a foot in his mouth. Then again, wasn't exactly sure how to fix it.

"And why must I fit inside either box?"

"Well, I thought everybody …"

"No," Starsky shook while waving Nick to follow. "Believe it or not, there is a third group. We're called the enraged. Drifters who have found no solace in wasting our lives for the sake of some silly tradition—or who fail to appease those lazy cranks from their thrones—dictating to the rest of us through their legislative pens. It's all extremely obnoxious, don't you think?"

Nick suddenly stopped to process the rant, his frosted nose now pink from the chill. He tightened the top of his coat, staring straight back. There was one last thing he needed to know before parting ways. "Are you saying that my father was … a lazy crank? That he wasted his life all for some silly … tradition?"

Starsky's silence lasted seconds, shuffling his scarf to buy time. "No," he finally shook with a sincere shrug as if forced to back off a bit. "In fact, if you want the truth—Kris Kringle was the hardest working man I ever knew."

Nick could feel a glimpse of sincerity breaking up the cynicism. Starsky made longer eye contact to ensure it was real before pointing to a building in the distance. A semi-busy street merged with the quiet alley. Horse-drawn sleighs and old automobiles slowly crossed each direction over the snow. Nick could see the red brick rising above shorter rooftops attached to either side. A large engraving ran along the top. "Pole Training Center."

Chapter 28

The double doors creaked as Nick stepped foot inside the foyer. It was vast. Two floors were lined with hallways to either side. The centerpiece was a large statue of an elf, with a droopy hat carrying a water bucket. It was quiet, other than an eerie combination of trickling water leaking through a hole in the bucket—and the faint sound of holiday lounge music playing somewhere. Nick recognized it as Bing Crosby but wasn't sure.

"Hello!" his hollow voice echoed, uncertain anybody was even inside. Other than some Christmas light strands dangling above, the foyer was dark. He veered around the statue and through another set of double doors. The sound of the doors closing was loud and chilling in a mostly vacant building. "Hello," Nick tried again as a long hallway presented itself. A hallway that grew blacker and blacker the further it went.

"Can I help you?" a voice startled Nick from the side. A janitor in an old, worn jumpsuit had a mop in hand next to a rolling yellow bucket filled with soapy suds. The truth was, the interior reminded Nick a lot of a normal school, only spookier.

Vance

"Yes," the boy responded as the elf emerged from a shadow near some lockers.

"Careful," the janitor, with black skin that blended in perfectly with his surroundings, warned, as Nick nearly slipped. "The floors are still wet. It might be easier to skate than walk."

Nick eyed the gentleman, as if recognizing him from somewhere. "I'm in search of a room," he said, holding up the notecard.

Instead of speaking this time, the janitor's cheeks widened to a grin. He sized Nick up head to toe, as if waiting a very long time to do just that. "Of course, Nick Kringle. Follow me."

The janitor flipped on a couple of switches. They provided just enough light, before coming to a staircase. "Why so empty?" Nick spoke to make the walk up less awkward.

The elf shook, more than happy to keep the conversation afloat. "This time last year, nearly every room was full. Of course, the crash changed all that. Haven't seen a single student walk through these doors since," the janitor turned back to make sure Nick was still following. "All hands on deck in the factories."

Nick processed the information, continuing to wind in the man's wake. "Then why the mopping?" he couldn't remain silent forever. His curiosity often got the best of him. "Wouldn't the floors be clean already? You know, with nobody here and all?" This time the old janitor said nothing, only offering up another smile.

"Here we are," the janitor watched Nick stop to slowly peak inside. It was the first fully lit room he'd seen since entering the PTC.

"Thank you," Nick turned one final time to address the janitor—the mop still pressed tightly against his shoulder and the moist strings dangling off his back near his sheepishly white hair.

Inheriting the Sleigh

Nick gazed around his new surroundings. The desks were all empty, with the only other person inside currently writing a line on the chalkboard. It was the very same sentence scribbled repeatedly. I am bored. I am bored. I am bored

Nick gently knocked once on the partially open door. Smudge jolted around. He was stocky, with a thick set of golden curls that combed over and swirled out at the bangs. He was dressed in a sports coat, with a red tie that was loose around the neck.

Smudge stared for several seconds before swiveling back toward the board to erase the tower of fresh sentences. Nick could only stand and watch near the door as the professor rapidly rubbed the eraser against the blackboard.

"Are you ... Mr. Terpley?" Nick eventually couldn't wait any longer—all while squeamishly picturing the man alone, painting his toenails.

He stopped at the sound of a voice—turning around ever so slowly. "Yes," he went from a stale smirk to a half-grin. "Though my mother calls me Smudge. And you are?"

"Late," Nick joked, as if hoping that might break the ice. Smudge failed to even so much as budge a cheekbone. Instead, he pointed a hand to take a seat.

Nick took off his coat, finding one in the middle of the room. The desk was old, but attractive and joined by a small stool topped by a comfy cushion.

Terpley's large backside stood out through some sweatpants as he bent to retrieve something from a lower drawer at his desk. The comfortable cotton trousers were an odd look joined by the sports coat. Nick waited patiently in the middle of the front row as the professor stood back up straight, focusing on a clipboard in hand.

Vance

"Nefi Strong?" Terpley's gaze rose from the clipboard as he oddly peered around the classroom. He then took a pencil to mark absent on his roll sheet. Nick hesitated before glancing back. As expected, he saw no one. "Ike Twisselman?" Funda Newcastle? Stew Arrington?"

Nick instinctively followed Terpley's eyes, as if there simply had to be others behind him—only there weren't. Smudge quickly checked more boxes.

"Excuse me," Nick raised a hand.

"Yes."

"Sorry to be rude, but is there a Nick Kringle somewhere on that list?"

"Nick Kringle? Well, let's see," he dropped his pale finger down with each line. "Doesn't look like it. Nope, don't see one."

Nick was as confused as ever, before handing the quirky professor the reminder notice given to him that very morning by the toy soldier. He perused it over. "Why of course," Terpley thought nothing of dropping his clipboard to the ground—once again crouching to search his bottom drawer. "Wrong list." A new clipboard was pulled out. "Yes, here we go. I've never actually taught this course before. Santa Claus Prep."

Nick nodded, as if relieved they were finally getting somewhere— only once again—Terpley gazed broadly about the room. "Saint Nicholas Kringle?" Nick waved his hand before watching Smudge's eyes slowly veer in. "Nicholas Kringle ... tardy, but present," he checked off the lone box next to the lone name on the roll in front of him.

The uncomfortable stare between Nick and Terpley permeated far longer than a naturally paranoid Nick would've liked. "What? Is it something I'm wearing? Because really, this is all I could find on short ..."

Inheriting the Sleigh

Terpley nodded. For just a moment, the professor's quirkiness was replaced by a sense of genuine wonder. "I'm sorry, but this was your father's calling." Smudge sounded rude but suddenly became even more emotional.

Nick on the other hand couldn't help but feel inadequate, and even somewhat guilty. "I didn't ask for this, Mr. Terpley." His return stare was half-bitter and half-sad.

"No," the elf snapped from his daze, flipping his whimsical bangs up off his round forehead. "Of course, you didn't, my boy. Should we start then?" Terpley approached the chalkboard.

Grabbing a piece of broken chalk, the board squeaked with a pitch that didn't seem to bother the professor. But it did Nick as he stuck a hand over each ear. Nick was relieved to see him finally stop writing, simply to get the noise to stop. It was written largely opposite some of the "I am bored" scribble from before. "Tell me, what does it say?"

"Time," Nick read.

"And what is, time?"

"What is, time?" he had never really thought about it before. "Ugh … a continued progression, maybe. I don't know."

"A continued progression of what?"

"Of … events that occur."

Terpley locked his fingers together while tapping his knuckles against his chin. "And does it ever stop?"

"Does it ever stop?" Nick paused, figuring it had to be a trick question. "No."

Terpley was right back at the chalkboard. "100 years a century. Ten years a decade. 365 days a year. 30 days a month. Seven days a week. 24 hours a day. 60 minutes an hour. 60 seconds a minute. One second being the smallest increment of time. Do you know how many seconds it took for me to say all of that, Mr. Kringle?" He did but failed to give Nick a chance to answer this time. "19. And you're right, by the way. You know, from before. Time doesn't stop. For 364 days a year, anyhow. But what about on the most important day?"

Nick wasn't sure if he was supposed to be taking notes, or just listening, wondering if Smudge's latest question was rhetorical. "I assume you're referring to Christmas. What about it?"

"Surely you've contemplated how little logic there is in a man delivering millions of presents from one end of the earth to the next over the course of mere hours," he emphatically pointed to the word "hours" on the chalkboard as he said it. "Why, it's in your very DNA to think about such things, is it not?"

Nick paused for a moment, looking about the classroom. "Matter of fact, now that you bring it up. Never really came to any conclusions though. A friend of mine back home, Loopy, always had a theory that it was due to some sort of four-dimensional spatial continuum involving alien help ... or something like that," Nick felt ridiculous even saying it out loud. "But to be honest, I usually tuned him out whenever he talked. Which really was all the time."

"Russell would say something like that," Terpley mused.

Nick was flabbergasted how he knew Loopy's given name, having been corrected on that technicality once before.

"I will tell you the kid isn't far off. Without the aliens, of course." Smudge faked a cough, pointing to a framed quote on the wall. It had font big enough for Nick to read many feet away. "Go ahead," he pointed.

"Be not ignorant of this one thing. That one day with the Lord is as a thousand years, and a thousand years as one day. Sure," he added after quoting 2nd Peter. "God's time is different from our own. If you know

Inheriting the Sleigh

Loopy's rarely used given name, then you must know I spent ten years going to Catholic school."

"I'm aware," Terpley seemed bored by Nick's sudden feistiness; and unlike others, unimpressed by either his name or his birthright. "But what your Highness does not seem to conceptualize, is that when the Christmas magic settles in during the early hours of the 25th, man's time becomes God's time."

Nick's candor suddenly morphed into silence as the truth struck hard and quick. A truth that for centuries had been left entirely to theory and guess work.

"That 19 seconds," Terpley alluded back with a wide grin.

"Yeah," the boy said with several follow-up questions since popping into his head. "What about it?"

"At 19 seconds—within a 24-hour period—let's just say I could have repeated what I did precisely 4,547 times. Multiply that by a thousand, and you get 4,547,368. In translation, that's more than four and a half million times your original 19 seconds. You know ... to perform the impossible all over the world."

Chapter 29

S o … you're finally offering up the courtesy of an explanation, I see," said Mauv, gazing up from a cement pad below. His hands were shackled with his jumpsuit the same bright color as the orange clown streak across his ears.

After a fierce battle, those unable to escape were bunched together behind him in the large, open prison corridor, awaiting Isaac's reply.

But Isaac didn't respond, at least for many seconds to voice his irritation through his stare—even more so through his silence. "Do you wish to know the death tally? Or do you not care about how many elves perished at your order?"

Mauv laughed—his way of reminding others he was still in charge. "You call it murder. I call it self-defense."

Silva moved forward, peering down over the railing. "You were in the middle of executing them," she reminded with quiet anger as Corbin then stepped into view from the left. Corbin was now staring directly into the eyes of the Speaker—no longer amused.

"47," uttered Corbin.

Inheriting the Sleigh

"Excuse me," said Lyman with his cuffed hands raised up together near his neck.

Corbin shrugged casually, with little malice in his eye. "Just answering the Chief's question. It was a good one. 47 elves are no longer with us."

An Elite with large green eyes and a nose ring fit for a bull, chimed in from the incarcerated throng. "So, what now? Surely there must be a trial or something."

"Right, a trial," Corbin mused calmly. "Like the one you gave me."

"And who's the judge?" shouted another.

"I bet you wish it were Kris himself," Isaac uttered. "Because you knew his heart. Knowing him, he would have forgiven all of you after a mild sentence."

"If Kris were here," Mauv corrected. "There would've been no need for a trial. Because there would have been no war to begin with."

"It's the boy, isn't it?" asked Silva. "It bothers you to know he's taking over."

"It bothers all of us that Mr. Newell here defied a strict order. First, crossing into the outside. And second—bringing an unwelcome intruder back with him. An imposter who has no business at the North Pole. We have strict laws against that these days, and for good reason. Who knows what virus or parasite they carry in."

"You were waiting for this, weren't you?" Isaac resumed calmly. "You know, for the Claus to die. You figured it had to happen sometime and so you bought time until it did. The only question being your intention. Was it truly to put an end to Christmas? At least in phases. Perhaps it all makes sense now."

"You just made many assumptions," piped another Elite. "I hope you plan on backing them all up."

"I don't need to," said Isaac. "At least not now. Too busy prepping for an important year. The year where we rightly return Christmas."

The Elites shouted at his back as Isaac, clearly fed up, walked away. Silva stayed to process the mockery before catching up—along with Corbin.

"So, what now?" she inquired. "File the paperwork for a quick and speedy trial? Or do we make them wait?"

Isaac failed to speak until fully exiting the confines of the penitentiary. "Honestly, after the stunt they pulled, I don't really care. What I do care about is finding Nick. Have either of you seen him?"

"Still nothing," issued Corbin. "I'll re-trace the surveillance activity; though it could take a while."

"Do it," Isaac ordered emphatically. "And Silva, go check in with Smudge Terpley." Isaac stared at a digital stopwatch with the frame-by-frame countdown changing rapidly. "I'm beginning to think we're not going fast enough."

With an uncertain step, Nick casually emerged out an alleyway onto a quaint street. He was bundled up in a long coat, scarf and hat—hunched over a bit—afraid his height might give him away.

Snow was lightly falling, with the shopping district quiet enough to make Nick feel safe. The old street sign—Bethlehem Way was perched next to a vintage lamppost and bench—though a horse-drawn carriage, one with black leather startled him. Nick took a step away from the approaching hooves.

"Excuse me," said the driver, curious if he knew Nick from somewhere.

Many storefront windows were lined in bright red; others in black, and some in green and blue, and most had festive displays. There was a pharmacy, a bookstore—a candy shop and law office above that. Nick felt as if he'd been transported back a century and a half by the old Victorian architecture that offered a charm more in common with old London than Manhattan.

"Flavored cocoa, sir," said a voice Nick initially didn't see—his eyes caught reading a dangling sign.

"What?" Nick turned to find it.

"I said, a steamy hot cocoa for you?" A young elf with blue knickers and long yellow socks manned a splendid street-side stand. There were several barrels stacked on top of one another, each with its own faucet. A series of funny, zigzagging pipes weaved over and around each one.

"Ugh," Nick's initial instinct was to reject the offer, but quickly fought it upon realizing how cold and thirsty he was. "Sure. I mean, thank you. That would be nice."

"Milk, mint, peppermint? Dark, pecan, hazel mint? Marshmallow, caramel, caramel mint? Coconut, toasted coconut, coco mint? Pumpkin, pumpkin spice, cherry mint? Orange, raspberry, cinnamint? Malt, Eggnog …"

"Whoa, whoa," Nick held out a hand, unable to take much more of the rhyme. He tried looking up, only to see a sign with more flavors listed than he could possibly ever compute in the moment. "I'll just a take a … regular. Do you have that?"

The elf shrugged, as if never having been asked for a "regular" before. He circled around the stack of barrels to the back before locating another keg and quickly filled up a cup. "That'll be 17 orbs then."

Nick hadn't even considered needing to pay for anything. "Oh, of course. Uhm …," he reached into his right pocket to find little more than lint.

Vance

The elf watched as Nick tried the other, only to pull out a handful of coins he'd never noticed before. Having no idea how valuable an orb was, he eventually just held up a palm full of mismatched coins—some silver and others bronze. The elf oddly looked up, reaching to pick a couple out. Nick was growing unsettled by the elf's curious stare, as if he could no longer hide who he was much longer.

With a band of street-goers making their way up the road, a paranoid Nick quickly grabbed his steamy cup. He slipped behind a tree and up the sidewalk, before walking into more traffic. He panicked, opening the nearest door—desperate for a place to think. He was relieved to see not a single soul inside—but what he did notice were crystal balls displayed over every shelf.

"Snow globes," he whispered, eventually with the courage to take a step or two further in. Nick glided about an aisle where there were hundreds of random globes.

Inside one, a cherry red cardinal clung to a snowy branch. There was the Taj Mahal, and a carousel horse. Nick was taken by the beauty of each one. Most of them looked old with scuff marks and streaks worn by time. Others had intricate bases with beautiful etch work.

"Anybody here? Anybody home?" Nick tried again to no response. He could hear faint chatter outside on the street; but inside, only an occasional chime.

After setting down his cup, Nick built up the courage to wind one. It was "O Holy Night." The globe was large with fake snow clouding the glass as he shook it. When it dissolved, he could see a small nativity—an open barn with a lifeless tree and a couple of sleeping animals. And then there was the manger. He watched the snow gently descend through the water and over the makeshift stable.

Inheriting the Sleigh

It reminded him a lot of the display inside St. Patrick's Cathedral, but Nick soon wondered if his eyes were playing tricks. The faint image of a face appeared in the glass. Nick jolted around, assuming it was just a reflection—though there was nobody behind him. The face gradually got more distinct with moving creases in its jaw—even blinking eyes. Nick wanted to drop the globe but managed to hold on. He fearfully pushed it back onto the shelf while slowly backpedaling away with the face still gazing straight at him. It was smiling—a warm smile, but the oddity was still hard to absorb.

"Santa," Nick called out as he backpedaled, bumping into another shelf and smashing a globe of Japanese fairies at the same time. Water suddenly trickled under his boots.

Nick, in a panic, crunched over broken glass before bolting for the door. His inclination was to run—and he did, right down Bethlehem Way, with his speedy exit scampering off through the snow. This time he didn't really care who was watching. He just kept going—then some more until being swooped up into a set of awaiting arms.

"Whoa, it's alright! Just calm down there," said Ezra hoping to prevent a public scene. "Everything's just fine." Nick was heaving and taking a while to stop—but Ezra's face and gentle disposition were exactly what he needed to see at that moment. "What happened? Are you OK? We've called out search parties."

"I'm sorry, Ezra. But I think I just … I think I just saw …"

"Saw who?" he asked as Nick was overwhelmed by what he couldn't understand.

"I think I just saw my father."

Chapter 30

I believe you, Nick," Isaac had to raise his voice a bit to get him to stop rambling. "But trust me, right now I have bigger candy canes to curl."

"Bigger than this? Like what?"

"For starters, Christmas is a mere 191 days, eight hours, 34 minutes and ...," the elf had to suddenly glance down at a stopwatch held low in his hand. "Boy, I really wish Ezra were here. 26 seconds away, maybe. Give or take. Well, you get my point."

"What in the world is everybody's fascination with time around here?" Nick vented under breath. His hands were raised in disbelief down a long and well-lit hall of wood planks. Elves passed, forcing the two to keep the conversation to a whisper. "But I'm telling you, I saw my father."

"Nick," Isaac stopped to grip him by the shoulders. "You could truly be hallucinating; or then again, you might not. The veil is spookingly thin around here. But really—if you understood my day, you wouldn't be pestering me with a bunch of small potatoes."

"What happened?" Nick wondered what could possibly trump his own story.

Inheriting the Sleigh

"Where do I start? It began with the insanely popular Pax Doll design not passing inspection. An assembly line track in factory 4G broke down out of nowhere. One which still hasn't been fixed by the way. And then I just heard about a flu outbreak coming from one of the south dormitories. Trust me, we're understaffed as it is," A flustered Isaac instinctively started to crunch more numbers with a hand nervously strung through his already thin hair. "Again!" Isaac exclaimed in frustration. "Where's Ezra?"

The elves were in uniform: name badges, droopy hats and all—every last one failing to hide their stares as they sauntered by. Isaac stopped in the middle of the hall where a wall suddenly opened, presenting a toy factory below. He waited for Nick to say something.

"OK," he relented. "I guess this means it's a bad time."

Nick peered down inside the factory, observing an elf using a lathe to make a baby doll crib. "Keep following me," Isaac resumed walking, with Nick left to wonder how much further down the seemingly never-ending hall they intended to go.

"By the way," Isaac was still disinterested, but at least tried to show some level of concern. "How's school going?"

"Professor Terpley says I need to learn over 25 hundred languages." Isaac laughed, humored by the sarcasm. "Why is that funny?!" Nick was almost glad to see the elf smile. "I told him—unless you're C3PO—that's not possible."

The two finally turned a corner into another interior log hall, this one with festive wallpaper. "Und was soll ich sagen?"

"Huh?" he squinted. "What do you mean?"

Isaac wanted to slap his forehead but instead whispered "good grief"—all as Nick failed to interpret what'd just happened.

"Let's try again. Ve ne ben sag oldugunu soyleyerek simdi?!" Isaac repeated the question, this time in Turkish instead of German.

Nick shook in confusion, as if stumped by a logarithm back at Lourdes Academy. He stated the obvious. "You just asked me, 'What am I saying right now?'"

"Yes, I did," Isaac confirmed as they reached an elevator. "But not in English."

Befuddled would understate Nick's stupored look. "Then what?'

"Try German? And some other tongue very few humans even speak."

"Are you sure?"

"Let's just say, I doubt you're fluent, but you clearly know enough." Isaac's head did its own swivel as Nick continued to process the odd fact he was apparently already multi-lingual. "And add to it, Japanese, Yiddish, Romani, and however many others. Put a little faith in Smudge Terpley," he advised. "He's quirkier than Zooey Deschanel, but a magician at his craft. And older than Moses."

"Older than Moses. My mom used to say that about my grandfather."

"No, I mean literally older than Moses. The poor guy nearly goes back to the flood."

Isaac flashed a security badge to open a new set of parting doors where others were waiting. "There you are," Gib noticed as he exited the break room. He was guzzling a bubbly beverage. The elf then tossed some grapes into his mouth, impressing Nick after nearly hitting the high ceiling on their way up.

"Somebody please tell me Corbin fixed that map hologram!" Isaac yelled with crossed fingers across the room—one that looked like the inside of a spaceship.

Inheriting the Sleigh

Corbin almost immediately popped up from behind a long, white desk. It was lit bright purple around the edges. He was holding up a cord with a smile on his face. "Ready for business." The three-dimensional globe shot out a projector as he plugged it in.

A startled Nick reacted by taking a full step back, with a bright blue and green circle suddenly only an inch or so from his face. Or so it appeared. He took a few more subtle steps but couldn't seem to get far enough away to see the entire earth. The circle was the size of a small house, with the top rounding up near the vaulted domed ceiling above. With a remote, Corbin began pushing buttons.

"What are they?" Nick asked, as what seemed like endless red dots began popping up over the green landmasses. They gradually began filling up in concentrated areas. Nick focused his attention on the United States where there were dots virtually everywhere, though more so bunched together on the coastlines. Pockets of Texas were full—as were some in Florida and other states.

"Every dot signifies a Christian household," said Ezra, suddenly emerging through an arched opening. "At least enough so to where they lay claim to the holiday."

"Good greasy giblets," Isaac conceded the floor. "Where have you been?" He wanted to rub it in, though Ezra was good at ignoring the agitation. He clicked on a remote instead. Yellow dots were added to the protruding image, though they were much scarcer, appearing only here and there.

"And what are those?" Nick asked.

"Converts. Those new to the tradition for the first time. You see, every dot has a number, with another number inside of it.

"And what do those numbers mean?"

"Let me show you," he said moving the hologram via remote. The globe was twisting horizontal and diagonal until Australia was now in Ezra and Nick's direct line of sight. It was now zooming deeper like Google Maps from space through the clouds and eventually down onto a beach before settling in on a simple, one-room residence. The hut's roof was thatched, with crumbling stucco on the sides.

"Where is this?" Nick asked.

"This is House One, Nick," informed Ezra as the image now sat still in the hologram. Utirik, an atoll on the Marshall Islands. Population, 409.

"It doesn't look like much," Nick observed the sands and dry weed growth around the hut. Green palms provided some color.

"And that's because it's not," said Gib matter-of-factly. "But trust me, it will be a very happy place come December 25th. That's if you can pull this whole blasted thing off."

Ezra cut back in, zooming even deeper until seven different headshots appeared in one straight horizontal line. Five of them were siblings. "Father, Feto. 47-years old. Fisherman by trade. Has requested some rubber boots for Christmas." Nick watched the next face get highlighted in the hologram. Her skin was equally native and dark, and her hair just as black—only much longer. "Mother, Lota. 45-years old. Homemaker and seamstress. Has thus far asked for nothing tangible, only that her youngest son, Wiki make it through the holiday."

Nick could only speculate what that meant, though it didn't sound good as Ezra spat off the bullet point information like a police chief mundanely reading off the morning crime file.

"Oldest son, Rangi. 24. A fisherman like his father. Has requested only to find companionship this year."

"Lover boy," Gib intrusively leaned over Nick's ear with a smile as he tossed a few nuts between his cheeks.

"Next son, Manu. 21." Nick's mind naturally phased both Gib and Ezra out as his eyes shot down to the end of the hologram row.

"Are you OK, Nick?" asked Isaac after getting to daughter, Ailana.

"Little Wiki," he said staring at his hairless head. "What's wrong with him?"

Ezra was forced to skip ahead a bit, getting straight to the sad part. "Wiki just turned 11 this month. Diagnosed with stage four leukemia."

"Is that as bad as it sounds?" Nick bit his lip through the conformation.

"Worse," added Corbin. "Let's just say, there is no stage five."

"The Ngoriakis have no access to the complicated and expensive medical care needed to prolong life—the village patriarchs not expecting him to make it far into next year," Ezra informed. "And unlike most kids his age, has asked for only one thing."

"One thing?" Nick quickly followed up—almost not wanting to know. "What is that?"

Ezra paused this time before answering, as if impressed himself by the mature request. "Eternal life." There was more silence around the brightly lit room. A room that almost reminded Nick of heaven itself. Lights occasionally flickered over various machines in the background.

"Sounds like a fine name for a new line of cross jewelry." Nobody was sure whether Gib was joking or not.

"And how could we possibly ever grant that?" Nick asked as the others only stared down at their feet.

"We don't," Isaac whispered, finally pulling his head back up. "Only God can do that."

Vance

"But obviously we have to drop off something," Nick rudely swiped the remote from Ezra to zoom in further on the boy. The hologram movement made a futuristic noise as Wiki was now the only face in view—the number seven in the top left corner, with Wiki's life-history etched across it in small print below his picture. There was a half-smile frozen across his face, as if desperately trying to stay strong.

"If only he were the one kid we had to worry about," said Gib taking a seat. "Unfortunately, personal tragedy extends miles deep."

"Sir, the letter bin has just been restocked," informed an interrupting elf from an open door.

"The letter bin?" Nick probed.

"Yeah," Isaac pointed to a thick, red string—hanging off by itself from a nearby ceiling. "Perhaps Wiki has asked for something else. And," he paused. "There's only one way to find out. Go ahead. Give it a tug."

Nick gently did, which is all it took to release a flap above his head. He had no time to react—the pile descending into an avalanche over his face. The thousands of falling letters didn't stop for many seconds before Nick could finally open his eyes again—suddenly covered neck-deep in a mountain of sealed envelopes. They were postmarked with stamps from all over the world.

Gib then quietly stood up from his rolling chair, handing him a chrome-colored pick about ten inches long. With Nick's arms all covered up, all he could think to do was open his mouth as Gib placed the letter opener between each row of clenched teeth.

"Better start crack'n then," Isaac smiled. "This could take weeks."

Chapter 31

Between a framed picture of Buddy Holly and the hood of a T-Bird protruding out the diner wall, a potted orange tree blended in. The tree was scarcely decorated, with themed bulbs spread out across its few branches.

Marie sat alone. She was dressed for summer with her fingers woven together on the table—her eyes aimlessly staring out the window into the yellowish-green foliage.

"Hello, Marie," Vienna, a bit awkwardly approached the red booth—as if not exactly sure what to say or how to say it.

"Oh, hello, Mrs. Crest."

Vienna took a seat. "I appreciate you meeting me here. How have you been?"

Marie was dressed much more casually—in a T-shirt and ponytail. "Hanging in there. What can I do for you?" Marie asked, having trouble maintaining eye contact.

Vienna intimidated Marie with her dangling earrings and Gucci handbag placed beside her on the table. She didn't take off her sunglasses, pausing before the words slowly trickled out. "You know something, don't you, Marie?"

Her eyes veered back toward the sidewalk traffic. "Marie, talk to me. He needs his pills. If he doesn't get them, you know as well as I what happens."

"I'm not sure what you want me to say, Mrs. Crest." Marie's tone was out of character. "Because the truth is, even if I did know something, I'm not sure you'd believe it."

Vienna's interest peaked further. "Try me then. After all these months, I think it would help your grief to finally let it go. Because the truth is, we're all grieving here."

"One Elvis Burger," a waitress in a white apron and short baby blue dress cut off at the thigh, plopped a big greasy burger down in front of Marie. It was joined by a basket of thick fries and a large chocolate shake. "Anything for you, ma'am?" The waitress asked Vienna, who shook in mild disgust at food she wasn't at all used to eating. Marie only offered a slightly guilty return stare.

"Where did he go, Marie?" an equally beaten down Vienna hastily tried again. "Because at this point, I'm running out of options—and honestly, don't know if I can go on another week."

The legendary Platters song suddenly took its turn streaming through the jukebox. "Only you … can make all this world seem right. Only you … can make all the darkness bright."

"He left on a Russian oil tanker," Vienna was surprised it came out so abruptly. The two made rare visual contact across the booth, with Marie nervously taking a large bite. The tomato, onion, and a gob of mustard all spilled out the bottom of the loaded bun as she did.

"An oil tanker?"

"Yes. Somewhere in Jersey. Elizabeth, I believe," Marie slurped her straw, somewhat relieved. "I saw him leave with someone. A male that looked like he might be in his 30's, I don't know."

Inheriting the Sleigh

"And you didn't recognize this man?"

"No," Marie shook. "And I'm terribly sorry I didn't say anything, but Nick told me not to worry. Said, that if he didn't go … millions would be disappointed."

"Millions would be disappointed?" Vienna repeated as her way of digesting the reveal. "Why would millions be disappointed?"

Marie shook again, this time in confusion with fries jamming up her mouth. She desperately wanted to give up the final clue, but this time managed to keep it to herself.

Meanwhile, Vienna had her own secret to divulge—and without thinking, pulled the trendy Aviator sunglasses off her face. Marie was shocked by what she saw. A swollen eye with tears streaming down the other one. "Mrs. Crest, are you alright?"

Vienna wiped a wet streak off her cheek, knowing the ruse was over.

"Did you … you know, fall down the stairs or something?" Marie asked, wanting to believe it.

Vienna broke into a forced smile, as if appreciating the glass half-full innocence—all the while, processing what she had just learned.

Nick's stare was deep inside a room—one with fine portraits of Elites perched about the old walls. He held up a large ornament with Nat King Cole's picture on it. It perfectly matched the ornament hanging off the potted tree inside the diner.

"Perhaps you should give that to me," Isaac uttered each word slowly and distinctly as he gently pried it away. The two of them were alone, and Nick masked his anger with silence. "Forgive me for not warning you about the dangers of eavesdropping. Sometimes you see things you never intended as a result."

But Isaac never received a response. Nick instead was clamming up, even panicking. "Nick," Isaac called out more than once as he watched him nervously fidget with his fingers.

"I'm sorry," his eyes finally lifted to meet Isaac's. But Nick's apology was masked by a sudden change of heart—as if watching his mother in real time was simply too much to bear. "I think I might have to go home now."

Isaac, familiar with the natural stages of shock and grief, was confident he'd soon break from it, only to find Nick already speeding for the Congressional House exit. "Ugh, Nick. You need to relax. Wait, where are you going?"

Inlets were positioned all down the hall, with decorative figurines and cheery splashes of color, but Nick was in no mood to observe the interior design. Isaac watched him bolt for the stairwell and massive lobby doors. He was off so quick he'd even forgotten his coat as he descended more steps—this time out into the exterior chill leading away from Chimney Sweep Square.

Nick, consumed by unhealthy emotion, suddenly got turned around. Unsure where to run, he had to go somewhere. Heavy winds beat across his exposed face as he sprinted out an open, high-arching iron gate. The further he went, the less familiar things became. He just wanted to find a fast and safe transport back into civilization, and yet his panicked brain wasn't relaying any signals steeped in reality.

With wind soon morphing into a storm, all other forms of humanity had since disappeared off the Pole's streets. But for Nick, he was just running. Heavy snowdrifts blinded his vision, and his skin was turning pink from the frost. His adrenaline carried him forward, until a mean gust suddenly swept him off his feet. The boy was now blowing away with little control. His back eventually rocked into an old, British-style phone booth, one with peeling red paint. His head was dizzy, now left to wonder where he was, and if this was how he might die.

Unsure how long he'd been passed out, a shard of light suddenly caught one of his slowly moving eyelids. As Nick forced it open, the light got brighter.

On a quaint street, the humble framework was simple—with an open door flapping mightily both in and out.

Nick winced as he got up, caught off guard by the sudden pain in his back. He hobbled forward through the still-beating wind. With his hands cupped over his eyes to see in the suffocating snow, he lunged the last step for the welcome warmth, before immediately dropping, desperate to kick the door shut with his feet.

Nick could feel the popping embers of a fire somewhere though didn't have the initial strength to lift his head to see exactly where. All he could hear was a reoccurring drip filling up a can.

Soon inching upward, it was now obvious. Nick was inside a small chapel. A large cross was the centerpiece behind the pulpit, with perhaps 15 hand-carved pews. It was plain yet inviting enough as several dripping candles provided just enough light. Nick slowly walked down the center aisle, though saw no one. What he did find was the welcome fire, which he rushed over to de-thaw his frozen limbs.

"Baaaaaa," Nick thrust around after finally hearing a sign at life. A farm animal had caught him off guard. It was a sheep poking its head over the small corral of a short, barnyard fence.

Nick approached and it embraced the attention, nibbling on loose straw inside the enclosure—one with a trough and a roof of brittle branches. Nick gently laid a hand over its black ears and wool, sinking his fingers deep inside the soft carpet for more warmth.

But then something else caught his eye. It was an old, dusty pipe organ that looked like it might have been plucked right out of a 16th century monastery.

Itching to play on something—anything other than a key whiz—he eagerly stepped onto the stage platform separating the pulpit from the pews. The organ was painted a cheerful pink with Bavarian accents, and the pipes rose tall toward the ceiling.

Softly pulling out a bench near the four layers of keys, he had never played on anything like it before. Nick could have started with anyone but first chose a key at a comfortable level on the second row. A burst of hollow sound arose through a golden windpipe. Nick, not wanting to draw attention to himself, naturally stopped. He waited for several seconds to see if he'd alerted somebody, but the only thing he seemed to hear was the onlooking sheep trying to lure Nick back over for some more affection. He tried another one—and then another—with music soon forming a melody through the various pipes shaped like a mountain above the keys. Nick didn't stop, as he tinkered with the pressurized air that almost sounded like he was entertaining a circus. He was enjoying the solitude; only he was no longer alone.

Nick jolted up, with the organ bench screeching backward at the sight of an elf. He wore a brown cloak under a healthy set of white locks. "No need to stop," an outstretched hand emerged through his loosely-fitted sleeves near the back pew.

"I'm sorry, I was caught in that storm," Nick built up a rambling apology. "But then I found this place here and went to pet your sheep before spotting this wonderful instrument and honestly, couldn't seem to help myself. But I'll go ahead and see myself out," he concluded with thoughts of his mother still filling up his cluttered head.

Inheriting the Sleigh

The older gentleman with a touch of medieval in his face widened into a smile. "There's little need to explain," he assured. "In fact, that's exactly what this place is intended to be, a refuge from all of life's storms." The priest picked up the can under the leak—only to dump it into a larger bucket.

Nick froze as he attempted to determine his next move. He could tell by the sound of the wind the storm had weakened but still was very cold and sore.

"My name is Clovis Finch," the kindly man introduced. "The caretaker of this godly house." Nick continued to exhale from the platform as Clovis resumed. "And you shouldn't have stopped … Saint Nicholas," he swung his head toward the organ. "We certainly have our own concert pianists here in the north, but your abilities might well surpass them all."

Nick hesitated but scooted in again. It was effortless. It was soothing, and when it was over, Clovis couldn't help but clap from a midlevel pew.

"Thanks," he said as playing music again helped him calm down.

"Of course. And you do realize that everyone in the city has now been graced by it too?" Clovis said, pulling down a lever near the organ—one that confined the sound to the church only.

"You mean … everybody?" Nick grew embarrassed, afraid he may have broken his own rule by causing a disturbance.

"Forgive me for prying, but is there something troubling you?"

Nick wanted to tell him everything but hesitated to broach—a story full of many complications. Clovis instead reached into a barrel to feed the sheep. "His name is Joseph."

"Joseph?" Nick repeated, joining him at the short fence.

Clovis affectionately stroked Joseph's black nose. "This animal is as old as it is special. Used to belong to the Master himself. He named it after his stepfather."

Nick froze at the thought, still forced to blow into his hands every few seconds for warmth. "Did you just say it belonged to … you know … Jesus? Of Nazareth?"

"That's right," Clovis nodded. "After escaping the Isle of Patmos, your father dragged him all the way up here himself. To be honest, I figured ol' Joe would have perished centuries back. And he came close once. He was quite sick back during the Crusades, but the blessed thing just keeps breathing. Perhaps he'll never die—all the way into the Millennium."

Nick stroked the sheep again, only this time with an entirely new respect. "Are you familiar with the parable of the lost sheep?" the Priest asked.

"Excuse me," Nick was in too deep a thought pattern to not need stuff occasionally repeated.

"The Savior himself gave it at a time when the corrupt tax collectors clung to his every word. They just waited to pounce on the very first thing they felt might contradict the Law of Moses. And then the Pharisees came along to accuse Jesus of befriending sinners."

"Yeah," Nick agreed. "I'm sure at times he felt like he just couldn't win."

"But he had his friends too, Nick. Like Joseph here. Suppose a man has a hundred sheep and loses one," Clovis quoted Jesus directly. "Doesn't he leave the 99 in the open country to go after the lost sheep until he finds it? And when he finds it, he joyfully puts it over his shoulder and goes home."

Inheriting the Sleigh

Nick was listening, but his eyes had since closed, as if suddenly fighting a series of unpleasant flashback. *"Nick, why don't you at least try football. Are you afraid to find out you might actually be good at it? Taking on a challenge is what we Crests do."*

"Then he calls his friends and neighbors together and says, Rejoice with me for I have found my lost sheep," Clovis resumed, despite Nick's grimace.

"And is it really necessary to play that damn piano right now? You're just like your mother," Snippets of Arthur's emotional abuse continued to eat away at his mind. *"I just cashed in a stock portfolio that surged over a thousand percent in one week. I would listen to what I'm telling you, Nick."*

"I tell you in the same way, there will be more rejoicing in heaven over one sinner who repents, than 99 of the righteous who do not."

"You really expect an inheritance!? I can't always be there to save you."

"And so it is among you. What man if he has a hundred ..."

Nick's mind then worm-holed to the Blue Owl. *"What are you doing here? Don't ever speak to me that way again! Don't ... speak ... again ... ever ... speak ... don't ... again."*

"And loses one ..."

"You're fighting the wrong person. I'm just looking out for you."

"Does not leave the 90 and nine ..."

"I mean it, Nick. You can't keep living this lie."

Clovis' concerned voice trailed off as he finally finished his sermon with a breathtaking whisper. "Until he finds it."

Nick was suddenly squinting and drenched in a sweat. Clovis gently helped him into a pew, draping a blanket over his jittery limbs. He waited for Nick to settle down, unsure the boy had heard a single word—although Nick soon put all that to rest.

"Clovis," he said softly. "Sometimes, I feel as if I'm the lost sheep."

Vance

A knock interrupted any chance for a response. A droopy knit hat then poked through. "Is he here?" the elf curiously inquired. Clovis only nodded. "Good, because they've followed the music," the elf said with a grin. "And I'd really hate to disappoint anyone. They're asking for more."

Nick wondered what he was talking about as the elf slowly opened the chapel door. The storm had now completely ceased, with hundreds of elves holding candles behind him in the thickly-fallen snow.

"I told you," said Clovis. "Perhaps it's time for an encore."

Chapter 32

A chime rang on cue. Nick had been inside once before and finally built up the courage to go back—though just like the first time, saw no one—only a wide assortment of snow globes.

Nick's boots crunched over the broken glass that still hadn't been swept from the last time. He snooped around until locating a broom in a small janitorial closet—wiping a finger across one of the shelves to expose the heavy dust. But that was not what he'd come to do. Nick was looking for one globe. And sure enough, there it was in the very spot he'd left it.

To its left was a Coca Cola globe with a polar bear sipping from an old bottle; and to its right, a miniature replica of Buckingham Palace with two members of the Queen's Guard standing patrol. But Nick paid little attention to either one.

Instead, he wrapped his hand around the familiar bronze base. Lifting it up to eye level, he was expecting something to happen—though once the shaken snow settled, all he saw was the old barn and manger.

Partial jingles occasionally startled Nick, with his eye shooting up every time something made even the slightest sound. He eventually felt confident enough to wind it up. "O Holy Night" graced the room before something began to cloud over the glass. Nick looked nervous, unaware of what was happening. The only difference is—this time he was braced and ready for whatever it was.

Something was playing out inside the glass—something cinematic. Nick tightly gripped the globe, as if watching a scary movie, though it wasn't scary at all. He was looking at a scene right out of what appeared to be ancient Rome. Sound accompanied the visuals through the globe, with heavy marketplace chatter since replacing the carol.

The great Colosseum, and a series of white columns rose tall in Rome's backdrop—but in Nick's immediate view was a tunneled arch of cement and brick, opening into rows of commerce. The sequence then cut to a tighter shot of a boy with his eye on a basket full of pears near a fruit stand. The boy was clearly an orphan, with a dirtied face and dressed in rags. He looked desperate.

Behind him, a man released his hood. His eyes were interested in the orphan. He looked familiar to Nick and pulled a coin bag from his belt while walking to approach the child. Maneuvering through the masses toward the row of colorful street tents, the man no longer saw the boy— failing to get there in time as he'd already made his dash. He had stolen the fruit.

"Guards! Guards!" cried the clerk to passing legionaries with bright red, bristle brush crests atop their helmets—and plates protecting their cheeks. Townsfolk were pushed over in the chase as the soldiers responded feverishly to the whistle, scampering after the fleeing feet.

The cloaked man, meanwhile, carefully observed every step of the chase. But instead of just watching like the rest, he followed it.

"Thief, stop!" They pulled their swords. But the barefooted boy couldn't afford to, weaving in and out of traffic as the center of attention.

Inheriting the Sleigh

He slid underneath a rolling pushcart and hopped over a barricading stack of crates before turning onto an adjoining street. But the Romans were right on his trail as the boy took another bite from the fruit and threw it back. More soldiers followed the alarm whistle, with the boy now running out of places to go. Eventually, he emerged into another wave of traffic.

Laying low amid many sets of encroaching sandals, he looked for someplace to hide—only to be swallowed up from behind. The man who had been watching from the beginning had forcefully pinned the child underneath his cloak, suddenly concealing his small frame. With a poker face, the stranger continued to walk slowly with a firm arm draped over the boy's mouth.

Soldiers jostled their heads. They bent to check every crevice and under every ledge as the rescuer continued to casually make his way out of the danger zone. He turned several corners before finally lifting his robe, gripping the child by the shoulders up against a vacant clay wall.

"I'm not here to hurt you," he affirmed, though could tell by the boy's frightened return stare he wasn't convinced. The man pulled out his sack of coins, holding it only inches from his face. "Do you see this?" The boy slowly shook with his eyes widening big—as if never having seen so much money at one time before. "OK then. It should feed you for a year. I want you to take it and run away for a while. Perhaps leave the city entirely. They'll be looking for you, you know."

The boy failed to say a word, only nodding every time the man spoke.

"Looking is in the past," a voice startled them both as he slowly approached from behind. They turned to find a young soldier releasing his helmet to expose a set of bright red hair. He held the helmet under

239

his arm with his sword extended. The boy wanted to run again, but his rescuer wouldn't allow it—holding him close.

"It's alright, just stay here. Please," the man then turned his attention to the soldier with the tip of his sword now just feet away. "You must understand, this boy will die if he receives nothing to eat. He just needs leniency. I promise, you will hear nothing more of him."

"In the name of Emperor Titus, justice must be carried out on this thief."

The man and boy both watched the soldier, with neither making a move. "You look familiar," said the legionary. "What is your name?"

"Perhaps I will tell you should you tell me yours. I always care to know to whom I converse with."

The soldier shrugged, as if to suggest "why not." "If it means that much to you. You'll be in the dungeons soon anyhow for abetting a crime. My name is Mauvtavious. Now your turn," resumed the soldier. "But I must say, you look eerily familiar to someone I was once told was deceased. Someone that passed long ago in Ephesus. Have you by chance any relation to John himself? You know, John the Beloved, or John the Revelator as the legends call him?"

To Nick, it clicked as a younger version of his father calmly felt the soldier out.

"What if I told you that John wasn't dead? Would you believe it?"

Lyman didn't know what to say but tried. "Impossible. He'd be more than a feeble old man by now."

"And yet you're looking directly at him. Have we crossed paths before?"

But Mauv had no time to respond as the rustling skirts of more soldiers could be heard close by. John took one more look at Mauv, frozen in his return glare.

Inheriting the Sleigh

"You must go," John moved his haste attention onto the boy—for the first time releasing the grip over his frightened shoulders. "Do as I say now."

Mauv Lyman raised a hand only partly to stop him, but then suddenly resisted in a surprising moment of mercy.

Officers rounded a corner from the opposite side to notice Mauv and John completely still. They were facing one another and waiting for the other to act. "Any sighting?!" they yelled from afar.

Lyman briefly glanced into the rich eyes and gentle face of John before exclaiming, "No. Nothing here!"

"May you forever be blessed," said John softly as the soldiers hurried away.

"Blessed? I am no saint, I can promise you that. But if you truly are, as you say, the great apostle himself, then what are you doing in Rome?"

"Just passing through … on my way north."

"North. Why north? Isn't it cold there?"

"So, they say," John admitted. "Though that is precisely where I am being called. A lost people awaits."

"A lost people? The Roman Kingdom only extends as far as Germania. Beyond that, savage tribes are all that exist."

John smiled. "Perhaps there are others. Others you're not aware of. The word 'lost' has great meaning, you know."

"Others? Others who live in any form of civility without the great influence of Roman rule. That's absurd," he chuckled.

"You think Rome is great?" John kept his voice low so others along the quiet street could not overhear.

"Of course," Lyman answered. "It is the most powerful societal and economic dynasty the world has ever known. Rome can conquer anything or anyone."

241

"Perhaps that is true," John shrugged as he leaned back against a wall to rest. "Unless of course that 'anyone' is God himself. Then suddenly Rome becomes powerless."

Mauv smirked at the first mention of God. "God may not approve of Rome, but the Gods certainly do. Like Diana and Apollo."

"Diana and Apollo offer little reward, and demand nothing in return. Which are precisely why injustices occur all around you," John waved his arms for emphasis.

"Of what injustices do you refer?"

"How about we start with grave social inequality. A land where emperors live lavishly off the backs of slaves, while for many, they can only wonder if food is an option that day. Where Christians and Jews hide their worship to survive, while savages cheer inside the Coliseum as one man kills another for sport. Please do not take this personally, but I have seen plenty enough of Rome to know little good exists here."

Mauv was slightly offended. "Well, it has treated me just fine," he arose from a crate, picking up his sword near his feet to bid farewell.

"Have you seen anything else?"

"What was that?"

"I said, have you seen anything else? "John inquired louder. "Perhaps you say what you do only because you fail to realize how much greater things could be."

"And I assume greater things await … in the north?" Another band of soldiers suddenly approached again.

"Mauvtavious!" yelled a Centurion. "March and report!"

Lyman quickly gathered his helmet and whispered something to John in passing as he barricaded the view of the boy. "Then I offer you only one request," he paused to breathe. "Please do not embark. At least until I have the chance to join you then."

Inheriting the Sleigh

A familiar sound coming from outside the globe was beginning to distract Nick. It was growing louder and harder to ignore—as soon the scene was suddenly washed away by a dark cloud. "No, come back!" Nick was annoyed and saddened to see it all end, as nothing but faux snow now fell over the old barn again.

Nick kept his eyes up waiting for the miniature train to make its way through a hole in the wall. The shiny black steam engine emerged in a crack near the ceiling. Steam rose as the track dipped down on its way for another corner on the opposite side of the room.

"Whoa!" a voice cried as a signal to quickly pull on the brakes. It was a toy soldier sticking its helmet outside the locomotive to get a better look.

Unlike the inside of his bedroom, there was no train stop this time—and yet, the miniature, four-car locomotive was screeching to a sudden halt over the open track. "What's going on here?!" cried another soldier, this one from the caboose. But his inquiry went unanswered until the train came to a complete stop.

"I'm sorry. It's just that, I believe I saw someone!" said the soldier at the front.

"In here? Impossible. Nobody's been inside these walls for years."

But the soldier continued to gaze around, as if swearing he'd seen a face. "Yes, there!" he pointed to a crouching figure who couldn't conceal himself quickly enough between two shelves.

"Where?!"

"There!"

Nick, with no choice, finally stood, stepping closer. "Hello," his call was filled with confusion—and some guilt.

"Is that you … Nick Kringle?"

"It's me."

"And what are you doing inside this unsavory place?"' the soldier asked. "Why, there's even black mold running up and down the walls."

"I have my business," Nick wondered why he was having to justify himself to something small enough to smash with a shoe. "But is there something else I can help you with?"

"Matter of fact, there is?" said the engineer in the rear. "Since we haven't been able to track you down. Pun intended," he smirked. "I believe you've got some mail here."

"More mail?" Nick grew nervous after having poured through a never-ending number of toy lists back at headquarters.

"Don't get too excited," said the conductor. Lieutenant!" his yell carried across the train.

"Hmmmm," another soldier snorted. This one rising from the second car with drowsy eyes.

"You have a good nap?" the conductor quipped facetiously as he spread his arms in disbelief.

"Did I really just doze off again?"

The soldier in the locomotive managed to roll his eyes. "Hey, the boss here needs his mail."

"Sure," he said, using two arms to lift some neatly bundled mailers with Nick's name on them. They nearly filled up the entire car. "Here. Here you go."

Nick approached the track along the far wall, holding up both arms to retrieve a wad of paper bound by a ribbon. The soldiers watched Nick slowly and hesitantly read each piece. "Sewage bill? Voter Registration renewal. Used car blowout. Everything from side cars to vintage vans. Liquidation sale of the century." Nick continued to flip through, hoping to eventually see something that might catch his eye. "Is this it?"

"Figured," said the engineer with his hands draped over his defeated cheeks. "Sometimes I feel that's all we're good for anymore … junk mail."

"Well," the conductor snapped. "I guess we should get out of here then. Say," he turned back toward Nick once more before they did. "What are you doing in this weird place anyhow?"

"Why? Is there something wrong with it?" he was beginning to think there might be.

"Well, no," he said after scratching his helmet and thinking about it some more. "That's if … you know, you don't mind the paranormal."

"More like pola-normal," added the sleepy soldier in the middle, as he once again comfortably leaned back inside his mail car.

"What do you mean?" Nick was anxious to receive another clue.

"Well, I'm sure you've heard of Jacob Marley?"

"Jacob Marley's a fictional character?"

"Perhaps," the soldier admitted, as if to say, 'touché.' "And yet, you're the only one I've seen who's bothered to spend time here. Coincidence? Think again."

"Now that you mention it," Nick was somewhat glad to have somebody to talk to about his recent experience. "I have, in fact, witnessed some odd things."

"Like flickering lights … weird echoes … strange reflections?" asked the engineer.

Nick was fully ready to tell his story, only to feel his heart jump at the sudden wail of an alarm. He dropped the mail as a red bulb inside the abandoned store began to flash every other second. More obnoxious than a car alarm, Nick was forced to cup his hands over his ears.

"What is that?!" he yelled loud enough for the soldiers to hear.

"Sounds like there's been a prison break!"

"A prison break?!"

"Yeah. I don't recall those alarms going off; at least since the breakout of 63."

Nick could barely hear the train's departing wheels as he hurried outside into the snowy air to escape the noise. The problem was, he couldn't. There were similar caged alarms sounding on every block along the cobbled street. Pockets of elves were equally flustered.

"Where's the prison?!" Nick asked the nearest elf.

With an arm pressed over his mouth for warmth, he pointed the other way to a cross street. Nick just ran, a jog that eventually took him down into a valley where a large concrete mini-city rested alone. It was surrounded by a high barbwire gate, very much like any penitentiary, only with garlands woven across the top. But it was the commotion that stood out.

"What's going on in there?!" Nick's eyes veered up.

"Not now!" cried the guard atop a platform, his firearm firmly pointed toward the chaos.

"But I need to know," Nick was persistent enough to eventually force the guard's attention.

"Mr. Kringle?"

"I need to get down there?!" Nick pried. The lookout appeared hesitant but knew he had little choice but honor Nick's request. "Please."

After a brief radio message, he carefully escorted Nick through several locked gates. Many layers of flustered security observed Nick proceeding closer into the danger zone, with war-torn sounds getting louder the further they went. Fists and clubs were exchanged. Some were in headlocks, with others being dragged across the prison yard snow.

Only a single chain link fence now separated Nick from the fight. Old guardsmen in burnt orange jumpsuits were skilled in their charge against a makeshift prison staff that had clearly been taken by surprise.

Inheriting the Sleigh

Escorted through a door on the second level, the altercation was even more intense. Nick looked down through one last protective barrier into the row of cells where Elites were relentless in their escape.

Guards used stunners with colorful rings—guns that looked eerily like toys, though there weren't enough of them to control the uprising. "I truly do apologize, but I think I need this," Nick yanked a barrel from a startled guard's grip in passing. He had occasionally been forced to play violent video games with Loopy O'Brien, but other than that, had never actually held even a fake firearm before—let alone a real one.

His first shot sailed high, sending a bunkbed collapsing instead. Despite feeling an uncomfortable vibration against his fingertips, Nick tried again, and this time was successful in picking off an Elite in the act of strangling a guard. He moved in closer toward the chaos with his eye over a scope. In the back of his mind, he knew it was stupid; but was also extremely tired of all the conflict. He just wanted it to end.

Faces whisked past on either side—but Nick just kept going— swiveling the barrel to his right, then the left. Many elves began to take notice, as did the enemy. An Elite with a purple beard loaded his shot and had a great look, but the protective instincts of the elves kicked in even quicker, dashing to shield Santa Claus from any incoming fire. Nick was shoved back into an open cell, with more elves rolling in like commandos. They tore off a mattress from a bunk, propping it up as a temporary buffer.

A welcomed period of silence ensued before a man slowly emerged. He had bizarre hair, but an authoritative eye. Since being privy to a scene from his far distant past, Nick couldn't help but want to see Mauv Lyman in an entirely new light. Then again, he also struggled to quantify exactly who he was, or what he was trying to do now.

"I think it's time to open up the gates," Mauv issued a threat from his own hiding spot. "And should you not, expect more to die."

Since his arrival, the elves had since deferred to Nick. "Mauvtavious!" the boy soon called out from behind the mattress.

Mauv recognized the voice, though was surprised to hear Nick use the long version of his first name. "Well, look who decided to show up again. Wherever there's trouble, Santa Junior is there. You were clearly fortunate to escape once, but the odds are never great you escape my wrath twice."

"Correct me if I'm wrong," Nick's retort was quick. "But you're the one escaping now."

"Consider us even then. Tell your men to open the gates and let us walk free. Perhaps we can spare us both anymore of that unbecoming scent of death."

Nick cringed as he slowly peeked out overtop, only to notice deceased elves and Elites both dotted about the cold, cement floor. "After everything you've done, you want me … just to release you?" he was shocked by Mauv's bold request.

"Aren't you a Kringle?" Mauv's manipulation began. "A name defined by what … mercy and love, as they say."

The scene inside Rome interrupted Nick's thoughts—his father meeting the soldier and pleading on behalf of the starving boy. The speaker was more so shocked by Nick's response. "Perhaps your own history is documented by similar episodes of love."

Security and inmates were now separated off into two bodies like rival gangs as Mauv contemplated the sentiment. He wondered why Nick would say such a thing—the hunkering elves to either side, wondering the same.

Inheriting the Sleigh

A door above suddenly interrupted the verbal back-and-forth. Isaac and Blaine had an urgent step, along with a stream of new backup to control the uprising once and for all. "Where is he?" Isaac was angrily looking for Mauv. The House Speaker knew his time for an escape had run out—slowly emerging into the open. "You'll need to tell your cronies there to drop their weapons," he instructed with guns now outnumbering the prisoners by five-to-one.

As they clanked against the ground, Nick felt confident enough to stand up again. "Look who beat you here," he joked as Isaac rubbed his forehead.

"I believe the last time I saw you, you were … running away from conflict, not toward it."

"I'm OK now," Nick promised.

"And you," Isaac turned to Mauv with a birds-eye view. "It didn't take long to stir up more trouble. Don't you know I'm in the middle of a logistical nightmare, with little to no time or patience for stunts like this?"

"You really expected me to give up that easily? We all know you're smarter than that, Isaac Newell."

The very same doors shot open again. Blaine was the first to turn around to behold a new band suddenly strutting in to overcomplicate the matter.

"Starsky Skiles?" Nick breathed upon witnessing the last person he ever expected to see. Their black and gray wardrobe lay a stark contrast to the color displayed all around them.

"And how is our next sleigh driver?" Starsky confidently greeted from above.

"Occupied," said Blaine, a little put off by the dramatic entrance.

"And good day to you too, Cross. How long's it been?"

"Not long enough," Blaine whispered with Mauv and the Elites doing their best to listen below.

"Perhaps you can quickly explain what you're doing here, Skiles?" Isaac was peeved himself by the interruption, as the entire rhythm of his rebuke got squashed.

"Honestly, I have the same question," Mauv issued.

"There's your answer," Starsky suddenly peered down at the Speaker with a half-smile.

"I'm sorry to inform you, but my visitation hours have already run out. You'll have to come back later," said Mauv, never letting an opportunity for sarcasm slip away.

"And miss this? I don't think so."

"If your goal is to be an annoyance—I can assure you—there are much more innovative ways to do it."

"OK, I think that's enough," said Isaac, tired of being a third wheel and losing all control of the dialogue.

"We mean no disrespect," Starsky said as his groupies leaned over to get a better look at the surrendered Elites. "We just didn't want to miss out on history. You know, where the two-tier ideological system finally comes to a blessed and long-awaited end."

"What are you talking about?" Blaine could only guess.

"Perhaps there's a third party that has earned the right to start making some decisions around here," Starsky added, with his pointy nose and clever eye.

"You … making decisions?" Mauv mocked. "We'd all be dead of frostbite."

"You don't think it's our turn?" Starsky was more straight-faced this time. "Besides … no dynasty lasts forever. Shoot, even Rome fell eventually."

Inheriting the Sleigh

Mauv grew reflective and silent for the first time, as if Starsky had suddenly just struck a nerve. The look in his eye had clearly changed, but he wasn't the only one. So had Nick's.

Who was he? The man that believed enough in his father to follow him through the deep tundra? Or the ruthless enemy that had nearly crucified him? They were only a few of Nick's questions.

The three-way conversation continued, though Nick could hardly make out what was being said. He was too focused on the flashbacks overwhelming his mind; the lost sheep, and the mercy Mauv showed in the marketplace. That is until being shaken to the point where he had no choice but wake up to what was going on directly in front of him.

"Nick. Nick!" Isaac had since descended to the surface—pinning the boy by both shoulders. He had spent the last few minutes assuring the Elites that additional charges were being added to their already long rap sheet; but as Nick's eyes opened again, he whispered something inaudible. Isaac thought he heard correctly, though hoped he hadn't. "What was that?" he gave him a chance to correct himself.

"I said, I think we need to release him."

Isaac desperately wanted to escort Nick into another room, though there was no opportunity for that here. "Excuse me," was all he could think to say, with a host of startled onlookers to all sides.

"Yeah ... Lyman. I think we should release him," Nick repeated, leaving little doubt this time.

"I, for one," Starsky was content with being the first to offer up an honest retort. "Certainly did not see that com'n."

"Mercy?" Isaac whispered into Nick's closest ear. "Have you lost your ...?"

"Mind? Perhaps. Let's just say ... I've learned a few things since the last time we saw each other."

"Have you now?" he squinted, beyond curious where Nick had been all this time. Isaac stared deeply into Nick's eyes, needing a second to read just how serious he was—before giving up and asking no further questions. After months of it being the other way around, he knew he needed to sit back and perhaps place his full trust in Nick.

Meanwhile, all heads turned to find Mauv and the remaining Elites sharing a satisfactory victory lap. "This is what you're giving a pass to?" Blain was equally dismayed by the smug look on their faces. "You really want to extend an olive branch to the heartless scum that showed none to you?"

Isaac stepped in, as if already being at peace with the decision—though in the back of his mind was struggling just as much as the rest. "If we do release you," he addressed the prisoners. "Then you must agree to some terms first."

"Wait," said Blaine. As one often inclined to defer to authority without challenge, he uncharacteristically stepped forward. "I can't go along with this. I mean, Corbin. Not to mention," he waved about the various dead lying between cell blocks. "Honestly, how many innocents can draw their blood back to this man?"

Starsky cut back in with plenty more to say. "You know me. I've rarely gotten involved in your squabbles. But he's clearly more pathetic than an injured sewer rat," he pointed to the Speaker as Mauv's return glare suggested he was ready to bite Starsky's head right off.

Isaac desperately wanted to agree but was caught in a no-win. He knew it was Nick's call, and though he didn't completely understand it, the Chief of Staff was intuitive enough to know there had to be a reason.

Starsky broke a period of more silence, tired of the awkwardness. "I may have an idea here," he spoke up with a large grin, as if just conjuring up a Nobel Prize-worthy compromise. All heads turned. "I say, we have a race. You know, down Dead Man's Pass."

There were few initial words from those listening—only oohs and aahhs.

"Wait a minute," cried the Elite closest to Mauv. "We seem to be digressing back into the absurd here."

"Dead Man's Pass?" Isaac repeated. "What do you think we want to do, kill another Santa Claus?"

It was a reply that didn't make Nick feel particularly good about the implication. "What is Dead Man's Pass?" the clueless boy asked nervously.

Isaac and Blaine looked to each other—and yet it was Starsky who beat them both to it. "It's only the Pole's highest mountain."

"You want me to race down the Pole's highest mountain?"

"Us. He wants us to sled race down the Pole's highest mountain," Mauv clarified with a slow-rolling explanation. "An idea as terrible as it is treacherous."

"It was once a popular sport," Isaac added. "That is until your father phased it out. In fact, he eventually banned sled racing altogether."

"Without getting too graphic," informed Blaine, beating Nick to his next question. "Let's just say—competitors were turning the ice red."

Nick grimaced. "Then why would I ever agree to such a thing? I say, we just release the prisoners as a one-time extended hand of mercy."

The best idea the boys ever had," Mauv piped in quickly. "What need is there to bring back such foolish traditions of sport?"

"None, that's what," added one of his yes-men.

"I'll tell you why," admitted Starsky, with the devil's advocate argument on ready. "Because as Cross here suggested, your constituents won't take kindly to the act of you just releasing a scoundrel." Isaac listened closely, letting Starsky resume with his logic unchallenged. "Believe me, you're gonna need a reason to grant his release, and a damn good one at that. If Mauv Lyman does, in fact, beat Nick here down the mountain, and yet lives to tell the tale," Starsky slowly spun to address the entire gathering—using hand motion to drive his idea home. "Then you grant him a full pardon. But if Nick wins … well. Let's just say, you lock the villain up and bury the key."

There was silence all around. Some of it, content, and some of it not—though not a soul countered the premise. And that included Mauv, who was forced to bite his lip to keep silent. The race, like it or not—was on.

Chapter 33

The mountain was misty, tall, narrow, and steep, with a curvy peak rising through the gray clouds. To Nick, it seemed like the entire Pole had joined in the caravan—at least as spectators. The white trail was now full of off-road vehicles, all with military grade tires. It was one after the next, winding around the snowy cliffs like a spiraling shell.

The grand marshal sat next to Isaac in the back of the limo-style cab, with Silva and Gib directly across. Nick wore a stretchy, long-sleeved tunic, and a vest of fur over that. The yak hair was coarse and fuzzy. An attractive designer knit hat covered his ears, with the strings dangling down over his chest.

"Does anyone … you know, have anything to say?" the boy desperately hoped to hear a story, maybe a joke, as the fact that even Gib was quiet made him uneasy.

But Gib shook awkwardly, as if having trouble playing games with the truth. Silva hated when he acted weird and clubbed him over the shoulder to prevent the loose cannon from saying something inappropriate for the moment.

"You're sending me to my grave, aren't you?" Nick uttered.

Vance

Silva's heart was softened by the sincerity. She turned to Isaac, suggesting he perhaps try and comfort the poor boy, though the Chief elected to take a different approach. "No," Isaac shrugged, less than convincingly. "You'll be fine."

"I wonder how that dirty crook's doing, anyhow," Gib shrugged, wanting to believe Lyman might be trembling violently.

"Look behind you," Isaac whispered with little emotion, his eyes fixed straight ahead.

Gib couldn't help but pull down the window, his mustache now blowing back in the blustery wind. He squinted in the heavy snowdrifts to behold Mauv standing proudly inside the roofless vehicle.

Nick gauged Gib's reaction, having to see for himself. Mauv was on a pedestal, his hands braced over a bar. Nick saw him waist-up—grinning ear-to-ear with a bright purple cape flapping in the wind. He was dressed for show, paraded alongside former Guards who had all been incarcerated just days before.

"As expected," Gib dipped back into the stretch car. "Clearly wetting his pants right now."

"He's raced and survived before, hasn't he?" Nick continued to prove he wasn't dumb.

The other's silence told Nick all he needed to know as everyone was suddenly bounced up off their seat by a loose rock. Isaac gripped Nick's arm to prevent an injury.

"What was that?"

"It means we're close," Isaac remained focused.

Nick grew dizzy as they spun up the last, narrow stretch for the top. Isaac was anxious to open the door, and despite the cold, couldn't wait to exit—if for nothing else to smell the fresh air again.

Inheriting the Sleigh

Nick peered out and down the endless line of vehicles, some with tires taller than he was. He felt the deep tread of his own car as elves began making their way up the last stretch of lonely mountain.

"Best of luck," said a disoriented elf in passing. Others offered him equally nervous glances on their way for Dead Man's Pass.

"Thanks ... I think," an increasingly nervous Nick stuttered back.

"C'mon," Isaac broke Nick's trance. "It's this way."

It was slick as they passed up the final set of stony steps. After turning a rocky corner, there it was. An elf in the front wiped a streak of snow off an unevenly cut sign fastened to a post—as if to make it official. The font was enough to frighten Nick, with "Man's Pass" covered up by powder, revealing only one unsettling word.

Nick watched Mauv skip like a boxer strutting toward the ring. His groupies hovered close. He looked like an arctic superhero in a costume of bright reds, blues, and greens. He dropped the goggles over his eyes as his comrades cinched up his gloves. Even Gib and Silva couldn't seem to keep their attention off the spectacle.

"Is it just me, or does he look like something straight out of a comic book gone wrong?" Silva smirked.

"Keep your eyes on me," Isaac had to pull Nick away from the circus by relocating his lost concentration. "All you need to worry about is getting down this mountain, understood?"

"I will say this," Gib piped in. "If you do make it down this beast of a bluff, you'll turn into an instant folk hero yourself." Both Isaac and Silva stared, as if to suggest, "not helping," with Isaac changing the subject as quickly as he knew how.

"OK, I think we're ready."

Nick's heart was beating so rapidly he hadn't even noticed the hoard of elves simultaneously packing their way into the oddly shaped bleachers welded into the front side of the rock. They were skiwampusly off-kilter, as if straight out of a Dr. Seuss book, but allowed spectators to get a decent view of the track below.

And there he was. Nick wanted to pummel Starsky right down the mountain for concocting the stupid idea to begin with. The rogue elf looked happy to be there as he staked out a good place.

"Let it go," Isaac pulled Nick's mind back from instinctively wanting to do what his body was already trying to. Instead, he was guided for the starting line, Silva assisting with his own goggles. Things were happening so rapidly that Nick wasn't even given the time to speak up—should he have a sudden change of heart.

A hip elf with a droopy patch of hair at the chin suddenly greeted the large crowd with a bullhorn. He reminded Nick of a mountain goat perched high on his cliff. "And Dead Man's Pass lives on!" his voice carried and echoed to a ruckus applause. "Welcome all, to the race of the century. Let me introduce our two high-profile, and need I say, daring contestants. To my left, he's a product of ancient Rome. The longest serving Speaker of the Elvish House, and currently on trial for attempted murrrrrrrrr-derrrrrrrrrrr!"

Mauv rolled his eyes, wishing that last part had been left out, but still managed to grin with cocky pride as he batted snow off his mittens. "A Scrooge if there ever was, but as shrewd a politician the Pole has ever seen!" This time he took the line as a compliment. "Maaaaaaauvtavious Lymaaaaaaaaan!" His last name echoed over the frosty mountaintop.

He was handed a small sled as Lyman stepped forward into the starting chute.

Nick, rather, was doing the best he could to block out the noise. He noticed elves not only filling every speck and crevice of the bleacher rows pressed up against the boulders, but cramming shoulder-to-shoulder on the outside of a rope corralling off the track as well.

"And to my right, his adolescent challenger!" The emcee resumed in his best voice. "He's the flesh and blood of the great Kris Kringle himself. An American citizen raised as the son of a multi-millionaire. The reigning Young Pianist of the Year, and the next Santa Clausssssssss!" The rockstar applause was starting to appeal to Nick. It was an adrenaline rush he had never quite felt before—one that even began to quell his nerves a bit. The elves were all on their toes with their fists pumping in the air. He was suddenly being treated, less like a concert pianist, and more like Bon Jovi.

"The last great hope for kids all across the world! Everyone stand on your feet for Saint Nicholas … Kringle!" The thin air got even thinner as the race announcer shouted his name.

Lyman shook, disgusted by the elated applause, while Silva handed him his sled. It was nothing fancy, with a wood base and red runners.

He stepped toward the starting chute that was little more than an old set of bars. It was obvious it hadn't been used in a while. A team of elves cleared some last remaining snow as the crowd was getting antsy. They were ready for the race.

"Happy trails, Santa Claus," Mauv antagonized with a departing snicker.

"Your instincts will try and convince you to brake!" Isaac yelled one last piece of advice into his ear over all the cheering and jeering. "Don't," he instructed. "Just keep going. Trust your sled around every turn. Got it?!" Nick just nodded. He was bundled up and having trouble seeing, with his goggles already fogged over. "OK then," Isaac paused, with one last reassuring nod. "We'll see you safely at the bottom then."

Vance

Isaac, Silva and Gib all slowly faded away into the hazy mountain drifts as Nick was left to process a series of life-consuming thoughts. If he really were ever to be the last great hope for kids all across the world, he would somehow have to survive what was coming next as the chute suddenly shot open. The sensation nearly took his breath away. Like it or not, Nick was plummeting down a steep embankment right next to Mauv—his cape lifting as he dropped alongside.

Nick was in control of the initial descent, but just as he was beginning to feel like everything might be alright, the Speaker stuck out his left arm. The subtle nudge wasn't much, but enough to send danger signals to his brain. The crowd noise was now just a muffle as Nick realized he was pouring right over a cliff.

"Don't brake, don't brake, don't brake, don't brake," he repeated with his eyes in a squint and his teeth tightly clenched. Nick's heart sank, with nothing but air any longer underneath his sled.

Seconds later, fresh powder spit up into his face, relieved to feel the surface again. He heard an encouraging roar from the crowd—but this time—Nick struggled to locate Mauv as he wiped a streak off his goggles.

Unsure whether he was now in the lead, or well behind, he continued to zig and zag around orange markers placed along the way. That is until he felt a tug at his sled. Lyman had reemerged from around a corner, clipping him from behind. It sent Nick spinning, and he quickly grew dizzy as Mauv turned back with a competitive fire.

Nick was forced to gather himself fast as he brushed past a prickly bush. The thick snow was now turning into an icy track, and he could feel the crowd getting nervous. He attempted to follow Mauv around a corner, before shooting inside the cavity of a rock. It was pitch dark—which wouldn't have bothered him much had he not been moving at an unnervingly swift pace.

Inheriting the Sleigh

A shard of light started small but quickly widened the closer he got to the cave's exit. A white fox darted in front as he whisked through a breathtaking grove of green. Nick wasn't sure how much track he had left, but even at intense speeds couldn't help but admire the beauty of the mountain. But again, the question kept coming back. "Where was Mauv?"

Flipping his head around, Nick couldn't see much anymore. No bleachers, no mountaintop, and no Speaker—just tree branches as he weaved in and out, around one corner and over the next. He did as instructed and never stopped, just kept riding the icy track. But there was only one problem. It looked like it was coming to an end tilting up into an incline, as if intended as a launchpad.

"Don't stop, don't stop, don't stop" his whispering repetition resumed. Taking the frosty ramp head-on, Nick soon generated air big enough to replicate a daredevil's stunt; but if there was another side to the track, Nick wasn't on pace to make it. He was plummeting right into a deep snowbank.

Crashing with a thump, the landing sent shockwaves to his body. His face took the brunt of it, and he wasn't stationary for long—Nick sliding uncontrollably down the mountainside. His sled since got caught over a bush, though he kept tumbling—then tumbled some more.

How long Nick was face down in the snow, he couldn't answer. A blurry light woke him from a slumber as he spit out a mouthful of ice pellets. The light had a red hue and hit him right between the sealed eyelids.

Nick instinctively held a hand up as a shield to block what felt bright even over his goggles, before dropping his neck again in fatigue. The truth was, it was easier to shut his eyes and just lie there. But the light was soon joined by a gentle nibble over the cheek. Nick concernedly shoved himself back as much as possible—apparent that a creature was now invading his personal space.

Though fuzzy, Nick yanked his goggles off and forced his eyes open. He could hear something sniffing and puffing and then felt a gentle poke. But it was the smell that eventually put his mind at ease—his nostrils having taken in that scent before. He reached his hand out, inadvertently grabbing onto the dipping antlers. Then, as the blur subsided, Nick could see the red light again. It was blinding.

"Rudolph?" There was no fear in Nick's voice. For some reason, he knew.

Rudolph bobbed her horns in excitement as Nick's eyes adjusted. Her nose wasn't black, but bright red, as if a small bulb had been twisted right into it. Her coat was dark around the face, off-white through the neck, and dark again at the back—but it was the nose that was captivating. Nick reached out a hand, and the reindeer responded, letting him stroke the underside of its mouth.

Nick was beginning to gather how much pain he was in as Rudolph started to scoot away. But the deer stopped once she realized that Nick wasn't following. Eventually getting the idea, he forced himself to his feet. Rudolph watched Nick stumble in the thick forest snow—retreating to help and eventually hunching down to scoop him up over her back. Nick helplessly hung on with one arm draped around Rudolph's fuzzy neck as she hauled him away through the dense foliage.

Nick had no idea where they were going but desperately could have used a hot drink or some fresh clothes.

The mountain trek extended for many minutes until a treeless valley opened in the distance. In the middle of the valley was an attractive red barn. A higher loft rose out the middle of the barn with small towers

Inheriting the Sleigh

shooting up out of that. Banners silhouetted with reindeer horns flapped in the wind from every corner of the attractive edifice.

Rudolph stepped foot from the brush, onto the trail leading for the barn's partially open sliding doors. Over a red carpet that ran up the middle of the barn's interior, new sets of antlers curiously poked through the stables on either side as the reindeer gently dropped to release Nick's weak frame. Everyone was clearly interested to see who had arrived.

Nick eyed each reindeer. It was his way of saying, "hello," but his mind was also beginning to de-cloud. Flashbacks of his rolling plummet down Dead Man's Pass were replaying backwards in his mind.

The other eight reindeer watched Rudolph, with her nose no longer glowing. She was affectionately sniffing up and down Nick's legs—her way of making a connection. Nick didn't hear, "What's wrong? Are you OK?" Nor anything else for that matter but did feel her concern.

"I don't know," he whispered out loud in response. "Perhaps not. I think I lost the race."

Chapter 34

L et's say you're crossing the Indian Ocean on your way for the mainland of Indonesia," Smudge whipped the glasses off his eyes. He was squinting wide as he continued his hypothetical. "What do you do?"

With his hand underneath his chin, Nick paused. He had an answer. "One, avoid Vietnamese airspace. Two, keep the defensive shield up and on the lookout for aerial pirates."

"And three?" Smudge turned his back, pacing the other way across his classroom.

"And three, keep the sleigh low. It's monsoon season in the South Pacific, and you must be prepared for an unexpected landing."

Smudge only hunched to deliver his approval before moving on to another scenario. "Flying into modern-day North Korea would be suicidal for anyone. And yet, you'll find a way. Why?"

"Because I'm Santa Claus," Nick mumbled with his bored forehead pressed down against his desk.

"That's right," said Smudge in his own brand of hypnosis. "And Santa Claus can do anything. According to Mr. Corbin Creel's recently updated database, there are precisely 9,007 closet Christians within the borders of the DPRK. You are the only thing in life they have to look forward to. But if you get caught delivering gifts inside North Korea, what happens?"

"I die?" Nick was quick and monotone with his reply.

"Certainly true, heaven forbid," Smudge shrugged. "But if you do … then so does the recipient. Or at least sending them to spend the rest of their days in some squalid prison camp somewhere."

With his head now back up off his desk—Nick gulped at the thought—sick by the immense pressure. Smudge let him mull it over a bit before continuing. "Alrighty, ready for the lightning round?" Nick said nothing in a mild spell. "In England, they call you?"

"Father Christmas." Though monotone, he didn't skip a beat.

"In France?"

"Pere Noel."

"The Republic of China legally let you in when?"

"1992."

"And what is that called?"

"The Treaty of Sheng dan lao ren."

"What percent of the Chinese expect your presence on Christmas Eve?" Or is that … presents? I never do tire of that one," Smudge loved to throw out an occasional pun.

"1.2 percent, give or take a thousandth of a percent."

"And where do the children's stockings turn to wood?"

"Holland, Professor Smudge. They place their shoes out instead."

Smudge paused, as if impressed by Nick's quick memory. He wanted to stump him. "The time difference between Chicago and Budapest?"

Nick didn't hesitate. "Seven hours."

"Montreal to Sydney?"

"15."

Vance

"Which reindeer has the gassy problem?" Smudge lifted an eye.

"Comet. Keep the carrots to a minimum, and I should probably bring him down in Madagascar—then again somewhere between Peru and Ecuador for a potty break."

Smudge, in a wrinkly T-shirt and ugly purple blazer finally stopped his line of questioning; instead, clapping with pride, as if impressed by his own efforts as well. His golden bangs were as out of control as ever. "Very good indeed, my boy. I never in a millennium thought I would say this, but you are well ahead of schedule ... I must say."

But there was no pride or excitement. Nick rather looked exhausted and concerned, with his glazed eyes lost in Smudge's sloppy penmanship. "Are you ready for the hardest test of your life?" was scribbled over and over again on the chalkboard.

"I also must say, I'd expect a little more pep from someone who just aced one of my examinations. I'd have to check my records to be sure, but perhaps a first. And that's going back to the Salem Witch Trials."

"I'm sorry, Professor," Nick stood, finally ready to open up. "It's just that ... I'm the laughingstock of the Pole right now."

"Laughingstock of the Pole?" Smudge squinted. His portly and oddly shaped frame, with trousers that never seemed to fit right, scooted closer to Nick's desk. "Whatever do you mean, boy?"

"I mean—not only did I lose the race, I didn't even finish it," Nick wiped some sweat off his forehead. It pained him to imagine Mauv celebrating at the bottom, all while he was being rescued by a reindeer.

Terpley signaled Nick to have a seat—apparent that he had something to say. Only this time there was less quirk and more wisdom. "The truth is," he put his glasses back on. "That nobody with even an ounce of sanity really expected you to ever win that race."

Nick perked an ear. "Nobody expected me to what?"

Inheriting the Sleigh

"That's right," Smudge pulled his bangs back in almost a flippant way. "Not a one. The former Speaker has lived a long life. He's a savvy and shrewd politician, let alone sled racer."

"Then why did I ever …?"

"Ever what?" Smudge held out an arm. "Risk your life … and your pride?"

Nick said nothing in emotional defeat. "Yeah."

"That's just it, good ol' Saint Nick. Technically, you did win that race."

"OK, if you're trying to confuse me, Professor Smudge …"

Terpley stopped him before he could say another word—taking his small, pudgy fingers and gripping Nick's face like an obtrusive aunt at Thanksgiving. "Why, you're alive, aren't you?"

"Am I?" the boy was suddenly forced to grip both wrists, slowly prying them off his cheeks.

Smudge continued in a slow and soft drawl. "The fact that you're still breathing right now says to me that you won and won big. Does it not?"

Nick slowly stood from his chair again, this time approaching a window where boisterous chatter was heard on the other side of the walls. He stared down into Sleigh Bell Street, all while pondering Smudge's analysis.

Horns honked as a band of former Elite Guards stirred up a scene below. They were parading in from the cross streets of Blitzen Boulevard and Manger Way.

"Oh yes, what a wondrous celebration," Smudge got his own look. The working elves on the street could only stand and watch as Elites arrogantly waved in passing. But Terpley didn't seem as bothered by it as Nick was, instead smiling from his birds-eye perch.

"Why is that amusing?" Nick finally mustered up the courage to ask.

Smudge hunched. "I tend to chuckle whenever someone is having a good time. Don't you?"

Nick's eyes rolled, though he wanted to bang his skull against his desk. Terpley changed the subject. "Do you know what today is?"

Nick shook. "Honestly, with the whole 24 hours of darkness and light thing around here, my sense of calendar and time has always been a little out of whack."

"Why, it's the 25th of September, Nick," said Terpley pointing to a calendar on the wall.

"The 25th of September," he uttered. "But I just ..."

"Got here? And yet we only have three months left." Nick needed a moment to mull it over, quickly growing even more anxious by the thought. "But don't worry," his attempt to calm Nick down was working. "As I said before ... you're ahead of schedule."

"Right ... ahead of schedule."

"And yet, so much more to learn."

"Right, plenty more to learn," Nick was suddenly entranced again.

Smudge grabbed his coat from a rack and handed Nick his—followed by a scarf, hat, and gloves. "Here, you'll definitely need these."

"Where are we going?" Nick wondered as Smudge had since hopped up to pull down a dangling string in the ceiling. A collapsible ladder was suddenly folding toward the floor.

Terpley turned as Nick was still racing to zip up. "Oh, one of my favorites, Nick. Chimney training."

Nick's eyes suddenly widened. For some reason, all this time he had failed to even consider having to go down a chimney. Smudge by now was already well up the ladder, with Nick forced to catch up. They continued climbing through a narrow, square hole; a hundred feet maybe until eventually spotting some natural light at the very top of the PTC.

The roof was vast, though not much to look at. There were some solar panels and exhaust fans. Here and there was a locked-up mechanical closet, with occasional railing for support.

Pulling himself the last of the way through, Nick dusted himself off. He swatted away at a cobweb or two, peering side-to-side in the brisk air. He was looking for Smudge, but with barriers in the way, couldn't seem to find him.

"C'mon," Terpley retreated with his head back above the surface, before descending another metal ladder. Nick caught up, following down onto a lower level. They turned a few corners along an edge, before rounding what looked like a greenhouse. Down a few more steps was a section of nothing but chimneys.

"Here we are," Smudge excitedly raised both arms out wide. Nick followed down the steps, slowly weaving through and around each one.

"There are certainly a lot of chimneys here," he observed. Each one was different. Some standard, others not so much. Even some a little bizarre.

"There are 195 countries across the world," Smudge informed. "Well, 196 if you count Taiwan. And that means a lot of different ways to ventilate a fire."

The traditional red brick rested in the middle of them all, but there were others Nick had never seen before. Varied sizes and widths, shapes, and materials. Nick stroked a thin, circular aluminum pipe, wondering how anyone bigger than a small child would ever fit through it. There was an adobe-style clay chimney next to that, with another made up of ground-up glass. Chimneys of color stood out—many painted in bright shades of red, orange, and yellow. Nick approached one. It was shaped like a mushroom, oddly bulging out near the tip.

"What do you think?" Smudge was a child in a candy store.

"What do I think? They're … nice," he moved onto another smokestack, but had a hard time sharing the professor's enthusiasm. "I guess."

"Fire has been around for many a good moon, you know. Since that very first lightning strike, in fact. And that means a long time for warming feet, hearts, and hands," said Terpley following behind Nick as he continued to weave through the tens, if not hundreds of chimneys. "A combination of oxygen and fuel sustaining life. But then man soon found a way to contain and infiltrate that natural, God-given element inside our own homes. Hence … the chimney," he dramatically waved a hand to unveil what stood before them.

Nick turned back toward a still-grinning Smudge. "But I'm assuming you didn't bring me up here just to tell me all that."

Smudge defogged his glasses. "Impatient, are we?"

"So, what do I do now?"

"Take your pick."

"My pick?"

"That's right. They're all fair game."

Nick's squint was uneasy at best. "Meaning you want me to … jump?"

"Certainly. That's what you do, isn't it? You are Santa Claus, after all."

"Right. Santa Claus," he mumbled, stopping in front of another chimney. It was cobbled and square with a wide base. He leaned over to glance inside but could see nothing. "It's all dark." Smudge just nodded as Nick slowly scooted up onto the concrete edge. "But I can't just …"

Inheriting the Sleigh

"Sure, you can," Smudge gave him a little unexpected tap from behind. It was all that was needed to send Nick plummeting.

He screamed as he suddenly felt himself descending into an unknown abyss, only to soon land onto a moving slide. Nick continued to twist and turn in the pitch black, before dropping the last few feet.

Patting at his startled heart, Nick covered his mouth, coughing from all the soot and ash kicked up from the rough landing.

Irritated to say the least, he gathered himself. As his eyes settled in, he could finally see some light. Nick winced in pain, while slowly stepping out of the fireplace and onto an attractive stone ledge. One more short jump to the floor succeeded that, before a sudden noise made him turn. It was a velvet red bag barreling down from behind, kicking up even more charcoaled dust. Nick hesitantly looked up into the pitch blackness. He quickly reached for the bag to pull it out, with toys spilling out the top.

He noticed he was now inside a living room. A cozy one with just enough light. Decorative candles were lit on the mantle over hung stockings. In fact, the entire room spewed Christmas cheer. A ten-foot, fully decorated tree was pressed up against the wall—one full of wrapped gifts underneath—though all Nick wanted to do was lie down over the soft, leather sofa that enveloped the room.

"Is it just me, or is he injured?" asked Blaine with his attention glued to a series of monitors showing every angle.

"Definitely limping," Corbin observed as Nick slowly hobbled over to sit down on the nearest accent chair. "Might have sprained an ankle during landing."

"Can he shake it off, that's the question," Blaine curiously whispered inside the small room—intently spying on Nick's every move. He was taking notes. "Because let's be honest—an ankle sprain is all its gonna take to throw off a rookie during Operation Return."

Corbin turned to Blaine in agreement, blowing a large bubble with gum that eventually popped all over his face once it got too large.

They'd only taken their eyes off the monitors for seconds, at most, but Nick was no longer resting. "Where'd he go?" Blaine squinted.

"Number three," Corbin rolled his chair over, pointing to a new camera. Nick was pacing about the room in a dark corner, holding his head.

"I think he's beginning to feel something," Blaine stared at Corbin, who simply smiled back. A focused glaze took over Nick's eyes as he was attempting to figure out what was going on inside him. "I'm calling the Chief," Blaine immediately grabbed a red phone on the wall. "I would get over here if I were you," he advised as Isaac was quick to pick up.

Nick, for the first time turned his attention to the sack of gifts. He dumped the pile of toys out over an ivory rug to see what he was working with. He was looking for something in particular.

"What's he doing!?" an anxious Isaac soon burst through the door—searching for the right monitor.

"I think he knows," said Blaine.

"What house number?"

Corbin handed him a laptop. "1,698,525,442."

"Littleton, Colorado," Isaac read what was pulled up on the screen.

Nick was now holding a toy in each hand. "Looks like he's narrowed it down to two," Blaine observed. A classic, All-American doll with a ponytail and cheerleading outfit was in his right. A brown doll in tanned leather in his left.

Nick held up the cheerleader, but his eyes were clouded by uncertainty. "He knows it doesn't feel right," said Isaac.

Inheriting the Sleigh

"Who's the little girl?" Blaine inquired. Isaac showed him a screen that Nick didn't have access to.

"Nara Norris," Isaac read. "Age nine. 75 percent Cherokee. And the only thing she's asked for this Christmas …"

"Of course," Blaine nodded as Nick gently set the Pocahontas-style doll, with slits in the sleeves underneath the tree.

Chapter 35

Isaac sat directly across from Mauv. "So … you asked me to meet you."

"Yes. And to my mild surprise you showed up," Lyman returned in a pink and yellow checkerboard suit—tailormade.

"Well, your persistence paid off. You badgered me into it more times than I can count." Isaac had both arms crossed inside the semi-dark room. "So … talk."

"Hasty," Mauv had a cane resting at his side and a matching handkerchief in his coat pocket.

"You've had your moment, and there's no reason to take this personally … but I don't have time for you."

"Perhaps you should make some. Remember, I won the race."

"Which means you temporarily escaped incarceration," Isaac reminded. "More than reward enough. It doesn't mean you can start calling shots again."

Isaac had struck a nerve as Mauv glared back. "Perhaps you underestimate how much influence I still wield around here."

Inheriting the Sleigh

Isaac laughed, which Mauv certainly did not appreciate. "You need to be more specific. Causing mischief? Sure, you can do that, but we all know your power all but doesn't exist anymore."

Mauv watched Isaac stand. He couldn't remain silent for long or risked cutting the conversation short. "As two men who have wielded their share of power in the past, let's talk then. Three months' time will be here before we know it."

"Agreed," Isaac surprised him by sitting again.

"And yet, still plenty of time to abandon this mission. The world remains uncertain we're coming," Mauv picked up a remote from a small wooden table, turning on a television set fastened to the wall. Wolf Blitzer was reporting in studio.

"We now join correspondent Donna Brass down in Philadelphia. Donna, you've been following this all year. What's the vibe there right now as folks start to think about the holiday season again?"

"Yeah, Wolf," said Brass with the CNN bug in the bottom corner. "I'm here at the grand opening of a new, state-of-the-art Toy World debuting in the brand-new refurbished section of downtown Philly. "This has been in the works for about four years now, long before the unexpected disappearance of Santa Claus last December. Now as you can see," the camera pulled away from the reporter and onto a long line parallel to a city street. "Many have been patiently waiting to get in, including these folks here."

"Hi," said a mother with twins at her side—a boy and a girl.

"Can I ask how long you've been waiting?"

"Oh, since about five this morning."

"Five?"

"Yeah, the kids have all seen the commercials, and the first 500 in receive a free giftbag. So, I said, 'why not'. We're hoping we make it. I hear it's gonna be close," the mother laughed as the twins shied away from the camera.

"And if you don't mind me asking, what's the mood like with your family right now? You know, with Christmas just a few short months out?"

"Well," her optimism seemed to all but disappear. "Not great. You know ...," she tipped her head down toward her toddlers, clinging to each leg.

"Of course," said Brass with a human look of remorse.

The screen then popped with static fuzz, transitioning to another news team. "Many Brits here in the south London area have signed a petition to cancel Christmas," said a male reporter with an English accent next to the River Thames. "Here it is, and as you can see," the petition unraveled toward his feet. "There are hundreds, perhaps even thousands of signatures, all in protest of what they see as an overly commercialized holiday not worth celebrating any longer. Perhaps Christmas has finally reached its shelf life."

The static broke again. "Mate, what is your name?"

"Mick. Mick Hackett."

"And what are you doing here, Mick?" asked the intrusive reporter.

"I'm feed'n the crocs, just like everyone else," he said from a dock overlooking a swamp. The dock was full of rugged men, each carrying long poles.

"I see that. But why the Santa hats attached to the poles?"

The man with camouflage pants and cutoff sleeves, stuck a fish inside the hat, dangling it down into a swarm of hungry crocodiles.

"'Cause it's sweet as," he smiled giddily, just as a croc lunged to rip away the golden perch. He was chewing away at the red hat as the feisty reptile tore away the fabric to gather the squirming fish between its jaws.

"But isn't that a little sacrilegious?" the reporter inquired with a raised voice to be heard over all the competing noise.

"I don't even know what that means, mate," the man anxiously stuck another hat onto the pole. He had a whole bucket full, with another bucket of fish next to that.

"I mean, disrespectful perhaps?"

"Disrespectful?" he perked up to meet the reporter in the eye. "The jolly man didn't even show up last year. Talk about disappointment. You weren't the one that had to explain it to the little ankle biters."

The TV suddenly shut off as Isaac made a dash for the remote. "I wasn't done making my point," an annoyed Mauv, cried.

But Isaac wasn't happy either. "Why are you showing me this? You above anyone would know I have a fairly good handle on what's going on across the world. In fact, that's precisely my job."

"And yet you're in denial."

"Denial of what?"

"Of the truth!" Mauv raised his voice.

"Look, the people are not expecting Santa Claus to show up this year. This is our chance to change course and go another direction. Don't you think the very descendants of Asher himself deserve that?"

Isaac this time didn't have a quick reply. He acted as if what Mauv said actually carried a little weight. "Perhaps. But this isn't about what we want. This is about what God wants. This is his holiday after all; and like it or not, we're the ones tasked with the responsibility."

Mauv toned it down a little. "What God wants? If there are three words Kris never stopped repeating, it was those." He softly bit his lip, annoyed by the thought.

Vance

"Whatever happened to you anyway?" Isaac asked as Mauv paced about the small room. "I don't know your complete history with Kris, but I think I know enough."

"Do you now?"

"I know you followed him here."

"Which has extended my life by thousands of years, by the way."

"Some would consider that a gift."

"Don't count me among them. I should have tasted death in the first century."

"So that's why you're bitter?" Isaac clarified. "Because you're not dead like he is?"

Mauv turned to face Isaac. "No," he shook.

"We can pretend for as long as you like, but I think we both know exactly what it is. The kid boils your skin."

Mauv blew off the thought, soon admitting it indirectly. "Come now, the whippersnapper couldn't even beat me down Dead Man's Pass. And suddenly, he's stepping into the boots of Kris Kringle himself? Please," he scoffed.

"You don't believe in predestined callings, do you, Mauvtavious?"

Mauv since took a seat again, staring at a wall. "I don't know what you're talking about."

"The original Twelve … do you really think they just happened to be in and around the holy city at the time of Christ, by mere chance? And that includes John. You say that Nick can't do this," Isaac looked straight-facedly. "And I say, he's the only one who can. You can cherry-pick events across the globe all you like—but the truth is, if we don't make it this Christmas … we'll never again gain the trust of the people. This is our one shot."

Chapter 36

Nick sat on the edge of his velvet couch. The sofa had large, brass buttons along the top and sides. Old, dusty *Life* magazines rested on a coffee table over a well-used rug— one of them with a mushroom cloud cover, dated August 1945. The long forest-green drapes were down, exposing only a shard of light as Nick slowly spun an old tan globe with the base resting on the table. Once he made it 360 degrees around, he spun it again to absorb every detail.

Meanwhile, the cottage fire—one that oddly never seemed to die continued to burn inside the stone pit. It was underneath the long mantle with imprints of reindeer chiseled into the centuries-old wood. Nick was bored. The popping embers were soothing, but this time he was forced to pull his head up. A face was slowly forming in the fire. Nick should have been frightened, but at this point was used to experiencing strange things. He stood, slowly approaching the bright orange flames. Nick shielded his own face from the heat as a mature male with a trimmed beard and drooping hat was now staring his way.

Nick rubbed his eyes, guessing he might be hallucinating. The face was smiling and blew a stream of thick smoke out his mouth, all before morphing from a face into a full-body view. Kris Kringle then reached inside his shirt pocket, pulling out a smoky image of an old key. He placed the key between his teeth, slowly pointing upward, before dissolving away just as quickly as he came.

Nick knew the outline in the flames was his father, and in a cough approached the mantle. It had a series of old, decorative pieces mixed in with strands of pine. A framed painting of John conversing with Jesus, was propped next to carved figurines of the Wise Men on camelback. But in the direct center of the mantle—at the very spot where Kris had pointed was a glass lantern. And inside the lantern was a half-used candle.

Curious, Nick carefully opened it, reaching his hand inside. He pulled the candle out, only to be met by dripping wax. He examined the candle to find nothing unusual; that is until he flipped it upside down. A rusty, dark brown key was molded into the underbelly. Nick pulled it out, with the imprint of the key now all that remained in the wax. But what was it for?

The cottage was generally so quiet that any noise, no matter how faint caught his ear. He knew he was starting to hear something. "The train," he whispered, while quickly tucking the key inside one of his jean pockets to hurry up the creaky steps.

It took a few seconds, but the miniature red and black steam engine soon made an appearance through its hole in the top corner of the master bedroom. Nick watched the locomotive roll through the snowy tracks for the woodland station. The engineer pulled on the brake to bring it to a halt near the bench and lamppost.

"Mail for Nick Kringle!" the conductor announced.

He raised a hand, only to hear the conductor cough into his fist. "Uh hum." But the soldier in the mail car continued to snore. "I said, uh hum!" The conductor's wakeup call from the lead car was loud enough this time to wake him from the slumber.

"Oh, sorry, Boss," he jolted up, standing half-asleep in a salute.

"At ease, soldier," the conductor slowly muttered in frustration, rolling his eyes at the same time. He waved his synthetic green hand toward an awaiting Nick.

"Of course," he searched for the stack, only to suddenly freeze in place. The conductor again patted his forehead in disbelief as the engineer scaled over the couplers transitioning the cars, to see what had happened.

"Looks like a dead battery, sir," said the engineer. "He must not have been properly charged overnight. I'll conduct an internal review."

"Time to head on back to base then," he said as they began to ready the train. "But before I forget," the soldier finally delivered the fresh stack— one bound together by twine.

Nick flipped through it like a financially strapped worker in search of his bi-weekly check, but as usual, there was nothing of interest. He was hoping for a clue that might coincide with the key he'd just found.

"Were you expecting something?" the conductor sensed something wrong.

"I guess ... not," he mumbled.

"Wait," cried the engineer. "Looks like there is one more here. The slippery thing must have fallen right off the pile."

Nick fully expected to see another donation request mailer, but this one looked noticeably different from a piece of mass mail. It was a normal envelope with a stamp of the twin towers, and a handwritten address in the top left corner. In the center was a familiar name and city.

Nick Crest: North Pole

Vance

But it was the name in the top-left that jumped out like a searing flame. Seeing **Marie Bayliff** spelled out in familiar handwriting nearly melted his homesick heart.

He looked up to see the conductor and engineer still staring. They were taken by the emotion from the way he held the envelope. He hadn't said a thing, and yet, Nick's eyes spoke for him. "You're free to go now," the boy hinted.

"Of course," the engineer fired up the shiny locomotive. "Much business to perform, as you well know."

As the train disappeared through the hole in the opposite corner, Nick was anxious to plop onto his canopy bed to rip into the envelope. He lit a lamp before pulling out a handwritten note and picture. It was he and Marie ice skating in Central Park. He stared at Marie longer than normal before propping the photo up against the lamp near the framed picture of his mother.

Dear Nick, it began. I pray earnestly this letter finds you. First, alive—and second, well. Apparently, there's no specific address for the North Pole. And believe me when I tell you, I've looked. Just like when I was a little girl, I trust it finds its way there—somehow.

A lot has happened in 9 months. I regret to tell you your parents have separated, though I guess that's only the beginning. The drugs and abuse continued—your father finally forced into custody over the summer. His fate is now a waiting game with court in recess.

But now the good part. I wanted to be the first to wish you a happy birthday. It's coming so quickly. Stepping onto that ship, I don't know if you'd assumed you saw the last of me yet—but perhaps we just might see each other again.

Inheriting the Sleigh

Nick's emotional dam nearly burst after seeing the trademark smiley face next to Marie's name. In fact, the only thing that contained the floodwater was an interruption at the cottage door. A knock that was quickly followed by another. Nick quietly inched down the creaky steps to peak through the peephole, only to see two elves he didn't recognize. They were slender—their suits pressed. He made them knock again before finally building up the courage to open it.

"Hello," Nick only inched it forward, with the chain still in place.

"Nick Kringle."

"Yes," he hurried to hide his remaining tears.

"The name's Agent Cumberly," he hastily flipped open a badge. "And this is Agent Moose," he pointed to the taller elf with shaggy hair—though each was shorter than Nick.

"And why are you here?" he asked to Isaac's replayed warning to be careful who you trust.

"Can we … you know, come in?" the elf did his best to see through the small gap between the door and chain, barely able to make out Nick's eyes. "It's pertinent."

Nick took a few seconds to think and gather himself before removing the chain. The two agents instinctively glanced behind them before stepping in to meet Nick inside the entryway. "Who are you?" he finally asked.

"We're E.I, sir."

"E.I.?"

"That's right. Elvish Intelligence."

"Elvish Intelligence. I don't understand. Is something …"

Vance

"I'm sorry to inform you, but we believe your life may be in … immediate danger." Cumberly's voice was brought to a whisper.

"In all due respect, my life has been in danger since the moment I got here." But Nick's nerves soon jumped by a sudden rustle in the nearby trees.

"Get down!" instructed Cumberly, with a mustache and part through his slick, black hair. The other agent, Moose, quickly pulled a large gun out from underneath his coat. It was bright orange—and like others he'd seen—looked more like a Nerf toy than something law enforcement might use. But Nick knew it was real and ready to prove fatal as Moose dropped to one knee with his eye pinned to the scope.

"Have you ever felt like you've been … you know, watched?" Cumberly inquired.

"Watched?" Nick's confusion bled through as Cumberly was now treating him like a threatened president, shielding his body near the door.

"I think he's gone," Moose interrupted, standing back up again. "Probably a spy."

"Yeah, you've had company in and out of this property for days now. See these?" Cumberly pointed to the shoeprints near some thick bushes.

"What do they want?"

"What do they want?" Moose repeated. "They want you gone, that's what."

Nick froze. "And who are they?"

"I assume, elements of the old Elitist Guard. Yeah, from now on, I don't think you have a choice. You're going to need a protection detail."

"Who sent you here anyway?" Nick didn't like the sound of any of it as another rustle caused Moose to immediately pull his gun back out, the barrel tucked tightly into his chest. But a white snow owl shooting out of the weeds proved a false alarm.

"Look, are you sure this is necessary?" All Nick wanted to do was get back to his letter and perhaps find out the true purpose of the mysterious key.

But another rustle cut Nick off. "Go, take a look," Cumberly instructed Moose. He obliged, but hesitantly. Nick and Agent Cumberly followed him over the stone walkway and eventually out the front gate. Moose pulled another object out from underneath his coat—this one a long, white stick with a handle and red light at the tip. He rubbed it against the surface like a treasure hunter searching for lost coins. Nick expected nothing to happen, but sure enough, the gadget suddenly started beeping—enough to give Moose and Cumberly instant concern.

"We gotta move!" cried Cumberly as he pulled Nick's arm for the snowy banks outlining the pathway. An explosion rocked their eardrums as they dove into the fresh snow. The force took them further than they could have gone on their own, with kicked-up powder burying their exposed faces on its way down.

Cumberly was the first to pull his head up, yanking both Nick and Moose up by the hair. They were disheveled, confused and breathing heavily from fright.

"What just happened?" Nick asked, banging cold flakes out his ears.

"A snow mine. As expected," Cumberly quickly jumped back to his feet. "They've tampered with the property."

Agent Moose pulled his gun. He had broad shoulders and thick hair that hung halfway down his neck. "This way!" said Moose as they all trudged through several feet of snow—until meeting the road ahead.

Vance

Nick was now sandwiched in between the two agents on the run though had no idea where they were going. The road was secluded and quiet. "What is it?" Nick wondered why Moose had suddenly stopped.

"They're coming this way," Moose flipped his free hair back as a loud engine could be heard beyond some trees.

"What now!" Nick was no longer patient. "Can't we call for help or something?"

"Sure," Cumberly pulled out a colorful gadget—one the shape and length of an old cordless telephone. "But even if we did, they wouldn't get here in time."

"Then what do we do? Run?" Nick stared off into a wilderness to either side.

"Sure, we could run," Moose said. "Or we could look for a slightly more comfortable alternative." Moose pulled the white stick out again as the band of engines was growing louder. "If my memory serves me," said Moose, as Cumberly nervously looked for any sign of the trouble he knew was well on its way. "There should be a sewer lid somewhere around here."

"If memory serves you?" Cumberly stared as Moose pointed the wand at the ground. "And how would you possibly know that?"

"I'll save it for another time," said Moose as a sound—one quite different from before started to alert him to exactly what he was looking for.

"C'mon, follow it!" Cumberly cried with the incoming vehicle too close for comfort. Once again, they trudged off-road in a game of "hot and cold" to a noise that sounded like a sound effect from an old video game.

Inheriting the Sleigh

"Ugh, there they are! And we're outnumbered," Nick warned as a vehicle turned a bend in the road—one that led to a dead-end. It looked like a military Jeep designed for the backcountry.

"Quick, drop!" Cumberly instructed with a hush as all three of them were now lying still and face-up in the snow. They sank a bit, hoping not to be seen as the car passed along the road.

Freezing, Nick was the first to jump back to his feet, with the vehicle far enough ahead to where he felt safe using his voice again.

"Ugh, this cavalcade isn't done," said Cumberly with another vehicle trailing behind.

"It's gotta be right around here ... somewhere," Moose waved an imaginary circle around his body, with the alarm continuing to beep.

"Quick ... dig!" Cumberly cried as they scooped whatever snow they could out from near their feet. Nick pulled his face back with a squint as his eyes got struck by a flying wad of frosty powder.

"I think I found it." The agent's hand felt the metal plate. Cumberly reached to pull up the lid, only to fall backwards. Blood was now splattered everywhere in a vivid contrast to the solid white.

"Agent Cumberly!" Nick cried, hopping over to help—though Moose, for his own protection pulled him back.

"He's gone!" Moose informed. "Here, help me with this!" The two desperately pulled up on the heavy lid together. "Get in!" Moose waved down with a connecting medal ladder leading for an abyss.

Nick ducked as he jumped down for the top rung. "Here, take my hand," Nick offered to assist Moose, whose body was suddenly timbering right toward him. But there was no control in the descent as a red wound had since punctured the sizeable agent's chest. Seconds later, Moose landed at the bottom of the hole with a heavy splash.

Vance

Unable to see what awaited at the bottom, Nick was mortified but managed to reach up with all his might to pull down on the lid. It was now unnervingly black.

Chapter 37

Wet and shivering, it was his Gethsemane moment. All Nick could do was put one sopping foot in front of the other, up and over the shallow slosh inside the dark tunnel. And even worse, he knew his pursuers weren't far behind. But Nick could handle the rest—just as long as he had some light—even a glimmer.

A speck finally appeared in the distance. He didn't hesitate to follow it, picking up speed. His boots splashed up as he ran, just hoping the light would soon lead to more. And it did—building up to a flame the size of his fist.

"Excuse me. Is someone there?" Nick desperately asked in a stuttering shiver. He rubbed away the distortion from his eyes but could see nothing, only a lit candlestick hovering in midair. "Anyone?"

Nick vaguely heard echoing chatter behind him and didn't have time to keep asking himself questions regarding the oddity. He walked over and put a hand over the candle, waving it around and embracing the newfound light. He ran again, knowing the splashing was certainly giving him away.

Vance

"Hurry!" the tracking voices moved at the same frantic pace. Nick slipped, holding up the candle as high as he could to avoid putting out the flame in the knee-high water. Thrusting back up to his feet, his whole body was now wet—nearly to the point where he couldn't carry on another step. His desperation willed him forward to a fork that split off into two separate tunnels. He stopped, wondering what to do.

"I'm curious. Why do you hesitate?" asked a man he did not recognize—inconspicuously resting on a floating log in the middle of the fork.

"What?" Nick's frightened eyes shot down to pinpoint exactly who was speaking to him; first and foremost, to determine whether the voice was a threat. The man was dressed in little more than drenched rags and was gruff and unshaven around the chin and cheeks. But he had a smile that was genuine and unintimidating.

"You knew which way to go, and yet you hesitated. Why?"

Nick was as baffled as ever. Unsure whether he should play the stranger's game—or keep worrying about the danger moving fast in his wake. "Why do you assume I know anything?" Nick inquired, with his frigid arms wrapped around his wet shoulders.

"You are Santa Claus, are you not?" the man hunched.

"I'm sorry. Who are you?" Nick could hardly refrain from asking any longer.

He simply smiled in return before changing the subject. "You're worried about them, aren't you?" he pointed.

"Them?" Nick turned back, and then forward again with the echoes growing louder and louder with time. "You better believe it. I've been told they want to kill me."

"Kill you?" The man hunched, as if unafraid of anything. "Interesting. Unfortunately, that is a reality I myself am all too familiar with," he said. "But why would they ever want to do that? You seem like such a nice boy."

"I don't know," Nick suddenly found himself being soothed when he should have been growing more concerned. "Perhaps, because … I believe in Christmas."

The man with large brown eyes and an endearing fuzz around his lips, smiled again. "You do much more than just believe in Christmas. You are Christmas."

Nick tried not to blush and instead stared as deep as possible into the veering, off-chute tunnels. "You asked earlier about my first instinct," he said, keeping his head up. "But the truth is, I'm not sure I remember having one."

"Sure, you did," said the mystery man. "You just gave into that small fraction of your brain consumed by so many other voices, that's all."

"Other voices?"

"That's right. Thousands of them." An intrigued Nick slowly veered back over the log. Nick was all ears. "You know what I'm talking about, don't you?"

"Yes," he admitted.

"Do you know who they are?" The boy said nothing in a puzzled fog. "Or let me put it this way. Do you want to?"

Nick's response wasn't immediate. "Perhaps," he shook slowly and methodically—still very much distracted.

"They're the voices of desperate children, Nick. Children from all over the world. Children who see you as their only hope. But there are certainly times when it is necessary and appropriate to block all those voices out," added the stranger. "Because there's another voice you must also pay attention to."

"Another voice?" Nick was confused.

"Yes. It is called the Spirit of God. And it has already told you which way to go."

"It did? I didn't mean to miss it," said Nick in a childlike submission of error. "It's just that I honestly didn't hear anything."

The stranger failed to respond. "Mr.?" Nick looked down, only to see the man had since vanished. But he couldn't dwell on the disappearance for long, snapping from a mild daze. The splashing was right around the corner.

Nick took one last glance at the fork in the tunnel, but this time it was brief. There was little hesitation as he dashed right. Still holding the candle, he ran with a new energy and didn't stop.

"C'mon! He's been here!" Nick, this time, heard his hasty pursuers clear as day.

Chapter 38

Tell me you have a sighting," Isaac frantically signaled Corbin, who only shook as he barreled into the room.

"Not since last night."

Blaine followed into the glowy interior. "Don't worry, the rest of the snow mines have all been disabled," Blaine stuck out a hand, getting the news out before Isaac could follow up with the obvious. "Curnuckle's got E.I stationed all around Cottage One."

"Here," Gib rolled up a chair. He gripped Isaac by the shoulders, forcing him to sit. "Take a breath."

But that didn't last long. "How many minutes now?"

A much calmer Ezra poked his head out from behind a square machine, one with many blinking lights. "118,601," he glanced down at his watch with the rolling time.

Isaac gasped. "Just under 2,000 hours left till Christmas and we can't even find Santa Claus."

Meanwhile, Blimm was fidgeting in seclusion from a nearby station. The awkward elf was eavesdropping on every word, before soon, unable to stay silent any longer. "And what if he's dead?" he popped up over a cubicle wall, proposing to a collective stare. Blimm adjusted his glasses and flipped a loose string of bangs up off his forehead as he endured the lull in the exchange.

"Why would you ever say that, boy?" said an aghast Gib.

Blimm stuttered. "For starters, it's no secret I was the last one to actually hear Father Kringle speak before ... well, you all know what I'm ... getting at," he was anxious to start slapping away at his keyboard again.

"Isn't he still an intern?" Gib quietly shielded his eyes from Blimm, pointing with a back-tilting thumb.

"He's not dead," Isaac broke his silence. "But time isn't the only thing we're fighting right now. Because truth is, if we don't find him soon—Blimm here might actually be onto something."

A chime broke up the concern. "I'll get it," Corbin took a remote to open two new doors.

"Sergeant Curnuckle," Isaac addressed as a mature and stern elf had his fingers clasped. "Any updates on the sleigh?"

"No. The investigation has not yet been finalized."

"If not that, you must have other pertinent information," Blaine was anxious to ask.

Curnuckle's scalp was as bare as his shoulders were broad. His chiseled cheekbones and straight posture rose tower-straight as he updated the edgy group. "We've found the two agents called in to retrieve Mr. Kringle."

"And?" said Blaine—figuring by his prolonged leer the news wasn't good.

"Both, dead." A nervous Blimm slowly lifted his eyes out from over his monitor to listen in again, nibbling at his already polished off nails.

"Where?" Isaac needed to know quickly.

"Both outside and inside a sewer lid," Curnuckle felt silly saying it. "Just beyond Cottage One. But the boy unfortunately wasn't found."

"Are we …?"

"Yes," the sergeant confirmed behind a distinguished, navy-blue suit. "We've got a team inside the sewer tunnel. We're certain he's somewhere inside."

"And do we have …? You know…?" Isaac turned to Corbin.

"Cameras? Inside the sewer tunnels?" Corbin would have laughed had it not been so serious.

"And what about these rogue brigades?" Ezra inquired. "Do we know how many are out there?"

"Hard to say," said Curnuckle. "At least a dozen, probably more."

"And are they taking orders?" Blaine inquired. "You know, from Lyman?"

"No." But it wasn't Curnuckle who answered this time. Rather, Isaac with his eyes dead-fixed on the floor.

"And how would you know that?" Everyone wondered, though it was Gib who asked.

"Because I've met with him. Privately, in fact." Isaac fully expected the rest of the group to be as taken back as they were. "I was just about to tell you—I cut a deal with the former Speaker."

"What kind of … deal?" Cumberly asked with a stern stare.

"Yeah, I second that," Gib stepped forward.

"Full immunity," Isaac just came right out and said it. "For any past crimes prosecutors seek to bring forward."

"Full immunity?" Gib was unable to hide his astonishment.

"I needed his help," Isaac raised his voice over the collective disbelief. "There are still Elites out there, including powerful senators who will be the first to bite us in the back if we don't have mediators on our side."

"And Lyman is suddenly one of those mediators?" asked Blaine.

"Whether we like it or not," Isaac paused. "Because now that some of this Elite Guard has gone rogue, we're gonna need him. If anybody can identify who they are, and perhaps even convince some to halt their murderous plight, it's him. Perhaps this way, we can avoid a war at the worst possible time."

"And just how is he ever about to do that?" Ezra wondered after a few more seconds of dead air.

"Well, it starts with a public address. He promised to deliver a speech by tomorrow morning to quell the uprising. To encourage peace. At least until after Christmas."

"That's preposterous," Gib spat.

"I know this is difficult for many of you to understand," Isaac resumed, hoping no one might feel betrayed. "But the truth is, it's complicated. There is more to the former Speaker than meets the eye."

The doors then split again with Silva's security badge held high in her right hand. "And where in scathing Scrooge have you been?" Gib was the first to ask as she sped in quickly.

But Silva didn't say anything. "What is it?" Isaac could tell she had an urgent message.

"It's Lyman," she slowly addressed the curious group—one since forming a full circle around her. "He's been … murdered."

Chapter 39

The sewer tunnel oddly morphed into a wall of clean glass, but it was beyond the glass that puzzled Nick. There were bunkbeds and furniture—all the decorative trimmings being in primary colors. It reminded Nick of a preschool, maybe a nursery as reds, blues and yellows filled the bedspreads and rugs. Wooden blocks aligned the shelves, and it was cheerfully lit.

He wanted to analyze it further but resisted, instead banging on the glass in hopes of finding a sign at life.

To Nick's delight, there was movement. A young elf in long johns curiously stuck his head out from an adjoining room. He was frightened by the noise he hardly expected to hear. Nick half-smiled, as not to frighten him further. The elf looked to either side before scooting closer—past a toy train set and over a basket full of loose toys.

"Please!" Nick didn't know if the elf could hear his plea but tried anyway.

The elf stared, as if deciphering whether he could trust the face beyond the glass. He had something behind his back and slowly revealed a remote. And with the punch of a button, a round section suddenly shot open to expose the cozy interior to the damp, wet tunnel.

Vance

Drenched, Nick desperately leapt through the yoga ball-sized window in a somersault, all as an unsure elf leapt back at the same pace.

"The light?!" Nick cried. "Shut off the light!" They could both now clearly hear stampeding feet fighting the current through the tunnel. The elf stared at Nick with innocent fascination, before using the remote to close the window and kill the fluorescents.

In a flash, everything went dark and quiet. Nick lay flat and still for several minutes over a soft rug.

"I believe they've passed," the elf eventually felt compelled to whisper after a group of sloshing feet swiftly moved on by.

"Are you sure?" Nick's voice was shivering to the point where he could barely pronounce long words.

A flashlight struck up near Nick's face. The elf was now only inches away from his blue cheeks. "Are you really … Santa Claus?" he asked, intrusively analyzing every crevice of his face.

Nick forced his weary head up, before plopping down again in fatigue. "Yes. Now, if you could … get these clothes off me."

"Of course," it finally clicked that Nick was near hypothermia.

"What is your name?" Nick shivered as the elf propped him upright to rip off his coat and shirt.

"Trumbo, sir."

"Thank you … Trumbo," Nick finally had a chance to act cordial. He expressed his relief as the last of the wet cloth was pulled up over his outstretched arms, replaced with a warm, red towel.

"Certainly. But if you don't mind me asking," the elf was too puzzled not to inquire. "What were you doing in the sewers?"

"Fair question," Nick admitted while pondering what an odd view it must be. "And even longer story."

Inheriting the Sleigh

Trumbo lit a match into a fully stocked fireplace, with a series of toys aligning the mantle. Nick continued to rest over a mat near the flames as Trumbo then brought in a tray of piping hot tea.

"Thank you," his hands shook as he reached.

"Who are they?" Trumbo couldn't wait any longer to ask. "It's not every day I see people chased outside my apartment window."

"To be honest, I'm still not sure." Nick didn't want to scare the elf any more than he had to, changing the subject. "What about you? Is this a good time? I never meant to intrude."

"Actually," a bird interrupted on cue.

The cuckoo squawked, "Time to get ready for work. Time to get ready for work," before shooting right back into the hand-carved clock on the wall.

Trumbo approached a dresser. "My shift begins here in just a few minutes."

"Your shift?"

"Yeah. I work inside the Classic Toy Division."

"Classic Toy Division. Of course," Nick picked up a Slinky within arm's reach.

Trumbo grabbed a pair of golden, knee-high socks from a drawer, followed by some blue overalls and a red T-shirt.

"Ugh, if you don't mind me asking. Do you really plan on leaving me here?"

"Oh … well, I …" the elf scratched his head. "Really haven't had much time to think about that."

"I mean, I could come with you. You know—if you think that's OK."

Trumbo again was plenty confused. "Well, assuming you are the boss," he pulled up his bright yellow socks. "But you will need some clothes, now, won't you?" He stared at Nick's bare chest with his index finger tapping his chin. "Here. Try this one," he tossed him a green one-piece with a red belt and Robin Hood-style cap.

Nick held it up, with the bottom of the suit stopping at his calves instead of his ankles. Then again, he was left with no better choice.

"Ready?" Trumbo asked.

"I think so," a still semi-weak Nick cinched up his rope belt. "So, how do you get out of this place anyway?" The residence was small, with a kitchen and bathroom accompanying the bedroom and closet, but as far as Nick could tell there was no door anywhere in sight.

Surprised he didn't know, Trumbo opened the closet again, parting the colorfully hung garments to either side. A round opening—large enough to fit a body through was discreet over a wall. "And what is that?" Nick pointed.

Again, Trumbo was perplexed. "Why, that's how the journey begins," he said with a metal lunch pail in hand. "We'll see you at the bottom then," he smiled, clearly concerned about the time— before, without hesitation, jumping through the chute. Trumbo laughed like a child down a slide; only this was far from something you'd find in any schoolyard as Nick would soon find out.

A swirl of pitch-black awaited him on his way down, until it opened into a clear tube. But it wasn't the only tube. There were hundreds of tubes swirling over, around and through a massive range of what seemed like endless nothing below.

The lighting was dim, with occasional bulbs of color flashing along the way. Nick felt as if he was floating through space but wasn't the only one. Elves were spinning in various directions all around him—some whizzing so close he feared a collision might occur. It was apparent the other passengers had made the trip before as they managed to lie flat in a slumber, simply enjoying the ride. Nick, rather, had no idea what awaited as he continued to helplessly turn and twist.

Synching his eyes tight was all he could think to do, just hoping for a safe end. That was before the epiphany hit.

"Aghhhh!" Nick cried as interior light suddenly emerged at the end of the tube. There was no flat landing—neither any way to stop his momentum. Before Nick knew it, he was falling, just as others to his right and left bounced upward.

"Hello," Trumbo smiled gleefully as they passed midair from opposite directions.

An unsettled Nick didn't have the wits to smile back. He just wanted to be on his feet again as elves continued to pour out the many holes at the top of the large factory.

The springs of the trampoline gave way to each bounce until he gradually came to a stop. Though unlike the others, Nick was frazzled and needed a moment.

"Are you OK, Santa?" Trumbo asked before getting cut off.

"Trumbo," an old elf with a clipboard and pencil tucked behind his large ear was all business as he passed. "You're 97 seconds late."

"Coming," he addressed his supervisor before attending back to Nick.

The weary boy was hunched over, holding his queasy stomach while lowering the tip of his pointy hat down over his blue eyes.

Nick was able to get a wide view of the factory for the first time. It was massive, with the rafters rising a couple hundred feet in places. A series of interconnecting pink and mint green carpets covered the pathways as thousands reported for work. But there was order and fluidity to go along with the bustling chatter.

Vance

Vacuums shaped like horns sucked up footballs and Frisbees. More tubes, some thin—others wide, dropped and zigzagged at straight angles, carrying objects from one place to the next. Some studiously assembled model airplanes, with others sewing doll dresses—and each section was identifiable in its own space and color scheme. Nick slowly walked along a conveyer belt full of Etch-a-Sketches exactly a foot and a half apart.

"This here is mine," Trumbo whispered next to a jazzy sign with a lab coat and beaker. There was only one sloping desk—surrounded by presses producing copies of the very same comic book.

"The Adventures of Farly Frye," Nick repeated with nostalgia. "I grew up reading everything Farly Frye. Farly and Professor Lockstep and all their ..."

"Crazy scientific escapades."

"Yeah," Nick breathed as Trumbo filled in the last part. "Unfortunately, I was always forced to find one at the library or manage one on my own." Trumbo listened intently as Nick picked up a fresh copy to read the cover. *Farly Splits Atom's Apple.* "I mean, my father certainly had the means to buy me whatever I wanted ... don't get me wrong," Nick shook, afraid he was making himself sound spoiled. "And he did. Only something different from what I hoped. For example, 'truck' was often on my Christmas list. So, hearing that ... what would you assume he got me?"

"Maybe one with a remote control. Or perhaps a Tonka," Trumbo guessed.

"Believe it or not, he actually paid somebody to build me a mini F350. I'm not exaggerating. Happened to be friends with the CEO of the Ford Motor Company. It was a specially engineered truck for young kids to drive on private property, and yet I was still too small to even reach the pedal. Believe me, that stupid thing wouldn't even fit inside our apartment."

"So, what did you do?"

Nick shook, as if still soured by the memory. "Just kept it locked away in some storage shed in the Bronx."

"I see," said Trumbo. "One of those dads who always supposed you wanted what he did. The newest and biggest."

"And so, when I asked for Farly Frye," he held up the comic again. "What I really got was some bad Farly impersonator showing up at my door one day. An out-of-work stage actor in a lab coat, paid to put on a show for myself and the kids of his office staff."

Nick oddly felt a little better after saying it out loud; self-therapy that was followed by a much-needed breath. Trumbo, meanwhile, sat down at his desk and grabbed a quill. "I really am sorry to hear that," said the elf. "But perhaps you were asking the wrong father. I assume you had one all along whom would have loved nothing more than see you receive one of my comic books."

"You," it finally registered. "You write these." Trumbo could only smile.

"Though clearly not writing now," the supervisor passed by again with stern eyes for his clipboard, hoping to complete his long list full of checkmarks. "Comic books don't create themselves, you know."

"Yes, Mr. Dusi," said Trumbo from his personal workspace where a sketchpad and set of colorful paints awaited. "And may I help you?" Drab Dusi transitioned his thick unibrow toward Nick.

"No sir," Nick kept his head tilted as low as possible, afraid to make eye contact.

Dusi tried to dip lower, only to watch Nick do the same. "Don't you have somewhere to be now?"

"Yes, he does," Trumbo spoke up after Nick failed to. "He'll soon be on his way."

A skeptical Dusi stopped and stared suspiciously once more. "You are rather tall, you know. Are you on the bear unit?" he pointed to a nearby section where elves stood atop small ladders, reaching to sew black buttons over the eyes of man-sized bears.

Nick's eyes darted over. His only thought was how such a massive toy would ever fit through a standard chimney. "Yes," Nick eventually spoke, though softly enough. "I should be getting back to it."

Nick couldn't have been more relieved to finally see the supervisor scooting on to his next checkmark—a checkmark he could no longer see as the factory suddenly went pitch black. In fact, the only available light was now coming from the flames inside the nearby brick kilns.

"The power's gone!" cried another manager in passing as all production suddenly came to a sweeping halt. Not a single conveyer moved, nor machine blinked.

"What happened?" a frustrated elf in charge struck up a candle alongside an engineer.

"I need to get into the electrical shed to find out," he insisted in a hurry, though never actually had the chance.

The interruption was all part of a staged entrance to the tune of a high-pitched voice. "No need for alarm. Goss Gizer here. Full disclosure, a former congressional whip, not to mention, rabid opportunist," the voice was amused by himself, feeding off the fear that wailed across the suddenly dark factory. "Have you heard of my Black Capes? A feisty band, for sure, though I must say—their discipline … amazing," Gizer drew out the last word for effect.

Nick froze like a popsicle, listening to every word alongside the hundreds of suddenly disconcerted elves. A part of him wanted to believe there had to be another reason for the intrusion, but deep down, knew what the elves did not.

"Anyway, where were we again? Terrible time for a brain fart, isn't it? Oh yes, Nick Kringle, is he around?"

Holding a flashlight, Trumbo naively pointed straight at Nick, with the boy fearfully pushing it aside.

"My ultimatum is fairly simple. Give him up, and no one dies," Gizer stated plainly. "Resist rule number one, and everyone does."

"Goss Gizer!" An elf finally took control in the dark following an awful gasp.

"Yes, who is this?"

"Ebony Stalwart. General Manager of the Classic Toy Division.

"Ebony Stalwart," Goss' greeting was just as cheerful as it was creepy. "Didn't we cross paths once? I believe it was at the signing of the infamous Sleigh Bill of 1742."

Ebony, in glasses and a green visor did his best to sound strong, but his nerves were showing through his retort. "What silly stunt is this? You've killed all our power. You do understand we have a toy quota to meet—where even minutes of lost production could make all the difference."

Gizer's amused laugh soon morphed into a squeal. "Toy quota. Good one, Ebony Stalwart."

"I'm deathly serious. Isaac Newell won't be happy about this. Besides, shouldn't you be back at the Capitol? You know, slogging through some pointless new legislation or something,"

But Goss' ensuing silence was even more unnerving than his laughter "You would think," he mumbled. "And yet I'm watching your every move—having already made my mandate quite clear."

Vance

"Quite … of course" Ebony soon whispered in defeat. "Nick Kringle, you say?" he repeated the name. "And why do you assume he's here? There are over a hundred factories in this district alone. He could be inside any last one."

Gizer chuckled. "There is really so much you do not know, isn't there, Ebony Stalwart? You really think I would make a fool of myself by insisting on something of which wasn't even possible? I know he's here. The Capes have been tracking him."

Nick clenched his fists even tighter. He was trying to remain calm, doing mental exercises and taking deep breaths through the exchange.

"I don't seem to understand. What do you want with the boy Claus?" Ebony resumed.

"That is for me to know—and you to wonder."

"And remind me again. Why should I take this seriously?"

Just then, the lights kicked back on, only in strobing flashes. A series of tightly-fitted black suits swiftly descended the rafters. The ropes dropped, with the Capes hitting the floor and the confused elves soon realizing they were surrounded.

"I guess that's why," admitted the stunned factory manager in a startled gasp—now staring down a host of intimidating rifles.

"So," Goss said, still unseen. "Kringle. Perhaps you could be a doll and make this easy on all of us."

Nick slowly dropped his cap back over his eyes, while Stalwart circled around to reassure his jittery staff. "Supervisors!" he called with a snap of his finger as uncertain elves with clipboards, one by one stepped into view. They waited for Ebony to give his instruction. "Has … anyone, you know … ? The Claus, I mean."

Nick only had one eye open as he watched the approaching elves remain silent from a distance. That is until a face with a unibrow stepped closer—one that caused Nick to brace for a potential emergency escape. "Well?" said Stalwart again, all as Drab Dusi waited to speak. "Have you now?"

Dusi raised one half of his brow, as if not wanting to get ahead of himself and sound silly. "Has Santa by chance relegated himself to the bear unit, sir?"

"The bear unit?" Ebony squinted as Capes were already swiftly enclosing on a section of the factory—one where massive, half-stuffed bears sat upright with unstitched seams in their fur. There were deathly screams as Gizer's band wasted little time to tear away anything in sight.

"What is happening here?" Ebony was beginning to wonder if he'd made a grave mistake. Stalwart then leapt back as he was tapped from behind. Goss now stood only feet away. "There you are," he held his heart as every elf inside the bear unit had since been pinned up against a wall for inspection.

"Nothing," word of the search had already been relayed back.

"Time to try again," the pudgy senator had a full set of black hair, with an Elvis-like swirl at the bangs—one that spiraled out over his large eyes. His eyebrows were bushy, with a collar rising high behind the neck. It made him appear especially conniving.

Ebony now shook with fright as he analyzed what he was up against; though for Trumbo, he now sat still under his desk, trying to get Nick's attention through the cracks in its base. It took a couple of tries but Nick eventually flinched, with multiple sections of the factory now getting ripped apart. "What do they want?"

Nick's return stare was cold. The elf repeated himself, simply to give Nick more time to snap from his stupor.

"Me ... dead. That's what," the boy revealed with distinct pronunciation as Trumbo's eyes grew big. "And I'm afraid they won't stop until I am."

Trumbo could have panicked but instead kept his wits about him. He kicked into survival mode as Capes, with fancy goggles swiftly moved in toward the comic book workstation.

"Line up," voices behind the goggles instructed every elf in sight. Trumbo could only eye Nick as the two stood close with their backs turned. "I said, line up," it was clear a Cape was now speaking directly to the two of them both.

Trumbo communicated with Nick only through physical touch. He gripped his wrist, waiting for just the right moment as a Cape approached—more than ready to jam the barrel of his gun into their backs.

"Go!" Trumbo cried after counting down inside his head. He swiveled quickly, reaching for open cans of paint to toss into the bizarre eyewear.

The brave gesture gave Nick time to sprint. And he did, only skidding to a stop as an approaching Cape adjusted a rotating lens to get a better look. Nick could now do little but stare back in fear. More were moving in to blockade his path over the casino-style aisles; others filling in at the sides.

Nick's mind was now made up as he lost his hat, deciding to slowly raise his hands in surrender. That is until the masses swapped out their sounds of fear for sounds of war. Nick personally watched a rotund elf fearlessly blindside a Black Cape through the wall of a collapsible cubicle. Automatic gunfire sparked as a result of the uprising, with debris suddenly crashing in from the ceiling.

Inheriting the Sleigh

With his pursuers distracted once again, Nick noticed a new lane suddenly emerge in the chaos. He took it, bumping into an elf—or enemy—he couldn't tell which. The truth was, he didn't even bother to look back as elves watched with wonder in the realization that Santa Claus himself had really been among them.

"Watch out!" Nick cried as they attempted to step back from his path.

Slipping around a corner, he weaved wherever he could before ending up in a closed-off section with lower ceilings. It was constructed mostly of logs and old wooden tables, where many shades of paint dripped off the ends from years and years of use. Elves had flipped them over as shields, with handcrafted dollhouses getting instantly pummeled in the chaos.

A cape flipped up as the soldier suddenly stepped out in front, only to fall from the thrust of a pick leveled into his abdomen by a grizzly wood carver.

Nick recognized more boots as the enemy was converging. On the opposite end was a doorway that stood alone—but there wasn't much on the other side; only a narrow, dark hallway. Ducking behind the tables, he wiggled low like a soldier through a trench.

Nick slithered faster—and to his relief, made it. He stood back up, grabbing a portable lantern off a hook near the entryway to start down the bleak hall. That is until he found his momentum crushed by something in his path. Tripped, Nick fell forward while dropping the glass lantern that smashed into a hundred shards.

Nick felt his cheeks rub against the cold, hard surface, but managed to leap up quickly in response to the flashlight that was now pointing his direction. "You!" he waved his finger in disgust at the very sight of Starsky Skiles. "How is it that you keep getting in my …?!"

"I would hold that thought for another time, if I were you," said Starsky to the tune of more voices. "Here, follow my lead," Starsky curled his finger. Nick felt as if he had no choice but to do just that as an open entry emerged to their right. Starsky entered through it, before turning— then again. Nick could both feel and hear the converging boots, completely disoriented as to which way was which. He was now at the sole mercy of his guide, occasionally stopping to think and inspect a new opening through the labyrinth.

"This way," he hesitated, but took it anyhow. "Or is it this way." All the while, the approaching noise grew louder.

"I hope you know where you're going," said Nick, insulting Starsky's intelligence at the same time.

"Little do you know, I spent decades hiding out in these abandoned halls," he responded before coming to a ladder attached to a cement wall. "After you," said Starsky. Nick stopped to breathe before inspecting the top, which was little but a square hole. "I really hate American clichés, but time is of the essence," Starsky, once again, encouraged him to move.

Starsky flicked at his slick, black hair before following Nick. The opening was small. "What is this?" Nick asked, forced to hunch while standing.

"Would you believe me if I told you my boys and I carved it out decades ago, precisely for an emergency like this?" Nick didn't answer. "Now quick, help me lift up this ladder," Starsky instructed with Black Capes swiftly converging down every ensuing pathway on their trail.

They pulled up on the ladder made of scrap rebar, with Starsky discreetly peeking out the opening. Confused Capes turned to all sides, frustrated by what they could not see.

Starsky waved Nick further down the carved-out tunnel until he felt safe again; before eventually leaning up against a rough wall. "You know, you're hard to find, Nick Kringle. Which makes me think you're a little more elf than I ever gave you credit for. You wouldn't believe the size of the search party out looking for you. No stone unturned, if you know what I mean."

"Really?" Nick's guilt began to set in as he could tell Starsky was amused by his wardrobe.

Starsky took a rolled-up newspaper from his back pocket and batted at Nick's chest. He then flashed a small light on the headline.

"Santa Disappears Months Before First Maiden Voyage," Nick recited next to a picture of himself.

"Well, if people only knew what I've been through the last 24 hours."

Starsky challenged Nick to a staring contest. "Actually," he admitted. "Eluding scores of highly trained former Elite Guardsman through an underground maze ... one I'm assuming you've never navigated before ... is rather remarkable."

Nick was a little surprised by the timing of the compliment before the past suddenly flooded back. "But you," he pointed. "You nearly sent me to my death down Dead Man's Pass."

"Wait ..."

"No," Nick interrupted. "Everything was just fine until you forced me down that mountain. And putting aside I could have killed myself, Mauv Lyman has obviously instructed his henchman to come and finish the job."

"Nick!" Starsky yelled louder than he should have after receiving no luck cutting him off quietly.

"What?" Nick relented in a sweat.

"Keep reading," Starsky pointed to another line of bold ink on the front page of the *Ice Cap*.

Vance

Nick's eyes slowly wandered down for another headline. "Mauv Lyman: Dead at the Age of 1,995."

"What?" Nick squinted.

"Lyman was murdered in cold blood."

"By whom?" Nick couldn't read fast enough.

Starsky paused for added effect. "A rival senator. Perhaps you've met him. Goss Gizer?" Nick needed more than a moment to digest the abrupt turn of events. "Yeah, the old man apparently cut a deal with your pal, Isaac Newell. Which makes sense, doesn't it? It's no coincidence that a couple hours after the paperwork was forged, he found himself lying on his kitchen floor in a pool of his own blood. Kind of ironic, don't you think? That Dead Man's Pass is now long in the past; and yet Mauv's dead, while you live."

Nick couldn't deny it, watching in horror as Starsky smiled back with that sneaky, trademark grin. "We gotta get out of here," Nick uttered as he stood up in claustrophobic fear.

"You've got that right," Starsky confirmed. "Though if it were only that easy," he pulled him back inside the small, makeshift tunnel to another round of echoing voices. "In case you haven't noticed, we're kind of in a precarious spot right now."

Chapter 40

Vienna hid her emotion as she was escorted through the heavy gray door. The security guard pointed down at a stool where Arthur sat on the opposite side of the plexiglass barrier. Vienna hesitated before taking a seat, setting her Gucci alligator skin purse over the armrest.

"I didn't expect you to come," said a withdrawn Arthur picking up the phone. His eyes were distant, as if confused how fast he had torpedoed into the clink. He wore a light blue jumpsuit with his arms folded over the prisoner's side of the ledge.

"Honestly. Neither had I," she said, taking off her sunglasses to expose a lingering bruised face.

For the first time, Aurthur revealed some mild shame.

"You know it's his birthday. He's 15 now."

"Is he?" he whispered to another lull, as if not actually having any idea. "Still no word?"

Vienna couldn't fend off the tears any longer. "No. It's been over ten months."

"I'm sorry, Vienna," Arthur finally felt the need to apologize.

"You're sorry?" she asked as a heavyset black man scooted into the booth next to Arthur for his own visitation. "I've not only lost my husband, but my one and only child. Tell me, what on earth am I supposed to do?"

Arthur changed topic as quickly as he knew how. "The police still have no leads?"

"It's in the hands of the FBI. We do know he was taken out of the country. But who with or where … remains a mystery." Vienna brought her voice down to a hush after receiving a library-like stare from the woman sitting next to her. "For all we know, he's been forced into some awful child labor scam somewhere."

"But how are we sure he was even kidnapped? I thought they hadn't ruled out he went voluntarily."

Vienna sighed while reaching for her purse. "And with all the chaos in his life, could you really blame him if he had? He boarded a ship under a false name and they've managed to track him all the way to Norway. But that's sadly where the trail ends."

"Norway?" Arthur locked his fingers together with an idea, as if suddenly coming across a streak of energy. "Vienna, you need to call the governor. He owes me a favor. He'll get that search moving, trust me."

"As if the governor of New York is about to tangle himself up with someone on trial for domestic abuse and cocaine possession," Vienna issued sarcastically. "I can think of nothing better for a reelection campaign."

"You're on your own then," Arthur moved past it, as if to suggest he probably deserved that.

She glared back with a defeated eye. "You're right. I am."

"Nick's a smart kid, you know," Arthur concluded as Vienna abruptly stood up to leave. Vienna slowly sat back down again, desperate for any encouragement. "Always has been—from the time he mysteriously ended up on our doorstep. Remember? I mean, it's no secret I haven't always been the best father," Arthur sniffed heavily from the withdrawal. "But even I could tell almost immediately there was something different about him."

Vienna's tears were getting more and more obvious. "Yeah," she shielded her embarrassed face. "As did I."

Nick's back was pressed up straight against an uncomfortable wall. Starsky held his index finger over his mouth, signaling absolute silence as a lone Black Cape passed on patrol. Nick sweated out every step until the footsteps dissolved away.

"C'mon," Starsky waved as they scurried down a wider hall with many bright red doors.

"What's inside?" Nick asked.

"Material centers. The toys these elves make must come from something. Plastics, nylon, polyester, paints, the lumber yard ... you name it," he whispered, pointing to one sign after the next above the various entryways. "But this isn't where we need to be."

"It isn't?" Nick pressed. Starsky knew where he was going but needed some time to calculate precisely how to get there.

"Truth is, we have to make it back up to the surface," Starsky said, frustrated by his limited options for making that happen. "The underground factories seem to have been taken over," he suddenly pushed Nick back flat against a wall as more footsteps passed by again in the distance.

Sitting with his knees up, Starsky pulled out a map. "See here," he pointed as Nick took a glance at what appeared to be a cluttered blueprint of little more than lines and arrows. "This is where we sit," he pulled the

315

cap off a pen with his mouth to mark an X. "And this is where we need to be."

"We have to go all the way around," Nick observed as he ran his finger along the only route that made sense.

"The problem is—every exit is occupied. Meaning, we either wait out help, or risk sneaking through a checkpoint. And neither one really sounds like a great option to me."

Nick rubbed his belly, having nearly forgotten how long it had been since he'd had a decent meal. "But I need to eat ... or else I may not be able to go much further."

Starsky sighed before jolting his eyes back down for the map. He placed his index finger over a large misshapen area in the middle of the page. "Wait a minute."

"What? What is it?" Nick grew optimistic by his widened eyes.

"Follow me," he smiled, tiptoeing up some stairs and around a couple corners until arriving at a long wall of fine and sturdy wood. Starsky checked with the map one last time to make sure they were in the right place.

"They're engravings on here," Nick looked closer in the mild darkness.

Starsky took a lantern off the opposite wall and held it close to the cherry. The artistic designs seemed to reveal a thick, luscious landscape, with trees, and even elves at work. They were gardening. "This is definitely it. Has to be."

"Definitely what?"

"Let's just say ... this might be your lucky day. There's food in there," Starsky informed. "Not to mention water, and plenty of it. Now, if I could only find an entrance."

"But there's no door."

Inheriting the Sleigh

"Here at the Pole, there often isn't," Starsky replied while slowly moving his hand horizontal over the bumpy surface. "And yet, there's always a way in … somehow."

Nick watched as Starsky walked parallel, dragging his open fingers over the chiseled-out grooves portraying a shady grove. He then stopped, pushing a hand upward at the same pace before going back the other way. Nick found it odd but continued to observe as Starsky covered every inch of the short wall. And then he abruptly stopped to turn with a smile as his hand had suddenly latched onto something different. It was a ring the size of a doorknob—perfectly hidden inside the wood. Starsky didn't need any time to process what he'd found. He already knew, swiveling his grip to turn the ring.

Both Starsky and Nick stepped back as a light then spilled out a square hole. It was followed by the tile at their feet suddenly moving as well. The beautifully carved wooden wall was now rotating, along with the ground like a revolving door inside a shopping mall.

Nick reached to grab hold of Starsky's gray t-shirt, unable to keep his balance as they spun. A vibrantly green landscape was emerging as the wall rotated for the other side, before stopping again.

Nick could no longer see any trace of the wall as the once-minimal light gave way to a natural glow. It was as if they'd suddenly been transported right into the middle of a Central American jungle.

Even Starsky looked somewhat perplexed—the top of the massive dome resembling a natural sky. "Where am I?" Nick gazed as he pushed a large bright fern from his face.

"In paradise," Starsky wasted no time in pulling off an entire pod of bananas. "Here," he tossed one at Nick—who could not have been more content to rip off the peel and embrace the sweetness.

Vance

Nick finally had the courage to take a step or two deeper inside the tropical dome. The sounds of unseen birds chirped, and there was humidity inside he hadn't felt since his last vacation to Hawaii. Starsky followed, peering up at the tall canopy of palms.

"I can't possibly be in the North Pole right now," Nick whispered.

"Where do you think the produce around here comes from?" Starsky quipped as he gulped down another banana. "Last I checked, it wasn't growing outside."

"And so, you've constructed massive greenhouses," Nick observed in fascination as he pulled back a flowery pink bush to keep exploring through the dense vegetation.

"Hey, look—berries," Starsky stepped into Nick's view, exposing a handful.

"Are you sure they're not poisonous?"

"If they are, it's too late," Starsky admitted with red and purple stains around his mouth.

Nick only thought about it for a second or two before his stomach overruled his head.

"Has it sunk in yet?" Starsky asked with an inquisitive stare as they felt safe enough to rest. "You know, this whole fairytale you've been living." Nick said nothing at first, savagely shoving another round of berries between his lips. "I can only imagine how a rich kid from the States would embrace the odd societal dysfunction of a lost tribe of Israel."

Nick offered a rare smile. "Odd might be understating it. I mean, we have our political differences at home too," he found a nice spot to sit in-between the sprawling roots of a large trunk. "Republicans hate Democrats. Democrats hate Republicans. But they typically hash out those differences ... you know, without killing each other first."

Inheriting the Sleigh

"Sure," Starsky hunched. "What a concept."

"I didn't really pay attention to it much," Nick shrugged. "But I guess our method of choice is more of a ballot box kind of thing. Or perhaps a public debate forum. At least since the Civil War anyway."

"The Civil War," Starsky found his own tree. "I remember that."

Nick did a doubletake. Even though such a thought was no longer new, it was still strange to hear somebody who looked the same age talking about something a century and-a-half old—as if he'd been there.

"Yeah. It was back when I was still making toys. I remember your father gathering all his committee chairs together during the winter of 1863 and scripting out the safest possible routes through the various war zones. My father was responsible for approving travel permits at the time." Nick listened closely as Starsky reminisced. "I remember it like it was yesterday—all the bickering. For example, how was he ever supposed to ensure safe passage through the back countries of Tennessee during the Battle of Mossy Creek?" Nick was no longer consuming wild berries as Starsky now had passion in his voice, as if he actually cared about something. "It was a good thing Lincoln won that war," he continued, sweating from the wet heat. "Setting the stage for millions more to receive what even Santa Claus could not give them. Their freedom."

Nick wanted to reply, but was too busy agreeing in silence, instead. "That was rather brilliant."

Starsky was too proud to admit it as he rolled up his sleeves. "I will say this. Even in the 21st century, slavery still exists. Oppression … brutality. It all does … somewhere." Starsky then glared back at Nick, fully engaged. "And I don't envy the man who has an obligation to meet the needs of all those desperate people."

Nick soon turned away, hardly able to endure the depth of his stare much longer. "The survival of Christmas is anything but a sure thing, isn't it?" he exhaled with his eyes lost in a large swath of ferns. "I guess we're locked in the middle of our own Civil War." Starsky's silence implied he agreed when an odd sound interrupted any more train of thought. "Did ... you just hear that?"

Starsky thrust an open hand, with his ear waiting to hear it again. Nick stopped as the unsettling rustle stirred through the adjoining bushes. "I think we'd be wise to keep going," Starsky uttered—this time barely soft enough for Nick to hear.

Nick signaled back. "After you."

Following a third rustle, Starsky kicked up his heels.

"You kind of forgot to tell me there could be something alive in here!" Nick cried on the run as he tried to keep up, barely ducking a tree branch.

"Believe me. If I knew, it would have come up!" Starsky's voice trailed off as the noise appeared to be stalking them through some thick, adjoining brush. "Hurry!"

"Trying!" Nick hopped a boulder, fearing he was desperately close to losing his guide.

But rounding a large palm, the rushing sound of water stopped their momentum. Nick nearly bumped into Starsky's back with the two of them forced to jolt around to the tune of another sound—this one a snarl.

"Is that ...?"

"A panther? Appears so," Nick observed as the black cat exposed its teeth and long tongue. Starsky turned himself to confirm it. They were trapped between the large cat and a roaring river.

"You don't happen to have a weapon of some kind on ya," Starsky inquired, only for effect with his stringy bangs stuck down over his eyes. He already knew the answer. "A cherry blaster. Maybe even a snow pistol would work."

Inheriting the Sleigh

They paced back along the bank, only to watch the panther do the same. "If I die here," Nick uttered sincerely—the lanky feline looking desperately hungry. It was growling and ready to leap. "I want you to tell Isaac how extremely sorry I was. Sorry we couldn't finish what we started."

Starsky offered him an odd look. "Really? You're envisioning a scenario right now where you make it—though somehow I escape to tell the tale?"

Bumping into a tree as they backpedaled, Nick winced—only to experience another unwelcome sound. "Is that what I think it is?"

"Falls," Starsky confirmed as they ran a bit further to the rushing dump of water off the edge.

"This is like the movies," Nick shook in disbelief as the panther leapt forward around the same barricading tree.

"Here," Starsky daringly leapt onto a stone set a yard or two into the water. He reached a hand to pull Nick in as the cat slowly eased forward at the same pace.

The panther then rested upright, with all weight at its hind legs—staring at Nick and Starsky each straddling the small rock.

"Easy kitty," Starsky tried to soothe the large predator, only to watch it snarl again. They leapt back, nearly falling off the back edge of the rock.

"You have any other encouraging words?" Nick quipped. "Like perhaps how nice it looks today."

"Ugh, I think it's ready to pounce!" Starsky cried as he veered his eyes back. The panther was testing the moving current.

"Back, kitty!" Nick was extremely out of character as he did his best to hold up a threatening fist. "Get back!"

"Agh!" They covered their eyes as the beast lunged.

A bang followed. Nick slowly released his forearm, wondering what had just happened. He didn't feel like he'd been shot—though never did meet the claws of the panther either.

"It's dead," Starsky observed as it now straddled the bank with a gaping hole in its back. The two slowly and fearfully lifted their heads as a couple of Black Capes emerged through the trees pointing large weapons. Cobra heads sprung wide at the mouths of the curious firearms.

"Now THEY have guns," Starsky emphasized as another figure followed in from behind. He was shoving the two Capes aside to get a look at the pair—nervous, scared, and with little place to go.

Gizer oozed confidence. He swung his lofty hair, grinning wide at the sight of Nick. "This chase has lasted longer than I expected it might. Very veteran-like move of you to enter the rainforest. Then again," he looked down at the bloody cat. "Maybe it wasn't."

Nick wasn't sure if it was smart to respond as he wiped another sweaty streak off his forehead from the intense heat. Eventually something came out. "Is it really your intent to end Christmas? You know, forever?"

Goss softly tilted his guard's guns toward the sand while inching closer. "I see we're getting right down to it then. For centuries gone by, Nicholas, I have been duped into a life of what powerful men were always telling me was service and love. And I did it inside a wasteland where you can literally go half the year without even spotting a single trace of the sun. Yet, to be fair, I must admit, the temperature is rather pleasant inside here," Goss smiled to expose a gap in his teeth. "But that's beside the point. Where was I?"

"Duped into a life," a Cape got him back on track.

"Of course. Point being, the Pole has paid its dues."

"Dues?" Starsky scoffed while shielding Nick.

Goss hesitated before laughing. "Aren't you that pesky hobo kid from the Glacier District?"

"Hobo?" Starsky took offense.

"Yeah, you know. From the opposite side of the tracks, as they say."

"What hobo dresses like this?" Starsky instinctively pinched the once fine fabric at his shoulders—only to give up, realizing his recent excursion had taken a toll on his threads. "Well, if you would've seen me 48 hours ago."

"You don't think you owe anything to the children of the world, do you?" Nick steered the conversation back with a much more serious tone. "Because as you see it, they have nothing to offer you. The most selfish form of conviction, is it not?"

Goss sized the boy up and down with an awful smile. "You mean, children who grow old? Children who turn into thugs, criminals, and oppressive world leaders? Children who pollute the earth and overcrowd prisons? Children like ... Arthur Crest?"

Nick's eyes suddenly morphed into a daze at the very utterance of his father's name. In that moment, they didn't even blink, as if he were arriving upon a disturbing truth.

"Ugh, Nick," Starsky watched Goss signal his guards. He attempted to steal back the confused boy's attention. "I said, Nick," Isaac shook harder. "On the count of three, we jump. Ready?"

"Huh?"

"In fact, scratch that!" Starsky yelled this time. "We jump now!"

Nick felt a sudden splash as they hit the moving current. Swiftly pushed away, it was enough to finally snap him back into the moment.

"Duck!" Starsky cried as they heard rapid gunfire. Both heads dipped under the water, only to pop back up again once they could no longer hold their breath.

Vance

Nick's head emerged first, followed by Starsky's. They were just in time to see what they'd previously only heard. The waterfall was now so loud, they could no longer hear each other speak. And with gritting teeth, there was nothing the pair could do but spill overboard into the foamy, white suds.

Chapter 41

Nick forced Starsky's head above water inside a pitch-dark canal. With nothing to grip over the enclosed walls, all they could do was stay afloat with the help of some driftwood. But soon, a series of green bulbs, with jail bar protective shells provided minimal light.

Nick found a welcome stone ledge. He pulled Starsky up first. "Where am I?" Starsky gazed around the damp tunnel.

"I was gonna ask the same. You still have that map?"

A disoriented Starsky reached into his back pocket, only to watch the paper shrivel into a hundred wet fragments.

The ledge thinned and Nick straddled the wall in search of a way out. Instead, he found some glass above his head—a rectangle a few feet across. Nick pushed on his toes to get a better look over the mossy wall. It was murky on the other side of the glass.

"I think I found something," Nick mused, watching him lie flat in fatigue with feet still helplessly dangling over the water.

"What is it?"

"I ... don't know," he peeled away a semi-loose rock from the ledge. "But right now, I think it's probably our best bet."

Vance

A dripping Starsky slowly paced the wall before inching up toward the window. Nick gave the shorter Starsky a boost up to get a better look, but it was of little use, hardly able to see much detail on the other side. "Here, give me that rock," Starsky swung its jagged edge into the glass. He did it again until just enough of it shattered. Starsky grunted as he pushed his body up and over.

"Are you OK?!" Nick heard a painful grunt, but nothing else. He quickly did a pull-up, barely avoiding toothed glass as he wiggled his own body through the narrow hole. Hopping down, he found Starsky on the floor, pulling his still-exhausted frame off the broken shards.

But Nick had other worries; like figuring out exactly where they were. He slowly paced around the edge of what appeared to be a large, circular room, until finding a lever indented into a groove in the wall. Figuring he had nothing to lose, he pulled up—embracing the light that gradually brightened the circle. Strings of long bulbs flickered on one at a time.

The room was polished and tidy—but it was what was resting alone in the middle that immediately captured their attention.

"Well, all be. The sleigh," Starsky uttered with reverence.

Nick stepped back to survey with a wider view. "It's magnificent," he said, caught off guard by the size of it under a domed ceiling. A bright red base was perched high over glistening, silver runners. The unusual aerial transport had a very tall back and swirled downward before dipping up again at the dash.

"I guess this means you haven't seen it," Starsky paid close attention to Nick's admiring gaze as he quietly and slowly approached the ladder.

Open space separated the sleigh from the port wall, where a series of aluminum toolboxes and workbenches hugged the edges. It'd been freshly washed and waxed, as evidenced by the empty bucket and sponge pole leaning up against the high frame.

Anxious to climb up, Nick didn't hesitate, too excited to even notice the big gash across his forehead from landing over broken glass.

Standing in the cockpit, he slowly swiveled to admire the leather upholstery, followed by the dash. A control stick was in the center, with a black screen beyond that; but there was also a switch. Nick debated repeatedly in his mind but ultimately couldn't help himself. He immediately flipped it to a series of dazzling chimes and lights. There was a spinning half-globe, and digital map angles joined by dots and coded numbers. Small protruding bulbs lit up one after the next, followed by streaks of white light across the sides.

Starsky now sat upright on the floor, just as Nick playfully waved him in. He was suddenly inclined to have a little fun. "C'mon."

"Seriously, if they have yet to train you on that thing," Starsky's adventurous spirit all seemed to disappear. "Then I really wouldn't …"

Blinking red, accompanied by a siren immediately cut him off mid-concern. It caused Nick to jump from the driver's seat as stampeding feet followed the noise.

"What did you just do?" Starsky's escalating intonation was one of, "I told you so."

"Nothing," Nick wanted to deny it. "Well, maybe something. I'm not sure!"

"Nick," a familiar voice then shouted through a speaker somewhere—one that sounded as if it was coming directly through the sleigh itself.

"Who is this?!" he returned loud enough to be heard over the chaos.

"Nick, is that you?" Corbin's face suddenly appeared over a small screen on the dash.

"Corbin!" Nick smiled with relief.

"You have no idea how glad I am to finally…," the elf cheered as Nick bounced around wondering where the camera was. "I see you've stumbled upon the reindeer machine. Brand new, I might add. In fact, the paint may not even be dry."

Starsky soon leapt into Corbin's view—in no mood for calm overtones. "Creel, what the hell is going on here? There are men on the other side of this wall currently trying to break their way in!"

Corbin urgently checked an adjoining monitor with an update. "Yeah, it looks as if you're surrounded. I see you've got company on the opposite side of that barrier to your right, with enemy canal rafts soon to arrive at your left."

"Which means? How much time do we have?" Nick probed.

"Oh … I don't know. 90 seconds … if you're lucky."

"A minute and a half?!" Starsky panicked, with the noises getting louder.

"Yeah," Corbin's composure was obviously irritating him as he multitasked delivering an honest assessment, with a potential solution. "Possibly less."

"Possibly less? So, what do I do?!" Nick desperately hoped Corbin had a concrete answer this time.

"I guess it's time for your first sleigh lesson," Corbin informed— perhaps a little too casually.

"Sleigh lesson?! Don't I need reindeer for that?"

"If you want to move forward or back, yeah, you'd need horsepower. But for the time being—all you're doing … is going up. Way up."

Starsky shrugged, wondering why he hadn't thought of that himself.

"OK," Nick's hands shook as he processed the thought, waiting for further instruction. "We're ready … I think."

Inheriting the Sleigh

"I see that you've already fired up the dash. Now I need you to search the box below to your right."

Nick reached a hand. "Alright, tell me. What am I looking for?"

"There's a small remote."

"Got it!" Nick smiled as Starsky slung the portable ladder to the ground.

"There's only one button. Press it." The tip of the dome above suddenly separated into four rotating corners, creating a hole large enough for the sleigh to fit through. Nick was impressed by the spaceship-like engineering. "Now, turn the key."

Nick wasn't even old enough to legally drive a car but soon felt the vibration of a powerful engine fire up below the sleigh. "OK, now what?" He was getting excited, despite the distracting voices they could hear urgently banging away on the opposite side.

"They're gonna have that door up in seconds, by the way," Starsky couldn't believe Corbin was really popping a bubble as he said it.

"Then get us up out of here!" Starsky cried as a large section of the garage-style entryway was now lifting from the floor. Meanwhile, the sleigh's engine was beginning to grow louder.

"Have you ever used a joystick before, Nick?" Corbin asked. "No, wait, Atari was before your time, wasn't it?"

"Focus, please," Starsky plead as he could now see boots ready to burst in.

"I need you to slowly pull up on the stick in the center, utilizing the red button at the tip."

They could now spot plenty of black cloth as the sleigh awkwardly jolted upward at Nick's cue.

"Whoa!" Starsky was jostled by the rough acceleration as he dipped his head over the edge—only to spot a series of goggles now peering upward. He pulled his head back in quickly as Nick struggled to gain control of the sleigh.

"OK, steady it," Corbin instructed as he watched from afar.

"Trying!" Nick assured, getting the hang of it much slower than he would have liked.

"I think they might shoot!" Starsky couldn't help but take another peek below.

"OK. Now I need you to pull on the automatic vertical acceleration choke."

"Green or orange?"

"Orange."

"Orange it is," Starsky couldn't wait any longer, beating Nick to it by reaching across his body to tug on the small, round knob.

"I forgot to warn you ..." Corbin was too late as the sleigh suddenly shot up, nearly clipping the edge of the hole in the dome, all as ammunition clanked off the sleigh's bulletproof shell. "To hold on."

The sky above twinkled with a scattering of very bright stars. Nick and Starsky held onto each other with a scream as they slipped down off the seat into the leg space below the dash. It felt like a free-falling carnival ride, all while hoping they weren't about to plummet again.

"Now push the choke back in!" Corbin screamed loudly enough.

Nick gripped the edge of the leather, quickly thrusting upward to pop it back in place with a swat of his palm. The sleigh suddenly came to a rocking halt—now resting still in the freezing night air.

Starsky dipped his head out over the edge of the sleigh one last time, only to see flames shooting out large exhausts near the engine.

Lights were now only dots below as Nick, for the first time got a bird's-eye view of the North Pole. The clock tower was lit neon blue, and

Inheriting the Sleigh

Chimney Sweep Square provided a beauty only fully appreciated from the sky.

"Not bad," Corbin sighed with relief. His feet were kicked up over a switchboard. It was his way of calming back down again, knowing Nick and Starsky were no longer in any immediate danger.

Nick, rather, was petrified by the vulnerable feeling of being up so high; a feeling superseded only by his frigid discomfort. "Ugh, Corbin." Nick shivered. "It's a little ... cold up here."

"Of course," the elf flung back into medic mode. "Stand and lift up on the driver seat. There are polar bear skin coats and gloves inside. And don't worry," he assured with a tone Nick always came to appreciate. "I've got a rescue team on its way."

Chapter 42

Isaac did something far out of character, rushing over to give the shivering boy a hug. Nick wanted to insist that wasn't necessary but instead allowed his Chief of Staff to wrap his relieved arms around his waist. Isaac needed to ask questions but instead ordered Nick to be smothered with attention. "Can we get the blanket heaters in here!" Movement accelerated at the snap of his fingers.

Corbin, Ezra, Silva and Gib quietly stood in the background of a log interior, watching Nick's body vibrate from exposure to the unforgiving elements. The motherly side of Silva took over as she shed a subtle tear—knowing enough of what he was forced to endure to empathize with his unfortunate plight through the Pole's underground.

Nick suddenly found his numb feet soaking in a pool of steamy, hot water. There was a thermometer in his mouth and two more in his ears—and he was bundled up so tight he thought about crying for air. All the while, nearly forgetting all about another freezing body—one purposefully standing back, patiently waiting to be introduced.

"Excuse me," Nick mumbled through his thermometer as an approaching nurse checked a temperature reading. "I said, excuse me."

Inheriting the Sleigh

Nick was bothered his first two calls went unheeded, causing his third to sound rude. Rude enough for people to start listening again.

"Go ahead, laddie," Gib was the first to offer up the floor.

"I'm sorry," Nick apologized, suddenly feeling rather bad. "It's just …," he turned back toward Starsky with a subtle wave. Starsky stood alone, doing his best to generate warmth next to one of the many burning fires inside the lodge.

"Well," Isaac licked his lips as he thought about what to say. Silva and Gib stood back, uncertain how the greeting might play out. "If it's not one of the most complicated personalities in the world. What is it today, Starsky Skiles? Can we finally call you a friend? Or is it really just a roll of the dice?"

Starsky flinched as he was intrusively grappled by a team of female elves attempting to replace his old thermals with fresh ones. "If you don't mind, I think I'll just go ahead and keep you guessing," he quipped as Gib was the only one to appreciate the response.

Isaac wasn't done trying to beat an explanation out but instead was interrupted. "The truth is," Nick paused. "Starsky here saved my life."

The gathering absorbed the sentiment as Gib eventually had a follow-up. "Just to be clear—when you say, saved your life. Do you mean, saved your life? Or put you in harm's way?"

Starsky rolled his eyes as Nick repeated his declaration. "It's true. If it weren't for him, there's no chance I would have made it out of there alive."

"And yet," Starsky bit his lip, as if rather pained to say it. "Nick here saved mine."

"So …," Corbin broke the ice following some digestive silence. "Saving each other. It sounds like a great *Ice Cap* feature to me. Not to mention, one we can all celebrate," he said as Isaac continued to skeptically stare Starsky down head to toe—still unsure precisely what to believe.

"Perhaps we can get to that later," Isaac was in no mood to go down unnecessary rabbit holes. "As for the here and now, there are factories full of elves being held hostage by this invasion."

"Goss Gizer," Starsky just came out and said it after taking a sip from a steamy cup of terrible tea—tea he wanted to immediately spit out. Every face inside was listening—curious by the random name.

"Gizer," Gib repeated after a few long seconds. "Isn't he that fat senator who once proposed enforcing a 50 percent gift reduction across the board?"

"He's been proposing many measures to ramp down toy production for decades now," Ezra added.

"Yeah, that's him."

"Are you sure?" Silva probed, needing Starsky to be positive before expending the mental energy to process it.

"I should have seen it coming," Isaac mumbled. "Took a leave of absence from the Congress. Said it was to get his health in order—only to find out all this time he was really building an army. It makes sense."

"The question being, how powerful is this army?" Silva quizzed.

"Powerful and crafty enough to infiltrate the factory shafts without anybody knowing about it," said Corbin. "I think at this point, we have to assume he can get away with whatever he wants. We're obviously dealing with an intellect not just par for the course."

"But now to the bigger question," proposed Gib. "What bloody is it that he wants?"

After a pause, Starsky spoke again—hesitantly refilling his mug from a porcelain kettle—he was that thirsty. "Let's not kid ourselves. You know exactly what he's doing. Gizer will stop at nothing until he officially squashes Christmas, once and for all."

Another period of quiet lingered, with everyone wondering whether Starsky knew something they did not. "Of course, I think we'd also all agree, that can't happen. I mean … the show must go on … right?"

Gib rolled his fingers up through his bushy sideburns, watching him suddenly help himself to a pastry that was typically reserved solely for him. "Ugh, aren't you the same laddie that at a public street rally once called Christmas, a sucker's last lick?"

Starsky tapped a finger at his pale chin with a nod. He couldn't deny it.

A door to the outside was suddenly shoved open, with three elves struggling to safely make it inside past the beating winds. Everybody's nerves settled once they laid eyes on Sergeant Curnuckle, along with two elves in uniform. It took all their might to force the heavy wooden door back shut.

"Good, it's you," said Isaac.

"And you're lucky we found this place," Curnuckle couldn't help but sound curmudgeonly as he pulled off his gloves. "When you said, 'safe house,' I didn't think that meant having to cross the Barren Ridge to get there. We truly are out in the middle of nowhere, aren't we? And this must be …," he moved on quickly from his complaint—staring brazenly at Nick.

"That's right," Ezra smiled as Curnuckle's imperial mustache locked stares for an uncomfortably long period of time.

"Well, hello … Nicholas Kringle." Nick watched the sergeant make his initial assessment, as if quickly attempting to gauge his real chops. "You're a hard one to find, you know. Then again, many elves are. That's if … they don't want to be found."

Vance

A still shivering Nick wasn't sure what he meant, nor had much to say in reply.

The others hated the awkwardness. "We have much to discuss then," Isaac was anxious to press on.

"Yes, we do," admitted Curnuckle, holding up a rolled-up piece of paper in his hand—signifying its importance.

"And what is that?" Ezra inquired, having an idea.

"The results of the investigation." All ears immediately perked up, including Nicks'. "You know … into the suspicious death of … Kris Kringle."

"Perhaps we should do this elsewhere. I have a makeshift office in the back," Isaac was nervous to discuss it with Nick in earshot.

"No," the boy waved off the concern. "I can take it. Whatever it is."

Isaac had been waiting many months to receive the report—and after taking a moment to think—relented. "Very well," he signaled as Curnuckle let the written conclusion drop down his forearm.

His delivery was smooth and pronounced. "I could dive into the details—and there are certainly many. But honestly, who has the time?"

"Give it to us then," Gib could hardly take another minute.

Curnuckle liked the no-nonsense approach. "The sleigh … it was tampered with," the sergeant informed to a collective gasp inside the secluded cabin. "Somebody was clearly in control of that descent."

"How certain are you?" Silva gauged.

"You want a percentage? Maybe 110," the sergeant's mustache curled up with confidence.

"So then," Nick breathed, as not a soul dared speak this time. It was slow-building but Nick was trying to fight through his anger, as if never having considered it. "It was no accident, after all?"

Inheriting the Sleigh

Isaac assisted Nick down onto a sofa to process what he assumed might be a tough pill to swallow.

"Does the boy even know who Gizer is?" Curnuckle curiously turned to the Chief.

Isaac had his arms crossed. He was staring into a crackling fire, annoyed that now was the time to have to explain it. "No, Clive ... he doesn't."

"I know exactly who he is," Nick insisted, far more forcibly than he typically ever would have. "A shrewd and corrupt politician, that's what. Not to mention, a murderer."

"That he is," Blaine confirmed. "Only I'm afraid there's more."

Ezra looked to Isaac, as if needing permission to reveal the truth. "Gizer was the Roman judge who personally banished your father to the Isle of Patmos. Fully expecting him to die there, I might add."

"And I gather," a clearly distraught Blaine turned to Curnuckle. "The one you suppose had meddled with the sleigh. The very one I helped design."

Curnuckle didn't have to verbally confirm the suggestion as Nick put the pieces together all on his own. "So ... not only did he unjustly imprison my father—he's going after me next."

Silva took an interest in what Nick was now staring at. It was a large oil painting of Kris Kringle in a thick golden frame positioned over a brick mantle. "And how did he get here?" Nick turned back around.

"That we don't know, Nick," Isaac informed. "How he got to the North Pole remains a mystery."

"A mystery?" Starsky piped back in. "How could that possibly be a mystery? Every arrival here is strictly documented."

"Unfortunately, we're talking about a period long before our time," Isaac sighed.

"And mine," Silva added, followed by Corbin and Blaine.

"Am I really that old?" Gib hunched, as all eyes naturally turned to him. "All I remember is him mysteriously showing up here one day. Back during a time when men still dressed like women. You know, in those pretty little dresses the terrible fashion gods all dictated we wear."

Gib's head hunkered after Silva's stare. "I believe you're referring to robes."

"He wouldn't say why, or how he got here?" Nick was quick to veer it back.

"No. And unfortunately only one other person knew the answer to that."

"Who?" Nick's follow-up was obvious.

Everyone turned to Isaac as he finally lifted his lull from the flames. "Kris."

"You mean to tell me my father welcomed his future killer to the Pole—never revealing why he was ever here to begin with?"

"The lad's a quick learner," Gib couldn't keep his mouth shut forever. "I will give him that."

"His lineage isn't with the tribe of Asher, Nick," said Ezra, with glasses and a pencil behind his ear. "Your father hoped that he, as well as others might fully integrate and eventually become one of us. Unfortunately, in some cases that never occurred."

Isaac picked up the history lesson from there. "Over 700 years before Christ, Asher was a part of the Northern Kingdom of Israel. That is until the Assyrian conquest of 723 BC. Most were killed or enslaved, but for those spared death, they journeyed northwest." Isaac then reached for a gift he had sitting over an end table. It was one he'd been anxious to give him for days now.

"What's this?" Nick wondered why he was receiving it then.

Inheriting the Sleigh

"You didn't think we'd forget your birthday?" said Silva.

"My birthday?" Nick thought, realizing he had no time to even consider it in all the recent chaos.

"Go ahead, open it," Corbin suggested as Nick stroked the thick paper with a big 15 on the front.

A book?" Nick said as he tore off the ribbon to lift out an old spine and cover. The leather was soft and worn. "In the beginning, God created heaven and earth," he turned to the first page and read the first chapter and verse of Genesis. It was handwritten in partially faded ink—though very legible. He lifted his head to notice all eyes on him.

"Your father's Bible," Isaac informed.

He gently flipped a few pages, rustling the ancient parchment. "Asher was the eighth son of Jacob," Nick almost said instinctively from his studious days at Lourdes Academy.

"Very good. There's a marker there," Blaine pointed.

Nick found the ripped corner of newspaper holding the page's place, opening to Genesis: 30th chapter. "And Zilpah, Leah's maid bore Jacob a second son. And Leah said, happy am I, for the daughters will call me blessed. And she called his name, Asher."

"The eighth son of Israel, and the second for Zilpah," repeated Isaac. "Boys were circumcised on the eighth day. God saved eight people on the ark during the great flood. And Jesus showed himself eight different times following his resurrection."

"OK," Nick looked confused. "And what exactly am I supposed to glean from all this?" Nick inquired in a whisper as he gently turned another page.

"It's the number of new beginnings, Nick. With two being the scriptural number signifying union—or witness. A witness of two coming together through the union of marriage. If you put both together, it makes 'a witnessing of new beginnings.' And that new beginning was here," said Isaac as Nick gently closed the ancient book.

"As you can imagine, making something of this hellish wasteland," Gib raised his arms out wide. "The outlook for the future was anything but easy. But when John arrived, that all changed."

"How so?" Nick raised.

"For many reasons," said Ezra. "But every one of those reasons boils down to one. He introduced us to the new law. He introduced us to Christ."

"Which brings us back to Gizer," added Corbin.

"Yes," Curnuckle had been waiting to hear that name formally introduced. The enemy certainly has risen—as you can attest," said the military man turning to Nick.

"He's on a killing spree," the boy responded, pulling off his blanket.

"That's why I'm here," offered Curnuckle.

"Besides, you don't have time to worry about that," Ezra said gazing down at the old watch chained to his belt. "Looks like we're down to 4.6 million seconds."

"In all due respect, days might be more of a helpful measuring stick right now," Starsky did his best to sound polite.

"Certainly," he recalculated. "Considering it's the 30th of October, we're look'n at ... 55 days till Christmas."

"And production?" Nick posed. "I saw it with my own eyes. Many of the factories were empty."

Isaac turned to Curnuckle. "My men have regained control over most of them, though some on the northern end are still held hostage. As for Gizer," he paused to deliver the most important part. "I'm sure he and his henchman have all since fled back into the deep underground."

"The deep underground?" Nick squinted as he asked. "I thought Starsky and I were in the deep underground."

"Oh no. It gets deeper," Gib shrugged. "Much deeper."

"So, what now?" Starsky sounded like he enjoyed being part of the conversation.

"Does he even have clearance to be here?" the skeptical sergeant asked Isaac—with a look suggesting he still wasn't sure. "Anyway, what I need now are reinforcements."

"How many?"

"Hundreds, maybe thousands. There are more hiding places down there than one can count."

"What if we pull a unit off the dark chocolate line?" proposed Silva with a pen and paper in hand. "Or perhaps we could spare some men from Teddy Bear Five. Maybe even Blocks Seven. They're both ahead of schedule."

"But many other units have already lost production with the latest retreat," Blaine countered. "If we pull more off, we may not make it."

"Yes, we may not," Isaac agreed. "But of course, that is a call you'll have to make." He turned to Nick, who took one last sip, finishing off the last of his tea.

He thought for a moment, making eye contact with every elf on down the line. "I say we pull whoever we have to. You know—to provide the reinforcements. How many seconds did you say?" Nick found himself looking to Ezra this time for a concrete answer.

"4.6 million."

Nick computed the number, as if it now all made perfect sense. "As long as we keep Gizer occupied with a counterattack, I still think we can do it."

Chapter 43

Nativity Way had a festive glow for the holiday; just not the one Nick expected to see with hot orange lights trimming storefront windows. "Halloween?" he curiously stopped to inspect a display behind the glass—only to step back in surprise. A skeleton, with frizzy hair popped out of a giftwrapped box, its eyes spinning red.

"Nick, relax" said Silva acting as his escort. Spiderwebs hung from every corner with neon flashes and autumn wreaths over every downtown door. Jack o' lanterns provided an ambient glow, with many sticking up out of recently fallen snow piles.

"Trick or treat," a young girl dressed as Little Bo Peep playfully tapped Nick from behind with her shepherd's cane.

"Huh?" he turned.

"Sorry kids," Silva informed as a walking pumpkin, a mummy— even a boy wearing a homemade crayon box all joined in with their burlap sacks opened wide and ready for more. "But the candy is that way. You alright?" Silva turned her attention back toward Nick as the children dispersed. "You seem chock-full of the jitters."

"I know. For some reason, all I seem to think about is ..."

Inheriting the Sleigh

"You don't have to say his name," Silva shook. "I'm no shrink, but it's not hard to see that your recent excursion through the sewer tunnels has been more than traumatic. Just breathe," she soothed as Nick followed her over the charming streets and past more spooky displays.

"Breathe. Right," he exhaled past a monster on stilts. "What is all this, by the way?"

"Scarefest," Silva informed as a werewolf swiveled its claws. A howl then caused him to turn and hold his heart as three witches whizzed past on motorized brooms. "You won't find those anywhere," Silva pointed. "Still prototypes—but the hover technology of the future."

"And what about that?" Nick pointed to a squirmy slug lit up by a series of neon bulbs. Pattering feet wiggled it forward as elves along both sides of the street cheered loudly.

"C'mon," Silva laughed again. "We're in the middle of a parade, that's all. What—you not a fan of Halloween? I thought that was as American as apple pie."

"No, it's not that," Nick admitted as they forged a path through the chaos. "I'm just a little antsy, that's all."

"All the more reason for a distraction. I know we've ramped up production, transferring some additional factory staff to Curnuckle's new marine units; but the truth is—the elves still occasionally need things like this to keep them motivated. Human nature, of course."

Silva knew exactly where she was going, short cutting through some unoccupied streets. She was armed and took each corner slowly to carefully inspect each one.

"Now are you going to tell me where we're going?" Nick grew impatient as he passed another temporary view of the parade route between alleyways.

"To do something I'm afraid we should have done weeks ago," Silva admitted, forced to pull Nick's attention away.

Around several more corners they found the parked carriage. It looked like something out of the Wild West, simple and black with some fine horses at the front. Gib was fidgety as he waited from the driver's seat.

"About time," he signaled in a fine suit. "I can't take another whiff of this fresh pile."

"C'mon, Nick," Silva waived for the door that was already open and ready for entry.

"I feel like a sitting duck out here," Gib griped, gazing around in paranoia as they stepped inside. The parking space was secluded and quiet, with only a faint trickle of the parade now within earshot.

"Let's get out of here then," Silva yelled up.

Nick felt transported back in time as they navigated through the old Dickensian streets—past vintage lampposts and under a small tunnel. An old sign signifying a law office and tavern, along with a printing office made up the narrow stretch—the road eventually dipping under a bridge. "What time is it, anyway?"

"Looks like we just hit two in the afternoon," said Silva in view of the old clock tower.

"Two … and it's pitch dark outside," Nick stared as Gib already had the carriage down a more secluded road. "But can you finally tell me where we're going?" Nick wondered as he could now see little more than dead trees over a quaint stretch. The road was plowed, but just enough.

"Of course," Silva knew she couldn't keep it from him forever. "For your own protection, Isaac asked me to refrain from revealing any destination secrets until we arrived upon the outskirts. We're off to Reindeer Ranch. A place I understand you've been before."

"Once, by freak chance."

"I assume you know why it's time to go back then."

Nick had a feeling, growing unsettled by the thought.

Let's just say that due to your most recent disappearance, we're now well behind schedule on your flight training," Silva informed as an unexpected gunshot interrupted her. It caused Gib to pull up quickly on the reigns. "That's IF we can get there," Silva sighed with concern. "What was that?!" she yelled with her head and neck stretched out the window.

"Wish I knew," Gib cried. "But if I had to guess, I'm left to assume we have company!"

Gib and Silva shared a moment of equal concern before Silva's lips finally moved. "What are you waiting for then? Go!" It was as if the elf needed her to freak out before definitively processing the threat inside his own head. Gib swiveled back around in his full-length coat to get the carriage moving—only this time the horses were in a gallop.

"Hold on, Nick!" she advised as the wooden wheels were now turning at a speed that made them sound like they might fall right off the axles. "This could get dicey."

Another gunshot punctured the snowbank in front of them, causing Silva to yank out a small device. "Route me to the Chief of Staff's office please. And however fast you feel inclined to do that, times it by ten!" she cried.

"Routing now," said an operator.

"Silva, is that you?" Isaac asked as she shed some relief he picked up so quickly.

"Ugh, yeah, and let's just say we're not alone out here," she warned to the unnerving sound of more gunfire. "I thought you promised me protection between routing points A and B!"

"Just tell me where you're at?" Isaac did his best to sound calm.

"Too far. About 3.6 nautical miles from the stables."

"Have you been hit?"

Silva instinctively patted across her own body in search of unwanted holes—all while inspecting Nick. He was also unscathed, but deathly nervous. "No. Not yet."

"Just hold tight then. Curnuckle's call'n in the air force."

"Hold tight. Yeah, we can do that ... can't we, Nick?" Silva tried to convince herself everything was going to be just fine as she pulled out a pink pistol. "You OK up there!" Silva yelled up to a completely vulnerable Gib—his eyes frozen in fear.

"No. A matter of fact, I'm not, dear," he cried back with little power behind his shaky voice.

A second round of ammunition struck the carriage—causing it to nearly tip over. "Whoa!" Nick howled, while swearing he felt the breeze of a bullet pass directly over his ear.

"Just keep going, Gib!" Silva could think of nothing else to say once the horses stopped to kick up their front legs. She then made her move out the window to fire off her first shot.

"Who is it!?" Nick asked the obvious once she dipped back in.

"Someone that wouldn't hesitate to shoot you dead," Silva smiled the obvious with a tough-girl grin. It was her way of satisfying the question without getting too specific.

"Corbin's gathering surveillance, though it might be difficult out in no man's land," Isaac stated via speaker. "Let's assume it's not some rogue bandit, but another unit of Gizer's brigade.

"You ever use one of these before, Nick?" Silva inquired, holding up her pistol.

"What?" he was caught off guard by the question as she handed it to him like a baton. It was bright, with a hot pink barrel and a tie dye grip.

Inheriting the Sleigh

"Wait, where you going?" Things were happening faster than Nick was comfortable with.

But Silva had already made her move out the window—this time permanently. "The weapons loaded. Turn safety off," she demonstrated only the Cliff's Notes version. "Point, aim and pull," Silva lastly held her index finger next to the trigger. "Sorry, but I know Gib." The carriage swerved erratically again, nearly sending Silva flying off into the snow. "And he's gonna need me to start driving real soon. The poor guy gets motion sick quicker than I get ornery during that time of the month."

More shots fired in their wake. Nick took a deep breath before quickly popping his head out into the danger zone—the gun now aimed at something he couldn't even see in the haze behind him. He fired anyway, hearing a car peeling off the road upon impact.

"That a boy, Nick," Gib squealed. "Keep it up." With a sudden burst of confidence, he turned and fired again at the faint headlight, only to have his head nearly taken off at the same time. Nick nervously leapt back inside—both arms draped over his rattled ears.

"I nearly got hit!" he cried in a rush of adrenaline.

"Yep, that didn't take long," uttered a loopy Gib. He was hunched next to Silva, now in control of the steeds.

A comforting sound swooped in. "Is that what I think it is?" Nick slowly gained the confidence to show his face again—this time looking up at a series of propellers gracing the starry sky.

"That it is," a wide torso then came squirming through the opposite side of the moving carriage. "Those pilots have waited at least a century to see some good combat."

"That's your air force?" Nick noticed the World War I style planes, only smaller to fit the elves' tiny frames. "The aircraft had top and bottom wings painted in red and green stripes, with white stars over the rear rudders.

"Silva, you still there?" Isaac radioed.

"It's actually Gib here. And yes, she is in control of the giddy-up," he said, still plenty dizzy, but alert enough to show his excitement. The bombers began raining machine gun fire down into the surface snow, with the aerial light now exposing the enemy vehicles.

"Gib, what's going on? Has the team arrived yet?"

"Oh, they've arrived alright, laddie. In all their bomb drop'n glory!"

"Good. I've made sure the ranch gates have been opened."

"Roger that," Gib was sprawled out over the floor of the carriage's leg space—having fun with the back-and-forth. He pulled the device away, casually talking to Nick, all as miniature bombs exploded not far away. "Looks like the Tundra Bird Squadron."

"Excuse me," Nick only heard half of it.

"Tundra Bird Squadron. Since the start of the 20th century, the closest they came to any combat was World War II."

"World War II?"

"Yeah," said Gib casually. "As you can imagine, we were watching the fragile fate of the earth along with everybody else. And you wouldn't believe how close we came to assisting the British with the Nazi assault. That is until the Americans finally stepped in and we didn't feel like we absolutely had to any longer. Believe it or not, war has never been our bread and butter. You know, with the obvious size deprivation and all," he waved his hands down his sides, as if admiring his own rotund frame.

"Gib, how far?" Silva yelled back, interrupting the story that was told only to distract from the real chaos ensuing all around them.

"Looks like half-a-mile!" he responded, reading his reverse odometer. "Anyway," he softened his voice again as explosions continued to rock. Nick wanted to keep watching the fire soak into the nearby snow, but Gib kept him distracted. "How did it feel?" Gib nodded toward the pistol that Nick forgot was still within his grip. The elf slowly pushed the muzzle away, only so that it was no longer pointed directly into his chest.

"Oddly, not too bad."

"Well, it won't be too much longer till you're back up there in the great skies again."

But Nick gulped this time. "Yeah … cannot wait."

"Is something wrong?"

"Oh, nothing. It's just that when I was hovering up there. You know … with Starsky … inside the sleigh," Nick felt dumb having to admit his greatest fear. "That I began to feel it. The butterflies fluttering up my bowels, as they say."

Gib was straight-faced with mild shock as he waited for his real emotion to build up to a point of no return. The elf was now laughing uncontrollably—so much so he was holding his substantial gut. "Wait, you mean to tell me, the blood son of Santa Claus himself is afraid of … heights?"

"I've only been to the top of the Empire State Building once," he admitted. "Because the first time, I think I may have passed out."

"Well then, this should be interesting," he pointed to the log overhang that Nick's back was now facing inside the carriage.

The horses slowed near a set of armed guards. They were waving them in as fighter pilots continued to fire away in their wake.

Nick could now see the barn in the distance—which was essentially a wooden fortress standing alone. The fenced-in grounds were semi-wooded, and a man was patiently waiting for their arrival as the gates closed, the carriage winding up the front road leading for the stables.

"Smudge Terpley," Nick was glad to see his professor quickly rush over to greet him.

Terpley was bundled in an Eskimo-style coat, with his cold hands in his pockets. Nick initially expected to receive a normal greeting; that is until he remembered that with Terpley, social pleasantries were rarely normal. He just stood completely still. "Choko Sasaki."

"Excuse me?" Nick was confused by the first words out his mouth. There was no, "how are you?" No, "how have you been?" Or even an, "I'm sorry to hear you'd just nearly been killed."

"Choko Sasaki. Who is she?"

"Choko Sasaki?" he repeated.

"That's right."

"But I'm not ..."

"Just tell me who she is," Terpley doubled down with his hand waving across his face like a hypnotist gaining control over a subject at the county fair. "Focus," he issued as Nick continued to look perplexed.

"The old man's finally lost it," Gib breathed next to Silva, observing every word of the exchange.

"And yet—there are those who have said the same about you," Silva whispered back.

"Just watch my hand," Terpley continued to soothe Nick as he slowly panned across his eyes. Nick remained still, with both corneas gliding at the same pace as his fingers. "Now close 'em." Nick immediately did as told in the dark, frigid air. "Now ... I ask again. Who is Choko Sasaki?"

"She is eight," Nick whispered, as if soon seeing precisely what the professor intended. "Or eight and-a-half, as she would have me believe. Lives in Kyoto, Japan with her mom and sister. Her father recently passed in an unfortunate fishing boat accident."

"Correct. And what has she asked for this Christmas?"

Nick kept his eyes closed. "A Pelly Trinket Doll."

"Correct again. And Stanley Studebaker. Who is he?"

Nick thought hard for a moment as if trying to locate another name across a mental database containing millions of human records. "OK," I think I have him," he smiled many seconds later—his eyes still closed. "Winnipeg, Manitoba Canada. He's … 13. Or at least turns 13 next month. Was devastated that Santa Claus never showed up last year," Nick's smile had since disappeared—replaced by a genuine sadness, as if he could suddenly feel into Stanley's troubled heart. He … left home." Nick's eyes finally popped back open, staring directly at Smudge.

"And why did he leave?"

"It looks as if he ran away as an act of rebellion to join a street gang. But has still made a Christmas request on behalf of his little brother, Scottie."

"He is rather good, isn't he?" Terpley made a point to look over at Gib with a smile. It was his own way of flattering himself. "But please, carry on."

"He wants Scottie to have a box of Builder Bots. But also, a copy of the Bible so that he doesn't end up making the same poor choices he did."

"And Catalina Machado?" Terpley quickly moved onto another.

"San Pablo, Chile. She's three. It'll be the first Christmas she remembers. Money is tight this year—so what she receives from us unfortunately might be it."

"He is good," Silva nodded with a genuine whisper of her own.

"Forgive me. I had to make sure your mind was still where it needed to be," Smudge lowered his spell over the sounds of unnerving bombs blasting away in the distance. "And just wait until we add that magic hat into the equation. Your recent absence has surely set us back, so let us be swift and efficient with our remaining lessons, shall we."

Nick briskly followed the professor toward the massive barn. "And now onto my very favorite lesson," Smudge locked his fingers together with a smile. "The nine first-teamers are waiting."

Chapter 44

Easy," Skeeta LeBelle soothed Blitzen's snout with her outstretched palm. The keeper pushed the feisty reindeer back as it lowered its horns. "All she's really doing is being playful," Skeeta reassured, knowing how frightened Nick was to feel the deer's head and back dipped—ready to lunge.

"Did you say, she?" Nick naturally retreated a step for his own safety, only now inching forward again.

"All of these flight reindeer are female," Skeeta informed as Blitzen restlessly rolled around in the sawdust. "The males lose their antlers by fall."

Skeeta's hair was long—her face rosy and fair, and she wore a brown, one-piece jumper while offering Nick a tour of the stables.

Each stall had a framed picture of a different reindeer next to their respective names. The word "Blitzen" was spelled out in fun, bright red font. Skeeta used a pitchfork to scoop some fresh hay into the clean stall, but Blitzen wouldn't touch it. Instead, she continued to keep her eyes focused on Nick; so much so that Skeeta found the connection fascinating. "Here," she reached into a pouch around her waist. "This is typically reserved for dessert but go ahead."

Vance

Nick took the carrot and waved it slowly across Blitzen's frozen eyes. Her nostrils caught the scent, though her eyes remained where they were as Nick inched forward with his hand stretched flat. He was nervous the antlers might suddenly catch him across the arm but kept going until his hand was now directly over Blitzen's ears; gently stroking the black stripe over the nose.

Little did he know that Smudge had been watching every second of the exchange. "Ugh, what are they doing?" Terpley whispered as the greeting grew awkwardly slow for his impatient taste.

"Quit chattering," Skeeta scolded, put off by the professor's typical reaction to anything normal. The keeper of Reindeer Ranch enjoyed the precious back-and-forth—evidenced by a smile that soaked up every last minute.

Blitzen wanted to bob again, but this time Nick's hand was quick to latch onto the antlers—keeping them still. "I know you took it the hardest," he seemed to be suddenly reading the reindeer's mind. "You know, about my father's death. You loved him, didn't you?" Blitzen's nostrils puffed hard. "The truth is, I wish I'd known him as you did."

"I'm afraid he's rambling," Smudge said, desperately wanting to step forward to distract the boy. Skeeta, however, wouldn't allow it, with a look of "don't you dare."

"You're still a bit uncertain ... aren't you? You know, about me. I would too. A complete stranger ... young and naïve. Truth is, I don't even know if I trust myself." He then put the carrot up to her mouth as Blitzen's lips salivated—swallowing it whole. She chomped away, with her eyes still watching Nick ever so close. "And that's why I need you." Nick could feel the reindeer begin to relax away in his hands. "Does this mean I can count on you then? You know, to take me wherever I need to go. All around the world?"

Inheriting the Sleigh

Nick heard a honk. It was loud enough to cause him to turn, not even realizing the other eight reindeer were now out of their stalls, each harnessed and standing next to a different elf. "I think they're ready now," Skeeta admitted with pride.

"Let's see how they respond in the air," Terpley added, still annoyed by the delay. Nick gulped after realizing he couldn't prolong the inevitable any longer—an inevitable he'd been extremely nervous about.

The combined whiff of sawdust, pellets and hay was replaced by the fresh, frigid air as the caretakers made their way out of the barn. The very same sleigh that Nick and Starsky once used to escape the Black Capes was now parked and ready in the back.

Blaine was up top testing out the control deck, with the sleigh's recently polished frame sparkling over a launchpad under some artificial light. Elves were already at work securing the reindeer.

"Nick," greeted Blaine with a smile after hopping down the ladder.

"Cross."

"I revved 'er up for you. Both engines working. Fresh fluids and fuel. Everything you need to conduct a successful test run."

"Well, not everything," Nick stuttered.

"Oh, you'll be fine," Blaine said, loud enough to be heard over the sound of the roaring engines. "It's really not that much different than the simulator."

"I'll just keep telling myself that," he tried to break up his anxiety any way he could. "But I will say, that with the simulator, at least I had a safety net."

Blaine shrugged. "Nets are not designed for Kringles."

"Nick!" he heard a familiar voice hobbling into view from a distant vortex of blowing wind and snow. Gib was carefully holding onto a decorative box. "Forgetting something?" he reminded in the dark chill. "Don't worry, I learned my lesson. Not gonna touch it this time."

Silva and Blaine were now watching alongside Smudge as a light snow fell over the launchpad. They were waiting to see how Nick, after all his training would react to wearing the wine-colored hat.

Nick opened the lid for the soft wool. He was waiting for the right time to place the fur trim over his ears in anticipation of what was coming.

"Wellllllllllcommmmme baaaaaaaaaaaccckkk. The heir of Christmaaaaaaaas joy and cheeeeeeeeeeeer." Nick could feel the intense wind shooting across his temples. The odd thing was—the sweeping voice didn't seem to bother him as much this time. "Let us riiiiiiiiiiiiiiiddddde and gliiiiiiiiiiiiiiddddddde through the northern skkkkkkyyyyyyyyy."

"Are you alright?" Silva asked, running her fingers across his pupils.

Nick surprisingly answered right away. "I guess it's time to find out," he said with the fuzzy white ball now drooping off to the side of his neck.

A path was respectfully parted as Nick made his way for the ladder. The small crowd watched as he climbed, soon having a bird's-eye view of the others. The runway guide waved a glowing purple baton to clear the road and signal the beginning of the test launch.

Blaine pointed to his ear as a signal to pop in the earpiece. "Please talk to me. Somebody. Anybody," a fidgety Isaac called in, as if repeating himself for a while.

"Isaac? Is that you?" Nick greeted.

"There you are. Team One in place?"

"Team One?"

"Yeah. On Comet, on Cupid. Didn't your parents ever read you, 'Twas the Night Before Christmas?'"

Inheriting the Sleigh

"Dasher. Now Dancer. Of course. Yeah, they're in place," said a distracted Nick, as an elf below gave him the cue. The sleigh's dashboard was glowing, with much of it twinkling in patterns.

"Just to fill you in. The enemy has managed to infiltrate more than we'd previously thought. The good news is, Curnuckle's newly trained marines have since had some success flushing out the remaining Capes."

"In all due respect," he asked calmly. "If that were true, then why I would I still need so much protection?" Nick could now see the outlines of planes to either side.

Isaac knew it was a great question and desperately wanted to offer Nick a better answer. "Because these days, I can never seem to do too much to ensure it. Hence the escorts." Lights to his left and right suddenly emerged to expose a member of the Tundra Bird Squadron, each smiling proud from their open cockpits. The pilots had staticky hair and funny grins— joined by leather hats and their thumbs raised high. Nick felt silly raising a thumb in return.

Wave-like signals rushed past his thoughts. It was as if all his normal mental processes had suddenly sped up, causing him to focus to take it all in. But there was also a confidence he never really remembered before.

"Nick, are you still there?"

He knew Isaac had been talking to him, though didn't respond until now.

"Did you hear what I said?"

"Yeah. You went over all the emergency parachute procedures."

"That's right," a surprised Isaac confirmed before his voice softened—sensitive to the nerves Nick had to be feeling. "And remember, this is just a test run. Precarious circumstances, I know. But you also need so many flight hours, and to get 'em all in, we need to start now. But just remember, if something does go wrong … we've got all our accident control measures in place."

The reassurances were supposed to make Nick feel better—but the truth was he didn't need them. "Let's take it up then," said Nick with his focus having shifted to "all business."

A pleasantly surprised Isaac paused for a moment with a genuine smile. "In that case." The runway guide now had his neon sticks raised. "Just like the simulators," Isaac reminded as Nick was as perplexed as any to find he didn't have any more questions. He was fidgeting with numbers, graphs, buttons, and levers, as if suddenly knowing exactly what they all meant.

"Fuel RPG?" Isaac began his checklist.

"227."

"Exhaust fluid?" The gauge lights began to display one after the other.

"High."

"Supersonic speed reactor?"

"On."

"Net thrust meter?"

"Also, on."

"What about the jet coolant? It probably doesn't matter, but sometimes the mechanics forget to top it off."

"They didn't," Nick was getting anxious.

"Alright then." Isaac sighed from the control room as Vixen kicked up her legs in anticipation—excited to take flight.

Suddenly a flash of red lit up the runway in front of the sleigh. So much so that it made a noticeable difference in visibility. Rudolph looked like any other reindeer; that is until her nose turned on, glowing vibrantly.

Inheriting the Sleigh

The Tundra Bird Squadron had their propellers spinning, with the first one taking off. "Alright," Isaac piped back in. "They should be giving you the green light any moment now."

Nick exhaled with Rudolph's feet taking the lead over the runway. It was as if they'd done exactly that a thousand times before. The reindeer were now in a sprint, with the sleigh gliding smoothly over a light layer of snow.

Nick's hat blew back in the wind. There was a warmth he couldn't explain around his ears and a clarity to his mind as Rudolph suddenly leapt out at the open air. Dasher and Dancer followed—Prancer, Vixen, Comet, Cupid, along with Donner and Blitzen in the rear. Each reindeer had its hooves off the ground, and Nick was now officially in flight—his hands gently tugging at the reigns through a couple of holes under the dash.

"Tell me. How does it feel?"

Nick's back was tilted down against the tall leather backrest with his eyes staring up at the bright stars. He could hear the plane engines rumble as the reindeer continued to elevate. "This is actually kind of fun," his first instinct was to giggle.

"Feel free to give a little more juice with the stick but the deer should be so well rested, you probably won't need the extra horsepower. How's your elevation?"

"Approaching 6,000 feet."

"Making good time then. Once you hit 75, go ahead and level out. You look good in that hat by the way." Isaac said, now watching his every movement from a monitor.

The chilling rush of the night sky was almost refreshing as he let the reindeer do the grunt work. It gave Nick the chance to just be a spectator for the moment. He felt like Peter Pan gliding over an evening London sky. The clock tower was his Big Ben, and the small twinkling lights below were like a showering of fireflies.

"Alright, try not to get too awe-struck," Isaac knew Nick had his head giddily dipped out over the side. "There are four golden, residential rooftops—each with a different slope. The four street addresses should be listed on your screen now. See them?"

"Yes."

"Good. Plug in the first address and let the system do the rest."

The reindeer suddenly made a sharp turn that felt just like the rollercoasters he used to ride at Coney Island. Toy factories that resembled Moscow's Saint Basil's Cathedral, with towering and colorful, onion-shaped spires were now in view—along with rows of charming neighborhoods. The beauty was so immense that Nick, for only a moment assumed he was simply on a joy ride.

Nick lowered the reindeer into the heart of the dark city. He was looking for the first landing spot when he heard a noise inside his head. "Do yooooooooou have the keeeeeeeeeeeeeeeyyyyyyy?" It was longwinded and rustled like the wind. Nick knew it was the hat calling.

"What?"

"The keeeeeeeeyyyyyyyy? Dooooooooooooo yoooooooooouuuu haaaaaaave it?" The numbers and fuel levels once filling up the dashboard had suddenly disappeared, instead replaced by an image forming in its place. The digital picture was a replica of the old key Nick found inside his father's cottage, something he'd nearly forgotten about in the recent chaos. Worrying it had been lost some time ago, he frantically checked every pocket before, sure enough, feeling a bulge deep inside his coat.

"You mean, this one?" he breathed, now holding the iron relic. Nick couldn't understand how it had been kept safe all that time since finding it hidden above his mantle.

Inheriting the Sleigh

"Yeeeeeeeeeesssssss. It is tiiiiiiiiiiiiiimmmme."

"Time? Time for what?" Nick grew nervous, with the first rooftop now in his sight. He was no longer guiding the sleigh. He had suddenly lost control.

"Tiiiiiiiiiiiimmmmmme to unlock your paaaaaaaaaaaaaasttttt, preeeeeeessssssssssent and fuuuuuuuuuuuturrrrre."

"Nick, you do realize you're heading off course." Isaac was waiting for him to take notice and re-correct. "And what happened to the Tundra Birds?"

"I … don't know," uttered a confused Nick as the reindeer had suddenly sunk down in so low they were now breezing past the tops of chimneys. "They seem to have … disappeared."

"What do you mean, disappeared?" Isaac snapped from his casual position, trying to figure out what was going on.

Nick, meanwhile, punched away at a series of buttons, only to gather the effort fruitless. The graceful reindeer continued to coast in a wavelike pattern, pumping their legs two-by-two in stride. Meanwhile, excited elves from below pointed up at the streaking sleigh. They were fascinated, and possibly even a little worried by the fact it was gliding so low.

"Nick. Come in, Nick!" Isaac's call cut in and out—before disappearing altogether.

The sleigh was erratically dipping even more than before, this time toward the outskirts of town where lifeless trees sprung up in the snow. Nick knew he was entering dangerous territory—no longer with any aerial or ground protection at his disposal. But even more concerning was the fact he couldn't do anything about it. For some reason, all Nick knew was that he had to get home—and that the sleigh, like it or not was taking him there.

Vance

Now hovering directly over the stone bridge that arched over the frozen creek bed, smoke seeped out both cottage chimneys. "Alright, let's drop," he instructed as the reindeer slowly made the last descent into an empty patch of snow between the house and bridge. Reindeer hooves and the base of the sleigh both made contact with the surface, and Nick quickly descended the ladder. He stroked the noses of Dasher and Vixen on his way for the stone walkway leading for the thick front door. The door creaked as it opened. As always—other than the crackling fire, it was eerily quiet inside.

"Hello. Anybody home?" It made Nick feel better to say it. He passed the kitchen on his way for the living room where he'd since gotten used to the smell: a combination of must, wax, wood, smoke, and incense.

"Now what?" Nick waited for more instruction. "What do I do with this?" He held out the six-inch long key, panning from one side of the cottage to the next. Nick stared at every framed oil painting, as well as every trinket inside the dark room when the swirling wind inside the hat struck up again. Nick had learned not to let it bother him, but he knew it was trying to tell him something as his eyes couldn't leave the fire. His boots creaked over the wood floor as he passed the rocking chair and sofa. Nick grabbed a few fresh logs to stoke the flame. He was staring at the stones above the fire, gently reaching for one that nearly called out to him in silence. As he fully expected, the stone moved.

"A keyhole," Nick breathed. Having no idea what might transpire as a result, he placed the key inside. It fit perfectly and Nick was quick to turn it counterclockwise. He was confused to see nothing happen. That is until something did.

A picture of Jesus conversing with Nick's aunt, Mary Magdalene near a Jerusalem well shook over the wall. With one hand, Nick scurried to keep it from slipping off the nail—catching a wooden reindeer statue from falling off the edge with the other. The mantle itself stayed put, but the stone fireplace below was suddenly splitting in half. It was gliding away from Nick to create what appeared to be a new opening.

Once it stopped, he cautiously dipped his head down to get a better look, all the while covering his nose and mouth to keep from breathing in any unwanted smoke. He doused the flame with a bucket of water, but it never completely went out. He could see the reindeer foraging for food underneath the snow through a crack in the drapes, but his attention couldn't escape the suddenly formed hole inside his fireplace.

His boots slowly crunched over fresh ash and soot, with a short stairwell leading down beyond it. It was uncomfortable for Nick to duck that far down, but once he reached the bottom stair he could now stand completely upright again. He was inside what led to a narrow cave.

An old box of matches and a lantern sat on a shelf at the base of the steps. Nick struck up some light and rubbed his hands against the cold, chiseled stone walls. He proceeded deeper until the narrow pathway suddenly opened into a large room with a smoky layer. The ceiling was tall, and the thick fog rose almost like a movie screen inside a theatre—curving around like an IMAX.

Nick inched closer out of fear of the bizarre. An almost chilling rush accompanied the haze as it began to light up with faint images over the first third of the screen. "Is somebody there?"

Roman sandals suddenly stormed every house with ensuing screams as they kicked open the feeble doors. "Boy or girl?" probed one merciless soldier to the next as they held back the child's frantic mother.

"Boy," he informed.

"Please," the mother begged. "Don't take him from me! He's all I have!"

"Bring him," the soldier instructed as they went house to house, many of the residences carved directly into the red cliffs of ancient Bethlehem. Nick gritted as he watched a team of soldiers carting off the 25 toddlers to the helpless cries of their parents.

Patches of fire engulfed the small hamlet inside ancient Israel, but there was a well-to-do man whom Nick seemed to recognize arriving upon the dreadfully howling scene. His skin was black, and he quickly hopped off his camel dressed in fine clothes; a royal, turban-like hat wrapped like a thick towel, along with a complimentary robe embroidered with dangling blue knots.

"Excuse me, whatever is going on here?" the concerned man, with a beard connecting his sideburns asked a frightened citizen watching the march.

"They are taking away all our little boys!"

The wealthy traveler proceeded to storm away from his camel for the Roman legion. He was brash and unafraid of what might happen as he grabbed ahold of the Centurion's bare arm. "What is it you think you are doing here? What gives you the right to invade this village and kill their babies?"

The Centurion thrust his elbow to shove the traveler away. "Get your hands off me, Magi."

"You tell Herod the child is not the sort of king he's looking for," he plead from the sand. "We showed him the star only so that he might admire him with the rest." The Centurion did not look amused as he stopped to listen, being kept from doing his job. "Besides, the baby with whom you seek is no longer here. You're merely slaughtering innocents."

"You would know, wouldn't you, Magi," the Centurion mocked as the Roman band scurried away—each with a crying baby in its arms. "In fact," the Centurion swiveled to address the Magi one final time. "You never returned to Jerusalem as ordered. And come to think of it, where are the other two?"

The smoke suddenly washed the scene away for a brand new one; this one much quieter. "We need a place to stay for the night," informed a bearded but comely man to an innkeeper.

The innkeeper stared him down head to toe, unimpressed by the simple robes. "Go away. This establishment here costs money."

"I have money," said Joseph as the innkeeper surprisingly turned back around. Joseph pulled out a decorative box with a cushy red top and colorful beads.

"And so, you do."

"Yes," Joseph confirmed as his veiled wife then stepped forward with a calm infant comfortably sleeping in her arms. The innkeeper's eyes widened as Joseph lifted onto the lid to expose several shiny new gold pieces.

The screen then abruptly transitioned to a third moving picture. It was a woman's feet sprinting over the dusty dirt roads outside Jerusalem. Her run didn't stop as she entered the city, hurrying over the old stone streets.

Peter and John knelt together in a resident courtyard, surrounded by a short wall. They stood while meditating around a fig tree. "Disciples." Peter was curious upon hearing Mary Magdalene's exhausted cry. "Our Lord!"

"Yes?" John asked, with his hands now gripped over Mary's slumped shoulders as she gathered her breath. "What is it?"

"They have taken him away."

"What do you mean?" a concerned Simon Peter quizzed.

"I mean, he is no longer inside the sepulcher. And I know not where they laid him."

Vance

Peter and John eyed each other for a full second, maybe more, before making a sudden dash. They didn't even bother using the gate, instead hopping over the wall to save themselves some time. They knew the path well and paid no attention to the curious stares from onlookers, amused by their urgency.

The much younger John couldn't help but race out in front, passing olive trees and grapevines before coming to a narrow and windy stairwell dipping down into an isolated and quiet garden. Wildflowers sprung up and around the short stone cliff. Small trees and patches of grass blended above and around the tomb as John skidded to a stop next to the heavy, round stone that had since been pushed open, exposing the tomb. Peter followed with an equally overwhelmed gut as they stared together at the small rectangular opening. John hunched to dip his head inside first. Seconds later, he turned back around and nodded at Peter—as if to suggest "nothing." A hasty Peter then sidestepped John to see inside the tomb for himself as Mary had finally arrived at the rear.

"You're right," Peter said, aghast. "The Rabonni is gone."

The scene suddenly faded as the hat spoke to Nick once again. "The paaaaaaaaaaaaaaaaaaaaasttttttttt leads intooooooo the present."

Nick's limbs were so numb he nearly felt like collapsing—which he eventually did.

Chapter 45

Each had a different job as assembly lines of elves worked at a rapid pace. From blocks to trikes—dolls to balls—and gaming systems to cleverly designed action figures, each was stamped or branded the exact same way; with a special seal—a swirling "SC" signifying where it was made.

Isaac marched alongside Silva through a factory, observing each station. "And what do you think compelled him to just abandon his training mid-flight?" she inquired, jotting down some notes about a broken conveyer belt near the army truck unit.

Isaac's sigh was painful. "Who knows. I mean, I could venture a guess like everyone else, but who has the time? I know I've said this before, but at this point, we just need to find him."

"You don't think he's having any … you know, second thoughts?" Isaac didn't say anything this time, prompting Silva to take that as a "no." She nervously gripped Isaac by the forearm. "Because look around you," she waved, watching elves in robotic motion. "Teams laboring around the clock. Imagine if I were to suddenly tell them, Santa Claus was having second thoughts."

Vance

Isaac just stared before bending to tighten a loose bracket. "Then let's hope he isn't," he slowly and gently pried her sharp grip away.

A squelch sounded over his radio. "Chief … you there? Over."

Isaac stopped again. "I am. But only if it's good news."

"Negative. Scoured the entire cottage. Both inside and out. Santa Claus isn't here."

Isaac rolled his eyes next to an equally engaged Silva—baffled to no end how they could keep losing him. "And the reindeer?"

"All nine … well and accounted for. In fact, they appear to be gorging on … apples," said the elf conducting the inspection as he reached to pull a partially chewed core from up out of the snow.

"Of course," Isaac whispered to himself. "Kris used to do the same— spoiling them with Golden Delicious."

Ezra joined from the opposite way. He held up his stopwatch, anticipating being asked for an update. "Is something wrong?" he could clearly see it in Isaac's worn-out face, though perhaps wished he hadn't asked.

The steeple led him right to it. The small church rested at the end of a dead-end street. The white wood blended in with the snow at either side, with the top of a cross sticking up out of some adjoining ice. Nick approached the door in a different condition than the last time he sought refuge inside; but as he searched for Clovis Finch, saw no one.

"Baaaaagh." Joseph popped out from between a pew. He was roaming free outside his pen.

"Oh, hello," Nick was quick to sink his hands deep inside the sheep's old wool. "Have you seen …? Never mind," he realized who he was talking to, unzipping the main pouch to his backpack. "Look, I brought something. Heard popcorn and gingerbread were two of your favorites.

Is that true?" He couldn't finish his sentence before Joseph excitedly nibbled out of his hand. It made Nick smile to see the sheep enjoying the treat. "There you go. And I've got more."

"Enough for me too, I hope," said Clovis, releasing the hood over his ears as he followed through the door.

"Oh, hello," Nick's guilt began to set in. "I know it's probably really bad for him, but I was just …"

"Bearing gifts, of course. Welcome back, Nick Kringle. Joseph and I were hoping you might return."

"I've been meaning to."

Clovis waved his arm to the nearest pew, suggesting Nick take a seat. The drip from the ceiling, meanwhile, continued to fill up the very same can. He sat and stared at a statue of Jesus praying on two knees. It was chiseled out of a log behind the pulpit. "If I remember the last time, you were having an episode into your past. And yet, the past still haunts you," he faced Nick like a wise and trusted shrink.

Nick thought hard about the day before, occasionally rubbing away at muscles that were still plenty sore—though it was also a great relief to have somebody to talk to.

"Clovis," he liked that soothing something in his eye. "I don't know exactly how to explain this, but sometimes I feel as if I'm liv'n directly inside the New Testament. And I'm not talking about the good parts where Jesus wins."

Clovis listened closely, not needing to suggest Nick offer up more detail. "Without the ugly stuff, there is no victory. For Jesus endured and conquered to ensure it."

"But what does any of that have to do with me?" he couldn't manage to get the terrible replay of slaughtered babies out of his head.

Vance

Clovis laid his eyes back on the wooden statue. "Perhaps we all at times must receive a taste of what it's like to see the very worst in humanity." Finch stood up again to approach it closer, as if analyzing every detail for the first time. "The past is there to teach us lessons about who we are and what our mission here on earth is. Your mission is clear," Clovis lauded as Joseph was still at Nick's hip—eating food unfit for a sheep.

"Have you seen him?" Nick looked confused, not entirely certain as to who he was referring. "Your father, have you seen him?" Clovis pointed to another piece of artwork, this one inside a frame over an adjoining wall.

"Is that … John?" Nick stood himself to get a better look. Clovis only nodded as Nick observed the pleasantly genuine features in his face. He knew it was a younger version of the man he once saw inside the snow globe.

"When I said, your father, whom did you think I was talking about?"

Nick's eyes nearly winced as he envisioned his adopted dad escorted along a lonely hall full of bars. The bitter thought morphed into one even more bitter as he recreated the sleigh crash in his mind. He let the pain pass before opening back up again. "Is it wrong to assume you were talking about both?"

Clovis smiled big. "Of course not."

"How could two people with the same title be so different?" he couldn't help but ask.

Clovis chuckled this time. "And you forget what they have in common. Arthur is sadly imprisoned. And yet, is it not also true that John once found himself incarcerated by sea?"

Nick hunched. It was his way of admitting he had never made the connection before. "But only one deserved his fate."

Inheriting the Sleigh

"Our parents shape and influence who we are, Nick. For good or for bad. But there are always things we can learn, even if that happens to be primarily from their mistakes," Clovis informed. "We covered forgiveness the last time if my memory serves me. Perhaps it's charity you have learned now."

"Charity?"

"That's right, which trumps even forgiveness. To forgive requires us to swallow our pride. But to serve takes a certain physical sacrifice."

Joseph caught Nick off guard by jumping into his lap to sniff out more popcorn.

"I've fed him corn stocks before, but it turns out he likes the movie theatre variety even more," Clovis joked. "Come, walk with me and tell me more about what you saw."

"The wise men," Nick uttered, baffled that Clovis had again beaten him to the point— all without knowing precisely how. He stopped at a stained-glass window of the three in magnificent cloaks, all offering up their gifts.

"Do you know who they were, Nick?"

"I know they were men of means from the south."

"Wealthy merchants of Arabia," Clovis added. "And you think they really needed to venture thousands of miles from their native homes to follow their consciences, let alone that star? Nah," Finch answered his own question. "They had a comfortable life, and yet they were called to leave." Clovis rubbed his chin. "But if anybody would understand such a burden, it would be you."

"They had to visit their new king," said Nick.

"It was a toiling sacrifice to deliver their charity—their wonderful gifts. But they also knew that the gold, frankincense and myrrh would be returned to them a thousand-fold."

Vance

"The Risen Lord rising again the third day."

"You're smarter than you give yourself credit for, Nick Kringle," observed Clovis.

He pulled the Santa hat from his backpack, placing it back over his head. "Here," he then reached for a handmade hammer; one with a red leather handle he'd spent his little free time stitching himself. It was wrapped in a bow. "I almost forgot."

"And what is this?" Clovis grasped—to the recurring drip he had grown so accustomed.

Nick pointed above. "I couldn't help but notice the roof needing a little tender loving care. Consider it an early Christmas gift."

Clovis smiled as he simulated the motion of pounding a nail. And it was then and there that he settled upon what was happening. Through all Nick's anxiety, he had naturally managed to begin the process of turning into a man Clovis knew well. "The others are looking for you, aren't they?"

Nick shook with guilt, as if they could both feel Isaac scouring every resource possible to find him. "I have to go now. The clock is ticking."

Chapter 46

O uch," Nick squinted as an elf with grayish hair had pins stuck up and down—ankle to neck. "Careful, Gretchen!"

"I thought I told you to suck in."

"But I have to take a breath, eventually. And that one really hurt," he winced as she continued to poke through the wooly red fabric that dangled off all four limbs.

"Believe me," said Gretchen in her shower cap and gown. "Come Christmas Eve, you'll be wearing this suit forever just beggin' for it to fit right. OK, stay just like … that," she froze, raising both arms up high with a pin in her mouth, all with Nick struggling to stand off-balance.

"How long?" he gritted, hoping for the agony to end.

"I don't know … just longer," Gretchen didn't mind being difficult. "You know, like father like son. You'd think he'd eventually get used to it, but year after year, Father Kris would wail up a storm whenever I hemmed his trousers."

"You mean to tell me I have to do this every year?" Nick griped as a prettier elf entered past the dressing room curtain to start filing his nails.

"Of course. Why, you think you're going to be this thin forever? Bodies change, you know, and not for the better. Just ask my tubby hubby."

Vance

An entire team was suddenly working on Nick, with new pieces of the uniform gradually being ushered in. "Ugh!" he was caught off guard by the thick black belt suddenly being cinched tight around his waist.

"Alright, I've finally found a nine and-a-half," said a feminine male storming in with two shiny black boots. Nick was forced back into a seat as the boots were intrusively pulled up over his feet. Others hauled loose fabric away once the measurements had been completed. "OK, how's this one?"

"To be honest, still suffocating."

"Why does he insist on being such a toosh?" the frustrated elf griped to Gretchen as he pulled the boots off again. "I'll go see if we have a ten."

"I'm truly sorry to put an end to ... whatever this is," Isaac had never been such a welcome distraction, poking his head through a curtain. "But Santa Claus is needed elsewhere."

Gretchen gave Isaac the look of death as a relieved Nick was quick to step off the small platform to start stripping off all the unhemmed fabric. "Oh, that's really too bad," Nick did a terrible job hiding the joy behind the sarcasm. "But I guess we'll have to continue this fashion show later, then."

"I promise I'll make it up to you," Isaac assured Gretchen, while silently signaling Nick to hurry fast. The truth was, he couldn't endure that uncomfortable stare a second longer.

"You knew she was gonna do that, didn't you?" Nick shook as he reached for his bag on the way out.

"Yeah," Isaac didn't even attempt to fib his way out this time. "My way of getting back at you for running away again. Or was it flying away, this time?"

"Have you still not accepted the fact I had no control over the sleigh? I'm telling you—it was possessed."

Inheriting the Sleigh

"And yet you keep making my job more and more difficult. Look, the truth is … I need somebody watching you around the clock. You know, in case you … or whoever it was," Isaac clarified. "Suddenly decides to dart off again." Nick couldn't argue as Isaac changed the subject. "I do hear you've been on a recent gift giving binge though. Just remember—the next time you spoil the reindeer with apples, it makes 'em gassy."

"Which reminds me," Nick's face lit up as they stopped near a green door. He unzipped a backpack off his shoulder, only to unveil the last thing Isaac ever expected to see; especially right before such an important meeting.

"What is that?" The elf didn't need to ask but did anyway.

"It's a dustpan," Nick had a child-like innocence about his face as he awaited a reaction.

"Wow," Isaac did his best to act excited. "I give you a Key Whiz, and you give me … a … dustpan?"

Nick gave him a moment to inspect it. "The last time I was inside your place—forgive me—but I noticed … well, anyway," Nick chose his words carefully. "I made it myself."

"Yes, you did," Isaac uttered slowly as he stroked the freshly carved wood. There were some obvious blemishes, but he failed to bring those up. "As much as I wish I had the time to clean my house right now—you really think you're ready for this?"

Nick didn't feel a need to answer this time. In fact, he pushed the awaiting door open himself, only to behold a series of unpleasant stares. "And the prodigal son returns," spat a cynical first observer. He had dyed, spiky blue hair and unpleasantly pale skin. "On your father's wretched time again, I see."

"And it's good to see you as well … whatever your name is," Nick showed his agitation with a crack of his own as Elites sat shoulder-to-shoulder around a large table. Another row of congressman crowded an elevated row against the wall, with a gap in-between.

"You call us all here at a half-days' notice, the least you could do is start this pointless exchange on time," said another with a Revolutionary War-era wig.

"I've been trying to entertain them," uttered Gib next to Blaine, with three colorful balls and a unicycle in hand. "But apparently juggling's not their thing."

Isaac wanted to roll his eyes—but before he could de-escalate tempers, Nick was already taking charge.

"You're right," Nick caught more than just Isaac off guard by admitting his error. "Perhaps I should be more punctual." Elites scratched their heads, unsure how to process the contrite gesture. "And now as to the purpose of this meeting."

"Dieeeeee-ing to know," a female Elite with long, fake curls twiddled her hair as she interrupted him.

"It shouldn't be a dirty secret to anyone any longer that my life's been under siege."

Blaine could only watch the brash Elites badger Nick as he stood through the silence.

"And I suppose you're so vain as to assume we care even a smidgen."

Nick didn't see where the smart aleck remark came from—again electing to ignore it. "As I was saying. I wanted to personally send my condolences for Mauv Lyman's murder."

"Condolences?" said an Elite with so much makeup, it nearly made his skin look pink. "You wish condolences on a man who once ordered your own death?"

Inheriting the Sleigh

"Well …," Nick thought, as if it were just beginning to feel natural to forgive. "Yes. And that's why I'm here. To forge a new friendship at the Pole."

"Friendship? Let me guess. You brashly think you can bridge the divide that's been in place here for centuries? How could you be so bloody foolish?"

Nick paused between thoughts, gauging the awkward reactions from all 25 or so in the room. The Elites were now silent and attentive—a most welcome change. "Because I believe we need each other." Isaac was surprised by Nick's retort. He was leaning back, watching him take command of the floor. "I mean, who really knows how dangerous this enemy is or could be. Perhaps it threatens both elf and Elite."

"What are you saying?" pried an Elite with a chiseled jaw and golden contact lenses that made his eyes nearly glow.

"I think it's clear. You're either with me in a new era of bringing the spirit of Christmas to the world …." Nick opened his bag again, this time pulling out a brightly patterned dog on wheels. "Or … you're not." The Elites had little idea what to think as he set the toy in the very middle of the table to make a point.

"Go ahead," Nick suggested a man with unkempt, Einstein-like hair take hold of the remote that went along with it.

The look on Gib's face was pure shock as he never in a thousand years thought he might see an Elite even so much as touch a toy.

"What, have you really never played with one before?" Nick quizzed. "Look, I'll show you," he took back the remote. The skeptical Elite almost lunged away, startled by the fact the dog's eyes suddenly lit up and barked. Its tongue was now wagging on its hindlegs, playfully waving its paws. Nick then spun the dog 360 degrees. "Here," he gave it back. "You try."

Vance

The Elite did eventually lay his own hand over the combination of rubber and plastic—but only after a slow pry and an uncertain glance about the room. Rolling the joystick in a circular motion, the robotic dog began to move its legs across the table. The motion was choppy, but the Elite was slowly getting the hang of it. That is until abruptly getting knocked off the table with a sudden swoop.

The Elite was jumpy again, as if finally knocked out of a trance—one where for only a short moment he had turned into a child. The rest of the room was equally startled as another stepped forward. He possessed a cane, with a brass rodent on the top—clearly perturbed and ready to make his case.

"And what was that for?" Nick made sure his question was both short and direct.

"Because we are lawmakers, Mr. Kringle," said the stout man with red suspenders dropping down over a large waste. His black mustache was thin—his grin, familiar and sinister. "And lawmakers don't have time for pointless play hour."

"But everybody needs to play," Nick countered.

"Why? Because you march in here and say that we do?"

"No," Nick shook as he attempted to read the man who had ruthlessly stepped forward to challenge him. "Because what really is the point of any of this if we don't manage to find things that bring us joy along the way? And …," he reached down to retrieve the K9. "If this doesn't tickle your fancy—perhaps you can tell me what does."

"A request? Of Santa Claus?" he laughed.

Blaine and Gib were never so fascinated as Nick slowly peered around the small room. "Perhaps I even have it in my bag at this very moment." But the Elite didn't answer this time. "What is your name?" Nick asked.

"He doesn't know?" the Elite laughed toward Isaac with big eyes. Isaac stood straight-faced as the intimidating Elite waved his cane back at the boy. "Perhaps all you need to know is my last name."

"Nick," Isaac broke his silence, tipping his head toward the mystery man. "Meet, Griswald Gizer."

The name alone was enough to stir Nick's heart. Goss' face had since replaced Griswald's—enough so to where Blaine could tell something was wrong. "Are you OK?"

"Yeah," Nick fought it until snapping back.

"Good then," said Griswald. "I understand you've met my second cousin."

"The man who killed the Speaker. And who appears to be coming after me next. Yes. Perhaps you can tell me where he is?"

"As if Clive Curnuckle himself hasn't already interrogated me a hundred times," Griswald scoffed. "The truth is, nobody knows. The Pole's underground extends deep. There are a million places for him to hide."

"Are you trying to scare the boy?" Gib intervened. It was his attempt at protecting Nick—but like it or not, the bloodline association was beginning to fester under his skin.

"Since you don't know where he is," Nick finally spoke back up in a whisper. "Then I'm left to assume you don't share the same allegiance?"

The rest of the Elites remained silent with keen interest in what he might divulge next—though Griswald elected to change the subject entirely. "So, tell me … what else is in that magic bag?"

Nick was more than happy to unveil a new toy. This time it was a wooden ball on a string. Nick pushed the classic Kendama into the air, catching the small ball into the groove attached to the side. That was before encircling the group—offering it to a watchful Elite on his way past.

"So, you say you leave the childish behavior to others; those beneath you," Nick had since fully made it once around the table. "And yet, perhaps therein lies the problem. You can go back to your fancy living quarters. Back to your exclusive chamber writing more legislation full of legal jargon designed to enrich yourselves, all as others labor for a cause. But in the end, except you become as a little child … your arrogance will certainly destroy you. Because in the eyes of God," Nick's preachy monologue flowed freely. "The elves are the higher class." Whether his audience appreciated it or not, he had a new toy for every flummoxed Elite listening with a cynical ear.

"Meek, submissive and full of innocent curiosity. Always willing to learn and embrace truth. Apt to giving others the benefit of the doubt. Forgiving quickly; not to mention seeing the best in people. And of course," Nick wrapped up once all the toys from his bag had finally been dispersed. His eyes sunk deep underneath the skin of every Elite as he caught a twirling pigskin on its way down. "Being a little playful never hurt either."

Chapter 47

Every second a robotic hand stamped the assembly line of T-Rex', branding a different dinosaur with the exact same seal.

"How many do you anticipate having by deadline?" Nick quizzed a factory manager.

"Target goal—around 450,000, sir."

"Hmmm," Nick hastily rubbed his chin. He stared at the parade of toys elevating over the moving belt. "Is there any way you can boost that number to 475? Let's just say, I've been receiving some late requests."

"Whatever you wish." Nick, with a quill slipped behind his ear lent a satisfactory nod. "And does that include the sister line of stegosaurus'?"

Nick gave him an encouraging pat on the shoulder before advancing deeper through the colorful factory. He was now looking upward with a sudden eerie feeling in his bones. There was a drift he remembered well following the last ambush and couldn't help but feel vulnerable to another. Now staring up at the ventilation shafts, the boy could've sworn he'd noticed the blur of something shuffling above.

The end of the scope was blinking like a real eye. It zigzagged through narrow tunnels—vertically, then otherwise. At the very bottom, a Black Cape held the periscope handle with two hands on each side of the viewfinder, as if inside an old submarine, tracking the movements of an enemy ship.

Gizer stood in a dark cavern watching Nick through a series of clever mirrors. "Hold," instructed Gizer, staring closely. "Hold the eye, steady."

"But look," said a Cape from behind. "It's as if he senses something off. I think he knows somebody's watching."

"Of course, he does," Goss mocked. "He clearly has the freakish intuition. The same one his father had."

"Should I retreat the scope then?" asked the Cape with his hands still gripped over the handle.

"No. Keep it there," Gizer snickered. "I want him to know we're watching. Hasn't anyone here ever taken a course in psychology before?" he turned to the small group of Capes inside the dimly lit cavern. "Of course, you haven't," he waved after not hearing a retort. "And that's precisely why I am here, and you are … well, never mind."

The door then opened to behold Griswald with a hand cupped over the brass head of a rat.

"There you are," said Goss as he stood outside the barrier between caves. "Holding that dreadful rodent as usual, I see. I prefer snakes. They eat rats."

"Pardon the delay … cousin."

"Second cousin," Goss clarified.

"Of course," Griswald shook. "As I was saying, the journey down here can make one a bit …"

"Disoriented?" Goss beat him to it with large eyes, as if quietly mumbling "lightweight" under his breath. "For some … yes."

Inheriting the Sleigh

"I personally pull the trigger on the Speaker, and you continue to treat me like a child?" uttered Griswald. "As if I take all the risk of doing your dirty work, while you reap the reward."

"Now, Griswald," Goss consoled. "For we are both of the great Gizer name and tradition. There is plenty of credit to go around. A beverage?" Goss reached for a cup over a table, lifting on a faucet. The glass brimmed with a bubbly green liquid.

"What is it?" inquired a thirsty but skeptical Griswald as he curiously sniffed the suds at the top.

"What difference does it make?" Goss shrugged as Griswald took a sip, only to immediately spit it back out.

"That's dreadful."

"Yes, it is," Goss sat on a bench carved out of stone to lay his hands over his snickering cheeks. "But to answer your question, it's a combination of whiskey and green punch. Oh, and I threw in a little carbonation for effect."

"That's not drinkable," Griswald used his cane to support himself as he sat next to Goss.

"Yeah, well, as you can see, the selection down here is limited. We consume what we have. So," Goss seemed eager to change the subject. "I heard there was a meeting."

"Your moles work fast," Griswald observed. "Then did they tell you what transpired, or simply what you wished to hear?"

After a seconds long pause, Goss laughed, still unsure if it was a joke. "You always were the funny one, weren't you, Griswald?"

But Griswald wasn't laughing. "Believe me, I would love nothing more than to report his spirits are down, but it appears to be the opposite. The boy is stronger than you give him credit for," said Griswald, casually walking across the room. He found a box of doughnuts on the table and helped himself. "Much better, by the way. Just wish I had something to wash it down with," he took another look at the whiskey. Goss didn't appear amused by the observation before Griswald whipped around to offer up a smile of his own. "But that doesn't mean there isn't still time to break him."

Goss suddenly stood back up, holding his cup high with approval. "To two failed Christmases."

But Griswald wasn't finished. "I will have you know that some of my colleagues appear to be somewhat sympathetic to their cause. At least straddling the fence at this point."

"I see."

"They have not taken well to the murder of the Speaker, and I have struggled to get them on board with your vision for the future. I assume they need more time but can't say for sure."

The Cape at the periscope swiveled, interrupting the one-on-one. "Look," he signaled the monitor. "It appears as if the boy is now … waving at us. If I didn't know any better, I'd think he's egging us on, sir."

Griswald waited for his second cousin's now violet face to burst, before whispering his own fuming reaction instead. "That's exactly what he's doing."

Chapter 48

Nick tinkered at his bench. Handmade clocks occasionally chimed on the wall as he fiddled with tools. The drapes were open inside the bedroom, exposing a fresh snowfall as he held a screwdriver and pick assembling a motorcycle sidecar.

Nick wound it up, watching the sidecar roll over the fresh sawdust shavings—until a loose hammer stopped its momentum. Nick hung the hammer next to the other countless tools dangling over the long, custom built workstation. Many shelves were filled with toys; most of which were made over decades. But just as he began to paint the sidecar he heard the train.

The miniature locomotive rolled over the tracks through the hole in the wall, only stopping at the wooded station in the corner of the bedroom. "A note for Nick Kringle," yelled the conductor with his green hand cupped over his mouth in search of the proper recipient.

"I'm right here," said Nick softly to the toy soldier. "You don't have to yell."

"Of course," he seemed somewhat embarrassed as Nick reached up to grab hold of the envelope.

Vance

"I haven't seen you for a while. Is everything alright?"

Nick could tell the conductor thought it odd, as if he'd never been asked about his personal welfare before. "I believe we've been just … fine, thank you."

"Actually," the engineer inside the caboose cut off the conductor with some surprising honesty. "It's been a rather tough week, you know." The conductor shot the engineer a funny look, wondering why he was going against protocol with a complaint.

"Really?" said Nick as a suggestion to carry on. "What happened?"

"Well, it all began with an essential fragment of the track freezing over near the Honey Baked Ham District. And that was followed by a blown regulator rod that kept us parked for at least a couple hours more. And I haven't even mentioned the clogged steam dome yet."

"Sergeant," called the conductor, suggesting they'd heard enough—though the engineer clearly felt much better after releasing the burdening secrets.

"I'm sorry to hear about your string of misfortune," said Nick. "But I'm glad you're back up and running now."

"Well, that's assuming we get that pressure gauge replaced. It's on its last leg, you know. And don't even get me started on the coal shortage. We're gonna need a new shipment here real soon—or else trust me— we're not going anywhere."

The conductor was flummoxed. "I'm truly sorry for all that," he whispered with impatience and guilt. "I don't really know what's gotten into him. Anyway, we've made our delivery. Clearly time for us to be moving on now," the soldier tugged on the whistle string as steam once again poured out the smokestack.

"Wait, before I forget," Nick ran to a drawer, searching for something. Nick pulled out what could barely be seen by the human eye from a distance. Between his thumb and index fingers was a small, wrapped gift for each soldier. "Perhaps these will make you feel better."

"What is this?" wondered the conductor as they received the present—each the size of a quarter.

"Go ahead."

"You do realize we're not even real?" reminded the conductor. "Just products of ingenuity and invention."

Nick hadn't even considered it, encouraging the soldiers to open the gifts anyway. The engineer tore the bright red wrapping paper off first. "A new pressure gauge?" Both soldiers seemed perplexed. "How did you know?"

Nick rubbed his head, somewhat unsure himself. It was as if he had since forgotten what it was he'd even wrapped.

The conductor was now more anxious to open his. "A new hat," he smiled as he inspected the glimmering black bill and flat top. It had a gold band across the middle. The soldier removed an old flimsy, jean-colored cap he wore over his plastic helmet, immediately replacing it with the new one.

"Look'n good, Captain," said the engineer with a wide grin.

"Really?" even he couldn't hold back a smile before turning back into his disciplined self. "I mean, of course I do. C'mon, it's time to go. We're now seven minutes off schedule."

"Wait, where's the other one?" Nick was referring to the third soldier—often seen slumbering inside the mail car. The conductor waved his helmet that direction and when Nick listened close, could hear him hunched down inside, snoring as usual. "Well, when he awakes, will you give him this?" said Nick, handing the conductor a third gift.

Vance

"Thank you ... Santa Claus," said the engineer genuinely one last time as the train quickly slid out of view over a fireplace through another hole in the wall.

Nick finally had a chance to open his letter. It was sealed with a golden sticker. The message was short and in large, handwritten font.

Do you still have the key? It's time now to see the present.

Nick thought for a moment before dropping the paper. He searched a drawer before barreling down the rickety wooden staircase for the cottage's main floor. After inserting the key into its hole, the main fireplace was folding in again under the mantle to expose the mysterious entryway inside.

Nick was even more nervous than he was the last time, but as usual his curiosity overrode all of that. With his forearm protecting his face from the dusty soot, he grabbed the lantern to descend the steps, proceeding through the cave. That is until finding the trail of mist that led to the smoky screen. This time, images quickly began to form over the middle third.

"Do you understand how much I'm paying you?" said Arthur Crest, unused to being the only one in the room not wearing a suit.

His attorney stared across the table as Arthur sat on the opposite end in his jail jumper. "And do you understand how much trouble you're in?" the peeved lawyer countered while trying to sound as respectful as possible. "I may be one of the most sought-after defense attorneys in the city, but I'm not God. I can't just do away with the law simply because you want an easy way out of this mess."

Arthur took a deep breath, attempting to calm himself down. "Go ahead. Continue," he twirled a hand.

"As I was saying, they want to cut a deal."

Inheriting the Sleigh

"What kind of deal?" Arthur couldn't remain silent for long. "Like half a million-dollar fine and up to six months in jail or something?"

Once again, the attorney rolled his eyes, as if hating to speak the truth and risk watching Arthur blow his top. "More like six years."

"Six years!" Arthur's chair screeched as he abruptly stood up.

"And a two and a half million-dollar fine."

Arthur bit his lip this time to keep himself from saying something he might regret.

"I tried to tell you, Mr. Crest. This judge is not messing around. He has a history of enforcing domestic abuse—coupled with other charges—as harshly as possible. But if it makes you feel any better, the prosecutor originally wanted to give you eight to nine. I bargained them down."

Arthur gave his lawyer the kiss of death. "And if we take it to trial?"

"Then you're looking at no less than 12, maybe 15."

The screen abruptly transitioned, with only a flash in-between. Nick squinted as he quickly tried to figure out where Marie was. She didn't belong in her current environment and wasn't the only one to recognize it, receiving odd looks on her way past.

Marie wisely and inconspicuously kept her head dipped down into the weedy sidewalk as she scurried over the trash-ridden streets and past a series of barred shop windows.

Nick watched with concern, knowing this was not some movie guaranteed to have a happy conclusion. He was observing in real time.

"How's the trust fund?" laughed a toothless hag. "Wouldn't care to fill an old woman's stomach, now, would ya?" she held out her hands for spare change.

"I'm sorry," Marie kept on jogging, only to encounter another vagabond. This one full of the shakes.

"Excuse me, but I just a need a couple of bucks … that's all. Just to get a bus ticket 'outa here. And then I'm never coming back," he pestered.

"I just need to meet someone," Marie looked at a piece of scrap paper in hand. "Again, I'm so sorry."

Though she couldn't see the creepy observance at her back, Nick could. "Marie!" Nick yelled out in desperation. He was surprised to find her suddenly stop before trying again. "Marie!"

The girl looked up and then out, as if having just heard a familiar voice. She pinched her arm to make sure she wasn't crazy before moving again. But this time, started to jog—past a burning trash barrel where boys kept warm in the evening winds.

"Lost, little girl?" laughed a man over some cracked steps. He was smoking a cigarette, but Marie didn't pay any attention to the mockery. She just kept running—stopping only to check a new street sign.

Nick watched with bated breath as she passed a tattoo parlor, followed by several liquor stores with lit-up lottery signs.

"Where is this place?" Marie finally vented after stopping at an intersection.

"Pssssss," A male startled her. He had blended in perfectly with a pole, releasing his hooded sweatshirt. "You, Ms. Bayliff?"

Nick was anticipating the worst, stepping closer to the smoke, as if he could actually do something to protect her.

Marie hesitated before nodding.

"Then follow me." Marie cautiously trailed a couple steps behind as he proceeded forward, crossing a street for several back alleyways. The further she followed, the more nervous she became with less and less people suddenly in sight.

"Where are you taking me?" she asked.

Inheriting the Sleigh

"Not much further," said the man who occasionally glanced around—as if making certain he wasn't being watched. "Alright, here we are," he did one last double-take before unlocking a door down a quiet alley between dumpsters.

Nick could barely stand it any longer as he whisked her inside, turning on the lights to expose a mostly empty warehouse.

"What is this place?"

"Never mind. You have the …?"

"Money?" Marie reached under her jacket to pull out several large bills. "Right here."

The man was glad to finally come eye-to-eye with the cash. "Look at that, you weren't play'n?" But Marie quickly pulled the money back as he lunged.

"First … what I need."

"Of course," he uttered. "What you need. And tell me, what is that again?" his mind had since become sidetracked by the loot.

"I thought we talked about this. I need to get out of the country."

"Well, you came to the right man for that," he assured with a tough-guy swag, tugging at his hoodie and nibbling on a toothpick. "I can get you pretty much anywhere you need to go. So, where are you trying to disappear to anyway? China? The Caribbean? I just got a guy into Singapore yesterday. Do you have any idea how hard it is to forge documents into Singapore?" Marie only nodded but failed to answer his original question. "Perhaps you'd like me to pick someplace for you then?" he asked in jest. "'Cause I could get you to Paris in two days. You ever seen the Eiffel …"

"The North Pole," she felt awkward cutting him off.

The street tough thought he'd heard correctly though repeated it for kicks. "Come again—did you just say … North … Pole?"

"That's right," Marie fought through her humiliation, saying it louder this time. "I'm trying to get to the North Pole." The man stared before bending over in laughter. "What is so funny?" she exclaimed.

"And I bet you want a little magical elf train with hot cocoa and butterscotch cookies to take you there."

"Are you done?" Marie had had enough.

"Perhaps for a few grand more I could even build you a sleigh. And wait, wait, wait," he could no longer contain himself. "I even know an old white dude with a beard. He's toothless and drunk half the time but would be perfect. We could fatten him up a bit, and then he could taxi you on over there himself."

"I'm sorry, I think I may have made a mistake," a humiliated Marie tucked the cash away, making a jolt for the door.

"Wait, hold on," he was quick to stop her as he dried up the tears around his eyes. "Man, you white girls don't know how to take a joke?" he stated to no response. "Look, you want to go to the North Pole," he waved her deeper inside the warehouse toward a world map pinned to the wall. Every continent was a different color and it was full of tack marks, representing years and years of use. "Now, take a good look at this," he used a flashlight for more light. "This here is planet Earth. Do you see the North Pole? Anywhere?" he asked, trying not to sound facetious as he used a fist to hide any more unintentional laughter. "Go ahead. Step closer."

Marie slowly approached the map, darting her eyes around for something she already knew wasn't there. "No," she shrugged with defeat.

"So how then do you ever expect me to get you somewhere that no one—not even agents inside the all-mighty government can locate," he asked seriously this time, wanting very badly what she had tucked inside her jacket. "It's like Area 51, or Atlantis or something."

All Marie could do was shrug. "But I was told you were the best. You know, that if anybody could me get me there, it was ..."

The man stopped, as if suddenly feeling his heart melted down by the compliment. "Hold up," he paused, retreating back toward the board. "You say, the North Pole?" he tried again. "OK, I guess that means we're dealing with ... this region ... here," he reached up to point toward the very top of the map. "We'll try Siberia. Assuming for argument's sake we're at least somewhere in the ballpark."

Marie continued to say nothing, but she did nod this time as the man smiled to reveal a golden tooth. "OK ... I think I can get you there."

"Wait!" Nick cried as the images of Marie suddenly gave way to a new scene. "Come back!"

But he stopped once he realized there was absolutely nothing he could do. An entire army was now positioned inside the rocky, underground fortress. "My sons! The true sons of Asher!" raised a familiar voice—echoing with crisp acoustics. Decorated Black Capes stood shoulder-to-shoulder listening to their leader speak charismatically over an elevated platform. "I hope you've checked your calendars," Gizer smiled to a collective cheer. "Do you know what dreadful month it is? Always saving the worst for last. That's right— December."

The Capes were bunched inside the massive cave deposit, with stalagmites dripping down like stone icicles. There was a frost coated over the rock, with an icy river splitting through the vast underground. "Let us prepare and then wait. We wait for our time to strike. And when that time comes, we go with all the merry might we can muster!"

Following a rousing, Nazi-like cheer, the last picture in the fog slowly faded away before disappearing entirely. Once again, Nick's mind and heart were both consumed. He should have been frightened most by what he knew was now taking place somewhere under his feet—though couldn't seem to stop mumbling the very same name. A name that trumped every other cause for concern. "Marie."

Chapter 49

And on that brisk but cheery day, the morning appeared as night. A night where time stood literally still," Smudge Terpley gripped a flashlight in front of his cheeky face. The classroom was dark, and the odd professor whispered slowly for dramatic effect. "The two hands working tirelessly to strike midnight at the old but glorious clock. The blessed eve of the morning giving clearance for the great Santa to commence. He would elevate the anxious team of flying deer through a lull in time, reaching every Christian home," Terpley raised both his voice and his fingers. "A token of faith for the traveler to make his annual living room dash—one bound with sparkling new ..."

Smudge opened his eyes just long enough to notice Nick clearly disinterested in the theatrical display. The boy was sitting still at his desk—both elbows propped, and his hands cupped over his mouth.

Terpley turned the flashlight off and the house lights back on, though Nick's eyes failed to move. Smudge hunched down to snap over his still face. It took a few tries before Nick's corneas finally budged. "That was ... wonderful?" he said with monotone assurance.

"Was it?" Terpley was offended by both the disinterest and the lie. "Because typically when one enjoys a legendary performance such as that, they at least act engaged."

"Was it that obvious?"

"So, what's wrong? Did you wake up on the wrong side of that king-sized bed of yours? You know, the one with the 2,000 thread count sheets imported directly from Cairo?" Terpley had a titch of jealous sarcasm in his voice.

"I don't know, Professor," Nick was unsure how to divulge the randomness of his thought. A thought that for whatever reason wouldn't go away. The book inside his head was unnaturally large; so much so he could hardly even tell how to read it.

Nick looked at Smudge, long and straight, as if he couldn't play games any longer. He needed answers and finally realized where to start as images of the Congressional House suddenly flashed across his mind.

"Tell me, what is it you see?" The professor wasn't blind to the fact something was bothering him.

"It's a book," he squinted. "Only one that I couldn't possibly ever hold, it's so big."

"I see." Terpley didn't appear to need another clue. "The Book of Names must be calling."

"Book of Names?"

"Of course. Have you not yet been introduced?"

"I guess not," Nick sighed.

"What have you and Mr. Newell been doing all this time?" Terpley's better judgement kicked in, thinking it best not to wait for an answer to the ill-timed thought. "But the bigger question is, why is it being impressed upon you now?"

Inheriting the Sleigh

"I don't ... know," Nick continued to look flummoxed. "What is in the book, anyway?"

Smudge offered him a perplexing look of his own. "Why, it's every name, of course. Every name and their coinciding story." Marie's eyes were unmistakably the next image to light up bright across Nick's brain. "Is there somebody's story weighing on your mind? Perhaps this could be a teaching moment. One we could go over together."

But Nick knew, as urgent as it was, this was something he had to deal with alone. "I'm sorry," he bolted out the classroom door like a chameleon's tongue for a sitting fly—pulling his coat off the rack on his way past.

"But you just used the ... latrine," Smudge's confused call trailed off once Nick was already too far out of earshot.

Nick scampered along the quiet schoolhouse halls and down a flight of stairs. Wreaths hung over empty doors and Frank Sinatra's "Have Yourself a Merry Little Christmas" was lightly playing; though this time, he noticed none of it. Past the statue in the entryway, Nick used a burst to push through the heavy double doors out into the cold, dark wind. It immediately blew across his face—all while having no idea his every step was being closely watched.

The janitor's mop was propped on the tile—a set of fingers firmly gripped over the stickhandle. He keenly watched from the shadows, having a particular interest in those urgent feet that sprang away into the coinciding street traffic.

There was a colorful glow on the outside to offset the never-ending darkness. Nick's face was hidden by the hood of his thick coat as he hurried through town, flagging a young elf on a bike taxi. "Candy Cane Square, please!"

The boy responded to the urgency, pedaling fiercely through a little-known shortcut. Bright lights covered the gated enclosure. Some elves played a game of pickup hockey over a frozen pond, while others just patrolled the festive grounds, drinking hot beverages and enjoying the glowing décor.

"Thank you," Nick flipped the boy a coin as he jumped off—entering underneath two giant candy canes that crossed diagonally to signify he was in the right place.

Nick walked swiftly but discreetly through the hazy grounds. He was forced to puff into his hands every few seconds for warmth as he approached the tall, white steps leading up into the massive dome. It took him several minutes to make it to the top, where the surface finally flattened out to a series of limestone statues.

Nick was met by security at the doors. He flashed his badge and was allowed in where the cement gave way to accented marble. The foyer was vast and high, and he sprinted the hall before finding precisely what he was looking for.

A vast, circular hole was protected by only a short rail. Nick stopped to peer over—beholding the countless pine needles at eye level and beyond. His breath was taken by the majesty of the giant Christmas tree full of glimmering bulbs—each one different from the next.

Nick only crossed paths with a couple of meandering Elites before proceeding to what was next on his to-do list. Bending around the center of the mighty tree, there it was—propped upright.

"The Book of Names," Nick uttered. It was the height of a very tall man and the width of a small car. It had a soft, leather cover and sturdy spine that made Nick wonder if the book went back centuries.

Nick stepped onto a stool to gain the needed leverage to flip it open, but he immediately noticed something unique about the pages. They weren't parchment as he expected to see—rather thin sheets of digital ink. The font was of vintage penmanship, as if coming from an old hand just having dipped a quill into fresh ink. The pages were full of many small columns, aligned top to bottom in names.

"Alec Aaebatoo," was the first one to appear alphabetically in the top-left corner of page one. Nick had to tiptoe to read it. He then flipped more pages that were remarkably thin for being digital. He used both hands to grab as many pages as he could, only to grow frustrated by his inability to even make it out of the A's. Nick read a few random names along the way for curiosity's sake. As he did, an image of a new child would form across his brain—each with a unique story. But for the sake of time was forced to press on with the one name he had originally come to search.

"Bay," a fatigued Nick got excited as he knew he was getting close. He ran his finger until finally locating Bayliff. But even then, there were hundreds more to sift through; that is until he found the accompanying first name. He tapped on "Marie," which brought up a picture, along with an exceptionally long number.

When asked for a print, Nick pressed his thumb up against the screen until the security protocol was approved.

Jumping from the stool, he had what he needed. It was now onto the nearby port where the vehicles were parked and empty. He entered the first one he saw, watching his step as he opened the gate with a warning sign to do just that. One clumsy slip and he'd fall right off the edge—into the massive hole toward the tree's trunk; most of which he couldn't see.

Now safely inside the silver carrier, he sat. The screen on a monitor asked for another thumbprint. A recent photo of Marie emerged again, along with her personal file full of bullet point information.

Vance

-15 years old.
-New York, United States.
-Father: Burton, district attorney.
-Mother: Marlene, homemaker.
-Sister: Claire, seven years old.
-Love interest ... Nick paused as he silently read his own name.

He broke from yet another lull, slowly coasting with the strange transport. It stretched out, gliding its way around the tree. Nick occasionally rubbed his hand across an unusually large ornament, with the vehicle bending further before elevating upward and inward.

It was getting darker as Nick ventured deeper, with the light generated from the monitor now needed to see. Nick noticed a flashlight secured inside and quickly put it to use, barely ducking to avoid a prickly branch. He was now weaving through and around ornaments, sometimes thinking he might crash right into one. Nick kept his light out in front as he continued to float across a programmed path—over layers of red mesh, and underneath a dangling wooden star.

But then it stopped. Nick knew the ornament when he saw it. It was a glass ball, with a twist of light purple that brought a kaleidoscope of more color depending on the angle. He had given Marie an exact replica, only much smaller just a few Christmases back.

The vehicle finally slowed to a stop. Nick stood from his seat and approached the hand-blown glass, waiting for something to happen. He gently poked at it, watching it lightly sway from its clear string over the branch. The ornament soon came to a stop again and began to glow. Nick was now seeing directly into an apartment he recognized very much. It was much less grandiose than the one he was raised in but still furnished nicely. A large painting of Mary, the mother of Jesus, hung on the wall behind the Christmas tree—and on the sofa next to it were Burton and Marlene Bayliff.

Burton held his wife's hand as she pressed a cordless telephone up to her ear in tears. Nick couldn't hear anything, but the picture alone told him everything he needed to know. Marlene then ended the call, dropping the phone as she sank her sad eyes into her husband's shoulder.

Distraught, Nick drove back for the platform, racing away on foot as quickly as he could. He was now running through another large hallway, this one full of offices adorned with festive wallpaper. Administrative elves passed him on both sides, wondering what all the commotion was about.

"Corbin!" Nick poked his head into one random office doorway after the next. "Corbin!"

"Not here," said the only elf in the room.

Nick then bolted for the next one in panic, only to get the same reply. He was too frantic to grant anyone the time—even if they could offer up a clue.

"Oh, hello … Nick," a passing Gib uttered with a pause in-between. Nick rudely whipped right by, causing Gib's top hat to fly off from the gust. "Of course. I guess that means we'll have to save the chitchat for another time then," he sarcastically grumbled as Nick didn't even have the courtesy to look back on the run.

At this point, the scared boy was drawing mostly unwanted attention; so much so it was beginning to embarrass those who knew him best.

"Nick," Ezra called to no reply, dropping his glasses further down his nose to make sure he was seeing correctly.

Vance

Silva poked her head out of an adjoining office to gather what all the fuss was about. Nick accidentally pushed over a woman on his way past. He was now coming directly for Silva but didn't have the wits to notice. Instead, he flew forward with his head suddenly hitting the ground with a thump.

"Ow," Nick winced as he pulled up to regain his composure. The tripwire had done its job, bringing the spectacle to a painful conclusion.

Silva was the first to rush to his side—followed by Ezra. "I'm sorry, Nick, but you seem to have gone raving mad," she said in a crouch, further inspecting his fragile state of mind. "Now tell me, whatever is the problem?"

Nick spit out a glop of blood. "I just need to speak to Corbin, that's all."

Wearing headphones, Corbin had finally caught word of the commotion, stepping out into the now-cluttered hallway.

"Then let your wish be granted," Gib was facetious with his mumble.

"Nick," Corbin squinted. "What is it? What's wrong?"

Nick finally exhaled. Looking back on it, he desperately wished he'd handled the situation differently, with so many elves since drawn in. After saying nothing more, Corbin simply nodded. It was his way of saying, "follow me."

Chapter 50

Corbin's office was a collection of neon signage and posters, with cords going every which direction. It was cluttered, to put it mildly by a series of old, dusty gadgets.

"What is this, by the way?" Nick curiously pointed to whatever happened to be in his direct line of sight, all while holding his nose from the musty scent.

"That?" Corbin offered up his trademark grin as he instinctively began turning stuff on. "Is an 8-track player."

Nick was already flipping through some cartridges stacked next to the silver-plated machine. "Jefferson Starship, Van Halen, The Ice Picks."

"Oh, you wouldn't know that last one," Corbin said, plopping back into his well-used roller chair. "They're an old grunge band here at the Pole. A one-hit wonder, really. 'I'm frozen to you …!'" Corbin's rocker voice caught Nick off guard by how on-point it was.

"So," he stopped mid-note. "Have a seat." The elf gathered that Nick was in no mood, pointing down at a disco-era sofa covered in mustard yellow flowers. "Sorry if the place doesn't look like much. I collect stuff nobody else wants." He was used to people acting unimpressed—

pushing a stack of records away so that Nick had a place to sit. "Call it a curse."

Nick usually didn't appreciate a mess but was so desperate for help was more than happy to look past it this time.

"Now, about this gasket you just blew," he popped a bubble while taking a rag and some window cleaner to dust off an old phonograph he just then realized desperately needed it.

"Right," Nick sulked, forced to quickly cast the embarrassment aside. He took a needed breath. "About that. And I'm really not even sure how to explain this."

"Perhaps start from the top."

"Right … the top," Nick tried again. "Let's just say, I know a girl."

"As do I," said Corbin once Nick stopped sooner than he should have.

"Well, this is more than just a girl. She's a close friend. A very close friend." But Nick paused again—this time for an uncomfortably long period of time.

"Is something wrong? Whoever she is," Corbin pried for another clue.

"I think … she's coming, Corbin" Nick finally just came out with it once he realized there was no better way. "I mean, I know she is."

Corbin usually had great control over the gum he always seemed to be chewing, but this time the stringy bubble popped all over his face. "Tell me you don't mean here?" Nick's silent nod was certain, causing Corbin to speed up his concern. "And who exactly are we talking about again?" he asked while instinctively pulling up a computer database.

"Her name?" Nick paused. "Marie."

The elf quickly concluded he didn't need any software. Having tracked Nick's movements for some time, he knew exactly who she was.

Inheriting the Sleigh

"Marie Torie Bayliff," he recited her full name, though Corbin's next question was important. "Tell me ... how exactly do you know this?"

"Because I saw her. She was running."

"O ... K," the elf was more befuddled than ever. "And that somehow translates into her making a sudden dash for the world's most secretive tundra? Forgive me, but you might need to help me out here."

If he hadn't before, Nick started to sound frantic.

"Alright," Corbin held out a hand as if forced to at least pretend to accept the idea. "Alright ... I trust you. Then perhaps you can tell me how far she's gotten?" Corbin slid his chair over to a monitor on the opposite end of the room, trying to appear productive.

"That's the thing," Nick explained. "That's unfortunately where my information stops."

Corbin got right to work with Nick immediately recognizing the various angles of New York City. The elf typed rapid finger, zooming in to get a closer look at any place he guessed Marie might be. There was one directly outside her apartment on 31st Street, and another both in and outside Lourdes Academy.

"The Poodle Skirt," Nick noticed as Corbin went in tighter on the diner.

"Yeah, your father and I noticed the two of you frequent there quite often," Corbin realized there was really no way of saying it without sounding like a creep.

But Nick, leaning in from behind, sighed, as the camera panned left-to-right, confirming every face inside the restaurant. "Not her," he shook once Corbin got close enough to confirm the young girl sitting at the table next to the T-Bird hood was not Marie.

"Load me up with some more clues then. Where else could she be? I can only monitor public places."

But Nick looked defeated, instead dropping back into the old sofa where a broken spring painfully caught his butt on the way down.

Corbin, meanwhile, tried to come up with something honest to say; all without crushing his tender hopes in the process. "Of course, you do understand, as noble as this ambition might be … it simply is not possible?"

"What?" Nick's eyes were sadder than a puppy.

"You know, to find this place. Some of the most experienced arctic explorers have all tried, only to return home empty—or in many cases … dead." Corbin hated to scare him with the D-word.

"So … what are you saying, exactly?" Nick asked the elf to clarify, simply to buy time.

"I'm saying, the Pole was designed not to be found. And if what you're telling me is indeed true … I assume with the intention of finding you again. Well … as much as my heart longs to hear it, let's just say the likelihood is high she dies trying."

Nick's fear reached its peak, springing back up in a panic. "Then we need to keep looking! Perhaps we should call in the National Guard. Or maybe we …!"

Corbin politely listened to every word as Nick wore on and on with a series of illogical solutions at best. His rambling didn't end any time soon, though the elf did eventually feel a need to cut back in. "You do know what you're asking me, right? The earth has a circumference of 40,000 kilometers. Not to mention 7.5 billion people in it. I can't possibly monitor everything."

"Then we're gonna have to narrow that number."

Considering his naivety, Corbin said nothing, as if giving Nick the benefit of the doubt. He wanted to say that it simply wasn't possible—

but managed to leave open at least a shard of hope. "You really like her, don't you?" Corbin didn't need him to say anything more.

Nick felt terrible having to push his luck at the worst possible moment. "There is actually one more little thing," he nibbled at his knuckles as he said it.

"Oh, boy," Corbin didn't like the sound.

"We'd be wasting time if I told you how I know this, but let's just say that Marie isn't the only one in trouble right now." Corbin forced himself to brace for whatever it was. "The truth is, we might all be in some. It has to do with Gizer."

"Gizer? And…?"

Nick's stare circled the room once or twice around as he mustered up the courage. "What if I said, he's not actually on the run, after all? You know, like we were told. Let's just say … his army …"

"Yeah," Corbin encouraged Nick to speed up the reveal.

"Is much bigger than we thought."

Corbin was given a moment to process the terrifying declaration before adamantly shaking his head. "Nah, Gizer's been around too long. Trust me, he's too smart for that. He and Curnuckle have a long history— and that weasel knows he'll get crushed. The guy's hiding like a mole rat in some deep crevice somewhere."

But Nick's return glare spoke a thousand words. "I need to trust you again on this, don't I?" the elf hesitantly admitted as Nick nodded slowly, north to south. "And you haven't told anybody else about this? Isaac? Nobody?" Corbin was flattered, but also a bit frustrated the burden was placed solely on him. "Truth is, I wouldn't tell the Chief either. With all these late toy requests, Isaac's a blasted mess."

"So, what do I do? What do we do?" Nick got more specific.

Corbin shook. "The deep underground's hard to monitor. But honestly, I'm not sure the others would believe you anyway." He briefly paused after catching a glimpse of Nick's confused stare. "You know, if we were to tell them a threat is imminent—without proof."

A knock at the door startled them both. Ezra inched it open. "Everybody OK in here?" he inquired underneath a flashing red sign with the word "Santa" spelled out above the entryway. It made Corbin's office look like an old radio station.

Corbin waited for Nick to speak first. "Only time will tell," Nick was content to use Ezra's favorite word.

"Well, I hope the answer's 'yes,'" Ezra slipped on his glasses to get a better look at his pocket watch. "Because, aside from the fact you've got the whole office wing buzzing about this recent   meltdown of yours, we're now down to our final week. It's officially only seven days till Christmas."

Chapter 51

Marie's journey was exhausting at best. Relishing the chance to rest her feet, she looked nervous and extremely out of place next to a potted cactus outside an old pub. Clotheslines stretched across tree limbs near droopy gates as goats meandered, looking for anything to eat.

"Quieres jugar?" asked some boys without shoes. They wore only shorts and sleeveless, hand-me-down, American-made shirts.

A scuffed-up soccer ball eventually rolled Marie's way. The teenage girl politely tapped the ball right back. "Lo siento. Yo no hablo ingles," she looked down at a notecard in hand to remember the last part.

"Lagarse!" a man told the kids to "scram" as he exited the saloon doors. A nervous Marie stood up as he approached with a belly exposed underneath an old, white T-shirt that was much too short to cover his flabby abdomen. "Come," he turned to Marie in broken English. "Follow."

Marie traced a couple steps behind over dirt roads filled with potholes full of fresh rain. An old Honda motorbike—with peeling paint zoomed over the road, kicking up mud as it passed. She shielded her face from the flying dirt, while her guide failed to even so much as recognize, let alone apologize for the fact she was now splattered in sludge.

"Hurry," he said as she did her best to keep up around some garbage barrels and tin roof shacks. Dogs barked as they passed. An unsure Marie treaded carefully, not wanting to get bit while her guide merely kicked a ferocious chihuahua out of the way. He lifted some ferns and proceeded down a steep bank. It was hidden from view by the trees. Marie nearly slipped and fell the rest of the way down before grabbing a tree root to brace her fall.

At the bottom was a small plot of sand bordering an isolated beach—with a run-down shrimping boat anchored to a small dock. Marie could see nothing else other than the trees shading the coastline.

A couple of men walked off the boat for the dock. "Su próximo cliente."

"Wait," Marie finally voiced some concern. "This is the boat? How long will it take to get there?"

"No worry?" her guide seemed put off by the tone. "Much faster than think."

The janitor was no longer perusing the schoolhouse halls. He was now far away from the Pole's Training Center in a dark, rocky crevice. He had swapped his mop and bucket for a gun—though continued to wear the brown jumpsuit as he was descending through a small hole.

Loose rock crumbled along with him as he scooted down through a chute. The janitor struggled to keep his balance as the chute opened into a vast cliff. More rock fell off the cliff's edge as he held onto a secure boulder overlooking a trail bordering the cliff. It was the only thing keeping him from plummeting overboard.

Inheriting the Sleigh

The old man with sheepishly cotton hair listened carefully once the rocks stopped shuffling. He heard an echo, slowly straddling the edge of the wall toward the noise.

He could only move so fast at his age but managed to hunch forward, climbing another boulder and up over a high stone ridge. The janitor was exhausted but kept going until he reached the top. And that's where he dropped in fatigue—left to hug little but the tip of the peak.

There was now a decent view of what was making the noise. A large waterfall gushed from a hole feeding a stream that carved a path through the interior valley below. But it was the soldiers on either side of the stream that was the janitor's primary focus.

"They're coming," his whisper was full of emotion as the Black Capes were now uniformly moving in disciplined rows from the valley surface. They were weaving up the steep trails on the opposite side of the cave.

The janitor opened a canvas sack and pulled out a camera. It looked old but was rather sophisticated. He cautiously snapped what he could before pushing back down into his hiding spot. The last of the Capes were now on their way up over the opposite mountain.

The janitor was sweating profusely with rolled sleeves before turning to a gadget over his wrist. The top flipped open exposing a digital screen. He pushed a button on the side that immediately called up Corbin.

"Hello," a mature face appeared. "Who is this?"

"It is me," the janitor kept his voice low. "The Magi."

"Magi," Corbin was pleasantly surprised. "Where are you? It's dark."

He held the lantern in closer to illuminate an instrument that gauged his depth. "Looks like 6.1 miles underneath."

"Six miles?! You're above the icy ridge then and could be near the molten zone to the west," Corbin informed with concern. "Magi, you

411

need to get out of there—or without proper gear you might die. It's too hot."

"Of course," he said placing the camera back in his canvas sack. "But you must warn the others. Tell them we now have our validation."

"You mean to say, you've seen them?" Corbin grew excited. "With your own eyes, I mean?"

"Gizer? Or in other words, Herod's personal baby killer? Yes," said the perspiring Magi—his confidence level at a hundred percent. "He and his men are on their way. They'll be there by Eve."

Chapter 52

Sacrifice and love are Christmas cheer. To see children glow once every year. Sacrifice and love are Christmas cheer. To see children glow once every year. Sacrifice and …"

"You can stop now," Isaac interrupted as Nick sat Indian style, with his eyes shut over a floormat inside a small room. He wore only street clothes, along with the signature deep red hat.

Nick finally popped both eyes back open. "But I think I just found that mental zone Professor Terpley keeps talking about. They were calling for me."

"I'm not even about to pretend like I understand what that means, but I do know they are literally calling for you … out there," Isaac pointed back toward reality.

The faint chant was beginning to trickle in from outside. Elves were layered for the frigid air—bunched shoulder-to-shoulder inside Kringle Stadium with their arms pumping above their thick hats. "Santa Claus! Santa Claus!"

"Surely, you hear that."

"Am I supposed to be giving some sort of speech or something?" Nick wondered as his meditative state finally wore off.

Vance

Isaac cupped his hand over his face in disbelief, as if flabbergasted he'd forgotten again. "Nick, we've been over this probably ten times. The last of which was only about a half hour ago, by the way."

The boy only hunched. "Well, if you don't mind, for an 11th … remind me. What I'm supposed to say out there?"

"This is the final week rally. Where you address the elves, personally thanking them for all their hard work and encouraging everybody not to slow down as we enter these last few days. Of course, feel free to throw in any other motivational cheese you can think of. Kris was a master at that."

"And if there ever was a year they deserve it," Gib couldn't help but eavesdrop from afar.

Nick paused for several seconds, as if still trying to wake up. "OK," he finally stood. Some she-elves held up his fitted Santa coat that he slipped into on his way down the transitionary hall for the balcony that overlooked out into the raucous, at-capacity stadium. Once Nick emerged through the doors, they were still chanting—a roaring applause rumbling over the red seats.

A young elf handed him a wireless stick mic as the crowd noise slowly died. Nick took some time to inspect his audience, though he couldn't for long. The stadium lights in the distance nearly blinded him.

"Hello," his mic screeched and popped as he attempted to address the thousands, still gathering exactly what to say. "Thank you for coming. I ugh …," he turned to see Isaac watching behind him on the balcony— his arms crossed—trying to stay warm.

Nick was still somewhat distracted by the reoccurring voices inside his head; kids across the globe on pins and needles, nervous for what was, or wasn't about to soon happen inside their own living rooms. "I see that we're now in our final hour," he resumed. The many faces in the crowd were now deathly silent, with Nick instinctively wondering if he was supposed to break the ice with a joke. He gulped as he struggled to come up with something.

"Not going well?" Gib always seemed to pop up at the most inopportune times, whispering into the Chief's ear.

"No. No it's not," Isaac for once, was inclined to agree.

The elves continued to patiently wait out his next line, however long of a pause they had to endure to get there. Nick looked back at Isaac once more, as if to apologize in advance. There was something else he was fighting, and fully soaked into the spotlight, figured now must have been the right time to say it.

"You all have been such valiant toymakers," Nick spoke to an occasional hoot and holler from the crowd. "But you've also been such valiant warriors as well. You saved my life, and on more than one occasion."

Nick's delivery started to smooth out a bit, though Isaac remained unsure where he was going next.

"So, it is with a heavy heart that I must warn you." Isaac's nerves were tightening some more. "I have seen something truly terrible." Nick paused again, wondering exactly how to divulge the truth.

"And?" yelled an elf from somewhere. "What did you see, Santa Claus?!"

"Our enemies," Nick just then locked eyes on a privileged section up front. The Elites lounged in softer and spacier chairs. Their wardrobes and scowls easily gave them away. "As I was saying," Nick gulped. "Our enemy will soon be coming back to greet us. I have had ample evidence to suggest the Black Capes are ascending. Once again, war could soon be in our future."

Isaac—no longer willing to take the risk—swiped a finger across his neck as a cue to pull the mic. It was a level ten emergency.

"And I only offer it as a warning," Nick was no longer able to project his jumbled message to the panicked crowd. "Ugh, I think it's off," he tapped at his chin, once again looking for Isaac.

The Chief of Staff swooped in, hooking his arm from behind. Nick was suddenly rushed back inside the green room where a Clive Curnuckle was already there waiting with an ill-amused scowl.

"Saint Nick, what have you done! Are you trying to set off a panic storm? And less than a week before Christmas, at that!"

"No, certainly not," a sincere Nick sounded flustered next to the distinguished face of Curnuckle.

"Then why would you even imply that the people's securities in jeopardy?"

"Well," Nick paused. "I just wanted them to be prepared—that's all."

"Ugh, Boss," cried Blain, abruptly bursting through the door. "I think we're seeing a stampede out here!"

"Send a message that everything's just fine," instructed Isaac. "Just a false alarm. And make sure the medics are on ready!"

"I'm sorry, but I also cannot deny what I saw."

"What is all this implication about our enemies coming back, anyhow?" Curnuckle changed the subject. "Every last one of my intelligence briefings suggest he has been locked so far underground, they are no longer of any immediate threat."

Nick took a breath. "But I've seen it. This is personal to Gizer. He's bound to make sure Christmas never gets off the ground."

"Nick," the physically stout Curnuckle respectfully gripped the standing boy by the shoulders, having to elevate his arms a bit to do so. "You certainly have a very important job to do. And I would assume you also understand mine to share some importance in its own right." Nick nodded. "Please, by all means, do yours. "But double please, by double means, don't take over mine," he stared deep, with his thin mustache partially entrancing the boy. "My men have gone to great lengths at not only pushing them beneath but cutting off all the entrance ports." Curnuckle kept his proud stare in place, before hastily with an agitated step scooting back out the door.

The Magi was still sweating profusely. Swiping at the humid air, his hand slipped off a rock as he attempted to climb up a steep wall.

"Agh!" he fell ten or so feet, wincing in pain as he dropped onto his back. "Come in, Mr. Corbin. Can you hear me?" he looked at his wrist. "Please, come in."

"Hello," Corbin answered. "Is somebody there? You're extremely fuzzy."

"It's me. The Magi."

"Of course," Corbin took interest in the call by quickly livening up. "I thought I'd lost you back at the cavern. Tell me … do you still have it?"

"I don't know if I can make it back up," his voice cut in and out as Corbin listened closely. Only a speckled fraction of the Magi's black face was seen due to the static swirling across his screen.

"What happened?"

"Never mind that. I'm still miles from the surface, so I'm going to have to transmit here."

"That may take days," said Corbin. "Days we don't have, by the way. The signals are weak."

"It might be our only hope. Most of the Capes are already well ahead of me—and I believe I'm being followed."

"You're just dehydrated—which breeds paranoia. You have any water left?"

"Maybe a liter," the Magi opened his bag to take another small, rationed sip from a canteen.

"OK, just rest there for a moment and then try and climb again."

"No," he insisted. "I must transmit, for I fear this could be the end."

"Not down there it isn't," Corbin insisted. "You simply have to make it out."

The janitor was already at work punching buttons, while incomprehensibly mumbling what he could. "Let's just hope by the grace of God himself they get to you in time."

"Magi?" any period of silence greatly unsettled Corbin.

"Yes," the old man softly retorted back.

"Tell me … what did you mean before when you referred to Gizer as Herod's baby killer?" But this time there was no response. Corbin sat shocked and numb as he settled upon what had happened. The Magi lay lifeless—all while images programmed inside the small machine continued to load and transmit; however slowly.

Chapter 53

"Where are you taking me?" a blindfolded Nick wondered as his boots crunched over fresh snow.

"You'll see," said Silva acting as his guide. Every building was adorned in bright Christmas cheer, with old English overwhelming the district. An unevenly cut sign dangled overhead where she and Nick suddenly came to a stop. It read, "Tiny Tim's Tavern."

"Please tell me this is it," said Nick outside a sturdy stone structure— one with high, sloping, triangular rooftops. The walls were half-stone and half-timbered. "Because I don't think I can walk a step further."

"It might be," she smiled, escorting him inside the round, mahogany door with thick, black hinges. A bell rang and Silva finally released his blindfold to expose a pitch-dark room.

"Silva, you there?" asked Nick once she failed to utter a single word. "Silva … I'm telling you—this isn't funny."

"Surprise!" Nick jumped as the torches lit up all at once, exposing a host of familiar elves. Silva approached first in apologetic laughter.

"I knew you were up to something. Where am I?" Nick smiled, patting his startled heart.

Vance

"Tiny Tim's," greeted Gib.

"It's tradition," Isaac added. "Every year before takeoff. It's our time to celebrate."

Nick gazed around the log interior—one with a large, dangling chandelier woven by reindeer horns as its centerpiece. It was filled with tables, benches, chairs, and plenty of barrels stacked both behind the bars and stored over high ledges. A staircase exposed a second level with framed pictures of old elves dotted about the chiseled walls.

"Now it's time to let loose a little, Santa Claus," Silva danced as Nick was suddenly whisked over to an empty table. Drinks with spewing suds were passed about the tavern in large mugs. Nick noticed Smudge Terpley standing in a corner. He was performing another one of his theatrical displays, only this time with a captivated audience.

Gib hopped onto an elm wood table dancing a jig that made Nick smile—all as Ezra was hard at work fixing a broken clock on the wall.

"This is fun," a partially distracted Nick admitted as a mug was plopped in front of him, along with a large basket of pretzels and salted nuts. "But don't we still have plenty of work to do?"

"Yes … some," said Isaac. "Though nothing that can't be done in an hour. Like I said … tradition."

An elf broke some freshly cued pool balls, and a large fire lit up the tavern behind the bar. It was like a touch of medieval splendor. "Aren't we missing somebody?" Nick couldn't help but notice as he waved to Blaine in the distance.

"Hmmm," Isaac said, mid-sip. "Yeah … where is Corbin?"

Corbin's glazed eyes were glued to a screen. A hot green bar was loading, but not fast enough.

Inheriting the Sleigh

In frustration he leapt up from his chair to check a notification on another computer. It was an email with the subject line, "Possible Sighting of Marie Bayliff." Corbin opened it immediately, copying down the long code number. He then plugged it into his surveillance where images of a Central American village began to display. At first, Corbin didn't see much other than palms and jungle leaves but dove in deeper on the file. There were natives inside the foliage, but also a Caucasian girl who stood out. "Marie," he whispered—relieved and ecstatic both.

Corbin checked the digital loading bar once more before cinching up his scarf and grabbing his coat on a hanger near the door. A square flap in the wall was concealed by a piece of furniture. He pushed the armoire to expose the opening, jumping into a short slide that entered a basement with a garage door where a snowmobile was waiting. Corbin used a remote to expose the outside and off he went, urgently speeding over the dark streets. That is until arriving at Tiny Tim's.

Corbin only inched through the weighty front door. The combination of a fiddle and the heavy clanking of mugs provided enough of a distraction that no one even saw him sneak in.

The tavern was glowing from the many candles. Skeeta LeBelle sat on a hay bale feeding Vixen a sugar cube and Terpley had not yet given up regaling—though his audience had since shrunk. Meanwhile, Corbin searched for Nick inside the patchy darkness. That is until he found him stroking the nose of a taxidermized moose above the fire.

Corbin slid over to avoid bumping into a waitress full of mugs, before approaching Nick from behind. He tapped him on the back as he released his hood.

Nick, for only a moment had forgotten about his many problems but was also plenty relieved to see his friend's face. "Corbin. You look tired."

"Do I?" the elf rubbed both eyes as Nick grew nervous for what he might hear, still adjusting from his temporary bout of silliness.

"You have a verdict then?" the boy asked.

"I hope you're ready for a batch of both good and bad." The elf chose his words carefully. "So … tell me; which one do you prefer first?"

Nick didn't know how to answer.

"I've found her," the elf elected to resume quickly regardless.

Nick exhaled. "Where?" Tavern patrons turned at the sudden rise of his voice.

"On a boat. A shrimping vessel of all the highly unsafe transports you could possibly choose from. I believe it was headed for Greenland."

"Greenland. Then I was right."

"That you were," Corbin admitted in a hush, with others inadvertently beginning to overhear.

"So, what now?" Nick truly was clueless. Then again, so was Corbin.

"I don't know. Honestly, it's something we should probably tell Isaac, but even if we do find her alive, I'm not certain how receptive he'll be to the idea of bringing her here. Marie has a life elsewhere, and it could be ill-perceived by the rest of the world. You know … looks a little like kidnapping if you know what I mean. Technically, we've already stolen you."

Nick's stare hinted that he clearly understood, and yet it was equally desperate.

"If I send a rescue unit," said Corbin. "It's a risk that could get me in a hearty heap of trouble. I mean, once Marie arrives at the port she won't survive long without help. Of course, that's assuming the boat even makes the trip across the icy Denmark Strait to begin with. I mean, I could lie to you, Nick, but that wouldn't be fair. The boat I saw is a pile of reindeer dung, to put it mildly."

Inheriting the Sleigh

Nick grew quiet in the ambiance of the tavern. "Marie, what have you done?" the boy's glaze got lost in the tabletop's many aged scratches. "I assume that was the bad news, then."

"Actually ... no," said the distressed elf as Nick's eyes widened. "A longtime friend of mine ... a trusted one," Corbin resumed as Nick had never seen him so emotional before. "Let's just say he bravely volunteered to find precisely what we needed. And unfortunately, gave up his life doing it."

Nick couldn't help but feel the need to apologize as Corbin saw his head instinctively sink into his chest.

"Again, you were right, Nick," Corbin's stare was stale once he lifted his fatigued head. "Gizer ... he's coming."

"And you have evidence of this?"

"Well, not yet. It's being transmitted as we speak. But that's just it. It's a slow process, and I don't know if we'll get it by Christmas Eve."

"Corbin?" an unusually peppy Isaac acknowledged his friend on his way past, half-tipsily interrupting their quiet conversation. "Where have you been? Tiny Tim's is your favorite bash of the year. You're always the first to arrive."

"Oh, hello, Chief," he rambled off a quick excuse with this year being vastly different than ever before. "I guess I've just been racking up some OT. You know, double checking the sleigh logs and lost track of time. Not to mention, feeling a little under the weather," Corbin faked a cough, though not very well.

"We're overworking you, aren't we?" Isaac parlayed how bad he felt with a friendly pat of the shoulder. "You have my word. I'll make it up to you. Promise," he said with a genuine smile—skipping off again.

Nick, meanwhile, waited for the right time to state the obvious. "This truly is the worst time for a party."

Chapter 54

Corbin and Nick's small hideout was little more than a residential room, with a few modest furnishings and just the right amount of equipment to work undercover.

"If I don't go get her myself, who will?" Nick's heart was conflicted.

"Leave that to me," the elf insisted. "Nick, the truth is—you can't even think about Marie right now. Today is December 23rd. You have any idea what that means?" Nick wasn't aloof but couldn't fault Corbin for making his point either. "Good. Cause a little over 15 hours from now, you'll be out in the open air doing something only one other person has ever done before. Not to mention for the first time."

"Yeah. Thanks for reminding me."

"Besides," Corbin stood up straight as if proud of his idea. "I think I may know of someone we can trust to get the job done. You just need to focus right now. Maybe do some more of that weird namaste introspection Smudge taught you."

"How much longer?" Nick pointed to his computer; the same one Corbin had his eyes glued on for days.

"My guess is … 12, 13 hours—maybe more."

Inheriting the Sleigh

"Perhaps we should try again. You know, to convince Curnuckle that this isn't just some figment of my imagination."

"Sure, we could do that. But if I know Clive, all he'd do is stare and smile. You know, basically his way of implying how stupid you are. Anything contrary to his own intelligence apparatus is ranked one step below obsolete, if you know what I mean."

Nick hated to bring up the obvious. "And if the transfer doesn't complete?"

Corbin had no answer this time, instead typing something on a separate keyboard. That is before a knock came at the door, startling him. "Tell me you know who that is," he asked as Nick didn't hesitate to greet the boy on the other side of the dark, adjoining hall. "Starsky Skiles?" Corbin squinted with confusion.

"You look surprised," Starsky retorted in his trademark leather. "But did I hear somebody say something about a street fight?"

"That depends. Are you looking for one?" asked Corbin as Starsky finally stepped inside.

"If it involves that weasel, Goss Gizer," Starsky cracked his knuckles—his gloves cut off at the fingertips. "Then ... yes."

Corbin was uncertain at best, turning to Nick for a little reassurance—though all the boy could really do was grin.

"I really hope you know what you're doing then," said the elf with a sigh. "Cause if you don't ..."

Capes scurried up the short tunnels. Using ropes and claws, they pushed up steep embankments until reaching the surface through discreet holes in the ground. The spies were equipped with stealth gear, emerging together.

"Surface One ready," the first Cape radioed.

Vance

"Surface Two ready."

"Surface Three ready."

"Surface Four ready."

"Surface Five ready," they reported in rapid succession as the soldiers were quick, efficient, and knew exactly where they were going.

A bored, yet unsuspecting guard laid wait at the entrance of a tall black gate. The city was quiet, sleepy, and cold, with little but tall stone buildings and statues rising high in the early morning fog.

A silent shot was fired—a rope fastening around the guard's ankle. He cried, but only for a second, immediately pulled toward the shooter with his mouth strangled.

The five Capes were climbing up different exterior stairwells, only stopping once they reached the top. They were now overlooking the city, with only the massive clock tower rising higher. They dispersed to various corners to open their bags, uncovering mushroom-shaped cylinders.

As they pulled up on the tops of the peculiar gadgets, the weaponry suddenly spun in rapid rotation, like miniature carnival rides. Glowing the brightest shade of pink, the cylinders made zero noise—tucked into discreet, unseen corners, with timers that started precisely at 12 hours.

"Surface One in place." Gizer waited in a dark, underground bunker to hear the confirmations for himself—simply to make sure the job got done.

"Surface Two in place."

"Surface Three in place."

"Surface Four in place."

Gizer stood with his head bowed and his arms crossed, patiently waiting for the fifth Cape to report. He was so confident in the flawless execution of his plan, he gave the lone Cape over a minute to respond;

but eventually started to feel a little uneasy, signaling his general with the radio to step in.

"Surface Five. Surface Five, report. I command you to report!"

"I wouldn't respond to that," Starsky heard every word. He blended in nicely with a shadow, patiently waiting for the right time to slowly step into the artificial light. "In fact, go ahead and drop it altogether … if you will," Skiles had a gun pointed directly at his chest. "You either didn't understand or are dumber than a hair searching for a carrot in the snow."

The Cape only slowly released his grip. He kicked over his communication device with the two now standing alone over a stone tower—one protected by a short rail. "That," Starsky used his head to nervously point down at the spinning cylinder. "What is it?"

"So, it looks as if Mr. Neutrality himself has finally picked a side," the Cape spoke for the first time, though failed to answer the question. "Looks to me as if you've chosen, Santa Claus."

"Surface Five!" the muffled voices on the other end were now sounding more and more urgent. "We need you to report, immediately."

"Over a loony zealot like Gizer," Starsky retorted quietly. "It wasn't hard."

The Cape remained perfectly still with his hands raised out as Starsky slowly bent forward to retrieve the radio. "Surface Five … in place," he whispered to a host of confused stares back inside the cobweb-full bunker.

"Who is this?" The nervous general repeated slowly.

"Please tell that fat, conniving friend of yours, it's the boy he ruthlessly turned into an orphan."

Gizer's eyes grew wide as he slowly approached the radio. "Boy Skiles, of course," he grinned. "Is that really you up at this early hour? I

427

assume because you believe deep inside that troubled heart of yours, you can actually stop what we're doing." Starsky said nothing, instead choosing to listen as he realized who was now on the other end. "Or rather, is this something personal between you and I?"

"Why can't it be both?"

Gizer smirked, as if to suggest, well played. "You wish to kill me, don't you? You know, for what you perceive happened to your good parents. You needed a scapegoat. Someone to blame for their unfortunate deaths, and so you chose me."

"I saw you do it," Starsky mumbled, while keeping a stunner pointed at the fifth Cape.

"And yet looks can be deceiving. But putting all that aside, I would get out of there if I were you." Gizer's warning was cavalier.

Starsky looked as if he was ready to pull the trigger at any moment. "You expect me to just run away? I could kill him right now, you know."

"I'm sure you could," Goss calmly agreed as the Cape grew unsettled by the look in Starsky's angry eye.

"In fact," Starsky's hand began to quake, overrun by a sudden rise of emotion. "Perhaps I will. If you ever want to see him again—you'll do exactly as I say."

Almost sensing Starsky's jitters from afar, Gizer chuckled. "I truly do doubt that," he said with Surface Five now pleased as well.

"What is this thing, anyhow?" he asked for a second time as the glow began to speed up even faster.

"Oh, that? Thought you would never ask. That is the Pole's newest toy. I call it a Death Racer."

"A Death Racer?" Starsky uttered, with the time now displaying 11 hours, 52 minutes.

Inheriting the Sleigh

"That's right," Gizer laughed again before casually offering one last warning. "And I wouldn't touch one if I were you. Surface Five ... it's time to be head'n back now."

In a blink, Surface Five turned to leap over the short railing. He was falling, with his arms spread out in a skydive—his cape flapping loudly in the breezes. Starsky rushed over to watch the suicidal descent before losing all sight of the plummeting body in the heavy darkness. All he could then do was shatter the radio in disgust.

Chapter 55

The resemblance is quite remarkable," said Corbin aghast as he stared at the four broad-shouldered Goddard brothers. They shared identical bowl cuts, all standing with reverence and respect. "I mean seriously, it's like your good mother, Gertrude, took a face she liked and cloned it three different times," they continued to stand still and straight. It was a line that formed a perfect slope. "The only difference, of course, being your height," Corbin placed his hand on the head of the tallest brother. "Gilbert," he said. "It's been a long time. You've really grown up since I saw you last."

"Yes," said Gilbert awkwardly, as if he could think of nothing more.

"And you, good Gabriel," Corbin moved onto the next brother, maybe half a foot shorter. "Named after the great archangel himself, I hear. Followed by the stout Gideon," Corbin kept going. "Stout like a tree. Your name means tree, does it not?" Corbin just shook after failing to receive a routine reply to his clumsy attempt at small talk. "Moving on then. And of course," he was anxious to get through his final greeting. The smallest brother stood giddy and wide-eyed, barely even blinking once. "The beloved little Gus," Corbin couldn't help himself from squeezing both rosy cheeks. "Tell me, how old are you now?"

Inheriting the Sleigh

"52," Gus' high pitch was the most excited of them all.

"52? Why, you're still just a pup. OK then," Corbin quickly changed subject by clasping his hands together while the four brothers remained in a boot camp-like line, awaiting their instruction. "You're probably wondering why I called you all here so suddenly on the eve of Christmas."

"Because you could find nobody else?" Gabriel said, with his robotic eyes fixated on the wall.

Corbin licked his lips "Wow. What you just said could not be more accurate. And now that we've established that, I'm sure you're all super anxious to hear about what this little mission might entail." Again, the response was deathly quiet. "Alright," Corbin resumed, still amused by the silence. "Why don't I just come out and say it then. You take me for a crowd that appreciates getting right down to the point. I need you to go to Greenland."

"Greenland. Population: 56.4 thousand," stated Gilbert.

"Greenland. A constitutional monarchy ceremoniously ruled by the Kingdom of Denmark," added Gabriel.

"Greenland," said the squeaky voice at the end of the line. "The world's largest non-continental island. A land split in ethnicity between the native Inuit and a much sparser population of European lineage. Possesses an ice sheet nearly two million kilometers squared, and at a volume of nearly three million kilometers cubed. Exports are 90 percent fish, with the remaining slice coming from the mining sector. And don't forget," Gus only paused for a second at most, with a raised index finger. "Has the world's largest population of musk oxen."

Corbin listened with awe and wonder. "Anything else?"

"Yeah. The suicide capital of the world," Gus did manage to have one more little fun fact left in him.

Vance

An aghast Corbin curiously watched the youngest Goddard take a much-needed breath. "Alright, now that we've wrapped up that highly informative geography lesson … it's time to reveal why I need you to go there." He pulled down a white screen, flashing an old film reel. Marie's high school yearbook photo appeared first, followed by some poses that were less formal.

"She's pretty," observed Gabriel.

"Yes, she is," Corbin did his best to keep them focused. "And she's also in trouble."

"Trouble?" Gilbert was concerned. "What kind of trouble?"

"Let's just say, the girl's lost. Or will be soon. And that's where the four of you come in. I need you to go rescue her."

"In Greenland," stated Gideon.

"He does speak," Corbin observed with a smile. "And listens too. Correct … in Greenland. You'll meet her on Ammassalik Island on the southeastern side. There is a port there."

"And you're confident she'll arrive … when?" asked Gilbert.

Corbin peered down at a watch. "A day and a half. Maybe less. Can you make it?"

"Over a thousand insufferable miles—and through an ocean of immovable glaciers?" Corbin, due to the adjectives being used started to grow nervous for what he might hear. Gabriel's nod, however, was sudden and quick. "Yes. We can do it."

The elf's grin widened by a mile. "Good. But I need you to go now. Or else … you may not make it."

Nick was startled by a wooden cuckoo. The collection of handmade clocks hanging about Santa's walls soon joined in a musical chorus.

Inheriting the Sleigh

Nick thrusted up underneath his bed's canopy; one held by four strong posts. He'd been sleeping so soundly he was still in the process of discerning precisely what day it was. But for the moment, he listened to the collaborating chimes that began to blend into an eerie carol. It sounded misty with a splash of old Irish.

The melody bounced across the room through many gadgets that had since come alive in the morning chill. And there was a rush that caught Nick off guard. It was heavily swashing up and down through his bloodstream as a series of windup toys had suddenly started to waddle over his work bench—all without being wound up at all. The entire room was now awake.

But it was the footsteps creaking up over the stairs that startled Nick most. He leapt out of bed, grabbing a wooden baseball bat by the door for protection. It was one he'd previously been compelled to carve as a gift. "Who's there?"

Nick, with disheveled hair, slowly crept down the stairs. The lanterns along the wall had already been lit—something he'd been used to doing every morning when he woke—though couldn't remember if he'd forgotten to blow them out from the night before. "Is somebody … here?" he called out again as a view of the living room emerged toward the bottom of the staircase. Nick stopped to swivel both directions.

A fresh pine tree now stood in the corner of the room. It was full of sparkly tinsel and decorated with a series of old, handcrafted ornaments. And there was even a stocking over the mantle. Nick wanted to know who was responsible—until his boyish excitement took over. He hurried to get a closer look at the tree, stroking an ornament with a lumpy border of real twigs; one with a picture of a baby in the middle of the frame.

He moved over to the knit sock with "Nicholas" etched across it in red. It hung alone over the fireplace where something strange was happening inside the flames. They appeared to be morphing into images. Nick knew the faces of his mother and father, as there were framed portraits of them everywhere, including directly above the mantle.

Another sound startled him. This one a crackle from the record player. The needle suddenly dropped into place over some vinyl. It was Elvis' trademarked southern drawl.

"Blue Christmas," a confused Nick approached the brown box. "Isn't that an oxymoron?" he muttered to himself as nothing but black was on the other side of the window—just as it had been for weeks now.

Nick turned back toward the flames to behold a perfectly discernable image of Kris and Martha. They were on the floor cooing alongside a small baby, with Elvis serenading in the background. But there were other noises accompanying the music; and this time they were synced up perfectly with the fire.

"Look, Kris," Martha smiled, as only a proud mother could. "He's crawling."

"I know," Kris proudly stroked his clean beard over the wool rug as baby Nick thought about it—pushing forward on all fours. Nick stepped closer to the fireplace, suddenly watching himself. It was as if he'd come across an old home video, popping it into the VCR for the first time.

"How can we do this?" Martha's smile was soon replaced by a tear—followed by another. "Perhaps we shouldn't. There's still time."

"No," Kris shook, as she expected he might. "You and I both know there are things he needs to learn—things he simply cannot learn here. If the boy is to one day serve the people, he must know precisely who they are."

"Of course," Martha succumbed with a sad sigh as she watched little Nick make it all the way across the carpet for her awaiting arms. Nick hadn't realized it yet, but he was shedding tears while listening to the track on loop inside the lustrous room.

I'll have a blue Christmas without you
I'll be so blue thinking about you
Decorations of red on a green Christmas tree
Won't be the same dear, if you're not here with me

Nick had his own fond memory of that song, slurping across from Marie inside the Poodle Skirt—but this time he absorbed every word.

It had only been a month when he'd first learned the truth of where he'd come from and yet didn't have a whole lot of time to dwell on the reason for why he was ever given up. It was as if his parents were speaking directly to him—only to have the vinyl finally stop. The needle was now in the very center of the record. It was scratching, but there was no longer any music, the flames having since returned.

Nick stood alone again in silence, as if expecting and wanting more—but other than another creak over the cottage floorboards, heard nothing.

"Get this shipment to Loading Dock 17!" Isaac instructed in the chaos of a crowded factory. "And make sure those completed checklists are all getting submitted for review!"

Forklifts were beeping around every corner with frantic elves not wanting to incur Isaac's wrath. He rolled a sweaty hand back over his light brown hair in exhaustion.

"What?!" he overreacted to a gentle tap at his back.

The scared elf leapt as he turned. "Unit manager number 209 is reporting a shortage of SheBake cooking sets, sir."

"Well then, what are you complaining to me for? There should be a surplus stockpile in the eastside storage bins." Elves scurried away at the sound of his stern voice, while other supervisors were busy directing traffic amidst pallets stacked many feet high with toys. "I said, what?!" he turned again, this time about ready to explode. "Corbin," Isaac forced himself to calm down a bit at the unexpected sight of his closest friend.

"Rough day at the office?" Corbin stood with wide eyes, not anticipating the overreaction. "You look like you've been hit by a freight train."

"Yeah, well … in my defense," he couldn't help but check the time. "We are only a few hours away from Operation Return."

Corbin smiled, wondering how he was ever about to break his news at the worst possible moment. "Which is why I'm here."

"What is it, Corbs?" Isaac could tell it was important. "Please tell me the surveillances aren't down."

"Oh, no," Corbin swatted his fingers forward. "The surveillances are working fine. This is much worse."

Isaac stopped to squint wide with concern. "Worse?" he quietly took Corbin behind a wrapped pallet for some added privacy. "What do you mean?"

Corbin handed him a stack of photos. "See for yourself."

"They're dark," he couldn't help but notice right away.

"That's because they're underground."

"Black Capes," Isaac said as he kept flipping through. "I don't understand. How is this news? It's precisely where we want them—locked miles deep."

"Keep going," Corbin expected that response as Isaac paid closer attention to the detail in every proceeding photograph. "They're getting easier to see, aren't they?"

"What are you implying?"

"I think you know what I'm implying," stated Corbin plainly.

"Nick was right. Is that what you're saying?" Isaac needed a moment to state it out loud. "Gizer's men are pushing back up?"

"Not pushing," he paused, meeting Isaac's shock. "They are up. Apparently Curnuckle didn't have all the surface ports sealed like we thought."

Corbin handed him one last photograph—this time with care. "I just pulled it out of the dark room ten minutes ago. It's not even dry yet." Isaac noticed a Cape plummeting for the ground—his arms spread out in a skydive. "Starsky Skiles himself confronted him just last night. I think an attack is imminent."

Isaac took a closer glance at the photo. "Corbin?"

"Yeah," he said after a much-needed breather.

"What is that?" Isaac pointed to the hot pink cylinder in the background. The Chief's curiosity soon morphed into a dreadful gut feeling.

"Oh, that," said Corbin, as if he'd spent considerable time mulling over the possibilities himself. "I honestly have no idea."

"I need to find Curnuckle," Isaac whispered with Corbin glad to finally hear those five words. He sprang away before stopping to address Corbin one last time. "By the way," he inquired, waving the photographs in front of his face. "Where did you get these? We don't have the ability to see that deep."

Corbin responded, but only with a load of lingering guilt. "The Magi," he said with a melancholy eye. "He offered up his last gift."

Isaac stuttered to Corbin's affirmative nod. "The Magi ... is dead?"

Chapter 56

This army is young!" addressed the gruff Curnuckle inside a dark, empty warehouse. Thousands of elves in white camouflage were scrunched together in the standing- room only crowd—awaiting their instruction. They had cherry blasters hanging off their shoulders and were ready to fight. "Which is precisely why I've gathered you all here today. During a period devoted to merriment and celebration. But unfortunately, this is not that," the sergeant couldn't help but sound short. "You may ask your questions now."

"How many does the former congressman have at his command?" a brave soldier leaning against a bare wall, eventually spoke up.

Curnuckle thought. "For starters, almost all of what I call the Elite Guard's bitter element. Those I was personally forced to let go back during my stint as mariner commander. And you can assume he's recruited many of the cronies stemming from the political uprising of 1322. And I haven't even mentioned all those lawless thugs already hiding underground. You know, those looking for a criminal enterprise to belong to."

Inheriting the Sleigh

Curnuckle nodded with his distinguished mustache proving an air of confidence. "And yet somehow, we will complete this mission in the interest of returning the great tradition of Christmas." He gazed from one side to the next before changing the subject. "Now … if you'll indulge me. Let me turn the floor over to …," he coughed into his fist, as if having trouble keeping a straight face while doing so. "One of the Claus' closest and most trusted associates," Curnuckle was forced to read slowly from a cue card. "Representing the Chief of Staff's office, a Mr. Gib … Findiggy will address us now with further specifics on a united course of action."

Curnuckle slowly exited the platform, though nobody appeared to be replacing him. "Findiggy," an embarrassed Curnuckle turned again, this time calling out a little louder. Hands were hastily at work behind the curtain, forcing Gib out onto the platform where his audience patiently waited.

Shoved out into the open, Gib dusted himself off and slowly inched forward, stopping only to face the warehouse full of soldiers. His shirt was only partially tucked—clearly not expecting to be such a disheveled wreck.

"I do apologize … but if you don't mind giving me a moment here," Gib awkwardly pulled out his pocket liners as he stood in the center of a makeshift spotlight. "I did have some notes, though it looks as if no notes appear to be on me. How funny," he stuttered with his cheeks growing red.

Just as it looked as if Gib might be done in by a severe case of the shakes, a second figure came hastily bursting of her own accord through the curtain. Gib turned, never more grateful to see Silva. "Where in burley's beard have you been?" he whispered with an agitated tone as she now stood at his side. "You know I don't speak in front of large gatherings."

"And now for what you've all been waiting for—involving our plan for a safe and successful launch in the threat of an enemy attack," Silva spoke quickly to make up for lost time. "What I'm about to do is divulge top secret information. Sensitive intel we must all keep close to the bulletproof vest. We're moving the sleigh to a secure location. However, the control operations will remain where they've always been—at headquarters. Sergeant Curnuckle and his generals will be giving orders as to your checkpoints. The seriousness of this threat is an alert red," informed Silva with a straight face. "Repeat … an alert red. And if we do end up completing this launch," the she-elf swiveled her gaze out across the room to make eye contact with every soldier crammed into the small spaces. "Well … you'll most likely be able to draw it right back to this very group here."

"Thanks for walking with me, Ezra," Nick expressed as they strolled past lampposts and dark storefront windows. They were alone along the quiet street.

"Of course," Ezra pulled his glasses out from under his knit hat, just long enough to defog them. "And how are you feeling?"

"Fine, I guess," said Nick stoically. "Just doing as Professor Terpley instructed and keeping my thoughts trained on the moment. I'm hearing a lot of outside voices that are painfully hard to block out."

"Hmmm," Ezra genuinely listened as Nick blew into his hands. "Those voices are making their final pleas, I assume."

"The sheer volume of faces. It's like seeing millions of people you recognize from somewhere, only you can't put a finger on exactly how you know them." Ezra chuckled, prompting Nick to ask, "What's so funny?"

"I recall Kris saying the same. I realize now why it was so pertinent to hear Isaac insist on bringing you back. The key to saving Christmas is certainly locked inside you."

Nick stopped to eye the endearing wrinkles in Ezra's face. The protection detail hovering around them also stopped, their focused eyes rotating 360 degrees in search of incoming danger. "They're coming, Ezra. I feel that too."

Ezra didn't want to believe it and instead chose to keep walking. "So, they say. But you can't worry about that now."

"I can't?" Nick said nervously. "The weight of half the civilized ...."

"Shhhh," Ezra propped a finger over his mouth as they rounded a corner. The shadows of tall buildings rose high in the fog, but only one was lit. Ezra checked the silver pocket watch hanging off his coat. "Watch it," he pointed toward the beaming clock tower above Chimney Sweep Square. It was lit up in its traditional blue. With the short hand nearing the 12, the long hand was moving past the six on its way back up toward the top of the clock. It was approaching midnight. "It's happening."

Ezra glanced at the clock with a reverent smile, as if in a Zen-like euphoria. The ticks were getting closer and closer until they struck 12, with Nick suddenly left wondering what was happening. The elf closed his eyes, reaching to grip Nick's hand as they stood in place together.

An odd energy suddenly pushed through the city. Most of the elves were tucked safely inside—but for Nick and Ezra, they were exposed out in the open exterior to feel the sudden rush. Nick squinted, still unsure what to think as he endured the tidal wave of thick air that suddenly made it difficult to even open his eyes.

Vance

"Nick?" Ezra called out, though his voice was now hollow and faint. It took a couple of times the elf repeating himself before Nick answered. "Are you alright?"

"I think so. But what just happened?"

"One day is like a thousand years to the Lord," Ezra pointed back up toward the majestic clock tower. It was no longer blue. It had since turned bright green—though that wasn't the only change. The long hand was no longer moving. It was stuck on the 12 directly above the short hand.

Nick gathered his thoughts as he adjusted to the new thickness. All movement was slower and more methodical; almost dreamlike. "Time has stopped, hasn't it?"

Ezra chose to simply smile. "Now, let's go get that suit on, shall we? Christmas Eve has arrived—and the world is waiting in their sleep.

Chapter 57

The sleigh was positioned for takeoff. "OK, on a ten count let's open up the Wall," said Isaac, spearheading the moment of truth.

"Activating," Isaac only could hear the reply.

"Blimm, focus. I need you right now," Isaac scolded the elf who was nervously fidgeting near the control deck—all as a series of lights went haywire. "You're the only one I trust who knows this stupid equipment."

"You mean, sophisticated," he puffed into the inhaler that Isaac threw into his lap to calm him down.

Outside in the frosty darkness, spotlights were abruptly turned on to expose the runway. The Wall had split open just enough to create a gap for the sleigh to penetrate. A beating snowstorm immediately poured in through the opening—with a sudden chill that took the mink coats down below a moment to adjust to.

"Alright, open the gate!" Isaac was anxious but composed. The tall, steel doors suddenly wheeled upward to expose the fabulous sleigh.

"Is Nick ready?" Isaac asked.

"As ready as he'll ever be," signaled Cross from below as Santa Claus now had his hands on the reins—his hat dipped down over his brows.

Vance

The reindeer bobbed in anticipation as they could now see the multi-colored runway lights glistening against the fresh flakes—flakes simultaneously shoveled out by tractors. The surface crew was clearing the way as a maddening storm wrought havoc on the launch.

"In that case," Isaac's breath was content. "It's time. Curnuckle? Sergeant, repeat. You there?" A few seconds passed before he heard a responsive grumble. "How safe is our path?"

"My generals have all reported. There is no sign of the enemy. Repeat, no sign. My recommendation is that we leave, now."

"In that case," Isaac swallowed with more than one butterfly inside his stomach. "On a new ten count. Did you get that, Cross?"

"Copy," said Blaine as he raised his right arm with an open palm inside the sleigh port. And with the seconds passing by, the arm dropped into an L. The sleigh was clumsily whisking off—the reindeer in a gallop.

"Wait," a confused Blimm popped up from his chair as he watched the launch from his monitor station. "Something here doesn't seem quite right."

"Sit down, Blimm," Isaac cried while biting his own lip, highly used to dealing with the elf's paranoia in stressful situations.

"No, I mean it. You need to stop the launch ... immediately!"

"We stop nothing!" Isaac insisted, with even more irritation behind his voice.

"What's going on out there?" Curnuckle wondered why there was so much sudden commotion across the conference call.

"Nothing. There is nothing going on!" Isaac assured as the reindeer were now beginning to elevate.

"But those aren't ..." Blimm was interrupted by an alarm that immediately caught his attention. It forced him to forget all about what he'd been complaining about earlier.

Inheriting the Sleigh

"What is that?" Isaac wasn't sure, though knew he didn't like the sound of it.

Blimm didn't even have time to respond, immediately sounding his own alarm. With the push of a glowing button, a series of warning lights suddenly ignited fear along the runway dock. Trained soldiers, never having heard the alarm outside a drill situation, went running for the safety of the thick outlying snow. They were sprints masked by the slow motion in the stalled time of Christmas Eve. "This is a Blimm Barber here, Launch Operations Engineer. We need the missile defense shield raised immediately!" his trained intuition kicked in, yelling into a radio. "Repeat, raise the missile defense!"

"Missile defense?" Isaac approached, as Blimm was nervously hunched over, straddling the edge of his control deck. "What are you saying!?"

Blimm was drowning in nerves as he quickly turned to face Isaac. "An incoming mini missile is seconds away from taking out the sleigh, sir!" The elf was suddenly even more pale than his natural skin tone.

Isaac looked concerned—but unlike his cohort—there was no panic.

The Death Racers abruptly stopped spinning. The now glow-less tops popped and swiveled like advanced droids in search of whatever it was they were looking for. They had already located their target.

From the control room, Isaac and Blimm could see the colorful warhead now spiraling through the black night. It was descending at a diagonal trajectory, ready to connect with the elevating sleigh. Before he could even think, Blimm was now silent and aghast in a twisted nightmare of déjà vu as the sleigh lit into a fireball upon contact, immediately plummeting into a patch of snow near the runway.

445

Vance

After seconds of silence, Isaac softly radioed a message below. "We need to close the Wall—now!"

In a split second, Blimm went from frozen shock to losing his mind. "No!" he banged his twitchy head against the control deck. "Not again! Please, not again!" he pounded both fists against some glowing buttons.

"Blimm, Blimm!" Isaac ripped his headset off to rush over and smother the elf's flailing arms. "Calm down! I said … I need you to calm down."

"Not again," the yelling was softly dying into a whisper.

There were no tears in Isaac's eyes. In fact, at this point he even forced a mild smile as he held Blimm back from losing it altogether. "He's fine, Blimm," Isaac's promise was unusually soothing. "Nick … he's just fine."

Blimm finally froze, looking up at Isaac with a deep squint of confusion.

Nick ran alongside Silva through a dark, underground corridor. He held his hat as he sprinted. "I don't understand. What was that sound?"

"Trust me," Silva huffed as she explained. "As much as I'd love to explain it you, it's best you don't know."

"But why are we running?" Silva didn't answer this time while rounding a hall, where Gib was anxiously waiting near an open door.

"Is that really as fast as the two of you can run?" Gib had to ask as they eased up toward the door. "Even I can hobble across a finish line quicker than that, and I'm over 300 bloody pounds."

"Where are we?" Nick inquired upon entering what looked like a mechanic's garage. The sleigh was propped up on a makeshift lift where engineers were hastily making last-minute adjustments to the propellant engines.

446

Inheriting the Sleigh

"The last place your enemy might expect you to be," said Gib, ushering him forward. "Let's just say, you're gonna need some extra juice to get out of here on time."

Skeeta was hard at work harnessing all eight reindeer—each of which grew excited as Nick walked in. He stroked each one near the antlers. "Aren't we missing somebody?"

A somber Skeeta looked up in her single braid. "I'm sorry, but Rudolph's not coming."

"Not coming?" Nick probed. "But Rudolph with your nose so bright. Won't you guide my ...."

"Exactly," Silva interrupted, grabbing a tight hold of his arm. "You can't be drawing any attention to yourself right now. Unfortunately, all exterior light needs to be quelled," she instructed, hastily leading him toward the ladder. As Gib was busy with the disgusting, last-second chore of cleaning goop out of Donner's eye, Silva offered a sympathetic glance. "Are you alright ... Santa Claus?" she smiled as he turned back around, now halfway up the ladder.

"I hope so," Nick's voice softened. "Though I probably don't want to know what's out there waiting for me ... do I?"

Silva smiled again, this time proud of his bravery. It was a moment interrupted only by Gib's painful wince from getting poked in the rear by Blitzen's antlers. Nick pressed the rest of the way up into the sparkling sleigh that glittered with an array of red. Nick could smell the fresh leather and was dazzled by the flashing lights from the dashboard.

The reindeer knew this was no drill, anxiously preparing for flight by moving in place. Then again, they also seemed to know someone quite important was missing. Silva, Gib, Skeeta and the two engineers all backed away from the sleigh as Nick fired up the jet flames in the back.

Vance

Unlike the sleigh port—which was large, flashy and fit for show—the garage was anything but. An engineer used a hand crank to open the door, exposing little light but the stars on the outside.

"Saint Nick, can you hear me?"

"Corbin?" Nick was always comforted by the sound of his voice.

"Listen," the naturally fun-loving elf was all business. "With the Chief distracted by a million other things, I'm gonna get you out of here, OK. But I will tell you—expect this to go nothing like we practiced. We're currently in the middle of a residential neighborhood picked at random along the south side. As you know, the only opening through the Wall is to the east of the city near the sleigh port."

"Translation. What does that mean?"

"It means we'll be forced to get you in position to make your way through it. And quickly."

"Where are they? I mean, Gizer and his men?" It was the obvious question, with Nick needing composure to wait so long to ask it.

"I wish I knew," he admitted. "But it appears Gizer now has his eyes on the skies. Honestly, it looks like he's willing to use any measure necessary to take you out."

"I see," Nick sighed with building nerves as he put on his hat to embrace a new rush of noise. "You're saying the sleigh could actually go down tonight?"

"You know," Corbin resumed with empathy after a drawn pause. "Isaac wouldn't like me saying this, but you can still back out. Perhaps even saving Christmas isn't worth your own life. I certainly wouldn't judge you for it."

The youthful voices took on a giddiness almost pleasant for Nick to listen to. It was why he was so calm when he should have been petrified. They were playful and excited—everything Christmas was truly about.

Inheriting the Sleigh

Corbin gave Nick a few dead seconds to make up his own mind, and when he had, it was obvious. Nick suddenly pulled back hard on the reins to get the reindeer's attention. "Let's fly," he issued as Dasher and Dancer didn't take long to command the lead.

Corbin blew a big bubble with a raised fist, feeding off Nick's sudden burst of bravery. "Alright then, I want you to fly low around this stretch. They shouldn't expect you here, but we don't want to take any chances."

"Roger," Nick was now having some fun as his adrenaline kicked in near a stretch of fine homes. He hadn't even paid attention yet to the large sack of gifts rising tall out the back of the sleigh.

With the thrust of a joystick, they were suddenly whisking up out of the garage. Silva and Gib watched it shoot into a quaint neighborhood, unbothered by any light. The only thing now exposing the sleigh were two massive flames.

Nick did as instructed, guiding the reindeer past some rooftops. He warmed up his pilot skills by casually weaving through some chimneys.

"How do you feel?" Corbin occasionally checked in.

Nick was surprised by his response. "Wonderful."

"Then I need you to start taking it up a bit until you reach the city lights. Maybe 50 knots. And when you get there—just stop and hover."

"Stop and hover?" Nick repeated, as if having done precisely that once before.

"Yeah. Rushing you out of here is too risky. The enemy could have something trained in on your exit path. Plan on coasting the rest of the way. You should have enough reserve power to keep diagonal until you reach the outside."

Nick couldn't help but feel the lack of confidence behind Corbin's instruction as he continued to move the sleigh through the quiet backstreets. "Forgive me for asking … but won't that mean I'm a sitting duck?"

Corbin gulped, hesitant to go there. "You know what one of your father's favorite words was?" The question was clearly rhetorical. "Faith. In fact, he brought it up a lot. I'm still no expert on it myself—trust me. But more so than I can ever remember… now might be the perfect time for some."

"Move!" Gizer shoved his way for the underground periscope pinpointed on the crash site. Teams were hastily at work in the frosty glow digging through layers of ice to locate the driver inside the butchered sleigh. Black Capes jumped out of the way as Gizer anxiously stuck his eye to the viewfinder. He watched as the rescue team propped up the mangled wreckage to pull out a body. They dragged it through the snow for the cleared runway, shining flashlights across his still discernible face. But it wasn't the face anyone expected to see.

Gizer kept his eye close to the lens as he finally got his own view of the driver. He was scarred, but Starsky was visible enough.

The Capes waited long for a reaction as Goss silently kept his eyes glued to the scope. A general eventually had the nerve to speak up. "Well—is it him?"

Gizer slowly turned in a way that answered that question in complete silence. His face was boiling over like a kettle. "Decoy!" Gizer yelled from the top of his lungs as the underground bunker immediately went haywire. "Get another Death Racer ready before the real sleigh makes its move!" The Capes went dashing every which way, though Gizer stopped the last one. "General Seevus," he called. The Cape carried a stitched scar extending his right cheek. He was tall, with an unnerving look. "I know you've waited with great patience to hear this … but it's finally time to release the Havocs," said Gizer with some desperation in his voice. "Christmas gets crushed once and for all … understood?"

Seevus was thrilled, and with a twisted grin sauntered off calmly through the cave.

"Are the shields up?" Isaac was much more edgy than he was moments before.

Blimm slapped away at his keyboard, pulling up virtual radar charts with a series of blinking dots inside the launch room. "They're up!" Blimm stuttered in his colorfully striped uniform. "But that may not be the only thing we need to worry about right now. Sergeant?" Blimm called. "Are you still there?"

Another grunt signified he'd been listening quietly to every word.

"What is it now?" Isaac piped in, not liking Blimm's tone.

"Look," Blimm was hyperventilating as he pointed to a series of blinking lights.

"Please dumb it down for me. What am I looking at?"

"There's sudden movement near one of the spots we've already designated as an enemy escape hole."

"You're right—big movement," Isaac's confirming whisper frightened the sergeant.

"What number?" Curnuckle cried.

"Looking," Blimm flipped the bangs out of his eyes. "Looks like 123. But wait!" Curnuckle didn't have time to respond before Blimm noticed some more rapid movement in the dots. "And 62. Along with 95!" Blimm strung his open fingers up through his scraggly hair. It was more than he could process all at once.

"All combat units report for immediate battle!" an urgent Curnuckle immediately took over, radioing his men. "The enemy is above ground. Repeat, the enemy is above ground. All units prepare to engage!"

Isaac stood back, helpless from his perched, control room hideaway. He glanced out a tinted glass wall, afraid for what he might see. Blotches of black were converging through the snow in more than one direction through the adjacent city. "Kris," Isaac whispered. "Forgive me for not being able to protect him. Your one and only child is about to die."

Chapter 58

Nick used some of the Pole's tallest buildings for cover as the sleigh moved up, ever so slowly. "How am I doing?" he asked after not hearing Corbin's voice for a good while.

"Probably better than you," Corbin radioed. "Just keep going until you see the clock tower."

Nick breathed with the reindeer nearly scaling parallel to a large dome.

The night was eerily quiet as Nick listened closely for the sound of anything—though all he could hear was a rustling wind. The sleigh now had a beautiful view of the arctic city. Lights were aglow underneath the northern stars as Nick laid eyes on the green clock tower. He kept the reindeer in vertical flight, hovering next to it like gnats around a porch bulb. "OK," Nick gulped, with the sleigh now only slightly swaying. "I'm here. Now what?"

"We wait," said Corbin.

"Wait? But what are we waiting for?"

Corbin didn't respond this time. Instead, he was anticipating a loud boom that suddenly rocked every eardrum in the vicinity. Nick leapt up to see what it might be and where it came from. "That," Corbin finally spoke up as danger was forthcoming. There was something vibrantly pink spiraling Nick's way.

"Corbin," Nick could barely get his name out. He had since gotten somewhat used to the stalled time but found it bizarre that he could now actually size up the massive flame. His first instinct was to bail out over the edge of the sleigh.

"Nick, no!" the elf cried, carefully watching his every move. "Sit back down!"

The missile, with a bright green, Saturn-like ring around the back was getting closer—though Nick couldn't ascertain whether he had five seconds or 20. But there were other sounds joining the fight. Large satellites positioned around the city's center—ones that Nick had never even noticed before suddenly took on their own glow, acting abuzz. They were raising and spinning in defense.

Nick now nervously gripped onto his fuzzy hat as he stood and watched a Death Racer fire from the opposite direction. All he could do was close both eyes and pray as the two missiles soon struck each other head-on, creating a massive explosion—raining a shattering of neon sparks for the surface streets.

Nick opened his eyes again, only to see soldiers and Capes alike suddenly emerging out of their hiding spots. War was breaking out at the Pole.

Crip Seevus brandished a sword—one with an impressively wide blade. "Release the Havocs!" he waved as a host of Capes at his command were anxious to shoot out across the red line and onto the snowy battlefield. Trained elves in white camo met them on the run from the opposite way, racing for places to blockade from incoming gunfire.

"But what about you, General?" said a departing, and somewhat curious Cape.

"Yes. What about me?"

"Aren't you coming?"

Seevus shook his unpleasant face. "No. For I get the honor of closing the Wall."

Isaac was escorted by two armed guards near the runway. He held a thick fleece over his bare face as he attempted to grit his way through the bitter cold.

"Sir, I don't know if this is a good idea," admitted one of the guards. "There are no safe zones out here!"

"Just cover me!" Isaac instructed, barely able to hear his voice over the howling wind.

Isaac was now amid periodic sparks of gunfire but didn't turn around. A medic was still attending to Starsky, surrounded by nine dead reindeer sprawled over the ice. He pushed his way toward the middle of the scrum, Starsky lying still and flat. "So, is he … you know …?"

"I'm sorry," the medic declared.

Isaac's heart went numb as he desperately hoped they'd have a chance to save their hero. "Let's get him out of here then!" Isaac was anxious to make his eulogizing short—all the while, wishing he had more time to offer his condolences.

"And is this one for real?" assumed the medic, hard pressed not to ask.

Isaac knew it was pointless holding back any more secrets before his handheld radio interrupted the exchange.

"Chief, come in. Chief Newell … please, come in."

"What is it, Blimm?" Isaac made his bodyguards nervous by leaving the protective huddle for some added privacy. "I thought I already warned you not to lose it on me. Everything's fine."

"Agh," he had to second-guess whether that was indeed true, or if there was something else Isaac had been keeping from him for his own protection. "Would you say the same if I told you an override is currently being enacted to unlock the Wall?"

"What?!" Isaac lifted the fleece rag from over his face, just long enough to blow his top and cover it back up again.

"I'll take that as a 'no,'" said Blimm from the protective comfort of his warm workstation. "Because right now … I'm looking at somebody in the process of unlocking the code."

"That's impossible," uttered Isaac. "I'm the only one that knows that code."

A vibrating hum suddenly rocked the ground at their boots. The medic crew still carting off Starsky's body, was nearly knocked off their feet. Isaac, having heard that sound hundreds of times before, knew exactly what it was. "Corbin!" Isaac called after changing frequencies.

Corbin had his feet kicked up, staring aimlessly into a poster on the wall. As startled as he was by Isaac's urgent scream, it was exactly what he'd been waiting for. "What is it?!" his gum inadvertently popped all over his face as he responded.

"The Wall's closing," a pale-faced Isaac said, staring across the distant battlefield.

"What are you talking about? Doesn't Nick have to be safely on the other side before that happens?"

Isaac couldn't believe Corbin was stating the obvious at a time like this. "Go—now!" he exclaimed. "Or we may not get it back open in time!"

Inheriting the Sleigh

All the while, Nick had nearly been lulled to sleep by the fireworks. The truth was the glow of war was anything but peaceful—but pretending it was something else was the only thing he could think to do to keep calm as he waited.

The word came into the sleigh, loud and clear, "Nick, you gotta go now!" cried Corbin as Nick could tell something was moving in the distance. He didn't know what but heard an odd rustling of something he couldn't see.

On top of that, loud engines were moving in from behind—only this time the noise was welcome. "Tundra Bird Squadron," Nick whispered as an old fighter jet stopped to greet him on either side.

Despite this being his first official takeoff, Nick was smart enough to know that being trapped inside much longer could prove fatal. "Let's do this then!" his hat magnetically sucked over his scalp as he immediately slapped at the reins. Pushing the reindeer forward, they were no longer hovering but dropping away from the bright clock tower in a quick descent. It was a freewheel that felt like he was plummeting down the initial drop of a great roller coaster.

Blaine noticed what was happening, stealing two flare sticks from the closest elf. He tried to get Nick's attention to guide him for the narrow, unseen trail leading outside the city.

The sound and smell of gunfire was beginning to feel normal to Nick as the sleigh was starting to level out about 30 feet off the ground over the runway. He noticed the flare and veered back in that direction as Cross waved him in. The Tundra Birds were furiously firing from the back of their double-wing planes, as if their own lives depended on it.

Looking down for only a second, Nick could see the slaughtered reindeer in pools of blood-soaked snow; but more importantly, knew he was getting close to the outside. The one thing he didn't know was whether he might collide with something he couldn't see.

As elves lay dead, those still alive couldn't help but stop as they watched the sleigh magically slide through the break in time. Alarms, sirens and the cries of the injured all added to the chaos as they waited. Nick instinctively shielded his face at the thought of impact, but there was none—only a noticeable breeze following one last rustle near the ground. Nick was only guessing the Wall had closed, with the lights quickly becoming dimmer and dimmer the further he sailed.

Only eventually did he feel safe enough to glance behind him again. The reindeer's hooves were now skimming against the arctic ice, before coming to a stop well outside the city. With the protective warplanes no longer in view, he was now alone in a barren wilderness—nobody at his side other than the trusty eight reindeer.

"Boy, do I need you right now, Rudolph," Nick sat still in near-complete darkness with the sleigh runners stuck to the ice. The cold was overpowering, and all communication had since stopped. "Hello," Nick radioed. He spent several seconds trying to think through what to do next before eventually feeling a welcome pop. A generator suddenly kicked on with lights at the front of the sleigh exposing the reindeer. "There we go," he took a deep breath, trying to block out the thought of anything truly terrible happening back at the Pole.

The light wasn't what he was used to, but it was enough to muster up the courage to get the sleigh back into the air again. Powering the jets, the dashboard was soon blinking as well. "Now Dasher, now Dancer," Nick had never actually recited Clement Clark Moore's famous poem in its entirety before. "Now Prancer and Vixen. On Comet, on Cupid, on Donner and Blitzen. To the top of the porch, to the top of the wall. Now dash away, dash away, dash away all!"

Inheriting the Sleigh

The reindeer were in a gallop, pushing forward, and eventually up. Nick felt independent and free as if he could suddenly multi-task, gaining control over his many scattered thoughts. He wondered how over the course of a year he had ever become Santa Claus—but could also feel a piece of every child. With the stars closer than he had ever seen them, Operation Return was now officially underway.

Chapter 59

N ick wanted to fall asleep. His head was bobbing to the tune of a raving techno beat to stay awake. And worse, it was in Dutch. "This is awful," he flipped the radio once it occurred what he was listening to.

"Welcome back to RTHK Radio, Hong Kong," the disk jockey introduced in Chinese. "The day of holiday reckoning. Will Santa Claus show up this year? Or was last year's absence just some bizarre fluke with a reasonable explanation?"

Nick kept turning the dial. "The Benedict nuns at the Elstow Abbey Monastery holding a special prayer vigil in Bedfordshire tonight, all for the safe return flight of Father Christmas," said a reporter with a British accent. "They've invited the girls of St. Theresa's Boarding School in Effingham to join them for an evening of faith and song, all in effort to entice the return of St. Nicholas to the many homes across Britain. Ritual Shaw—signing off for the BBC."

The sleigh was racing across Alaska into the Bering Sea. Nick failed to find anything holding his interest for very long and finally gave up. He could now hear little other than the bells jingling off the reindeer as their legs kicked back and forth in the brisk air—moving south.

Inheriting the Sleigh

"Nick … come in," the voice was fuzzy, but cleared a bit the second time.

The boy's excitement doubled. "Corbin, is that you?"

"About time," he cheered with his voice still popping in and out. "Our main antenna's been destroyed—a chore, to put it mildly to sync up the right frequency from a backup. But enough of that—where are you right now?"

"Taking the short route. My meter says I'm still about 25 hundred miles from the Marshall Islands," Nick informed with a mix of giddiness and angst.

"Still?" Corbin questioned his word choice. "You'll be there quicker than you know. How 'bout visibility?"

"So-so. The fog's thick, but I can see."

"You got lucky then—which explains the suitable time. That's why Kris would often go the long way through the Atlantic to avoid any sticky run-ins with Mother Nature. Which out there, can be more unforgiving than a hungry orca through a seal herd."

Nick noticed the sea ice become dark blue ocean—now able to visualize images below. Without Rudolph, he used a flare to see off to both sides, only to pull his head back in whenever he got too dizzy. But it was the churning inside his gut for what was coming next that was causing him to grow mildly sick.

A disinterested Arthur Crest was escorted inside a small room. It was dressed in cheap tinsel and a few donated decorations. A cheesy drape of the North Pole hung down off the center of the front wall, with a glittery sheet that was supposed to resemble snow over a small wooden platform.

Arthur had grown a beard, making him nearly unrecognizable. He hesitantly scooted into one of the many empty foldup chairs. There were a few others in matching jumpsuits already sitting, with a burly prison guard standing watch at the door.

"Arty," he felt a poke. "Yur' gonna love dis." A grinning inmate anxiously turned back to address Arthur from his chair in the front row. He was old and toothless but could hardly contain his excitement.

Some of the others were amused by him, though not Arthur. He remained emotionless with a stale glare. The old man then jumped as a side door opened—the guard having to force him back into his seat to keep him from running toward Santa like a small child.

"Ho, ho, ho," said the beard in a knockoff suit. Some of the inmates cheered, while others mocked.

"Santee!" The man with the mind of a juvenile held out both arms. "Did you bring me a present?"

"Why of course," Santa held up his round belly, stroking his stringy, white below the chin. "For those that have been good this year. Have you been good this year ... Benny?" He squinted overtop his cheap frames to read the man's nametag, all while taking a seat atop the snowy platform full of cotton.

"Promise I have." The toothless prisoner with scraggy hair used all his willpower to stay put as he waited for Santa to pull a small gift from his sack. "Is it shaving cream and beef jerky like you got me last year?" Another prisoner snickered with folded arms, getting a rise of the exchange.

"Patience, my good man," Santa chuckled. "But first I have to call in my favorite helper."

"Elfie? Is it Elfie?" Benny clapped.

A college student in desperate need of some spare cash looked embarrassed to have to play the part. He followed in through the same door wearing a loosely fitted shirt cut-off at the sleeves—accompanied by a tall, pointy hat.

Arthur remained stone-faced as Elfie delivered candy canes hooked over his frail arms. His mind was spinning, trying to figure out how to escape the nightmare—and once he realized how real it was, eventually snapped.

"Alfonso!" Everybody turned at the unexpected thrust behind his voice. "I've changed my mind," he said panning for the guard as Santa and Elfie temporarily halted their enactment. "Take me back to my cell. Please."

Vienna leaned over the plush carpet inside apartment 5116. During a normal holiday, Christmas would have been fully set up weeks ago, but not this year. A view of Central Park was over her shoulder. She sat next to a plastic tub full of Christmas ornaments—taking the bulbs out slowly—stroking each one. Her stare was transfixed, her expression both melancholy and confused by her memories. And then she came across the only bulb of the bunch that was not part of a matching set. It was silver with mint stripes.

As much as she tried not to, her mind veered. Vienna was alone, having just gotten out of the bath when there came an unexpected knock at the door. She grabbed her robe, looking through the keyhole. The carpeted hallway was quiet and empty, but she opened it anyway to be sure. Seeing nothing, Vienna nearly shut it again before realizing there was something resting at her bare feet. Not just a cradle, but something clearly moving inside the fine bocote wood.

Vienna looked down both sides of the hall but saw no one as the snuggly-wrapped baby made her feel numb with shock. Not being watched, she lifted the swaddled sheet to behold the beautiful brown eyes of the stranger. A note was tucked under its arm; one that would ultimately change her life.

Take care of this one, she read after ripping the seal. It was a swirling SC. Santa's trademark stamp. *A special boy from a special place. One with a unique heart ailment that will require the best physician. May you look after him, as we have searched long and hard, ocean to ocean for a suitable match. You have been chosen. I know you cannot physically bear one of your own. Consider him a gift. His name, is Saint Nicholas.*

Vienna heard the door swing open. She knew it was Arthur who waltzed in with a smile holding a fresh bottle of wine. His top button was undone and his tie was loose around the collar. "I've won the Schwartzman account!" he said a little arrogantly after a full day at the office, his arms open wide as if ready to playfully embrace his wife. But she did not extend back. "Did you hear me? I said, the Schwartzman account. The biggest real estate mogul in … Queens." Arthur stopped after sensing something out of place.

With a flick of her head and a nervous hand propped over her mouth, she pointed at the infant cooing inside the cradle as she gently rocked it back-and-forth with her foot. "And who is this?" he asked with startled eyes.

Vienna said nothing, only handing him the note. Arthur perused it quickly before turning back to address his new wife, who continued to rock the cradle with an entranced grin. "But that's impossible," said Arthur, his face now oozing with confusion. "There are only three people on earth who know you can't get pregnant. You, me, and your OB."

Inheriting the Sleigh

"I know," Vienna said as she instinctively reached down to pick Nick up with a now-heavy smile. She swaddled him lovingly inside the rich blanket as her heart had already been more than won over. "I know."

Chapter 60

Enter landing mode," said an automated voice as the reindeer made a sharp turn in line with a stretch of open beach.

"Whoa," Nick nearly lost his gut as the sleigh dipped. Stripping his plush fur coat several thousand miles back, Nick's thermometer now read 74 degrees Fahrenheit. There were no lights on well past midnight on the small island atoll, and he could only see the tops of the palms as he descended.

Dasher and Dancer were not used to taking the lead but held that key spot now as the sleigh diagonally sprang for the beach. Nick could hear waves crashing and seagulls chirping. It was a jerky ride as he kept his hands gripped tightly over the reins. He had a headache but did his best to keep his eyes locked on the dash, looking for any warning signals.

With the last stretch upon him, the rookie pilot couldn't help but scream in the pitch-black unknown. And after a thrill he could have very well done without, the reindeer abruptly stopped their death-defying plummet. Nick gripped his heart, patting himself to make sure he was still alive.

Inheriting the Sleigh

"Nick," Corbin's staticky voice returned. He'd been sitting on the edge of his seat listening to the entire landing sequence with bated breath. "You there?"

It took him a few moments to gather himself, never having felt such a rush. Reaching for the flare, he shined it forward to see the eight reindeer now hovering mere feet off the sand. Nick then slowly dropped the sleigh the rest of the way down into the soft, white grains that filled up the isolated beach.

"Nick, talk to me!" Corbin was growing more nervous with time.

"Yes, I'm here," he assured surrounded by curious gulls. Santa Claus stood up, gazing around to soak in the moment. He hadn't experienced a climate this pleasant since the autumn before last and nearly forgot what a cool morning breeze felt like. House number one lit up large and bright on his dashboard.

"Then, tell me … what do you see?" Corbin couldn't take it any longer. He needed detail.

"Not much," the flare exposed little other than beach and ocean. Nick descended the ladder, scooping up two big handfuls of sand—grains he anxiously let roll back through his fingers. He enjoyed the salt in the air though felt out of place in the suit.

The reindeer watched as Nick marched inland—that is until he noticed a thick layer of palm. And there it was. House One was little more than a one-room cottage. It had a sloping, thatched roof of fronds—the base sitting up off the sand with posts to keep it safe from the high tide.

Nick had his hat bunched up in his right hand before it finally occurred. He needed to have it on, which is all it took to receive an invigorating rush.

Vance

The six resident faces, clear as day immediately began floating off the top of his head "Wiki. Wiki," said his excited older sister, Ailana. "Do you know what today is? It's Christmas Eve."

"Am I ... you know, still alive?" Wiki asked from his humble bed, as if anticipating that day for months.

"Of course, you're still alive," said Ailana as she gave him a big hug. "And do you know what that means? Do you know who's coming tomorrow?"

"Ailana," the oldest brother, Rangi, quietly rebuked. "Don't be feeding him any false hope. What if he doesn't show up again this year?" a bare-chested Rangi said in passing, a fishing pole in hand.

Ailana turned back to reassure her little brother once Rangi walked out the door, all the gladder to see his pessimism disappear with him. "Don't worry, Wik. He'll come. You'll see."

"And will he have gifts?" Wiki did his best to force his excited head upward, though Ailana gently set it back down against his pillow after noticing the sudden jolt causing him pain.

"He'll most certainly bring gifts. Which—if anyone deserves, it's you," Ailana smiled as the vision faded into another.

Ezra slipped his old spectacles over his eyes as he got a better look at the hologram. "The Ngoriakis can't afford expensive medical care, let alone gain access to it," Ezra informed. "And the village patriarchs don't expect him to make it into spring," Nick felt himself weep internally as Ezra's voice was now hollow. "He has asked for only one thing."

"And what is that?" Nick could oddly hear his own voice echoing inside his head.

"Eternal life. Eternal life. Eternal life." It took many seconds before Nick broke through his trance. A pelican landed, wondering what he'd been staring at all that time. Santa took a deep breath, wiping the sweat off his brow before running right back to the sleigh.

"You've returned?" Corbin spoke as he could hear Nick pushing up the ladder. "Did you find it?"

"Yep," Nick responded as he used another foldup ladder behind the driver's seat to peek up into the tall sack of gifts—all neatly harnessed. He began filling up a smaller sack from the larger pool of toys.

Nick was now more focused and confident than ever as he descended with the sack. He sunk his boots into the sand, tugging his hat down over his ears to re-approach House One.

"Wait, are you sure you've …." But this time, Corbin's concern was disregarded.

He could hardly help but see every moment of Wiki's short life flashing before his eyes on the lonely walk up.

There was no chimney above the hut, and the door possessed no lock. With the red sack slung over his left shoulder, he inched up the short flight of rickety stairs, gently grabbing the handle. It was his golden moment—one where it fully occurred what was happening; the beginning of a renewed happiness all across the world.

Slowly cracking the door open, he saw a wax candle dripping in the center of the otherwise dark room. It exposed a small, leafless tree decorated in sliced coconuts dangling by twine. The tree was surrounded by a series of hammocks that hung off a log supporting the A-frame roof above. A hand-carved cross, the size of a tire was visible along the back wall.

Nick nervously stepped one boot over the wood plank floor, followed by the next. Never had he ever imagined that inside his very first house, the entire family might be lying directly front and center around the tree.

Vance

Feto and Lota shared the big hammock near the stairs leading to a small storage loft above. Rangi, Manu and Ailana's hammock completed a full circle around the room. But there was one not in any hammock at all.

Little Wiki was comfortably curled up in a small, patched quilt over a mattress near the tree. He hugged a wooden statue of Santa Claus, looking happy as he slept. Nick set his sack on the floor, slowly crouching to get a better look at the ill child. He gently pulled the blanket up a little higher over his bare shoulders, simultaneously prying the Santa figurine from his fingertips.

Nick reached into his sack to expose a toy soldier. The size of a doll was heavy and well-built with a rubbery face painted over to resemble dirt. The soldier was dressed in camo and wore an army-style helmet over his black locks—the straps hanging down over the ears. A semi-automatic firearm was propped over his shoulder, with a knife at his side and a courageous grin below two eyes that never blinked.

Nick had a tear in his own eye as he ever so delicately tucked the gift into Wiki's frail chest, along with a large candy cane and other treats. His head was spinning inside the hat, and he naturally stuck his fingers over his ears to brace for the mental whirlwind.

Wiki's timeline, from birth to the current day was suddenly whisking before Nick's eyes. It was a series of quick pops that nearly made Nick feel guilty about his own life. No matter where Wiki was, there was a playful joy in his eye and a wide grin across his cheeks. Nick could now see that same smile firsthand as he slept.

"Mama … Mama," Wiki carted a yellowfin tuna, one half the size of himself into the house. She hurried to help him hoist it up onto the butcher's table.

Inheriting the Sleigh

"Wiki, you are in no shape to be fishing right now," rebuked Lota as she quickly thrust a machete over the fish to keep it from wiggling off. "You should be resting."

"But I caught it for you, Mama." Lota's heart nearly melted.

Nick instinctively reached into his bag. It was an impulse, though one his brain never triggered. He pulled out a piece of thick paper. It looked faded and wrinkled, like old currency with a greenish hue, but also had a bold title. "Ticket to Heaven," read Nick off the top. Santa Claus lifted his head, as if looking beyond the thatched roof. "What does this mean?" he plead. "But it can't ...," his whisper soon faded away once he determined that Wiki's fate was inevitable. He knew there was simply nothing he could do to change it.

Nick silently wept as he peered around the circle of hammocks—ending with Wiki on the floor. He took a pen and wrote over the certificate. The words came freely.

Dear Wiki,

I have seen your plight and know your heart. Your seven years of earthly service has surpassed most in their 90th year. You are strong like this soldier. I call him Peran, or Brave in your tongue. Please, say hello to my father for me. You will cross paths once you get there. Like myself, he has a vested interest in your well-being.

With Love,
Santa

Nick, rather overwhelmed, then stamped the official seal of the North Pole—discreetly fading away from House One.

471

Chapter 61

The Goddard brothers stood in their traditional single file incline. Over a dock—frosted by a glaze of snow—they looked out into the distant mountaintops of eastern Greenland. There were glimpses of colorful homes dotted about the shoreline rock, though you couldn't see much of them in the thick winter freeze.

The Goddard's didn't say much either. They were on an important errand looking for any sign of life—though not at all surprised to see a scene void of movement. It was simply too cold, with every villager tucked safely inside.

A small vessel sat tied at the end of the dock. Its bright orange and green paint were peeling away, and it was graffitied over. There was even what looked like a bullet fracture near the back of the hull.

Gilbert, the oldest and tallest, left the others to slowly inspect further down the curious vessel. He took it slowly, his boots crunching the snow on his way there. Gilbert stroked his glove against the side of the hull, searching for evidence as his three brothers chose to look on from a distance. He then noticed something out of place. Patches of ice at his feet were soaked in red. Gilbert crouched to lick the wine-colored ice from his fingertip, only to chap his lips from the bitter taste of blood, hopping back up in concern.

But before he could make it back upright, the rusty metal door to the tugboat was suddenly thrust open. Seeing danger play out in advance, a gunshot fired. Gilbert turned to find the shortest and youngest, Gus with his arms extended out—his fingers clasped over the trigger of a pistol. An armed boat captain quickly dropped into the icy sea through the narrow gap between the boat and dock. He had a gaping wound, dead center between the eyes.

"And to think you're the most inexperienced shot in the family," Gabriel stated, without a smile or a frown.

Gilbert reached for his own firearm, discreetly stepping up over the bow for the main deck. The others followed, inspecting every inch of the boat. Gabriel silently signaled Gideon that he was checking the top. And he barely got his first foot up over the bottom rung of the ladder when another figure emerged. The second male leapt the rail, only to land with a thump on the deck. The sailor couldn't help but slip across the layer of sloppy ice, while the stockiest of the bunch, Gideon, responded like a linebacker after a retreating quarterback. With a merciless slam into the side of the boat, Gus now had his firearm at the boy's chest. The sailor's arms were up in surrender as Gilbert approached.

"You know who we're looking for, don't you?" he asked in Spanish.

The boy nodded fearfully. "Entonces dime dónde."

"Then tell me where."

He pointed toward an endless white wilderness, as if to suggest Marie could be anywhere. "Ella ya se fue," he explained as he lowered his arms to cover his shivering body.

Gabrielle's head stoically turned, along with the others for the barren tundra. His observation was obvious. "The pretty girl doesn't last five minutes out there."

Crip Seevus was much taller than Gizer. The former senator sat still and quiet upon a rocky throne engraved out of an underground boulder. He could see Seevus approach with mild shame. The distinguished Cape softly set his curved blade upon an altar below Gizer's feet. He kneeled on one knee, bowing up at his superior.

"I'm sorry. We have killed many elves, but not the target you wanted."

Gizer's chuckle surprised Seevus. "I have waited 21 hundred years to see it end," he began to step down the chiseled steps. "This was my best shot, and yet he who I thought was my finest assassin could not even stop a newbie."

"But we're not even certain the mission bred any success," Crip attempted to provide some optimism. "For all we know, the heir has since been turned into sea lion food."

Gizer laughed again now walking at eye-level next to a kneeling Seevus. "Let me ask you, General. Do you truly believe that?" But Seevus didn't answer the question. In fact, his scarred face didn't even bother to look up. "Besides, this project was not to satisfy me."

"It wasn't?" Crip appeared surprised. "Then who?"

After slowly pacing away, Gizer whipped around to face Seevus. "There is really much you don't know, isn't there?" Goss said to humble his hatchet man. "I fulfill the direct mission once set out by my king … Herod the Great."

Inheriting the Sleigh

A fit frame zipped up his nimble, one-piece, carrying only a single bag. Blain had a look of focused anger between his signature sideburns as he entered a very specific elevator—one that blended in nicely with the quiet building. It was small, shaped like a cylinder with a glass door. Blaine had the proper access codes to gain entrance to the elevator; one that only went one direction—down.

It was swift in its descent; so much so that Blaine was forced to grip a handle to keep from falling over. He could now see every level as he dropped underground—the first few of which were nothing more than old, dusty warehouses filled with crates full of discarded toys. But as he got lower, the manmade enclosures began to disappear. There was soon a period of nothing but blackness, with no story to exit through—only earthly rock.

Blaine flashed a light through the glass as the elevator suddenly exposed new levels again. He knew he was now in the deep underground. There were caverns and rocky cliffs, some with manmade entryways.

Blaine held a small machine in his hand, one that gauged human activity with sonar waves. It was beginning to vibrate heavily as to alert him to something. He reached up and pulled a string secured to the roof of the elevator, bringing it to a sudden halt. Blaine jerked forward, hitting his head hard against the glass and tripping over his feet as the clear doors suddenly parted again. He plopped onto the adjoining rock, taking a few seconds to shake off his dizziness. He could immediately feel the increased heat and rolled up his sleeves before perking up at the sound of voices. There was moaning and groaning—even an occasional scream. Blaine stopped once the voices were now so clear he could easily decipher them.

Down below a wall of loose rock, wounded men filled up a tented campsite. They were being escorted in, crying for help.

But Cross forced himself to ignore the wailing. He had a job to do. Inside his bag was a small vehicle the size of a mailbox. It replicated a modern Jeep, with a swirl of dark camouflage that blended in nicely with the cave. But it also possessed four thick, durable tires designed to off-road. They were nearly as large as the body of the vehicle itself.

Blaine also pulled out a remote to control the sleek toy—one that would have been high on any little boy's Christmas list. Only this was no toy safe for a child. It had another purpose. The gadget, by design, made no noise as its tires swiveled and rotated up, over and around anything in its path.

Blaine found a boulder suitable to sit on. He pulled out a portable unit that quickly powered up by battery, with small monitors, controls and even a keyboard. He could now see exactly where the vehicle was going from one of the monitors now perched over his lap. The truck was racing at a high speed through a small pathway in the cave, and Blaine seemed to know exactly where he was going.

As it raced, he pulled out a second vehicle; only this one was closer to its intended destination. The tires and four-wheel drive began maneuvering down the awkward terrain and stone wall leading for the campsite. Loose rock occasionally crumbled for the flat surface, but the 4x4 pressed on—sometimes meticulously stepping up and over earth that was simply too big to plow through. With precision, Blaine knew how to control the vehicles—two at a time going opposite ways, all by watching their camera positions from the monitors resting over his thighs.

"Where are you?" he mumbled as he waited for Gizer to show himself. The miniature vehicle continued to speed along until it stumbled upon an opening. It was a large room surrounded by funhouse-like glass. Blaine got excited upon seeing Gizer's face for the first time.

Inheriting the Sleigh

The only problem, that same face was everywhere, with a reflection bouncing off the many misshapen glass panes inside the cave cavity.

His swirling hair coiled up as he wore a fancy coat. He proudly held a gaudy staff with a glowing ball at the top, an image expanding and shrinking at the will of the mirrors.

"You!" a startled Blaine jumped at the sound of a Black Cape. His monitor station suddenly flew off his lap, smacking against the rocks near his feet. Cross reached for a gun at his belt that whipped a beam through the Cape's heart. But there were others, and they immediately fired back.

Blaine dove behind a boulder, knowing he'd quickly be outnumbered. He had to immediately set off the assassination bombs, but the handheld detonator had since dropped to the bumpy surface in the middle of the firing zone. Bullets ricocheted off the stone behind him as he continued to duck for cover, all as the incoming Capes inched closer.

Blaine knew his time had to be now. Peeking his head around to see where the detonators were, he bravely dove forward with both hands flying for the red buttons. More gunfire rocked his eardrums as he hit hard against the surface—though with a clean grip of the detonators. Before they knew it, two explosions simultaneously wrought chaos inside the cave. The mirrors shattered, with glass flying like a thousand shooting knives.

Cave deposits also broke loose from the effects of a massive fireball; but it also produced a rumble that rippled through the cave. It knocked the Capes off their feet, with massive sections of the stony ceiling soon crumbling down.

Blaine tried to roll from the path of a falling rock that smashed hard over his left leg. He couldn't move, wincing in pain as all the minimal light from the underground tunnel had suddenly vanished. Blaine was still alive but could do nothing but lie face down in the dark. The heat was sweltering—and over time the moaning came to a stop, leaving the elf to assume he was the only one in the vicinity yet alive.

But once the dust settled, a shadowy figure holding a lantern slowly approached. He paced the tunnel, discarding most of the dead bodies as irrelevant. Crip Seevus took his time to maneuver around every roadblock.

Blaine could no longer swivel or lift his head but knew somebody was approaching. "Hello," he called in desperation, barely able to utter a sound. Seevus didn't respond and instead pushed the rock up off his now-lifeless leg. He cried in pain, rolling onto his back to glare up into the sudden stream of light. His eyes grew fearful and large as Crip Seevus' scarred face now stood before him.

"So," Seevus bent to get a better look. "I have finally found the source of this unfortunate assassination plot."

"Crip," Blaine mumbled, as if acknowledging an old acquaintance. "It's good to see you again."

"Is it?" he smiled. "I cannot imagine that would be true."

Blaine forced a laugh, however mild. "I guess not. Do you remember?"

"Remember what?" Seevus acted aloof to what Blain was referring to.

"You and I … working on project 541879. Those were great times, you know."

"Project 541879," Seevus mulled. "Of course, the sleigh design," he said with a degree of genuine patronization before reverting right back to his wicked self. "The very same sleigh I helped bring down. And perhaps one day—God willing—will do so again." Seevus dropped his lantern near Blaine's exposed face, all while lifting his polished blade.

Inheriting the Sleigh

Blaine forced his own head up, just long enough to see what was happening. His reflection glimmered off the sword that was then thrust down over his helpless neck.

Chapter 62

Heeeeeeeeeeeee's bock!" screamed a Rastafarian DJ inside a crowded soccer stadium. His thick, natty dreads poured down his Mad Hatter-style hat as tens of thousands watched a news report over a big screen. "Big t'ings are happenin' once again on December 25th, mon," he charged up the crowd. "So now we go fulljoy in the festive return of Fatha' Christmas!"

An emotionally strung Vienna flipped the channel from one international celebration to the next. It was as if the entire world had broken out in a celebratory frenzy once word of Santa's return began to trickle in.

Nick's mother was becoming just as hopeful as she was broken. Unable to sleep, she curiously flipped the dial until settling on another report. "It is now Christmas Eve here in the city," a crowd in the background of Times Square cheered loudly. "Where Santa Claus, to the great relief of millions all over the world, has not only returned—but has already swept through two-thirds of the globe on his way for the Western Hemisphere."

She muted the TV after hearing a knock at the door. Covering up her loose robe, she checked the peephole first, not really in any state to receive company.

Inheriting the Sleigh

"Marlene," Vienna addressed with guilt as Marie's disheveled mother stood over the entryway mat. "It's late, but Merry Christmas to you."

"I'm sorry. I shouldn't have come," Marlene Bayliff suddenly went white with panic. She stammered something before jetting right back for the elevator.

"No, wait," Vienna called her back. "Please," she begged. "Won't you … come in?" Marlene froze but followed. "Coffee?" Vienna offered to no reply. "I have tea, or whatever you wish."

"Coffee's … fine," Marlene broke from her distraught stupor as her mind got lost in the 15-foot-long living room mirror—one with crystal trim. The rest of the apartment reflected through the glass.

Marlene had been trying for some time to build up the courage to initiate a meeting but always felt intimidated by Vienna's money.

"I'm sorry, I couldn't really find the spirit to decorate this year," Vienna forced a smile amidst boxes full of un-hung ornaments on the floor. Her attempt at small talk was failing. "Please," she extended a hand over toward a charming sitting nook near the skyrise window. Vienna soon carried in a tray with two mugs and some Biscotti cookies.

"There are people everywhere," Marlene eventually spoke after Vienna handed her a mug. "I mean there always are in the city, but tonight I could barely reach Trump Tower."

"I know," Vienna forced a sip in the heavy awkwardness as Marlene was clearly not doing well. She twitched as she sipped from her own steamy mug. "I ugh … truly am sorry. You know, for everything you and Burton have gone through."

Marlene finally broke down in tears. "It's a big world, Vienna. We don't even know where to look." Vienna knew it was her time to simply listen as Marlene needed a moment to vent—and possibly someone to blame. "I mean, we always knew how fascinated she was by your son. She loved that boy and would follow Nick to the ends of the Earth. And we liked him too," Marlene covered her eyes with her hands. "Little did we know our little girl would actually try and do that," Marlene paused, wondering if she'd finally crossed a line.

Vienna stared away from Marlene who took another sip across the large apartment; one with a short set of steps separating the many rooms. She herself had already gone through the five stages of grief and knew Marlene was in the middle of that dreadful process now. "I'm sorry, did I …"

Vienna stopped her cold. "It's fine."

"No," Marlene cut in. "I do need to apologize. I know I'm not the only one here to part with a child." The two mothers needed a moment to lock eyes in grief.

"Yeah," Vienna whispered. "Christmas will certainly be different this year."

"Do you have any …? You know, any idea where he might be? Any idea where THEY might … be?"

Vienna took a few seconds to gather her response, though her initial attempt was little more than a slurp of her brew.

Another round of flashbacks sprung across her mind where the glass ornament was front and center—one she now noticed dangling over the Christmas tree from her current view. It was the only bulb she bothered to put up this year.

As for Marlene, she couldn't see it, but Vienna's bare foot had been swaying the hand-carved cradle underneath the small table. The back-and-forth was slow and sweet, as if a real baby were resting inside. "I'm afraid you might think I was crazy, if I told you."

Inheriting the Sleigh

A perfect square the size of a small room was opening inside a barren ice sheet. The sleigh, with no visible sack in the rear, hovered above the emerging hollow as the four sides parted amid the snow.

They dropped vertically through the underground abyss, until some light finally emerged at the bottom. The sleigh soon came to a stop as the reindeer settled onto the floor. The bunker was oval with glowing red and green light.

An elf lay asleep on a couch along the wall, snoring and aloof to their most recent arrival. Nick, meanwhile, was disoriented and winced with a severe headache.

Dancer, after sensing nothing happening, impatiently approached the sleeping elf. She was forced to push against the minimal slack, barely able to reach him with the tip of her antlers.

"Ouch," The elf arose after being poked in the ribcage. "Oh, you're back already?" he quickly leapt upward.

"What's going on? Where am I?"

The elf, with thick, blonde hair, smiled, as if amused by Nick's confusion. "You still don't remember who I am, do you? We've been performing this song and dance all night."

"Hmmm," Nick wracked his cluttered brain for any recognition— only to ask a repetitive question. "Where's Corbin?"

The elf climbed the ladder to get a better look at Nick. "I'm Teeter, the Sleigh Load Supervisor and you're just a little mixed up right now, that's all. Let's just say that moving from normal time to … well, this, can be a little hard on the temples. Seriously, going back and forth between two dimensions really takes some getting used to. It can damage all five senses."

"What time is it?" Nick asked.

Vance

Teeter shook, annoyed to have to explain it all over again. "Midnight. Let's just say, it's been midnight for a while now, Nick. And it won't stop until you've reached your last house."

"My last house—of course," Nick uttered as something finally registered. All Teeter needed to do was sound the bell with sections of the wall suddenly parting. Forklifts emerged, carrying crates full of new gifts to refill the sack.

"How much more do I have left?"

"If you want my opinion, you're doing surprisingly well, Nick. In fact, me and my guys here all placed bets before you left. Let's just say the big money was on you not making it past Finland." Teeter stopped after realizing the information wasn't well received. "Well, never mind that," he quickly moved on with a smile. "It's time now for the final third. It's time for the Americas."

"The Americas?"

"Yeah, the Americas. You know, the New World. Columbus. 1492," Teeter climbed up to inspect Nick the best he could, his eyes barely blinking even once. He used a small light to inspect his corneas.

Nick eventually turned to face the elf. "The truth is, I'm not sure I can do this anymore," his complaint was sincere as thoughts of his parents, among others suddenly caused a tidal wave of emotion.

Teeter shook as the crew was now busy refilling the sack. "Oh, much too late for any of that, Nick," Teeter was pleasant as he shrugged off the honesty. "Believe me, they now know you're coming."

Chapter 63

The landscape was white and abnormally peaceful. The city lights resembled a starry night; only it was well below the sleigh instead of above as Nick and the reindeer were whisking directly into the heart of Manhattan. Nick could spot an occasional drunk perusing the otherwise silent streets but knew right where he needed to be—confident he could still park undetected.

"Easy now," he mumbled as Dasher and Dancer got a little overanxious in the drop-down for the top of the residential tower. "I said, easy!" Nick held onto his safety grips, with the tall sack now dipping horizontally over Nick's head. His safety harness was the only thing keeping him inside before the reindeer finally flattened out again.

He blew a sigh, as if to suggest he'd never get used to that—though for the reindeer, it was business as usual. Nick took a moment to soak in the fact he was really back home. He could see the new World Trade Center and the Chrysler Building from his current perch.

Having been to his old friend Loopy's apartment many times before, he'd never experienced it from this angle. The roof had two bordering walls from taller structures covered up by artisan graffiti.

Vance

"I don't know if I can do this, Cupid," Nick rubbed the reindeer's nose in passing. Slowly peeking down into the streets below, he felt over into the decorative molding of the cornice at the top of the opening. Blitzen bobbed her head. It was her way of moving Nick along, frustrated there was nothing to eat. "Alright, alright. I get it," he was forced to bite back on his emotion, taking his first step down the flimsy fire escape.

And Nick's instincts served him right. He didn't need any tools for this job amid the aged red brick. Loopy had thankfully left his bedroom window completely unlocked.

Nick rubbed away the fog to peek inside, though Loopy didn't appear to be anywhere in sight. Pushing the window open, he stuck his black boots down inside to jump near the rear of Loopy's bed. His Captain America comforter was pulled down—and his sheets were askew. Posters of Han Solo and Bilbo Baggins were tacked crooked along the walls, and there were clothes and toys strewn freely over the floor.

"Ouch," Nick winced as a bowling ball he recognized from years ago caused him to mildly turn an ankle. "I think it's time to get rid of this," he thought while quietly pushing the heavy ball into one of the few crevices of un-wasted space inside the cluttered bedroom. Nick reminisced back to a time when he chomped at the bit to clean Loopy's room for him—the unfettered mess simply driving him nuts.

"Focus," he reminded as Nick suddenly heard the toilet flush. Loopy hadn't even washed his hands before the bathroom door suddenly slung open. A nervous Nick dropped his sack, doing his best to quickly hide behind a bedstand. Loopy—in faded Batman pajamas wasn't even awake, though managed to subconsciously step perfectly into every nook and cranny of empty real estate through the maze of loose objects spilled out over his floor—before plopping right back into bed.

Inheriting the Sleigh

Nick wiped his forehead with a sigh, quietly closing the window before nervously scooting into the family room. He couldn't help but smile as he pictured his old friend waking up that very morning to see what Santa had left.

Opening his sack, he approached the lit Christmas tree inside the ordinary apartment pulling out a shiny new Crop Cube Five. It was the newest model and had the swirly SC stamped onto the bottom corner of the box. "*Viral Villains Seven*," Nick reached for one of the most popular games to go along with it. "Nah, too violent. And addictive. That won't be good," he was talking as if Loopy were right next to him. "Yeah, this is more like it," he tried another with a playful snicker. *Farmyard Fun: A farmer's quest to round up all his stray pets*. "Oh, you'll love it. Though I better throw in *Off-Road Race Face*. Don't want you accusing me of being too cruel."

But once again, Nick was startled by a noise. Footsteps were coming from the bedroom. "Oh, hello, Nick," said Loopy as if they were having a sleepover. Nick froze in fear, slowly taking off his Santa hat for a moment as he watched Loopy casually mosey on over to the fridge to get a drink of water. He then reached for a fork next to a small plate, instinctively taking a bite from a slice of chocolate cake from the night before. Nick said nothing in return, only watching him finish off the water bottle. He crinkled the plastic and tossed it in the trash, before resuming to sleepwalk right back into bed. "Don't stay up too late now. Remember, Santa's coming."

Nick nervously watched every step before his greatest fear became real. Loopy had snapped from his spell, forcing Nick to quickly put his back on and stand from his crouch near the tree. "Nick … is that … you?" Loopy rubbed his eyes with a deep squint.

"No, Russell," he for the first time, curtly called him by his given name. "It's not."

"But it looks like you. Are you a ghost?"

"Not a ghost," Nick hoped Terpley's hypnotic tricks might work this time. "In fact, Nick is alive—only very, very far away. Very far," he stuck two fingers out close to his face—moving them methodically across his cheeks.

"Very far," Loopy repeated like a confused Stormtrooper to a Jedi. "Well, that's too bad," his head dropped. "I've really missed him. To be honest, he was the best friend I ever had."

Loopy stood still with his eyes heavily glazed over, though Nick could barely hold back his emotion as he inadvertently heard the unfiltered truth. Nick, hardly a social butterfly, usually considered Loopy more of a project than a friend but wept in response to the compliment.

"Well, whoever you are," Loopy continued with a yawn. "I think I will go back to sleep now."

Nick took a moment. Though unable to tell you exactly how— having stepped foot inside millions of homes over a period of mere hours—this time was different. After a full year away, he had now ventured directly back into the meat of his past.

Chapter 64

The celebratory bells rang inside the Vatican. Cardinals exited the front doors of a cathedral with their hands raised above their robes. They were flanked by children, all between four and eight, giddily skipping out with gifts they'd received that very morning.

TV cameras captured the Christmas jubilee as the Swiss Guard stood patrol in their medieval suits. The fancy security detail wore blue berets and held axes on sticks,

As for the red robes holding the hands of the children, they suddenly stopped out of respect as a white cloak was the last to emerge through the holy door. In his ceremonial mitre hat, Pope Francis held an exquisite golden staff bearing a cross at the top. Francis proceeded down the carpet waving to the massive crowd.

"Che benedetta mattina questo è." It translated to, "what a blessed morning it is. For the great Santa Claus has come again." The Cardinals then whisked the children up to greet the Pope in front of the cameras. "Certainly, our many prayers have been heard. The faith which we have had in our Lord and his virgin mother," Francis extended his arms around the properly dressed kids—all clutching their fresh toys. "Has now borne fruit of the great giver of gifts on this wonderful Christmas day."

Nick observed the celebration from his own television set—one that Vienna always kept on. The truth was it made her feel better to hear consistent noise coming from his bedroom.

In direct contrast to Loopy's, not a single thing was out of place, nor had anything been moved—even an inch since last laying eyes on it. His musical note bedspread was neatly tucked underneath a framed, black-and-white portrait of Mozart, and his keyboard rested against the wall next to a shelf of decorative collectables he had gathered over the years.

Nick stepped inside to reach for a framed photo over the dresser. Both Arthur and Vienna looked happy, snuggled in tightly to each other high up in the mountains of Park City, Utah. Everyone was in ski gear, and it was the last trip he could remember taking before everything changed.

Vienna wasn't in her own bedroom, rather having cried herself to sleep over the ivory oval-shaped sofa next to the tall tree. Nick could see holiday boxes uncharacteristically strewn about the fanciest room in the house, as if she'd tried last minute to set up Christmas the best she could before eventually running dry of energy. She was conked out, holding her own frame—this one of baby Nick. It was tucked tightly against her chest and the best thing she could think to do to share this bizarre Christmas with her only child.

Nick, rather, could only watch with a glimmer of the tree lights in his peripheral. He knew he needed to leave something, only had little idea what. Vienna Shriver Crest had been given every gift imaginable over the course of her privileged life, but fixing her newest problem was a conundrum—that of mending a broken heart.

Inheriting the Sleigh

There were a few gifts already under the bare tree, most with Nick's name on them—as if holding out hope he might miraculously show up on Christmas morning. And he did, only not the way she'd envisioned. He had an extremely specific job to do, and after that job was complete was to fly directly back to his new home at the North Pole.

Gently flipping his sack off his shoulder, Nick pulled his gloves to reach inside. Among the many toys and sweet things, he exposed something soft and leathery. It was a book that looked old and worn; but on the cover, read, The Holy Bible. Nick knew his mother was a Christian woman. She took him to church every chance she got, and yet something inside was telling Nick exactly what to leave.

As he thought further, never had he ever remembered seeing her just pick up the Bible for casual reading before. Pulling out a pen, he wrote inside the cover.

Your moment of greatest suffering has come, and yet the answers you seek lie directly under your nose. Let hope and the scriptures be your guide. Remember the past but feel no need to cling to it. For the future that lies in wait is better. Sincerely, he failed to sign his signature Santa Claus, but rather his given name instead. Your Dearest Nick. But there was a p.s. at the end. Let it be known that my birth father authored five of these books.

But Nick wasn't done. He also placed a comic book under the tree. "*The Adventures of Farly Frye,*" he smiled. It was a nostalgic gift to himself.

Now ready to inconspicuously slip away, Nick suddenly felt enticed to grab something on his way out. He offered one more glance around, as if wondering if there might be a way to stay. That is before his better judgement overrode his nostalgic heart.

Vance

"I know … you don't have to say anything," Nick was now back on top of Trump Tower, annoyed by Cupid's impatient glare. "Like I promised, we can go now. You know—back home." Nick pulled out some treats. It was his way of apologizing; an apology all eight of them understood. Or maybe it was just to soften them up for the mild blow coming next. "Actually, if you don't mind," he added to the crunching of carrot sticks. "I need to make one last stop before we do. Promise though, it'll be quick."

Other than a simple wreath over the front door, you wouldn't have known it was Christmas morning at the Lincoln Correctional Center. Unsure exactly what was about to happen, Nick entered to spot an officer half-asleep near a metal detector. The truth was, he didn't have the heart to ruin his on-the-job nap.

"You're kidding. Another one?" a feisty voice startled Nick from behind a pane window. "How many of these fake Santa's are gonna come through here this year?" said an African American officer with her hair tied back in a bun.

"I'm not sure," Nick answered cordially as the officer attending the metal detector—a male with receding hair opened his eyes to the noise. "But do you mind admitting one more?"

"You know what time it is?" the security chief came strutting out of her security office with a clipboard in hand. "So, where is your beard?" she lifted her head and laughed—long before Nick could respond.

He nervously stroked his bare, boyish chin instead. "I don't …"

"How old are you, anyway?" her head tilted as she naturally interrupted him again.

Nick wasn't exactly sure what to say, wondering why in the world he had ever been compelled to stop at a prison. "15 … ma'am."

Inheriting the Sleigh

The lady scratched her head, intrusively glaring him both up and down. "Shouldn't you be in bed? Where's your family anyhow?" she glanced through the clear door to see if there were others straggling in from behind.

"Well," Nick didn't flinch this time. "One of them is actually detained inside this …," he took a second to peer around. "Very nice facility you have here."

There was a brief period of dead silence until the two officers suddenly locked beams, laughing hysterically. "Very nice facility?" she mocked. "Good one, kid. What's his name anyway?" she suddenly lightened up, endeared by his politeness.

"Arthur. Arthur Crest."

She flipped deeper into the stack of papers secured to her clipboard, still chuckling a bit. But there was no laughter this time as the officer dropped her glasses over her nose to squint in surprise. "Arthur Crest. You mean to say you're here to see that crazy money bagger?"

"Yes," Nick hesitantly whispered. He took off his hat, exposing his disheveled brown hair—only hoping they might let him in.

"As ornery and entitled as I've ever seen walk through this wretched joint," she admitted as Nick acted unoffended and equally unsurprised to hear it. "You do realize that most of the inmates are asleep right now?"

"Yes, ma'am. I figured. I can go if you think it's a bad time," Nick used his best puppy voice.

The officer stared at the small present in his hands. "I assume that there is … for him?" Nick nodded. "For your …?"

"Uncle," he filled in the blank with a fib and a smile. My rich uncle, Arthur."

Nick nodded again as the officer snapped a large bubble with her gum. "What the hell," she soon relented "After all, it is Christmas. Stu!"

493

she turned the other way to yell across the prison foyer on the other side of the metal detector.

"Yeah, what is it, Boss?"

"I need you to do something for me, no questions asked."

"Sure, anything," the jovial guard approached closer.

"Take ol' Saint Nick here to cell number ... 174," she glanced down to double check the number.

"Right now? But visiting hours ..." Stu immediately caught himself. "Right. No questions," he slurred. "You might want to take off your belt there," he pointed as Nick safely made it through security following the traditional pat-down.

Nick followed through every checkpoint on his way for the cell block. "Nice suit, by the way," said Stu, stroking his hand across the boy's soft sleeve and handing him his gift back after clearing the metal detector.

"Thanks."

"Here we are," the officer opened one last door, leading Nick down a flight of stairs. A few of the inmates were still up sitting on their bunks, finding it rather odd that someone other than a guard was walking by this time of night.

"Santa Claus ... on Christmas Eve? Nobody ever put those two together," mocked a greasy old man with tattoos inked across both arms.

"Shut your mouth, Skinny," Stu rebuked through the hollow hall. Nick tried not to make eye contact with the curious inmates, all of whom seemed to know that whatever was happening was against protocol.

"Well, here we are," said the officer stopping in front of 174, a six-by-nine-foot cell.

Nick approached to see Arthur in a tank top and facial hair curled asleep on the bottom bunk. Stu was curious by his reaction, as if Nick couldn't decide precisely how to feel. A rush of emotion swept his mind in both directions, first carrying him all the way back to the Blue Owl.

"So, this is your life now?" Nick boldly addressed his intoxicated father inside the secret underground lounge. "Are you aware at all that mom's attorney has filed the divorce papers. She's preparing to bring charges?"

"Is that so?"

"You truly do believe you can buy your way out of anything," Nick was now used to seeing the timeline of other people's lives playing out across his mind; though it was especially odd to see his own history.

"And you really think it's wise to talk to me like that?" Arthur whispered.

"How could you lay a hand on her?! What, just because I'm some kid, you think I'll stand by, while you self-destruct and ruin our lives in the process?"

"Don't you ever speak to me that way! Without me, you'd have grown up in some rat-infested foster home, you hear?! Foster home, you hear. Foster home, you hear," the line painfully echoed past his ears.

Nick suddenly had an unnaturally firm grip over the bars, with Stu nearly feeling the need to rip them away himself. But before Nick could build into a rage, another memory took over; this one peaceful.

"The past is there to teach us lessons about who we are," said Clovis inside his tiny church. "And what our mission in life is."

"But I've known him for a long time, Clovis, and yet a part of me wishes I never had."

"Our parents shape and influence who we are, Nick—for good or for bad. But there are always things we can learn, even if that happens to be primarily from their mistakes. Remember, charity trumps forgiveness.

To forgive requires us to swallow our pride. But to serve takes a physical sacrifice." Those final two words repetitively trailed off.

"Are you alright, kid?" Stu got to a point where he had to ask. Nick said nothing, instead peering up at Stu with a cold sweat. "Or, Santa Claus. Or whoever you are."

"Yeah," he took another deep breath, as if glad to have finally gotten through the crux of the memory. "I'm just fine."

"You know, I usually don't do this," he reached for a walkie talkie at his belt. "In fact, I never do. But if you want, perhaps I can make a call to open up this gate."

"No," Nick shook. "But if you could—just give him this," he handed Stu the family photo under silver paper and a red bow. Nick kept his eyes locked on his father lying over a thin mattress. "Tell him that somebody loves him … and believes in him. That second chances are real."

Stu nodded as he repeated it back. "O … K. Second chances … very real," he said in earshot of some eavesdroppers occasionally whistling in the distance. "Anything else?"

"Yeah," Nick hunched, fully content to walk himself back out. "And perhaps you yourself … you know, could use some of that same advice."

Stu suddenly had a confused and guilty stare, as if able to feel the boy reading into his own complicated life story.

"Going already?" said the female officer, whom had curiously been watching Nick's every retreating step from her security monitors.

"Yes, thank you … Gladys," Nick waved as he subtly dropped off a small box of earrings on his way past. It was his final gift before scooting back through the metal detector for the remerging chill of the brisk night. "And Merry Christmas to you."

Gladys' eyes bulged big at the fact he had called her by her real name, a name she never used at work. She rushed out to catch up. "Well, can I at least call you a cab or something?! It's like 15 degrees out here," she said, coatless and concerned—her bare arms crossed over her chest.

"No, thank you," he turned back around—this time with a smile. "I have my transportation."

With a primarily empty sack in his wake, Nick had the sleigh on cruise control coasting over the northern skies. His head was dipped back over the seat in fatigue; fatigue both physical and emotional as his task was finally complete. At least this year. But that didn't mean his peace of mind was where he wanted it—still rightly worried about many things. Start with Vienna and Arthur, both imprisoned—at least in one way or another. And then, of course, there was Marie whom he'd somehow forgotten all about in the rigors of the night.

Where was she? It was a question he pondered while folding some scrap paper into an airplane. If he only knew what was directly beneath the sleigh where an outline of something was gliding across the frozen sea. But it wasn't a polar bear. Marie was covered head to toe in Eskimo gear, more determined than ever—not only to stay alive, but to reach the elusive North Pole.

About the Author

Morgan Vance has spent the last two decades providing highlights and in-depth features for TV news as a sports anchor in Salt Lake City, UT. But the time has come to transition to the written page. Morgan is attracted to stories where the ordinary and fantastic clash—more than ready to scratch an itch that has been trapped inside his own head for far too long. When he's not writing, his world revolves around his wife, Stephanie and their three girls. He enjoys discovering the Earth's endless beauty, working out, a great sitcom, as well as anything Eighties.